AFTAN WHISPERS

An Estalia Novel

Phil Williams

MMXVIII

Cover design by Jessica Bell

ISBN-10: 0-9931808-3-3
ISBN-13: 978-0-9931808-3-5

Visit www.phil-williams.co.uk online for more information and
regular news regarding the writing of Phil Williams.
Join the newsletter to receive free content and be the first to hear
about new projects.

Part 1

1

Tyler perched on the roof, hammer in one hand as the other fumbled nails. The first drops of rain pecked him as the clouds grumbled. Old Ruke, on the other side of the roof, met the sound with a grumble of his own. "Half the roof to finish, we'll be soaked through."

"Better us than Kompter," Tyler replied lightly. "We can handle a little rain."

As he said it, the patter turned to a downpour.

"Happy now?" Ruke thrust his hammer into a toolbox. "And for what? Goodwill?"

"He'll pay when he's ready," Tyler replied, raising his voice over the rain. Ruke clicked his tongue in annoyance, but he'd know there was no arguing; you couldn't leave a man exposed to the elements, no matter how little money he had. Nevertheless, they weren't getting much more done now. Tyler sat back on his haunches. He scanned the horizon of black towers and chimneys, trying to see how heavy the cloud cover was above the distant smoke. Between the two, he spotted a gentle orange glow.

"Is that fire?"

Ruke squinted, his eyes all but shut, a hand at his brow like a visor. "Gotta be a big one, that far off." Another moment and the glow was hidden behind the rain. The canvas at the edge of the roof flapped in the wind. Ruke shouted, "Time to go, boy, you know it as well as I!"

Biting back irritation, Tyler grabbed at the tiles around him and thrust them into the box. Slick with rain, one slipped from his grip. He lunged for it – too slow – and grabbed on to the building's edge to stop himself from falling.

The tile spiralled into darkness, between the jagged network of roofs and walkways of the five or six tiers visible below. This late, with the coming storm, the streets should have been empty, but a rapidly moving shadow caught Tyler's eye, four levels below.

"Look up!" Tyler yelled.

1

The figure skidded still. A young, startled face glanced up. A girl? The tile smashed in front of her, making her leap back and drop something. As Ruke shouted a question, Tyler clambered across the roof. "Wait! I'm sorry!" He slid down a metal support onto the nearest walkway. Leaning over the edge, he saw the girl doing the same below. Whatever she had dropped had fallen further down. Tyler shouted, "Are you okay?"

She ignored him, flashing a look back the way she'd come. Then she ran.

"Hold up!"

Tyler leapt down to the next tier.

"Where you going, boy?" Ruke demanded, skidding to the edge of the roof.

"To see if she's okay!" Tyler called back, springing off the banister and dropping to the next walkway. He jumped again, quickly descending until his uncle's voice was barely audible behind the rain.

"I'll just finish up myself, will I?"

Four levels down, Tyler staggered to a halt next to the shards of his shattered tile. He looked over the edge to see what she had dropped. A box, as long as Tyler's forearm, sat on the fabric roof of a market stall below.

Searching the surroundings, Tyler caught a flap of cloak as the girl disappeared down some steps. Heavy footfalls drew his attention back the other way. Two figures pounded towards him out of the shadows. They barged into him, charging after the girl, the metal of their armour clattering as they moved. Tyler braced himself against a banister and shouted, "What's going on?"

They weren't guards; the man was dressed in sleeveless furs, with chain mail wrapped around his bare arms and one leg, and the woman had a short-tailed leather coat. They were both decorated with the dark paintwork of tattoos and an axe swung from the man's hip. At best they were mercenaries. The man shouted, "There, cut her off!"

Tyler spotted the girl racing between the covered market stalls almost directly below. She'd doubled back on herself, searching for the box. Tyler jumped over the edge, a marquee catching his weight, bending the poles that supported it. He bounced to the next stall, scooping up the box, then pushed off to drop to the ground. An old lady, tidying her stall, gave him a disapproving look. He smiled back. This late, the market was otherwise dead.

The girl rushed out from between two stalls and disappeared again. She hadn't seen him and didn't know where she was going. Even when empty, the market's network of canvas awnings was difficult to navigate. Tyler ran after her. He vaulted over a table, skidded around a corner and spotted her going up more steps. Stretching on her toes, she strained to search the roofs of the stalls.

Tyler held up the box and opened his mouth to call out to her, but as he did, the pursuing lady burst into the market from the opposite direction. The girl spotted Tyler, with the box, and her pursuer beyond him. She turned and sprinted, and Tyler gave chase, the woman close behind.

"Out of the way, kid!" the woman ordered.

He jumped up the flight of stairs and found the walkway split into three. All the paths led into darkness, flanked by dormant shacks, and the girl was gone again. The rain rattled against the metal roofs above. Little of it reached this far down, but Tyler was already soaked. The woman bowled into him from behind, almost knocking him to the ground. As he steadied himself he saw she'd stopped too; he tugged his sodden fringe out of his eyes to look at her. She had a pistol in her hand, a metal one with a circular cylinder at its centre. He didn't know weapons, but he knew it was fancier, probably deadlier, than their local Road Guard ever carried, typically armed as they were with stumpy metal batons. He looked at the box in his hands, then instinctively thrust it behind his back as the woman turned towards him to ask, "Which way?"

Following his urge to protect this girl, he said, "No idea. Who is she?"

Before the woman could reply, her companion emerged from one of the paths, with no sign of the girl. Getting a good look at his face, with its angry eyes and the spiky black shapes etched up his neck and over one cheek, Tyler was certain he'd already chosen the right side in this affair. The woman looked little better; her left cheek was decorated with something like an angular spiderweb, stretching from her ear to under the eye, and her eyes were bathed in dark shadow. The pair exchanged a look that somehow confirmed the girl had got away, and the man slammed a fist into the nearest wall, denting the metal panelling and making Tyler jump.

The man spotted Tyler, then, and demanded, "Who the fuck are you?"

The pair studied Tyler as he shrank against the wall behind him, averting his eyes and shielding the box. He said, "I dropped a tile. From way up on the roofs."

"Dropped a tile," the man echoed, unimpressed.

As they continued to stare at him, Tyler avoided looking at their faces. He focused on the tattoos on the man's arms, instead. The pattern that covered part of his face snaked down over his shoulder, visible through gaps in his furs and vest, and spread into an increasingly elaborate pattern across his left arm. None of it referenced anything in nature or machinery, except at the end, in the middle of his forearm, where the pattern separated to leave space for a kite-shaped shield. At its centre was a triangle, pointing down, its top edge missing. Tyler didn't know the exact symbol but he knew the general idea: a letter that identified the man as a slave trader. Before they could form any decisions about him, Tyler blurted out, "Want me to help you look for her?"

The big guy turned away. He said to the woman, "Fuck it. We know where she's headed. The boys will get her."

He padded off down one of the passages. The woman hesitated a moment longer, studying Tyler, then followed. Tyler breathed again.

What were slavers doing inside the city walls?

Tyler entered his hut to find Ruke sitting on a stool, the stove aflame. He pulled the door closed but remained in the doorway, dripping. His uncle held up a cracked mug in a shaking hand. Tyler stowed the box under one arm and dropped his tool bag to wrap his hands around the mug for warmth. Behind the liquid's sugary base he tasted the sharp bite of *glus*. Their sheet-metal home was like a drum in the rain. Not always a bad thing; it kept out the sounds of Bawkley, their north-eastern district of the Metropolis, which was alive most nights with drunken shouting, abusive screams and occasional eruptions of gunpowder.

"You survived, then?" Ruke muttered, staring into the stove. The old man was stooped and withered like a barely fleshed skeleton. His hair was mostly gone, but what remained he kept long, the few strands dazzlingly white. To look at him, no stranger would give him more than a few hours' breath before reaching his last, but Tyler knew better. Ruke could work heavier construction than most. Their family's thin bodies were built to last.

"Thanks for tidying up," Tyler said.

Ruke mumbled acknowledgement: "Wasn't sure if you were coming back. You find 'em?"

"No. She ran away."

"Not surprised," Ruke chortled. "Throwing tiles at a girl, some way with the ladies!"

"Very funny, Unc." Tyler sat on the mat opposite Ruke and inspected the box the girl had dropped. It was metal with no markings, just a line around the middle that hinted at an opening. There was no catch, though. No sign of a lock or a hinge. He took a knife and ran it along the crack, saying, "She was being chased. Slavers, by the look of it."

Ruke looked up. "Slavers? Here?"

"Guess she got away from them somehow."

Noting the box, Ruke widened an eye. "What've you got there?"

"She dropped it."

"And you didn't hand it over to these slavers?"

"They didn't ask." The box wouldn't be pried open. "She was wearing a cloak. Like the nuns, you know? The Sisters of Providence. But she was young. Kind of pretty, dark hair, dark eyes. Small. I mean, not short, but slim. Guess those slavers haven't been feeding her."

"Kind of pretty," Ruke repeated. "That's all it takes to get you in trouble, is it? Now you gonna quit yammering and hand that thing over to old Ruke, boy?"

"I'm trying to open it."

"Failing to." Ruke held out a spiky hand, opening and closing his fingers. Tyler gave him the box. The old man tested its strength, then gave it a flex and a tap. It sprang open.

Tyler scrambled forwards. "How'd you do that?"

"You learn these tricks as you get older." Ruke handed the box back without looking into it. Tyler opened it to reveal a single sheet of paper, nothing more.

"It's just a note," Tyler said, dumbfounded.

"Notes can be valuable," Ruke replied. "That thing's like a portable safe. They used to be all the rage; I seen them when I had that Grenevic job, before your time. Crackpot Aftan inventor by the name of Fenzoni brandished them about for two or three seasons. It became a sure way to know some rich fool had things worth taking. No need for keys, just a little puzzle."

"Which anyone could figure out?"

"Said they were rich fools, didn't I? They ran Fenzoni out of town, eventually. Sure he found some other con to string people along, though, took to the waterways. What's on it, then?"

The paper was fine, smoother to the touch than a shirt. Not like the thick stuff they used for packaging food or covering windows. It was real paper, the sort educated and moneyed people wrote letters on. All it had on it was a series of numbers, though, with something written below. Five words. Tyler knew the numbers all right, but the words could've been anything.

He held it up to Ruke, saying, "What do you make of this?"

Ruke peered at it, then mumbled, "Whole lot of numbers."

"Maybe the writing explains it."

"Yeah?" Ruke held out a hand again. He looked at the note carefully, then concluded, "Whatever it is, wasn't meant for us."

"Maybe those slavers were after it. Must be important if she was keeping it in this box."

"Then why'd she ditch it so quick?"

"She didn't mean to. Do you know anyone who can read?"

Tyler and Ruke shared a long look. Together, they slowly shook their heads.

2

Tyler had woken from dreams of the girl fleeing through the city, chased by the brute with the tattoos. Over breakfast he tried to convince himself it was all right. She'd given them the slip once; even if they said they knew where she was going, she'd evade them again. There were enough places in the city to hide. Trying to force the ill-feeling out of himself, he whistled on the way to work, skipping through the streets and fixing his face in a smile.

They were lucky, living in the miracle of the Metropolis. It was a vertical city, built high upon itself rather than expanding into the hostile countryside that surrounded it. Layer upon layer of shacks teetered into the sky, joined by intricately layered paths. It looked ready to topple in a wrong wind, but the towers stood firm, expertly put together by people like Tyler and his uncle. From the slums of Bawkley and Kelp to the affluence of central Grenevic, from the vast pits of the Mines to the ports lining the banks of the Drain river, this marvel of chaotic architecture was the work of men who understood how to make things last. There were no raiders, no warring factions, no slavers here. Those things were for outside. Beyond the security of the city, where the population were working hard to make life comfortable and sustainable.

Tyler made a point of winding through the bustling market as enterprising shopkeepers bellowed deals from every direction. Trapped animals, exotic clothing, old machine parts scrapped together into new tools: whatever you needed was there. Tyler checked for new treasures every morning but mostly came out empty-handed. This morning, he made the added effort to retrace his steps from the night before, picturing the chase before trotting upstairs to the work site.

The top tiers of the tower were owned by a trade manager, and at this height the walkway linked it to only two other towers. Kompter rented a small dilapidated outcrop at the edge, converted from an old animal shelter. Though leaking and grotty, it was practically private, with a fine view of the city, including the far-off Guard Towers on the other side of Grenevic. In the haze, they were little more than pillars of darkness, behind the rest of the city's artificial canyons, but Tyler still enjoyed looking at them. They stood taller than anything in the Metropolis, perhaps anything in the world. He was taking it in fondly when Kompter hobbled out. "Tyler? That you?"

"There was a fire last night, near the Towers," Tyler recalled, peering at the horizon. "Did you hear about it?"

"I had problems of my own," Kompter sighed wearily.

Tyler turned to him. Kompter wasn't as old as Ruke, but he looked every inch his age, skin deeply set with wrinkles, oversized ragged clothes hanging off him and whiskered face deathly pale. His eyes, surrounded by a mess of thick scars, were always open, always staring, irises creamy white and seeing nothing. Tyler said softly, "I'm so sorry, Mr Kompter – we tried to get it done in time. I should've come earlier. Did much water get in?"

"Tsh." Kompter waved it off. "Ruke said you shouldn't have been up there at all, not in that weather."

He turned towards the hut, an invitation to enter. He bumped the doorframe as he went, and Tyler hurried to help him in, taking one of his elbows. As Tyler guided him back to a seat, drips of the previous night's rain hit the floor every few seconds. In the darkness, Tyler couldn't make out exactly where they were coming from.

"Doesn't look so bad," Tyler commented, scanning Kompter's few possessions. A tatty mattress, a thick oak chest, and his old Guard armour hidden under a damp blanket. Tyler's eyes rested there. "It's not right, you being up here with barely a roof over you."

"You're too good for your own good," Kompter chuckled. "You do your daddy proud, Tyler, but he wouldn't want you slipping off a wet roof on my behalf."

"He'd understand," Tyler said, unable to keep a smile from his own face. There was no way his dad would've let a retired guard suffer, least of all one that'd given his eyes for his work.

Kompter pushed a lump of bread his way. "Take that for this morning," he said. "It's not much – but I'll make this right, believe me. Just need more time. More time."

Tyler put a hand on his. "Don't you worry about it, Mr Kompter. I'm sure the things you did for the Guard paid for this more than a hundred times over."

"The things I did." Kompter turned his face thoughtfully towards his pile of armour, even if his eyes couldn't see it. "Don't know if I'd have done them again."

"You would," Tyler said. "Who wouldn't do their bit, given the chance?"

Kompter let out a sound that might have shown amusement or disappointment. Tyler didn't press for the reason. The old guard rarely spoke about his past, and it was all Tyler could do to keep positive around him. Losing your eyes was a big burden, after all. It made Tyler feel guilty, watching Kompter slip into a regretful bout of remembering. He'd never lost anything that meant much, not really. But he'd step up, given the chance; he knew he would. Like Kompter had, through his life, and like his dad had done.

Tyler's mind ran to the girl again, fleeing from those thugs, perhaps for her life. He said, "Say, Mr Kompter, the Guard don't let slavers operate in the city, do they?"

"Huh? No need, is there?" Kompter still didn't turn to face Tyler, his voice distant. "We've got the Mine Guard for that."

He meant the Mine Guard would round up runaways, leaving no work for the slavers. Tyler wondered if there was something in that. Slave traders, whatever your thoughts on them, picked up the slack for the Mine Guard in the far corners of Estalia. Maybe that's what they were doing here? It still didn't seem right that that girl was up against those thugs, though. Tyler bit his lip, imagining her in trouble. He needed some time to think about this, to see if he could find her. But first he had to finish this job.

Between shifts on Kompter's roof, Tyler persuaded Sila to join him for an early lunch. There had been little spark between them since they'd been introduced, but Tyler was still trying. There was good in everyone, after all, and he was pretty sure when he found Sila's he'd like her a whole lot more.

At a viewing spot on the slanted roof of a tower at the river's edge, they watched the heaving activity of the Drain, the monstrous torrent that cut the Metropolis in half. A fleet of traders and travellers floated across it, the noise of their shouts and engines drifting up. The view had changed in recent weeks, with the usual traffic now navigating gaps between vessels that dwarfed them. The combined forces of Border Guard and Water Guard warships had been returning to the Metropolis, consolidating in an incredible display of gunboats and battle barges. Armoured seamen shouted orders at the surrounding civilian ships, all vying for what limited space was left.

The cause of most of the congestion sat at the centre of the crowded river: a floating castle, as large as a block of buildings. It was punctuated with spiked towers, patchily painted in Border Guard black, with barrels of weapons poking out at various heights. Guards dotted the vessel, armed with rifles, and a ramp ran from one side of the castle to the bank of the river, forcing larger ships to go all the way round. Tradesmen with carts were crossing the bridge in both directions.

"It's only a small one, you know," Tyler said, catching Sila staring at the fortress too.

She screwed up her face and said, "You'd know?"

"Well, that's what Keflo told me. It's Command Post 3, from the South Sea. On a good day you could see it from Brofton. It's old, not one they sent to war."

"Keflo wouldn't know Brofton from Mystle," Sila scoffed. "He's never even set foot outside Bawkley. I don't know why you listen to him. That thing looks plenty big to me."

Tyler held his tongue. He'd only met Sila because he listened to Keflo; Tyler preferred the simpler interactions of dice games and parties on Escule Avenue to mingling with the gossipy girls who worked in the fabric shops. Keflo had insisted.

A smaller ship was drifting past the fortress, pointed like a triangle with a huge cannon barrel across its top. Tyler held off saying what Keflo had told him about that one. The gunboat was supposedly Commander Dniren's ship. He was the boss of Post 3, so it made sense to Tyler, but Sila would find some fault in that fact, too. She'd moved on, anyway, pointing at an enormous barge. "See the circus? You can take me there later."

It wasn't a question. The barge blew its horn. A great part of its starboard side was taken up by a wheel and a steam chimney. A parade of carts were being shifted off by eccentrically dressed men and woman. A lanky man in a floppy hat waddled up and down, waving his hands, giving orders in a lampoon of the nearby guards.

"I might need to look for work this evening," Tyler said.

"You can look for work this afternoon, forget going back to that old cripple. There's no money in it anyway."

"That old cripple was a guard, once," Tyler replied, skin bristling at her comment.

"A Water Guard. What'd he do, line the walls of a canal?"

"He—"

"I don't *care,* Tyler," Sila huffed. "He's rotten, and no good for you. Get some real work. Isn't Hamersham hiring again?"

Tyler hummed. She had it easier, working in the fabric shop, never having to decide between good work and good pay. Tyler's eyes wandered back up to the dark monoliths of the Guard Towers. They were clearer, here, closer, but still stood resolutely featureless in their grandeur. Hoping to change the subject, he said, "You hear anything about a fire last night?"

"Oh yeah. Talk of the shop this morning. Rebel attack of some kind. A foreign *in serpent*, you know, people from out of town. Branded with a snake."

Tyler frowned, sure that she had the wrong turn of phrase but not sure what the right one was. Either way, he pictured the girl running through Bawkley and wondered if she was somehow connected. She'd come from that general direction, though it would've taken two hours or more to get from the Towers to his neighbourhood. No, it couldn't have been her – the Guard would've been after her – but someone like her, maybe. A runaway rather than a rebel. He said, "They find who did it?"

"No. Set it and run. Cowards, right?"

"Could've been an attack from the Kennel."

Sila laughed, but put a hand over her mouth when she saw Tyler was serious. She shook her head. "You believe in that? The Kennel?"

"Kids escape from the Mines," Tyler said defensively. "They've gotta go somewhere."

"Sure but they're not setting off bombs and starting fires. They're not living in tunnels building weapons and making food from – what – moss? Mould? Rocks?"

His naivety amused her. She'd tell her friends in the fabric shop about it. That'd give them a hoot. As though the idea of foreign rebels with serpents on their arms was more believable than a community of runaway children. She'd been told about the fire by her friends, though, hadn't she, and he only knew about the Command Post and the Kennel from people like Keflo. Rather than get deeper into it, Tyler tried to change the subject again. "I ran into a girl last night, being chased."

"A girl," Sila said. "Thought you were working?"

"Look." He took the paper note from his leather satchel. "She dropped this. In a safe box."

Sila scanned the numbers and gave Tyler a look. "What is it?"

"No idea. You know anyone who can read?"

"Ralph the Signmaker might, but I'm fairly sure he's a liar. You'd need to take a walk to Juliacre, get help in one of them fancy clock shops or something." She tapped the words. "I know what *that* is, though. You don't recognise it?" Something about her tone suggested he'd let himself down again. Tyler shook his head. "It's the sign on that Guard hangout. In Central. The Den."

Tyler took another look. Two of the words definitely looked familiar. "Yeah. You might be right."

"Of course I'm right," Sila told him firmly.

"These other words, then, maybe that's the name of someone there. Could be someone who needs to see this. I should go."

"Why?"

Tyler looked at her, not sure how to respond to such a simple question. Wasn't the answer obvious? When he didn't reply for a few seconds, she pressed the note back into his hands and continued, "What do you care about some girl the guards are after? Hand this to the local Guard or toss it."

"She wasn't being chased by guards. They looked like slavers."

Sila's face screwed up in an expression he was quickly coming to understand and dislike. "How would you know about slavers? You ever seen one?"

"I have now," Tyler said. Picturing the girl and those thugs chasing after her, he decided to tell Sila why, plain as he saw it. "No one deserves to be involved with those sorts of people. And she was protecting this note for a reason. It's got to mean something, right?"

"Could mean a beating," Sila said. "Or worse. Get you locked up in the Iron Hold for helping her. Get your nose cut off for sticking it where it don't belong. Give it up, Tyler. Go tell

Kompter to take a hike, get some new work, and spend the evening taking me to the circus. That's your day." She looked away from him to pick out the barge again, eyes lighting up. Tyler followed her gaze to the latest carriage trundling off the boat. A mismatch of thick wood and metal bars, the enormous animal cage was being dragged by its chains. Sila said, "We are *definitely* going to see that."

"Sure," Tyler agreed. However this might be going, he could at least see the circus making her happy, and that was something.

"Sure? You're done with this mystery girl and the stupid paper?"

Tyler nodded, slipping the note carefully back into his bag. Sila gave him a light kiss on the lips and told him, factually, "I like you, you know."

"I like you too," he replied with a smile, fairly sure he didn't mean it. Fairly sure she didn't mean it, either. He had a feeling she just liked the idea of him doing what she said. Still, that was a bridge he could cross later. At this point, he was happy to keep her cool so he could plot the best route to the Raskel Den.

Phil Williams

3

The Raskel Den was a landmark known throughout the Metropolis and beyond, to the wider stretches of the Estalian Empire. At the heart of Central, close to the river, the three-tier bar was passed by most people at some point in their time in the city, though only the bravest or most foolish dared go in. Steps scaled the front and the walls had random panels of wood and metal covering past damages. The erratic, empty windows were not all part of the original design. The paint from the massive purple letters near the top of the structure had run halfway down the wall. Holding the paper up level with the words, Tyler saw a clear match. Sila was right: whatever the numbers were, they had something to do with this place.

Tyler had heard all the stories of the Den, from the mass brawls to the black market in the cellar; from the time that Werner Skull brained a fellow guard with a mug to the time a knife-fight left three men with one hand each. The building's original owners, it was said, were long gone, and the patronage of the Guard somehow kept it going as independent traders stocked and manned the bar. The same way everything worked in the city. When a need arose, someone stepped in to fill it – and there was always a need for alcohol and entertainment in the Den.

In the middle of the day, Tyler hoped to find it more sedate than usual.

There was no clear single entrance, so he ventured in through a hinged panel on the second floor, one hand on his leather satchel as though it might somehow protect him. The interior was barely lit except for occasional candles and shreds of the dim outside light seeping through the holes in the wall. It was furnished with mouldy, rot-eaten chairs and dented tables, with ragged curtains covering some of the decay. The second floor was only half complete, a gap in the middle overhanging more of the same below, and drunkenly constructed scrap staircases heading up. Even at this empty hour, it felt full, with derelict drinkers slumped across the tables. They were mostly quiet, though.

Tyler shuffled through, staring without wanting to. At a table with three men in Road Guard armour, talking over mugs of *glus*, the nearest one snarled, "Go home, boy."

The men looked tired and miserable. They must have finished long shifts, their plated grey armour at various stages of undress. Tyler gave them a brief smile to show he meant no harm, and hurried to the bar – driftwood perched on unmarked barrels.

"Hi, good morning, how are you?" Tyler said with another smile.

The barman regarded him with contempt. "You're in the wrong place, scrubber."

"Can I just ask –" Tyler pointed towards the front of the building "– you've got the name written real big up there. Do you get a lot of people in here that can read?"

"Want your neck broke?" the barman growled.

"No!" Tyler answered brightly. "Just wondering. Where I come from, people ain't good at reading, that's all. Thought it might be different here."

The barman leant heavily on the bar. "It's different here."

"Okay, okay." Tyler backed off. "I've just got this..." He put the note on the counter and snatched it up again as grease soaked through. He held it up, instead, saying, "That's the name of this place, isn't it? This note is meant for someone here."

The barman said, "What business you got with a Border Guard?"

"The fucking Border Guard?" a slurring Road Guard demanded, standing unsteadily, knocking his chair to the floor. "You got a problem, you come to us."

Tyler held up his hands in apology. "I respect that, I do. The Road Guard are fantastic. This is something else, though."

"I'll give yer something else," the guard sneered, taking a step forwards and having to support himself on a table. His eyes widened in alarm. The surrounding crowd had gone quiet, waiting for an inevitable retch, but the man somehow swallowed his plight. Half the onlookers sighed relief, half groaned disappointment, and the guard forgot his quarry to lurch towards an exit.

"Twenty minutes earlier he'd have had your head," the barman warned. "Give it time, someone else will."

"Because of this?" Tyler frowned at the paper. "What's it say? 'Border Guard'?"

"Not *the* Guard. *A* guard. Deadbeat, used to be a tracker." The barman nodded his fat head upwards, to the third level. "You'll find him at the bar."

Tyler thanked the barman and picked his way back through the drunkards, onto one of the rickety stairways. As he climbed, he heard a shout from the ground floor. A glass smashed as a scuffle erupted. The stairs shook unsteadily as he hurried on.

The third level was even darker, and less populated. Tyler immediately picked out the man he was after. Sitting stiffly at the bar, he wore black armour that was barely recognisable under a layer of dirt and an array of scrap clothing, including a tatty scarf and what looked like half an over-shirt. The lean, silver-haired man nursed a tankard, a rifle almost as tall as a man propped at his side. Tyler approached from the side, so as not to startle him. Getting closer, he saw patches of congealed liquid marred the rags and armour, like machine grease or engine oil.

"Excuse me, sir," Tyler shifted a heavy stool out of the way. Another bulky, sullen figure stood behind the bar, with the same malicious glare as the one before. They could have been twins. This one remained silent, though, as Tyler made his introduction. "My name's Tyler. I'm a roofer. I wonder if I could take a moment of your time?"

The silver-haired man looked at Tyler tiredly. The skin under his eyes sagged, as though the things his striking blue eyes had seen added weight to his expression. His answer came in a croaky voice: "I don't need a roof. Save your breath."

"It's not that. I've got this note, see." Tyler held up the paper, careful not to let it touch anything this time. "This writing here. Is it for you?"

The man squinted at the paper. His eyes ran slowly over the words, then the numbers, then over Tyler. He turned back to his mug and said, "I'm not for hire."

"That's okay. Pleased to meet you anyway." The young man held out his free hand. The guard looked from his hand to his face.

"The sooner you tell me what it's about, the sooner I can tell you no."

"Sorry – I don't read, see – and I don't actually know your name. Yet." Tyler smiled again.

The man sighed but finally shifted in his seat to better face Tyler. He said, "Qait Seyron. As it says on your paper. If you don't know who I am, what are you doing here?"

"Um…" Tyler looked at the barman, who was watching their conversation, then across to the other drunks within earshot. "Maybe we could talk somewhere private?"

"Like where? Outside the city?" the man answered coldly. "This is as private as it gets."

"Well…I got this off a girl. Kind of. She dropped it, and she was being chased by these people who looked like seriously bad news. It was kind of my fault she dropped this, and if it was important to her, I'd hate for it to all go wrong on account of me."

Qait eyed him carefully. He looked at the note again, still held up between them, and said, "You dragged yourself down from, what, Bawkley? Braved coming into the Raskel Den, because you found this piece of paper a stranger dropped?"

Tyler shrugged as if it were nothing. "Trying to help, that's all."

"Well, this girl might've wanted me for a job, doesn't mean I know where she is, or who she is. If she was on the run, try the Kennel."

Tyler lit up. "You believe in the Kennel?" The guard stared back blankly. It hadn't sounded like a joke, but maybe Qait had a particularly dry way of speaking. Tyler hummed, slipping the note back into his bag. "You're still a guard, aren't you? Aren't you supposed to help people? What if they hurt her?"

"Why would they?"

"Don't know," Tyler said. "They had tattoos. The guy, he was big, he had an emblem here, on his arm. Looked like this." Tyler held up two fingers to form a V. Qait's mouth twisted to a smile, but he wasn't amused; he shook his head.

"Steer well clear."

"You know him?"

Qait nodded, turning back to his drink. Tyler stood still. "Sir, if you *know* she's in trouble–"

"I've got no love for the slave trade –" Qait cut him off without looking up "– but we've all got bigger problems than a slave who's escaped her master. That's all this is. It's no secret that I can fly; she probably thinks the gyro could get her there quickest. Probably right."

"Get her where?"

"*There*." He pointed at Tyler's bag, indicating the paper inside. "You've got coordinates for some place out of town. There's two problems, though. First, if she's a slave then she's got no way to pay me. Second, with all these people moving south and the skirmishes along the waterways, the last thing anyone wants to be doing right now is leaving the Metropolis. She's better off here. Let the Kennel save her."

Tyler let this sink in for a moment, standing resolute. He pictured her slight, harmless figure being mercilessly hunted. Qait wasn't joking, though; he knew something like the Kennel existed. And the slavers might've thought the same way. They'd said they knew where she was going, they had friends who would've cut her off before she got there. Tyler said, "You know these numbers. You're a tracker, right? Know how to find places? People?"

Qait nodded.

"What if I paid you? You can help me find her."

"What for? I already told you –"

"How much? Just to find her?"

Qait looked him up and down. Tyler puffed up his chest, determined to look serious. The tracker didn't soften, though. He said, "Here's what I'll do. I'll wait here. You go home. Take time to ask yourself if it's worth risking your friends and family and home because you saw some girl getting chased. Some girl who might have done something bad to deserve it. You still want to risk it all to help her, come back tomorrow and I'll see what I can do. I'll be waiting."

Tyler blurted back, "I don't need to take the time, I know –"

"You're not the first concerned citizen that's come looking for a favour from the Guard, kid," Qait said. "There's only so much any of us can do. There's war practically on our doorstep, you've got people burning villages in the country and you don't know half of it, trust me. You want to waste either of our time on this, you make sure it's worth the risk. Think about it. Hard. Trust me. It's the best offer you'll get."

Tyler bit his lip and slowly nodded. "Tomorrow, then. You promise?"

"On my word," Qait said. "But you won't be back." Tyler turned to leave, but he was only a pace away when the tracker called out, "You can leave the note. I'll check the location, to be sure there's nothing there worth knowing about."

Tyler ran a hand over his satchel, the paper safely stowed inside.

"It's got my name on it, doesn't it?"

"Doesn't mean it's yours," Tyler said, and walked away.

4

Deni looked up at the grey sky and squinted to try and judge how light the sun was beyond the clouds. She wasn't sure if the day was darker than the one before, or if she'd simply been looking up for too long, but it seemed worse. Day by cloud-covered day, the light seemed dimmer, shorter. Maybe the world was slowly dying, like some people said. The clouds would keep getting thicker, the light sucked away behind them, until everyone shrivelled up and died. Her master, Balfair, had predicted it. That was the only conclusion that made sense to Deni, in all the time she'd spent thinking about it since fleeing his estate. That was the reason he had given his life for his research – because to go through the clouds was to challenge that end. The rocket he had built, with that special fuel that could take it higher than anyone had been before, held the means to make a difference. To break the clouds – to reveal the sky, so everyone could finally see the sun. She had seen it. The sunlight. The colours. How special it was. The light wasn't gone, after all. Just hidden.

From what Dr Hodwick had told her, change was possible – and change was frightening, to some. The means to create that change, in turn, was a powerful tool, which made it the perfect bargaining chip. Wherever the information ended up, it could at least save *her*. After all, the other thing she'd learnt, or at least confirmed, since she'd set out on her journey was how rotten and undeserving the world was. If the people she traded with could make use of Balfair's research then so be it. If not, it was no matter, as long as sharing her information paid for her safety. It would be a long time yet before the world coughed its last – long enough for her to live out a peaceful life, at least.

She couldn't take it back to Hodwick; that blithering scientist had no means to relieve her troubles, and he'd already got her in this mess by making her carry that infernal box. She needed a fighter on her side, not a thinker. But first she needed to find the young man who'd stolen the box from her.

Deni had been waiting in the market all morning, watching

louts drinking early, tradesmen pushing food that stank of burnt fat, and women throwing water over stains they had no hope of removing. She tried to take in many levels of the city at once, but it was a chaotic menagerie. It was possible the young man had been through and she'd missed him, maybe many times. It was possible the slavers would be back through here, too, and she'd never see them coming. When the thought of them made her skin tighten, she tried to push them from her mind.

Yesterday's encounter was the closest she had come to the tattooed man since she had escaped from Balfair's estate. The closest since her earliest memories, even, when that monster had forced her into captivity. She had only known for sure that he was after her when she'd seen him on the bank of the river, before arriving in the city, and even then she'd hoped it was a coincidence. At the back of her mind she'd willed away the childhood horror stories that Sincade had told her: the bogeymen wouldn't come after her, they didn't care about her any more. But there they were. Hunting her as Balfair and Sincade always promised they would. The two of them were dead because of her, and the demonic force of the tattooed man had risen from whatever cave he'd been dormant in to drag her into some new hell.

It was a good thing, though, she promised herself. If they were this close to her, she could finish this thing. With her slave bangle gone, they were the only people left to care that she lived, or how she lived – she just needed to stay one step ahead of them. Needed to get someone to fight them for her. She couldn't count on the luck she had enjoyed with the bloody-minded mercenary she'd left lying in the mud by the estate.

Montgomery. His face a mess, at her hands. Cracked open. Another death because of her.

She screwed her eyes shut and tried to think of something else. She needed more people in her life. Others to replace the few she had known. Good people, like she'd believed existed somewhere in this hive of activity. The people she'd met since she escaped had proved no better than the ones before, so far.

She scanned the market stalls again.

The city was full of loud people, ordering others to buy their wares, or quiet, moody people, warning others away with wicked stares.

A woman came down the street carrying a long pole with a metal contraption at one end. She held the pole up to the tall lanterns flanking the boardwalk, sparking a light into them. Deni stared with wonder; not at the clever device, but at the simplicity of the work being done. When Balfair had been her master, she had single-handedly cleaned and maintained their estate, taking time each day to activate and extinguish the gas lanterns and to cook food and to sweep floors and to move equipment. Here, people seemed fully occupied doing just one of these tasks.

"You'll fall to your death!" a man shouted, and Deni snapped her attention to a level below, where a young man was dropping a few metres down, from one walkway to another.

The young man. Finally.

He gave a friendly wave back up, dismissing whoever he'd upset, then skipped through the crowd to catch up to the street-lighter. A few tiers up, Deni raced along her own walkway to keep her eyes on him. He was light-footed, and lightly dressed, with a white shirt and a flannel vest, a small crop of untidy hair on top. He joined the woman as she lit another lantern. "Hey, miss, excuse me, miss!" The lady held up the staff like a defensive weapon. He jumped back, raising his hands. "I don't mean any harm. I think you dropped this."

The lighter lowered her staff, the fear on her sooty face fading in the light of the young man's smile. He was younger than Deni had realised, perhaps even younger than her. Barely old enough to be called a man. That must've been where his friendliness came from. Too young to know any better.

He held up a small pouch, which looked empty. The street-lighter took it and slipped it into a pocket. Deni knew the look on her face; whatever it was the man was returning, she didn't want it. Probably dropped it deliberately. Still, she thanked him.

The young man pointed to a small patch on one of the lady's arms. Her clothes were typical of the city workers, scraps darkened by the air and sporting a cog emblem. The same one worn by the guards that visited the estate: the symbol of the Estalian Empire.

"You don't look much like a guard," the young man said.

"How's a guard look?" the street-lighter replied, like she was expecting a joke.

"Hard," the man shrugged. "Like they're looking for trouble. Like they can't smile." She smiled. He seemed too breezy to have thought this up spontaneously; was it a rehearsed act? He continued, "Not that I don't respect them. You like helping people, right? That's why people become guards, isn't it?"

"Yeah," the street-lighter said, less amused. "That's why I light up lamps. I need to get back to work – I got a lot of streets to cover before dark."

The young man pointed upwards. "You don't call this dark?"

The street-lighter shook her head and turned away. He spoke more loudly. "Thanks for what you're doing. People don't say that enough. I love to see these streets lit up!"

"It's a job," the street-lighter replied, even less comfortable as he drew attention to her.

With that, she disappeared into the crowd, leaving the young man alone but pleased with himself. He had bundled up to this stranger looking for some weird validation. He wasn't trying to hustle her, or seemingly get anything from her. Had he taken something when she wasn't looking? Maybe he was a pickpocket. That would make sense, since he'd stolen the box.

He sprang into motion, jumping up a pile of boxes to the next level. Another angry stall-owner shouted and he apologised merrily. Deni ran after him. It didn't matter what he was up to; he'd lead her back to that note, and she'd be done with all this.

The young man was agile, climbing up and down poles and jumping from one walkway to another like some kind of tree animal. Deni knew how to move quickly, slipping past people like she wasn't there, but the intricacies of the city made it hard to keep an eye on him. The day was definitely getting darker, too; not with the thickening cloud, but dusk.

He finally slowed down at the end of a long row of shacks, each barely bigger than one of the washrooms from the estate. The modest homes lined one side of a walkway, with rows above and below in a series of giant steps. The thin metal barrier on the empty side looked across an artificial valley to a similar set of stepped shacks opposite. Each of the homes was unique in its colours and the junk that made up its walls, but all shared the same rickety, impoverished style. Deni crept to the tier above the young man's, keeping low as she watched him approach a building.

She flashed on the memory of Balfair warning her of the wider world. Outside the estate, he'd said, people lived in homes a fraction of the size of her workspace. The kitchen she had spent most of her time in really was larger than a handful of these shacks. The estate's heating, their small gas stoves, and the dim gas lighting were luxuries compared to the metal-drum fires and candles of an area like this.

The young man came out from his shack with an older man, withered by age to skin and bones. The old man's grey and white hair hung around his shoulders in kinked strands, thinner at the front. He spoke with a bold voice that showed none of his age, pushing the young man away: "Out, come on out! See what you done!"

Smoke wafted out of the shack after them.

"Didn't mean to surprise you," the young man told him, more amused than apologetic.

The old man shook his head, leaning against a wall as he looked back inside. He said, "Ah, blast, you've ruined it."

"Be fair," the young man said. "Was there much to ruin?"

The old man went to cuff him but he ducked out of the way. They seemed happy in spite of the scene. Whatever luxuries they lacked, this was their home and they shared it with loved ones. They could come and go as they pleased. That mattered. Soon Deni would enjoy the same freedom. She was never going back to servitude, not for any luxury.

"Met a nice lady on the way back," the young man said. "A street-lighter. She'd dropped something."

"And you just had to give it back, I guess?" the old man raised a bushy eyebrow. "Why you always got to be talking to people? You're an interferer, Tyler, you know that?"

"I met a guard, earlier, too. Thought he might help me, but he was..." the young man stopped. Tyler. An interferer. Whoever else he'd met hadn't impressed him as much as the street-lighter. He went on, "The street-lighter was better, put it that way. I got a smile from her."

"Modo, a smile!" The old man invoked the god of chance with a derisive laugh. "You'd feel better if that guard had given you a smile, would you? What're these thoughts doing in there?" The man knocked his knuckles against Tyler's head. "There's no one burning down our homes or cutting our throats as we sleep, what more do you want? The Guard gotta make you happy, too?"

"That's not what I meant. Whatever. Have you been by Kompter's?"

Did he really just want to see those people smile? Did he really think that street-lighter had been nice to him? Crossing the outside world, Deni wasn't sure she had encountered anyone who really cared that anyone else was happy. They all kept their heads down. Too worried about their own lives to care about anyone else's. Same as it had been in the estate.

The old man let out a long, retiring breath. "Job's done, all right, but he's got no chips to pay. I told him it's honest work we've done and honest pay we're due. Him being a good man – at least at some point – don't put food in our pan, does it?"

"No sir, but we're putting some rightness in the world – maybe keeping a man alive longer. That's worthy pay, isn't it?"

"You've got your dad's stubbornness for all things good, I ever tell you that?"

"Enough times," Tyler stifled something approaching a laugh. "Every time you want to hide the fact you think the same way, right? I didn't see you walking away from the job."

"Bah, I was promised some fresh *glus* – that, at least, he delivered on. Ah forget it! I've heard there's a circus in town, what do you think of that?"

Tyler put an arm around his shoulders. "I'm already promised there. I'll get you dinner, what do you say?"

The pair dropped back into the shack, fanning out the smoke. They got themselves ready in whatever way they needed, then put a padlock on the door and wandered away. Deni followed at a distance as they went down a set of stairs. The old man was telling Tyler, "I got an idea for another job. Church going up in Harlow, they need a few extra hands."

"Providence, or the Old Gods?"

"It matter?"

"You don't believe in Providence."

"Don't believe in the People of the Flame neither, but I made a tidy profit fixing one of their carts two moons ago, didn't I?

Believe in getting paid, is what I believe in."

"You wouldn't put a roof on a fighting pit, would you?" Tyler tested him.

The old man chuckled: "How much they paying?"

A few blocks over, they'd left the tiers of Tyler's neighbourhood to return to the more typical pillars of homes. They knocked at a door five storeys up, a tower little wider than their shack, and a young lady came out. Though they were all hard to see in the twilight shadows, Deni could tell she was pretty. Long hair and nicely sewn clothes made from new materials. Not like Deni's cloak, which had become hard and full of holes from the weeks she had been wearing it without a change.

The girl looked stern, though, even as she smiled at the young man and they briefly embraced. It was a short hug, and a light kiss. Polite. The girl's smile vanished a moment later, as she gave the old man a quick hello. Like much of what Deni had experienced in the city, this seemed nothing like the companionship she'd imagined. The antique storybooks in the estate had suggested love was a warm and powerful thing. They'd also suggested strangers could be kind and caring. So much of what Sincade had told her was proving to be true; that those fantasies were just that. Perhaps her fellow slave had been bitter with good reason; he must have experienced some of this.

The world was a cold place. The Metropolis was as miserable as he had been.

"Wasn't sure you'd come," the girl said.

"'Course I was gonna come, it's the circus isn't it?"

"Though you might be chasing after that runaway."

Tyler hesitated, then shook his head. She didn't trust him, that was obvious. And he was uncomfortable. He said, "You ready?"

Deni watched the group pad off. She'd seen enough. Other people had been talking about the circus in the market. It was across the city, on the river. It would be a long evening, following them there and back. And difficult to keep track of them. There was no need, though. Deni crept back the way they'd come, to the undefended shack.

5

The circus spanned a space opposite Grenevic, on the bank of the Drain, where the charred remnants of a warehouse levelled by fire formed a perimeter of broken walls. The performers had pushed the rubble to one side and erected a circle of tents whose many faded colours came alive in the light of countless lanterns. In the largest tent, acrobats performed great physical feats; the smaller tents exhibited lesser spectacles of foreign machines, weapons and animals, or games and scams to trick less guileful punters. In the centre of it all were looming mechanical rides, scrapped-together chunks of driftwood and rusty cogs spinning people, raising them in the air, propelling them back and forth at speed. Tyler and Sila had already tried the steam-powered carousel, which spun them in a cloud of smoke and left them with a nauseous sensation that took ten minutes to pass.

Tyler tried to love it. Usually, he found as much joy in seeing people fleeced as they got from enjoying the games, but this evening he was distracted. Sila's combative attitude, scorning the idea of helping the runaway girl, only made his inability to help starker in his mind. Qait's words spiralled around his head, and his best efforts to stay positive were waning when he thought about how little everyone else cared.

The worst of it was them questioning why he cared. Having to justify it to Qait, Sila – even to himself – seemed wrong. He knew slaves and the rehabilitation of kids in the Mines were a necessary part of society. They gave industries staff and helped the people in charge to do a better job. And those kids and slaves would be out on their ears, starving in gutters, otherwise. There were horror stories about the things that the escapees in the Kennel did to survive, from stabbings right through to cannibalism.

But none of that meant people *wanted* to be in the Mines, or servants to rich people.

That girl had been running scared – and those people were terrifying. That wasn't right.

There were nasty crowds in Bawkley, from heavy substance peddlers to protection gangs, but the Road Guard kept them in line. Those people knew the limits of what they could get away with, mostly restricting their violence to themselves, and the city was essentially safe if you kept your wits about you. Slavers weren't of the city, though. They were outsiders: they traded in the country beyond the cities, making them more dangerous. The average guard dealing with city thugs and thieves probably wouldn't know how to handle a slaver. Maybe that was the problem. That girl had been looking for a Border Guard, after all, not just anyone. And she'd marked a point on a map that she wanted to get to. She needed help, but the person she wanted to ask was already set to turn her away.

That was devastating. *Someone* had to do something.

"Would you quit brooding and look at this?" Sila dug her elbow into his ribs.

They were in front of the creature in the large cage, a monstrous beast, taller than a man and emitting rumbling noises louder than a hide drum. Its skin was thick and dark, a living layer of leather, and huge wings of ears hung past its bulbous head, which extended into a thick tentacle. Surrounded by gaping onlookers, it looked as frightened as it was angry. Tyler wondered if they ever let it out to stretch its legs. Another trapped animal.

"Amazing, ain't it?" Sila said with delight, but her face fell when she looked at Tyler. "What's *up* with you?" She turned the question to Ruke. "What's up with him?"

"Got helping people on his mind," Ruke said. He pointed away. "We going up or what?"

An enormous wooden Ferris wheel stood to the side, slowly lifting people to view the circus and the centre of the Metropolis. Tyler frowned and said, "How's that any different to what we see on the job?"

"Come on." Sila pulled his arm. "We need to see the freaks!"

Sullenly obliging, Tyler let her take him to one of the larger tents. The parade of oddities inside were mostly formed by design rather than nature, with limbs and other additions manufactured by the circus physician, who proudly explained the devices when asked. One man had no legs, and rolled around on a wheelchair with pneumatic motors. A metal-armed man proved his strength by breaking through rocks, though he had to use his human arm to pull the levers that operated the artificial limb.

"From beyond the Aftan Boundaries, feared by bandits and loved by locals," a man suddenly boomed, bidding the occupants of the crowded barn to look his way. He was clad in a burgundy suit, with a fine moustache and a bulging chest. "The Frenzied Horde rides through plight to bring light to the darkening days! Our spirits stay strong! Behold – the Incandescent Man!"

Tyler watched Sila and Ruke's faces as they lapped it up. Lucky them – they could enjoy this without caring that others were in trouble. When the announcements were over and the barker had given names to some of the other inefficient human machines, and the trio had wandered back outside, Tyler recalled the announcer's words, and echoed them back to his companions: "Easy for our spirits to stay strong, what troubles have we got?"

"Just the one right now," Ruke said, distractedly moving towards a meat vendor, where some animal was turning on a spit. "My belly's got a hankering."

"Hold up," Sila said, hotly turning on Tyler. "You're still on this? When did finding something someone dropped get to be so serious? You sweet on this girl?"

"No, it's nothing like that," Tyler said. He knew she wasn't going to like the truth, but he had to tell her. The feeling wasn't going away. "There's a man's name on that note. He can help. But he won't. He thinks the people after this girl are too dangerous to bother with."

"You went and checked?" Sila demanded. "By the gods! You really *are* sweet on her."

"You don't get it –"

"I get it all right!" Sila snapped, voice rising. "We're just getting started – hasn't been, what, four dates – already you're looking after –"

"Dendra!" Tyler invoked the life goddess. "Can you listen to me for a second?"

"No – no – I told you let it go, and you're out here, and we seen these great things and not even a smile from you – and you're whining, like she's all that matters, and what about me?"

Tyler moved closer to her, trying to put an arm around her and calm her down. People were stopping to watch. He caught Ruke's eye, but the old man quickly turned his attention to a freshly purchased skewer of meat, not wanting to get involved.

"You're a rot, Tyl, you know that? Keflo said, you know –"

"Oh, give it a break!" Tyler cut in. "I saw someone in trouble – listen to yourself – you think it's all about you? She was running from *slavers*! If you'd seen them –"

"You don't even know that's what they were!" Sila got impossibly louder. "You just wish it, so you can play hero – Bawkley boring you, is it? You rat – you –"

"People who can do something to help others *should*!"

"Ain't that the truth," a rumbling voice cut in. Tyler and Sila looked up at the stern face of the man in the burgundy suit. They both opened their mouths to reply, but he continued, "Now, I don't care for this argument, other than that it's bothering my guests, but if the sticky point is this young gentleman wanting to help a slave, then help a slave's what you should do."

Sila started a protest he didn't give her a chance to voice.

"Come." The man put a hefty hand on her shoulder. "It seems clear the resolution of your conflict lies in following this boy's plan. That'd be right, wouldn't it?"

He had a hand on Tyler's shoulder, too, and was walking them across the path, away from the crowd. The onlookers slowly turned back to what they were doing, the surrounding hubbub returning. Tyler twisted back to Ruke as the old man trotted up behind them with a mouthful of food.

"You know," the showman said, "we travel far and wide to put on this show. One moon ago we crossed the South Sea, procuring animals in Afta. Over there, they've got a saying. *Those together last the longest*. It sounds better in the Aftan tongue. Rhymes. But still, that's not bad, is it, *those together last the longest*. You know why they say it?" Sila was too intimidated to talk, and Tyler waited for the lesson. Had they found someone who understood? The man's moustache arched upwards in a smirk. "Out there, it's icy cold, there's little enough food and for sure no industry – but the biggest challenge is how damned lonely it is. They keep each other going by telling stories around campfires, sharing their histories, sharing their resources. Really listening to each other. Those who stay together keep each other *sane*. Over here, there's so many people huddled up tight enough that you don't see the cracks. When you *do* see a crack, don't think of the Guard, those faceless parasites – think about those Aftan nomads, doing their all to keep each other going."

Tyler nodded eagerly. "My father used to say that, you know – always do the right thing."

The showman twisted back to Ruke, who shook his head, spitting food to say, "I mean, *I* say it – but the boy's dad's not with us no more. Did one good thing too many." Ruke creased up, realising his bluntness, but Tyler ignored him.

He had to secure the circus-man's help. He said, "Sir, there's this girl – she was –"

The showman patted Tyler's shoulder and nodded understanding. But with the comforting pat, he gently shifted Tyler away, and said, "Indeed. You do the right thing. Just – somewhere else."

Tyler realised where the short walk and talk had taken them. They were standing on the other side of the rope barrier that surrounded the circus. They had passed the ticket hut, where new visitors were still queueing to get in. For all the man's words, they were simply being ejected. Another person who didn't even care.

They made it almost all the way back to Bawkley in silence before Sila exploded. After a tense but quiet walk along the bustling ground level, Ruke set her off when he caught sight of one of his favourite eating joints. "Let's eat in the Slew Diner – seeing as we didn't get our fill…"

"You got us kicked out of the fucking circus!" Sila shrieked. "You selfish, cheating prick!"

Tyler stared back incredulously. She continued with a series of insults and accusations as Tyler held his tongue, resisting the urge to shout back. He already knew this wasn't working, and there was no sense spending more energy on it. How dare he think of someone else, she was saying, when they had themselves to think about. When he had *her* to think about. It had cost them a night at the circus, already, and he didn't have any work lined up, either. How was he going to show her a good time?

Tyler let her words wash over him. There was nothing he wanted to say to her, so he merely held on to the strap of his leather satchel, picturing his father telling him to keep calm. Ruke

31

tried to intervene a couple of times and she flapped a hand at him, screaming, "No! You know it's true! He's no good!"

They waited for her to run out of steam. Her tirade crescendoed, though, and concluded with a harsh slap to Tyler's face. With that, she stormed off. Ruke stared with his jaw open as Tyler touched a finger to his reddening cheek.

"You didn't deserve none of that," Ruke muttered. "Whether you're thinking on other girls or not. Let's grab a bite, lick our wounds, get some rest and start a new day of the morn. What do you say?"

"You go," Tyler said. "There's something I want to do."

"Don't tell me you still got ideas –"

"Why *shouldn't* I have ideas?" Tyler shot back. "I *know* what's the right thing to do."

Ruke considered him quietly. "Sure. but how you gonna do anything about it?"

"I'm gonna stop waiting on someone else to act," Tyler said. "I don't care that no one else thinks it's worth it. I'll see you at home."

6

The lock opened with a satisfying click.

Deni slipped her knife back into its sheath under her sleeve and pocketed the pin she'd found in the gutter. Of all the skills she'd taken from Balfair's estate, the ability to open locks was second only to the ability to go unseen. Not that she imagined the cheap padlock was really meant to keep people out – more just to hold the door shut. Her thoughts were confirmed as she entered the shack; Tyler and his elderly companion owned nothing worth taking. They barely had padding to sleep on, their food pots were dirty and their few items of discarded clothes were fit for little more than mopping up spillages. The gas hob was coated in dried stew in the aftermath of the old man's failed attempt at cooking. It was only partially responsible for the smell. The sort of scent old food and clothing adopted to warn you away.

After a moment of toeing filthy clothes out of the way, Deni uncovered the box. Hodwick's damned box. Empty. She would be safe, away, if she had just pocketed the note. If he hadn't insisted on using this cumbersome piece of junk.

She flipped the open box over a few times, then tossed through the rest of the clothes with less restraint. What'd these idiots done with it? They couldn't have known what it meant.

She sat down to think.

She could surprise them. Force them to hand it over, if they still had it. It would be two more people who knew her face and had reason to hate her, perhaps, but that was the easiest way. The quickest way. The tattooed man would catch up to her again, otherwise.

Deni toyed with her knife. It was the only thing she still had from the estate, perhaps still the sharpest blade in the empire. It had done bad things in her hands, and one terrible thing in Montgomery's. It could do terrible things again. They'd know it, somehow; feel it in the Universal Conscious. This weapon was a killer.

The images came back to her as she closed her eyes. There was so much blood. Across the tollman's neck, all over the guards, and where Balfair's head had once been. On Montgomery's face after she had swung the rock into his skull. Dark lines marked his cheeks like warpaint. He had deserved a violent death, but the image still haunted her. As frightening as the tattooed man's grimace. The bloody face of one enemy, the glimmering gold teeth of another. Demons threatening to claw themselves free from her imagination to reclaim her.

Deni tried to shake herself out of it. She created a space around herself, folding clothes without thinking. She straightened some of the pots. This was their home, why didn't they take some time to make it up? Get rid of the smell.

She left the shack and went to the railing to breathe freely. The estate's swamp air had been more appealing; natural, if not pleasant. Here, everything smelt like smoke and things thrown into fire. Burnt meat, burnt waste, even burnt metal. The Metropolitans had created their own, thicker, blacker clouds under the already dark sky, with their chimneys and flames.

The old man's grumbles brought Deni back to earth. She froze, keeping her face forward as he meandered onto the path behind her, muttering to himself. "Kids' stuff. Look at me, don't look at her, kids' stuff."

She didn't move, to avoid drawing attention to herself. His footsteps slowed at the shack.

"Didn't we..." the old man mumbled. In his distraction at the open door, Deni ducked under the railing and slid down. Her feet found the roof of a shack below and she eased herself onto it.

"Oh, seriously!" The old man's voice rose as Deni ducked into the shadow of the overhanging walkway. "Find anything you liked? May Hrute have you!"

A few tiers up, a lady shouted back, "Take your medicine and shut up!"

"There's thieves about! Idiot thieves, stealing from the poor!"

Deni crept further into the shadows as another neighbour shouted for quiet. The old man continued complaining as he went inside. He had come back alone. She had to wait yet.

Someone was crudely plucking a string instrument, which broke up the continual sounds of dull conversation coming from the surrounding homes. The musician wasn't particularly able, but it gave Deni something to focus on, until the uneven melody was interrupted by footsteps above. Expecting more residents returning from wherever they went to drink their problems away, Deni crept over the roof she was hiding on and supported herself on the overhanging walkway. Staying out of view, she listened. Two people. At least. Big or weighed down by armour. Maybe both.

The pair slowed as they reached her position. A woman said, "Looks like the place."

Deni held her breath. She recognised the voice.

The second person made a sound of approval.

The hinges creaked as they opened a door, and the old man's voice came out: "Here, what do you think you're – hey – you're –"

"Ruke, right?" the low tone of the tattooed man said. The hairs prickled over Deni's body.

"What are you after?" the old man, Ruke, demanded. He was brave but confused.

The walkway creaked as the slavers moved into the shack.

"Your boy, he's the roofer?" the tattooed man continued. "Climbs around the market?"

"Climbs around everywhere, what of it? Knock over something, did he? I swear –"

"He had something that didn't belong to him."

"The hell he did," Ruke spat back. "What'd he want with the likes of you?"

There was a pause. The old man must have been taking them in properly for the first time. Deni could imagine their ink-stained bodies filling up his home. If Tyler had told him anything at all, Ruke must've realised who these people were.

"You know what we're talking about," the woman said, her tone no softer than the man's.

"You can't just barge in –"

There was a thump and a crash of furniture; one of them had knocked him down. He complained weakly as the pair moved about the shack.

"She was carrying this," the woman said. "Where's the contents?"

"Nothing to do with –"

Another thump, and something snapping. Deni winced. Ruke

was frail; he couldn't take half of what these people could serve.

"Where's the boy?" the man asked.

"Got his own life," Ruke coughed.

Another shuffle and the sound of the wall shaking as he was pushed against it. If the neighbours hadn't heard the scuffle before, they must have heard that. Yet the area had only grown quieter since this pair arrived; the music and conversation had stopped. Didn't these people know this old man? They lived right on top of him, surely someone would help?

"He never went to the Guard," the woman said. "Which means you either wanted this thing for yourselves, or you wanted to help that girl. Which is it?"

"What girl?" Ruke wheezed.

Deni tensed at another thump, which shook the building beneath her. Someone moved nearby, startled by the sound. Whoever it was didn't venture out.

"That it?" Ruke said, and another thump followed, this time eliciting a great, pained grunt.

"That's enough," the tattooed man told him without feeling. "Help yourself."

No, not without feeling. Worse, there was something like sadness in his voice. Like he regretted his actions, even if it was how he lived his life.

The sound of Ruke's heavy breathing filled the air as they let him recover. Deni pleaded with him, in her mind, to just tell them what he knew. He didn't need to suffer. Not because of her.

Ruke said, "I told him to leave it well alone. You know what I said? This girl probably done bad. That your sort wouldn't be after her otherwise. Said he had no part in it. Right?"

"Absolutely," the woman said.

"And you know, he *did* go to the Guard, but they didn't wanna help. Said the same thing. Not their problem, let these people do what they're gonna do."

"He went to who?" The woman sounded surprised. They must have spoken to the Guard themselves. Tyler had gone to someone they didn't expect, then. Had he understood what it said on the paper? When Ruke didn't answer, the woman went on, "What, exactly, was in that box?"

The old man took his time, clearing his throat and regaining some breath. He said, "It wasn't yours, huh?" The slavers waited this one out, not hitting him again. He started chuckling. "Oh, the boy was right, weren't he?" *No*, Deni tried to project to him, sensing what was coming, *don't say it*. "This girl, she any less defenceless than this old man?"

Another pause. The tattooed man said, "Tell us where the boy is and we can all move on."

"I got a better idea," Ruke said. "Get the hell out of my home." The old man suddenly shouted, "Call the Guard, someone! These animals are trying to –"

Another thump and a crash and he went quiet.

A few doors opened, at last.

Come on, Deni pleaded. Don't let them get away with it. Stop these animals.

Whoever had come onto the walkway didn't come closer: the sounds of movement stopped as the pair left Ruke's shack. The walkway flexed near Deni as they paused.

"What the hell is going on down there?" a man called out from a safe distance away.

"Private matter," the tattooed man answered.

"Doesn't sound private to me."

"Your choice."

No more movement followed. No more remarks from the neighbours. Then the sounds of a few people meekly retreating. Cowards. Insular, selfish cowards. Doors creaked as they hid in their homes.

"Let's get a drink," the tattooed man said. "He'll be back."

They walked away.

Deni waited until they were out of earshot, then peered above the overhang. Ruke's door was wide open and the old man was sprawled across the floor, his lower half visible as a crumpled mess in the dim moonlight. She scanned to the side, to the backs of her pursuers disappearing down some steps. She couldn't pull herself up, or risk getting any closer; they might have people watching.

A little groan came from the shack. The old man twitched.

Thank Dendra.

Deni dipped into the shadow of the overhang and climbed off her platform, then crept through the darkness in the gaps between the huts, in the opposite direction to the tattooed man. She found another stairway and returned to Ruke's tier, then made the same shady dash back, as quickly as her caution would allow, checking the vantage points that looked down on her. There was little movement, though. The twang of the string instrument returned, uncertainly at first. Then it stopped again. No longer in the mood.

At Ruke's shack, Deni crouched by the wall and listened. He was gasping for air. Alive at least. She knocked on the wall and whispered, "You okay?"

He groaned, "...you think?" He continued muttering something she couldn't hear. Some of the words came out between his rasping. "...damned people. That what we get? I wouldn't... I would've done something..."

"Where's Tyler?" Deni asked quietly.

The old man stopped. He had enough energy, at least, to consider what was happening. That was good. He said, "You one of them?"

"No," she said.

He paused. When he spoke again, his voice was quieter, more careful. "It's you?"

Deni said nothing. He had to be thinking this was her fault. It *was* her fault.

"Right," said Ruke, into her silence. It made him cough again, and his legs scuffed the floor – he was trying to sit up. He pushed himself closer to the wall, until he was on the other side from her. He said, "Don't sweat it. Everyone's gotta take care of themselves, I don't grudge that. Just wish the boy understood."

Deni bit her lip. Tyler wanted to help her, was that it? It would make him the first. And it meant they'd treat him as harshly as her, if they caught him. *When* they caught him, she corrected herself. They'd be waiting for him to come back. She asked, "Does he have my note?"

Ruke snorted, not justifying the question with an answer. "Where's it gonna take you?"

She considered it. It didn't have to take her anywhere. It just had to make things change. She explained, "If I get it back, I can stop those people. For good."

The old man laughed, genuinely amused, making Deni flush. Was she that transparent, that to do something worthwhile seemed so unlikely? She told him, faintly, "I mean it. Please, tell me where Tyler went."

Ruke didn't respond right away. Like he was considering her, reading her presence through the wall. "Where you think?" he said, quietly. "Where'd you go if you were looking for a runaway?"

7

The Metropolis was fully alive as Tyler walked through Bawkley. Never mind Qait, Sila, or Ruke even. He was going to do something good this evening. He'd be happy, and helpful, for the rest of them. He passed crowds rolling dice in the gutters and pitting small animals against each other for sport, the dancing flames of lanterns casting wicked shadows over it all. Tyler returned smiles and greetings to lift his spirits. It didn't last. He slowed down to observe a man with bulging eyes arguing with a crowd. The man was protesting about a place called Fewhaven, a trading post a short distance north of the Metropolis.

"The Guard have corrupted the north!" the man raved. "They caused the Thesteran Fire. That's why guards are being strung up from posts; it's not rebels, it's our own people who've found out the truth!"

"You're mad," someone snapped. "They're the only thing keeping us from the Kandish savages. The Short Queen's psychotic – she's skinned people alive from Thesteran to Nexter."

"Then why are we barricading the city?" The man pointed feverishly north. "If people are running from Highness Elzia, we should be letting them in! But the Guard are cutting off access. They're blocking the waterways –"

"They're hunting for rebels!"

Tyler had heard the name Elzia in the same whispers that spoke of violence outside the city. Some held her responsible for the Border Guard ships crowding the Drain. They said she was beautiful but deadly, an insane woman who was carving a path through Estalia to avenge her murdered family. Fire burnt in her eyes that inspired others to follow her. So much so that the Guard were regrouping to face her as one unified force, rather than risk being caught alone. It was mad, but it caught the imagination of street-preachers.

"It's not just Kands that believe in her," the man continued. "It was *only* guards that were killed in Fewhaven, don't you see? Our own people are rising up – the Guard are falling!"

"We'd be damned without them!" someone disagreed.

"What have the Guard done for you lately? Have they fed your family? Or just *taken*?"

Tyler elbowed his way to the edge of the group, as other people jostled to be heard.

"They caught someone fixing to blow up the Grenevic Passage!"

"The Guard took a bucket of my carrots," a new voice protested. "Left me wanting."

The debate got hotter as the grey armour of two Road Guards clattered into view. A man shoved someone near Tyler. He scrambled back out of the confusion and pulled himself up some building supports to the next tier. The guards pushed into the centre of the group, fixed on the speaker as he shouted, "It's the ugly truth: this rebellion is not just upon us, it's *for* us! It's the Fall of the Guard –"

A guard struck him without warning. The crowd fell over each other to get away. Down on a knee, the speaker tried to shout something else, and the guard struck him again. Tyler surged forwards, but someone caught his arm and pulled him back, hissing, "Don't be stupid!" Tyler tried to break the grip as he stared into the face of an older woman. She shook him, her washer's muscles holding fast. "You don't wanna drink from that cup."

The speaker clutched his bleeding nose, half hysterical, as the guard pointed a finger to the people around him and said, "You're all responsible for encouraging these vagrants." The guard pulled the man up by his hair. "Check your pockets didn't get any lighter in his excitement."

The onlookers started patting themselves. One man leapt forward. "My purse! Where's my purse?"

The guards checked the speaker but found nothing. They dragged him away, insulting him as they went, and the victim of theft was left aghast. Tyler wrenched his arm free of the woman. She was staring at the crowd, no longer interested in him, muttering, "Third one this week. These lunatics wanna see the city burn."

Tyler glared at her. Right or wrong, the man had only been talking, and he certainly wasn't the thief, if there had been one. Tyler left uneasily, finding it hard to recover his smile.

*

Tyler crossed the open sewer trench that marked the boundary of Bawkley, over a rickety set of planks, and continued into the sprawling Low Slums. An expanse of huts followed, few higher than a single storey, perched in gaps between the pipe-system that took the city's waste out to country pits. The homes themselves weren't much worse than the ones in his ramshackle neighbourhood, but the ground here was muddy and loose, the air harsh and acidic, and the stench worse than any other place in the Metropolis. Most of those who lived here wore masks, and Tyler wrapped his handkerchief across his face in mimicry. His eyes began to sting as he coughed on fumes of melting rubber. Skeletal figures wrapped in blankets watched him without comment.

The Low Slums were ignored and forgotten by the rest of the city, even as they sat inside the walls. Tyler and his friends had ventured into the area on dares when they were younger, but it became sad rather than adventurous when they understood it for the living graveyard that it was. It was where the sick and mutilated came when they were shunned by others. Where retired crooks and unlovable whores came, when no one else would house them. The place Kompter would be destined for, if not for the charity of people like Tyler.

Tyler found a circle of residents gathered around a fire in the clearing between a few buildings. The conversation died as he approached.

"Excuse me, sorry to interrupt," Tyler said, pulling down his mouth-cloth to show a friendly smile. These people were not masked; perhaps they were more used to the smell than most. Their eyes looked hollow, though, drained of life.

"You lost?" an emaciated man with ashen skin asked, voice husky from dehydration.

"Sort of. I'm looking for someone. A girl. About my height." Tyler held up a hand. "With dark hair. And a roundish nose... she was quite young. Maybe a bit older than me?"

He met a lot of blank stares.

"Quite pretty," Tyler continued. "Not like an entertainer pretty but, you know, in an ordinary way. Maybe hadn't washed for a while." Still nothing. It wasn't a great description. None of these people had washed in a while. "She was on the run. Figured she'd come this way."

"They often do," said a bearded man with boils around his eye. "Better to leave them to it."

Tyler stared at him, feeling empty in the face of this apathy. "If it's all the same, I'd really like to find her..."

"Your age? She'd get picked up pretty quick." The bearded man turned back to the fire, speaking without interest. "Mine Guard or gangs. One or the other'll get you too, hang around long enough." His companions murmured agreement.

Tyler scanned what he could see of their surroundings. There'd been no hint of guards or gangs so far, and he doubted he would see any.

"What about the Kennel?"

The group seemed to shake their head as one. The ashen man said, "Lot of suffering happens here on account of fools spreading stories about that kids' paradise. It don't exist. Nothing good for you out here. Nothing good for no one."

"This girl – she wasn't being chased by the Guard or gangs. They had tattoos. Slavers."

The group stamped their feet in agitation, further burying their gazes in the flames. The skinny man spoke up. "Seen *them* all right. On the edges. Slavers wouldn't come out here. Kennel might not exist, but that sentiment does. Can't fight the Mine Guard, but slavers –" he spat aside to show his disgust. It was a dry globule of saliva that Tyler wished he hadn't wasted.

He turned away, thinking it through. If she'd made it this far, she might be safe, yet. She might have slipped past the slavers at the perimeter, and they might not have followed her in. They couldn't have covered all the entrances, after all, or he would've seen them himself.

Deni surveyed the slums from a high vantage point. There was no single clear entry point between the residential towers and large warehouses of Bawkley and the low-lying huts, but she'd found an abandoned watch-tower with a view that covered most of the passing points. The area approaching the slums was quieter and more industrial than the neighbourhoods she'd had to cross to get here, as though proximity to the poor region was enough to drive people away. Or maybe these large buildings, with their long flat roofs and tall chimneys, only operated during the day, and the area cleared out at night.

There were only a few plank bridges crossing the ditch that separated the more civilised regions of the city from the slums, and this had been the most direct route from Tyler's home, so he'd surely have come near here. Unless he'd already made it back into the labyrinthine walkways of the Metropolis, before she'd arrived. Assuming he made it back.

The Low Slums had shocked her when she'd first been through them, guided by Chetan's people, but the more she saw of the Metropolis the more they made sense. How could she ever have thought someone might help her, here, when they couldn't even help themselves?

Those poor people were a good reminder, though, of what happened when you didn't take charge of your own life. She would never end up like that, at least, slowly waiting for death. She just needed to find that boy; that note was going to change everything.

The countless derelict buildings stretched further than Tyler realised. The district ran from the west of Bawkley right across the city, north of Hunterwell and Wermblay, before reaching the Mines. Vast as their numbers were, and physically afflicted in uncountable ways, the people all seemed the same. Hopeless. Most shrugged him off. Some were more aggressive. One man tried to shunt into Tyler to swipe his money, but Tyler slapped his wrist away and ran. The mugger apparently had no energy to follow.

The further Tyler walked, the less likely the existence of the Kennel seemed. The children who escaped from the Mines would've been in even worse shape than these people. Fighting exhaustion, Tyler finally decided to turn back. His route took him over a small panel bridge, a fallen slab of metal that crossed a cracked pipe gushing with liquid. The bridge shook under his feet, making him slow down, giving time for a young man to appear in front of him, concealed in a cloak with a hood pulled up over his head.

Tyler paused. "Hey friend," he said. "You need something?"

"Heard you're looking for a girl," the figure replied, his high voice betraying his youth.

"Yeah," Tyler said. "You seen her?"

"What do you want her for?"

"Are you from the Kennel?"

"Ain't everyone told you there's no such thing?" the figure snorted. He hacked up something in his throat, coughed to the side and demanded, "You got something of hers?" The hood nodded to Tyler's satchel. Tyler tightened his grip.

"Don't even think about it," a second voice said. Another hooded figure appeared, crouched on a nearby roof with a long rifle pointing his way.

"Hey, take it easy." Tyler raised his hands. "I'm here to help."

"So hand over the bag," the first hood said. "Real slow."

A third hooded spectre moved out of an alley to the right. The figure on the bridge stepped forward, drawing a blade from under his cloak. Tyler stepped back and bumped into a fourth person, who shoved him. The first figure snatched the bag from Tyler's hand as he stumbled, and when Tyler tried to grab it the knifeman raised the blade, hood falling back.

The boy was at least a few seasons younger than Tyler, adolescent face dusted with dirt. His eyes were large and richly brown, highlighted by a nearby lantern. He bared his teeth, showing two gaps and one incisor replaced by dull metal.

"Stick him, Hazel!" one of the others snapped excitedly.

"I ain't gonna stick you," the knifeman growled at Tyler, jamming the bag under an arm. "I'll teach you a lesson. Go tell 'em all it ain't safe poking around for the Kennel."

Tyler said nothing. The bag was his father's, a fine leather satchel, but to let them know he cared would only make it worse. With only a few snacks and the girl's piece of paper in it, maybe they'd toss it aside when they decided it was worthless.

The knifeman looked him up and down one last time, then turned to leave.

"I'm trying to help someone," Tyler said, unable to help it.

"You just did!" the knifeman laughed, then let out a short, sharp whoop and ran. The other figures slipped back into the shadows, then scurried away. Tyler watched the various shapes flapping away into the darkness.

He took a step towards them, ready to follow, but someone called out from a nearby home, "Consider yerself lucky you still have your life." Tyler turned to a pock-marked man in rags. "Keep going and you'll lose more'n that bag."

Tyler hesitated, as the thieving children vanished into the shadows. Feeling utterly deflated, he remained motionless. There was no sense in following now, and he certainly didn't want to find their source. If the Kennel existed, after all, it was another blight the city would be better off without.

8

Maybe it was the moon.

Tyler looked at the ever-overcast sky and searched for the faint glow behind it. They said that when the moon was at its strongest, people acted strange. Animals, too; dogs howled in the cages around the market on the brightest nights. It was a better explanation than thinking all these people were as bad as they seemed. The moon's odd light, or something it put in the air, that'd be it. Give it a few days and they'd calm down, stop trying so hard to screw each other over. Qait might find it in him to track down this girl. Sila would see how unreasonable she'd been. Those kids, whoever they were, maybe they'd think about what they'd done and get the same attitude as him. Follow the note back to Qait Seyron, return his dad's bag and get the girl the help she needed.

Give it a few days for the moon to clear.

Tyler kicked a stone that ricocheted off a wall.

As *if*.

Sila had been needling at him since he first met her. He'd already given her time to soften, like Keflo promised she would. And those kids were what everyone feared they were. Rats. Stealing for no damned reason. Tyler kicked another stone, harder, this one banging against a door.

Returning to the city proper, he passed through a makeshift barrier, a couple of piles of crates with a faded sign facing out towards the slums, words painted in a scrawl. He didn't need to read to know it said something unwelcoming. As he huffed, his eyes fell on a man watching him from the corner of a building, half masked in shadow. He was short and bulbous, physically completely different to the others, but his furs and chain mail made Tyler pause with recognition. The man held a thick cigar with one hand, the other resting on the butt of a long pistol threaded through his thick leather belt. His hair was short on top with a fuzzy mess of black beard concealing his jaw.

Seeing Tyler recognise him, the man shifted to attention, taking the cigar from his mouth.

Neither said anything.

The man looked past Tyler, towards the slum, then back over his shoulder, towards Bawkley. He was drawing conclusions that Tyler was fairly sure he'd get right. The fact that the slaver was interested in a boy at all, when they should've been looking for a girl, said they knew something about him.

There was a little distance between them, at least. He still had a chance.

Tyler dived to the side and pulled one of the crate piles down behind him. As the pallets scattered, he kicked off a wall to spring up to a balcony. He caught the edge of the platform with the tips of his fingers and strained to keep hold as the man ran towards him. Tyler pulled himself up, his legs just missing the grip of his pursuer's clutching hands.

Tyler paused to look back – thinking he was out of reach – but the man had his pistol out, taking a few steps back to get a better angle. Tyler ducked as the gun went off.

The gunshot snapped Deni's attention to the opposite direction she'd been looking in. It came from behind the higher buildings to her left; no way to see to street level. Who else would be lingering out here, though?

She jumped down the steps, clearing half a dozen at a time and skidding at the turns. Halfway down the tower, she froze at the sound of another gunshot. In the alleys, closer now. They were coming her way. She drew her knife as she continued.

A man's voice shouted, "It her?"

"The boy!" Another shout. "That way, that way!"

Deni sprinted out of the stairwell, where the barriers opened to a path across a slanted roof; not a home, too big. A storage building. She skipped across it and flinched at yet another gunshot, the bullet audibly rushing through the air nearby. The second man shouted, "You trying to kill him?"

Deni listened for the sound of their scuffling feet – one shoved the other. "Get moving!"

She rushed to the edge of the roof and saw the pair sprinting across the street, one tall, the other wide, furs flapping behind them as they disappeared between two buildings on the other side. A few rooftops away, across the street, someone was climbing up.

The young man righted himself and gave one glance down, then looked up and spotted Deni watching him. His eyes lit up and he was about to say something, but was cut off by the men's feet rattling up metal stairs. Climbing after him. Tyler pointed to Deni, then away, further into Bawkley. She followed his gesture, seeing only the chaotic rise and fall of towers and walkways. No idea where to go.

She dropped back as the two men bundled up onto the opposite roof, shoving one another in their search. They spotted Tyler and ran after him, jumping across a gap in the buildings, heavier than the boy and less agile but bigger and more powerful, moving faster.

Deni ran in parallel, separated by the wide gap of the ground-level street as Tyler led his pursuers over a chain of buildings. The big storehouses stretched towards the more erratic rise of residential towers, which Tyler reached before they caught up. He clambered up a banister and onto the next tier up. The taller of his pursuers attempted the same, struggling to control his gangly limbs while the pistol-man stood back and took aim. Deni opened her mouth to shout a warning, but nothing came out as the gun fired. The bullet barely missed the young man, sparking off a support near his hand, and the surprise made him fall back. He reached out for a pole but missed it, then he fell, over the edge, back towards them. He slammed into the roof next to the men. The one struggling to climb dropped back down next to him, as the one with the pistol slowly approached. The young man was winded, rocking on his back with groans. As the wider man grabbed him by the arms and hauled him up, Tyler's head turned Deni's way. She ducked behind a rooftop sign, seeing the pleading look in his eyes.

The men made grumbling complaints she couldn't hear. One of them drove a fist into the boy's stomach. They dragged him back across the roof, to some stairs down.

They'd do worse to him than the others had done to the old man; he was younger and could take it. And he'd fight back. Deni descended, trying to keep track of the trio as they entered another stairwell. They reached the street and threw the boy down, into the open. There was no cover, nowhere for him to run.

"Where's the girl?" the bulkier, bearded man demanded. Tyler looked up defiantly. He and Ruke were clearly of the same stock. The taller man drove a boot into his face.

"Fuck it. Show us where you've been." The wider man put his pistol back through his belt and yanked his captive up by the throat. Tyler gagged as they shoved him ahead of them. Back towards the slums.

"She's not there," Tyler told the men as they frogmarched him. Now that the chase was over, they had slowed right down and he could take them in properly. The second man was tall and lean like a pole, and exceptionally ugly. His nose changed direction twice and his scarred face hugged tightly to the bones underneath. He was missing an ear, and beneath the mess of hard skin that replaced it was a smaller, cruder version of the V on their leader's arm.

"I was looking for her, right," Tyler said. "I didn't find her. She's not there."

"You're in trouble, then," the bearded one said. No less threatening with the gun put away. The tall one had never even drawn a weapon and he seemed equally dangerous. He had two sheathed swords hanging from his waist. Why would anyone need two swords?

"What do you want with her?" Tyler demanded.

"All you need to know," the bearded one said, "is that we've been waiting the better part of two days for that bitch. And if you don't show us to her, you pay for it yourself."

"I've got nothing to do with this," Tyler said. "The Guard will –"

"You see any guards out here, Grunberg?" The bearded man turned to the ugly one.

"Might as well be in the north, this far from town," Grunberg said.

Tyler fell quiet, watching their faces. The Bawkley limit was just ahead. Without the advantage of high buildings or Tyler's knowledge of the city layout, a getaway seemed impossible. He braced himself, looking sideways at the bearded man's pistol. The man pushed him ahead, spotting the glance. "Do yourself a favour, kid."

They weren't ten paces from the threshold to the Low Slums.

"Here's the deal," Grunberg said. "You tell –"

The tall man screamed as he twisted and dropped to a knee. One hand clutched at his back while the other drew a sword. The second man fumbled for his pistol again, but before he could draw it a cloaked figure darted into him and he let out his own agonised cry. He didn't go down, but lost his grip on the gun. Tyler leapt at the pistol as it hit the ground, only to get knocked back by Grunberg. The tall man's face was contorted in pain, but he was far from done.

The cloak flapped across Tyler's vision, his saviour grabbing his hand as she passed. Tyler was running without thinking, away from the men and towards the slums. Away from the safety of the city he knew. He glanced at the girl, her face fixed ahead, dark eyes full of determination. He looked back to the bearded man retrieving his pistol, one hand on his bleeding side. Grunberg was racing after them, staggering every few steps.

The girl moved even faster, making Tyler stumble. He looked up just in time to avoid a rapidly approaching rock. Hearing a click behind him, Tyler pulled the girl down. The pistol cracked and a bullet glanced off the rock they'd passed.

Trusting the girl's advance, focusing more on staying upright, Tyler didn't see the drop coming. They sprinted straight out from the building line over the edge of the dip and fell. Tyler hit something hard and flew off it into something else. He spun full circle before crashing to a stop. Damp seeped through his top and the stench of excrement filled his nose. He blinked to clear his eyes and regain his senses, looking back up.

They'd fallen down a sharp brick incline, perhaps twenty feet high, the bank of the great sewage ditch. Tyler pushed himself up onto his elbows, mentally checking his body up and down, aching. Blood tickled his brow. He wiped it off and looked along the brick trench. The girl was pushing herself up onto her hands and knees. Her knife lay a few feet away from her.

"You okay?" Tyler called out, triggering her into action. She sprang up and grabbed the knife, pointing it at him. Tyler scrambled back, well out of reach, and cried, "Seriously!"

The girl didn't answer, darting her gaze back to the lip of the trench as the two men limped into view. The bearded one fired down at once, barely aiming. The girl ran, splashing through a thin surface of waste liquid towards a wide tunnel opening.

Tyler went to follow, but another shot hit the ground behind her, separating them.

"Find a way down!" the bearded man roared. At the sound of the flintlock being reloaded, Tyler sprinted. He jumped over the central gap in the ditch, where water and waste had collected, and ran through the tunnel entrance the girl had used. The bearded man yelled from across the ditch, a shout that said they were getting away. Finally and surely.

Tyler jogged into the darkness, a grin spreading across his face as he let the adrenaline elate him. They'd done it – they'd escaped – this amazing girl had fought off those psychos and –

He was struck from the side and hit the wall. He froze there, a bony forearm pinning him in place as the tip of the knife teased his eye. Beyond the blade, the girl's wild eyes stared into his. They were pools of mad darkness, vibrating rapidly, somewhere between anger and fear, but he couldn't keep the smile from his face.

"It's okay," he started. "I'm –"

"Where's the note?" she demanded.

Slowly, inevitably, Tyler's smile faded. "I'm sorry..."

9

Neither of them had spoken for a long time. After the young man had nursed his minor wounds, he had taken to simply staring at Deni, with occasional smiles. She got the feeling he was still excited about their brush with the slavers, and he wanted her to know it. She tried to avoid looking at him.

"Thanks for saving me back there," he had said as they walked, rubbing his neck where the blade had touched it but never mentioning her threat. "I've been trying to help you, but damn – hardly looks like you needed it!"

She didn't want to talk to him. Didn't want to believe him. He wanted something from her, wanted to trap her somehow, with her secret, or with the debt of his so-called help. When she didn't reply, he continued giving her looks. She flashed him irritated and angry looks of her own that only seemed to make his smile stronger. But she caught cracks in his expression, in her quickly stolen glances. Under the excitement he was concerned, vulnerable. At least a little scared.

He should be.

They had stopped in a small cavern in the sewage network, where Deni decided there was enough space and a dry enough collection of scraps to get a fire going. If her sense of direction was right, they weren't far from the Kennel, but she didn't want to go straight there, not yet. They needed more light to continue by, to replace the torch she'd quickly fashioned, and they needed to dry their clothes. Most importantly, she needed to see this young man up close, to get an idea of his nature.

Deni looked up to find the whites of his teeth glowing in the dancing light of the fire. He said, "Where'd you learn to fight like that? I never would've guessed it – I mean, to look at you – what I mean is –" He was embarrassing himself as Deni frowned at him. He finished by blurting out, "I'm *impressed*."

His smile broadened. She glared back to try and force it off him. As if she knew how to fight – as if she was impressive. He was a flatterer, simple as that.

"What's your name?" he asked. She didn't answer, still watching him. He didn't seem to mind, waiting for her. Even if she wanted to talk, she didn't know what to say. Either he was like everyone else, and she couldn't trust him, in which case it was better to tell him nothing, or he really was as stupidly innocent as he seemed, and that was even worse. Because she could only tell him bad things. She decided to wait. At least until their clothes were dry.

They were safe here, at least. There was one entrance and one exit to their underground room, both opening into long echoing tunnels that no one could come down without being heard a mile away. The smell was unpleasant, but it was bearable.

Not like they had a choice. The men could've been tearing up the slum above by now.

She should have stabbed higher. Gone for the throat. It was harder to reach and she might have slipped, or missed, but it would have been worth it. She shouldn't have left them alive. But if she was capable of doing something like that, she wouldn't have needed help from the start.

The young man cleared his throat, looking into the fire. He'd taken the quiet time to reach a decision on the best thing to say. "I'm sorry I lost your paper."

Deni raised a questioning eyebrow.

"Sorry. I shouldn't have come out here with it." He sighed. "I didn't know where else to go. And sorry if I got in the way. The other night. I don't know how to deal with people like that."

"You're sorry?" Deni asked. He nodded, meekly, waiting for some kind of judgement.

No one had ever apologised to her before, not really. Not for anything that mattered. In his dying breaths, her master Balfair had used the word "sorry", but not for her. For himself. This boy, hurt and hiding for her sins, who she'd threatened with a knife, was upset because he thought he'd let her down. It wasn't possible. She didn't know what his trick was, but there had to be one. She said, "Why were you looking for me?"

He shrugged. "You looked like you were in trouble."

"So?"

His brown eyes glinted in the fire's light. Deni steeled her face against him, making sure to stay strong, to show no weakness. But she felt something, as his eyes rested on her. Something alien. The feeling she remembered from the stories Sincade had read to her. Hopeful stories, that talked about good people and how it was to know you were near one.

He finally replied, thoughtfully, "You're a person, same as anyone else. People in trouble need help."

Deni prodded the fire with a stick and stirred orange embers between them. "I'm a free woman. You understand that?"

"Did they try to take you from your home? I thought slavers only went after people with nothing."

He said it like it made sense. People were forced into nothing when they became slaves, not before. She kept quiet, though, too unclear about his intentions to start arguing.

He waited a moment more for a response, then asked, "Where is it, the place you want to go? What's there?"

Deni gave him another questioning frown, not following.

"Your paper, it pointed to a place. You wanted that tracker to get you there? He told me –"

"No," Deni said. "It's not for me."

Tyler's brow creased in confusion. "What do you mean? These coordinates –"

"It's to trade," she said. "That's all. I don't want to go there." Tyler was still staring, not seeming to follow, and Deni felt her face redden. She didn't know how to explain, and didn't really want to. What would he know of the sky, and the machines of a man like Balfair? She averted her eyes. "Maybe they'll still do a deal, even if they took it from you."

"The children?"

She nodded. "I need to get to Chetan. He can finish this."

"Who's Chetan?"

"The leader of the Kennel."

Quiet again. Tyler considered this, then said, "I'll come with you. It's dangerous. And the ones after you –"

Deni cut in: "It's nothing to do with you." It came out more curtly than she intended.

"After that," Tyler suddenly smiled again, pointing the way they'd come, "I'd say I'm involved, wouldn't you? They tried to shoot me! Think I'm not going to do something about that? Besides, I owe you, after what you just did."

He had a look of childish enthusiasm. Was he *enjoying* this? Deni said, "You don't know what you're doing."

"I want to help," Tyler insisted, shifting closer, around the fire.

"No one wants to help."

"Yeah, I get that. I mean, I don't get why, but I know how it is. That's not me, though. That'll never be me. I don't know you but I can see you're not doing anything wrong. Who wouldn't run from those freaks? And sure, you don't know me either, but we can change that." He held out a hand to her. "I'm Tyler. I fix roofs. And other things. Where'd you come from? What's your name?" Deni stared at the hand warily. He added, "You're supposed to shake."

Deni stood and took a few steps away from him.

He rose after her, saying, "No need to worry, I'm –"

She had the knife out again, without thinking. "Stay back."

Tyler's face fell. "I swear, I just want to do the right thing. I'm a good person."

"I'm not," Deni told him. "I'm bad. You need to stay away."

He didn't move as she backed off, towards the tunnel. "You expect me to just forget about this?" he said. "I went to the Guard and he didn't care, right? I've always thought they were out there, for people like you, but here we are and you're alone. If you can't count on the Guard, you need *someone* to count on. I couldn't sleep knowing that should've been me and wasn't. You can't ask me to just go home."

Deni froze at that. No, she couldn't. However dumb or brave he might be, she couldn't let him fall back into the slavers' hands. "No. You can't go home."

"Damn right, you're in trouble and I –"

"They're waiting for you."

Silence again as she let that sink in. He drew the right conclusion, weakly. "My uncle? Ruke?"

"He's okay," Deni said. "But they're there. And they'll get you if you go back."

"If my uncle –"

"He's okay. They won't hurt him." Any more, at least. She took a breath and said, "But they'll hurt you. To get to me."

Deni watched his fists clench and she stiffened, fearing he might try and hit her, never mind her knife, or that they were half a room apart.

"Ruke means everything to me," Tyler told her, straining to keep his voice level. "He's all the family I've got."

"I saw him, he's safe. Wait here, until I finish this. You'll be safe, too."

"Safe nothing," Tyler said, his conviction only strengthening. "They come to my home, they pull guns and push girls around... I'm not hanging around *waiting*. No argument."

Deni had nothing left to say. There was no trap he could lead her into, not in the Kennel, and he'd said nothing to hint of her debt to him. Her concern, she realised as she voiced it, was more honest: "I don't want you to get hurt."

Tyler raised a hand for her to lead the way, though, and said, "So let's finish your deal safely."

10

Tyler was more interested in watching the mystery girl than the tunnels. Difficult to talk to as she seemed, he was sure that helping her had been the right choice. She was alone against this violent force, and had gone to great lengths to hide herself, yet she'd come out of the shadows to save him. Even if she called herself bad, he already knew she wasn't.

Her flaming torch illuminated her cloak, which was unmistakeably that of a Sister of Providence, as he'd thought; a dark habit that would once have been hemmed with white, identifiable by a small emblem on the chest, now black with dirt. She was no sister, though. When she'd been preparing the fire, her sleeve had slipped and revealed raw red flesh lining her wrist. It was the mark of someone who had recently removed a slave bangle, though her resourcefulness in fashioning the fire and a torch showed she'd been no ordinary maid. Whatever her background, Tyler was sure she was hurt and lonely. She was afraid of people, so much that she hadn't even told him her name.

Tyler felt a change in the air as the girl picked the route from the drab brickwork of the sewage system into the children's domain. The tunnel dipped down carved steps into an unlit, stony cave. Tyler heard hushed whispers before he saw anyone, an eerie sense of life around them. Faces peered out from carved side-rooms. He slowed down, but the girl strode on. As the cave-dwellers stirred from sleep, the pair passed stained mattresses and torn bedding, unwashed cooking pots and broken furniture. Children shied from the torchlight; they might've been part of the shadows if not for the whites of their watching eyes.

"Who's moving?" a voice said ahead. At a turning, dim lantern light showed at least one person was standing guard. A boy, barely a teenager, emerged into the tunnel, dressed in a heavy overcoat and a red woollen hat. The light stayed somewhere behind him. He held a gun in both hands, a flintlock rifle that had been sawn short.

"What's your business here, sister?" the boy demanded, putting on an air of more confidence than his cracking voice could support.

"I need to see Chetan," the girl replied.

"Yeah?" the boy said, puffing up his chest. "I could shoot you just for trying."

"He's got a debt to pay me."

The girl took a step forwards and the boy raised his gun. "Don't move – not one more step, right? No one just walks into the Kennel."

Tyler put a hand on the girl's arm and she turned to him with alarm. He whispered, "He's scared, take it easy." She looked a little angry, but let Tyler move past her. He addressed the boy: "Look, what's your name? I'm Tyler, this is –" He nodded to the girl, and finally got an introduction.

"Deni."

"Deni," Tyler said, brightening. "That's nice." She frowned as he quickly turned back to the boy. "This is Deni. You?"

The boy shifted uncertainly. He said, "Roller."

"Okay, Roller. We've come a long way and we've got people after us the same as all of you down here. Deni knows Chetan, they've got a deal. We don't have to come in. You can bring him here."

"Chetan don't come out for chats," Roller said.

"Well, then, we *do* need to go in, don't we?" Tyler said. "He knows Deni. Might even reward you for bringing her in."

Roller stared sceptically. He said, "You're not neckers?"

Tyler shook his head without hesitation, having no idea what the word meant. "Absolutely not."

The boy held off a moment more, but Tyler's smile had already worn him down. He shouldered his sawn-off rifle and said, "Follow me. But the smallest bit of funny business and you're dead – you understand?"

They walked into a taller, wider cavern, where a boy on an elevated platform nudged another from slumber, both with guns at their sides. Roller waved and one of them pulled a lever. A pair of chains pulled a spiked gate up at the far end of the room. It was a scrappy sentry-point, but it would've been hard for even the Guard to break through.

Tyler whispered to Deni, "You got in here before?"

"I was invited," she said.

Tyler watched her face, hoping for more, but she said nothing.

They continued past more side-rooms, into narrow halls. The Kennel was a remarkably intricate set of alcoves, a carved cave essentially unfurnished but civilised, with occasional oil and gas lanterns perched on outcrops of rock that served as shelves. Hungry eyes looked out at them. A few of the youths clutched guns: old pistols that needed to be loaded with bags of powder and a stick, not the slicker cartridge weapons the Border Guard used. Mostly, though, the sleepy children had tools for weapons. Blunt knives and hammers, at best. All of them looked frightened.

The Kennel was real, Tyler reflected. And of course they hadn't overthrown the Mine Guard or caused any serious damage to the city. They weren't here to lead a violent uprising; they were just kids, struggling to survive. Tyler felt his shoulders tightening at the realisation.

Roller led them up the ladder of a mine-shaft, taking them into a sequence of taller tunnels where the children seemed older, and watched them more attentively. They walked through a wide room where half a dozen tired teenagers sat playing cards. No one said a thing. The trio continued through a cave that brought them to a pair of massive wooden doors. Two more teenagers were sitting there, one holding a chipped wooden club, the other a dull metal blade, both dressed in clothes that looked like they'd been made from a dozen different rags. The sentries stirred as though they'd been dozing, and Tyler recognised the one with the blade as he yawned. The boy with the knife from earlier – Hazel.

"Who let the pray-sister in?" the boy with the club snarled at Deni.

"Says she knows Chetan," Roller said, quietly. The other boys were older, more sure of themselves. They stalked up to Tyler and padded around the pair.

"This guy…" Hazel's voice brimmed with hostility.

"Thought we told him to get lost," the club boy said.

"What you took off me, it was hers." Tyler nodded to Deni.

"Big deal," the one with the club snorted. He pressed close to Tyler, making his skin crawl.

"You know why I'm here." Deni glared at them. The boldest Tyler had seen her all night.

"Yeah," Hazel said. "We got no need for you."

"We had a deal," Deni said. "Open this door if you want to live."

Tyler looked at her with surprise. Her voice wavered with barely restrained anger. She seemed just nervous enough that she might do anything. The most dangerous kind of person. The youths were too caught up in posturing to notice, though, ready to cause trouble. Fortunately, someone else was listening. On the other side of the door, an older voice called out, "Modo, let her through. I'll deal with this."

The self-titled King of the Underdogs, Chetan, was famous across the Estalian Empire. They said he turned liberated children into soldiers. He had an army operating from the shadows, unseen, picking at the Metropolis through theft and random acts of violence. He had stolen half the riches in the Metropolis for his people, and would one day use them to overthrow the Mine Guard. They said he was responsible for the drought three seasons ago, and the fires five seasons ago, and half the accidents and deaths wrought upon all four of the Guard institutions. They said he stood two metres tall and could wield a sabre faster than any man alive.

As myths went, he was as infamous as the Short Queen, Elzia.

Chetan didn't live up to the stories. His cavernous lair was decorated with rich spoils, certainly, with candles in sculpted stands and chests overflowing with precious metals and curious contraptions, but the man himself was less impressive. He sat on an armchair tall and wide enough to be a throne, the centrepiece of the room, but when he stood he was decidedly less than two metres tall. Chetan was shorter than Tyler, in fact. And pot-bellied. More notable than his height and level of fitness, however, was his age. He was balding and wrinkled, and a patchy beard straddled his chin. His velvet clothes, once fine, were too tight, and faded from age. One button was missing, exposing his gut. His left eye was larger than his right, and it widened as he clocked Deni.

"Made it back, huh?" Chetan said, his voice dry. His smile revealed at least half a dozen missing teeth. He looked to Hazel. "Didn't I say she had gumption?"

"You have my note," Deni said.

Her voice was more resolute now, faced with this den leader with his twitching eye and fidgeting child-guards. Her fists were clenched and she was unafraid.

Chetan sidestepped to a desk covered in maps and papers. Tyler saw his dad's satchel, lying by the side, open and seemingly empty.

"This?" Chetan picked up Deni's piece of paper.

Tyler moved towards it and Hazel jumped in his way. He froze at the sight of Hazel's blade, but snarled, "That's not yours."

"Lesson One in the Kennel," Chetan said. "What comes here, belongs here."

"It's hers," Tyler said. "Whether you took it or not."

Chetan stepped towards him, hand on the hilt of the sword at his belt. "Lesson Two of the Kennel. Chetan makes the rules and *no one* questions him."

"I did what you wanted –" Deni started again, but Chetan waved a hand.

"Sure. And I'm impressed. I didn't think you'd make it. But you really think I need this? You brought me a fairy tale." Chetan ran his hand around the sword hilt. "And the price you asked, that requires a whole lot more than a fairy tale. We don't go up against the man with the V for a *fairy tale*."

Deni went quiet, some of her passion dying as she read Chetan. Tyler frowned, trying to understand. She drew a grim conclusion. "You're scared of him."

Chetan laughed, too loud, and turned to his boys. "She thinks we're scared?" The others joined the joke, laughing too. Chetan turned back, finger raised. "You know how many neckers we've killed? We string 'em up by the dozen, ain't no necker safe from us!"

A chorus of agreement came from the others.

"Ain't *no one* says we're scared, not of nothing!"

As the leader became more animated, Tyler tensed in front of Deni, ready to push back, even without a weapon. Anyone who made a point of telling you they weren't scared was normally lying – he'd seen enough of that in Bawkley. They usually did stupid things to prove otherwise. He said, "Well, if you're not scared then you're rotten. The lot of you. Where's your honour?"

"Who the hell are you? She sold you on this story? Or you just got a bone for her?"

Tyler glared, trying to look dangerous himself, but it only made Chetan laugh again.

"Yeah, there it is. A *million* like you. Tinkering about in the above-ground waiting for some adventure. Where? Harlow? Bawkley at worst. She comes along with a crazy story –" he nodded to Deni "– and you think you got what it takes to join the Kennel?"

"It's not a story," Deni replied.

"It's trash," Chetan said. He flapped the paper again. "This has one use, if you're willing to go with it. It proves *you* are worth something. You got this from the Towers? Truthfully, like you said? *That* impresses me. That fire, was that you?"

Deni said nothing. Chetan smirked, taking it for a yes.

"And here you are. Not dead. You even get hurt? Shit. I don't know if you were running a scam or you really believed your idiot ideas, but let's face it – you couldn't have thought I'd go for it, not really. Time to get to the real bargain, ain't it?"

"We had a deal –"

"There's only one deal," Chetan said. "The deal I give you. Right now. You've done something few would dare, and that's bought you an in. With a little guidance, I can make you hard enough to fight for the Kennel – hard enough to fight for yourself, even. Then you can stick your own knife in that necker scum. But this is just the beginning, you understand?" He put the paper down. "The real work starts right here."

He stopped, giving it a moment to sink in. Tyler searched Deni's face. What he was offering must have been exactly what Deni had run from in the first place. A promise of servitude. She was silent. Chetan's eye twitched as he waited. His men tightened their grips on their weapons. Expecting trouble, and at least a little afraid of it.

"Maybe we should just go," Tyler whispered to Deni.

"Ah, now, you don't just go," Chetan said. Before he could continue, Deni interrupted.

"This was a test?" she said. "You want to recruit me?"

Chetan widened his twitching eye again. "Let's not go that far. This errand shows your potential, but that's all. You want to be a part of this?" He waved a hand at the cave around them. "You're damned sure gonna earn it."

"I can work," Deni said. "As long as one way or another, the tattooed man dies."

Chetan smiled crookedly, as if he'd known all along that they'd end up here. He nodded.

"And Tyler stays, too?" Deni asked. Just like that? Tyler opened his mouth to speak but Deni didn't let him. "You have to take both of us."

The den leader watched Tyler carefully, and said, "Still feeling chivalrous now?"

Tyler stared back at him, mind racing but nothing clear coming through. There were four armed people, each as big as him, and he wasn't sure he could rely on Deni now. He wanted to meet her eyes, to read exactly what she was planning, but she wasn't looking his way, eyes fixed on Chetan. He swallowed his fear, not daring to speak up; not if she had some other plan, or even if she didn't. Surrounded in this room, they had to keep these boys happy. They were waiting for him, all of them. He said slowly, "Yeah. I am. You were right, before. I'm done with that above-ground life. Give us a chance, I guarantee you won't regret it."

11

Tyler and Deni were placed in a circular room barely big enough for two people to sit on the floor. The torch in the hallway cast them in vague silhouettes as they waited for Roller to leave. He had told them they would like it there, then closed the door and turned a key in the lock. As Tyler moved towards it, Roller called out, "Till we're sure you can be trusted, that's all!"

Tyler spun back to Deni, finding her calmly staring at the door. He hissed, "They're crooks. The stories about this place are true. Thieves – troublemakers – worse. They're not just kids who ran off from the Mines, they're people who *couldn't* work down there. Couldn't work anywhere. What are you thinking?"

Her eyes were on the doorway, but her focus was elsewhere. Circling in her imagination. When she spoke, her voice was distant. "He's got rules like a master."

"And you're a free woman, right?" Tyler said with relief. She focused on him, then, surprised that he'd remembered her words. He repeated, "What are you *thinking*?"

"I'm getting my note back," she told him simply.

Tyler paused. That was her plan? Stay here to steal from them? It was hardly better than her wanting to join them – they were locked up either way. He said, "These kids might be run-down, but they could still kill us. How's your note worth that?"

Deni said, "I need to find someone braver to trade it with."

"Trade *what*? What's at that location?"

Deni went quiet again. Still holding out.

"I'm stuck in this, aren't I?" Tyler said. "Tell me why."

She hesitated, whatever secret she was holding on to seemingly painful to share. When she answered, it came out in a rush. "It's what my master was working on. They killed him for it." She stopped, looking at him as though she'd revealed a terrible truth. He stared with his mouth open.

"Yeah?" he said. "Sure you don't want to be a bit more vague?"

Deni's brow creased in irritation. "It's... dangerous."

"I've been shot at and trapped here!" Tyler answered, almost laughing at how cryptic she was being. "I don't need to know it's dangerous, I need to know what it is!"

She still hesitated, but took a breath and let it out. "I've seen the skies part."

Again, she stopped like he'd been told all he needed to know. It wasn't getting any easier. The clouds shifted, thinned at times, let light through in varying glows, but they never parted. Not in the Providential sense, the opening of heavens the preachers shouted about. From the look on Deni's face, he got the feeling that was the sense she meant. He could see it wasn't easy for her, though. She didn't seem to like talking. He said, "Tell me, properly. Like if you were thinking it to yourself."

"It's bad," she replied. "I told you I'm bad. My master created something... that went through the sky. Then they all died. They all died because of me. Because I wanted to be free."

"Something that went through the sky," Tyler repeated.

"A rocket," Deni said. "That's what I have to trade. That idea."

Tyler paused, not sure what to do with this. They were getting somewhere, but it was sounding worse by the moment. The sky parting, rockets – maybe it was a thing of fairy tales, like Chetan had said. From the look in her eyes, even in the hour or two he'd been with her, Tyler could see she was drifting in and out of her thoughts. Was it dreamy recollection or simple invention? The only rockets he knew of were the ones that exploded in colours below the clouds, the sort they sold for ten chips apiece on Lambaste Street. A boy from two tiers above his home had lost three fingers firing one from his hand during the last Feast of Hrute. It would take a huge accident to kill multiple people with one, though, especially when it had flown into the sky. He asked, carefully, "How did it kill them? Something went wrong?"

She shook her head gravely, and said, "The Guard. They killed Balfair and Sincade, and Frinz, even the other guards. Everyone. Because of this rocket. Because of the clouds." She spoke hesitantly, and despite his doubts Tyler knew she at least believed it herself. He tried to give her an encouraging look. Perhaps if she could get the story out, properly, they could start to make sense of it together. Sharing that look seemed to help; she continued, more determined, and the sense behind it started to come out. "It was a special rocket. Massive. The Guard are afraid of it because it broke through the sky. Because it made the clouds part and – and I think it could do it again. It can tell us things about the sky that the Guard don't want people to know, that's what my master said. It can do something big – maybe bring back the light, stop the days getting darker – if it can draw back the clouds. And that makes it valuable. I... I need to use it. To trade it and get someone to stop the tattooed man. Chetan promised he could do that, if I got him the rocket's location. He hates the Guard – it made sense – he might do something that could bring about change, with the rocket's information. But it was a lie. You heard. It was a stupid test. He doesn't care about the rocket and he's as scared of the slavers as me. No one can help."

"Hey." Tyler stepped slightly closer, as near to her as he could get without invading her space. He spoke softly: "I'm helping you, aren't I?" She looked at him uncertainly. He continued, "But everyone knows nothing can go above the clouds. Remember the Fulcorn airship disaster, three seasons ago? It climbed too high, all those people on board – they found pieces as far west as Wermblay."

Deni shook her head. "I *saw* the sky. I *saw* the clouds part, and what was beyond them. Colours I don't have words for. Light, more than you've ever seen. And I've spoken to a man who understood; it's *real*. He found the rocket."

"All right," Tyler replied. "Then why would the Guard hide it? The Guard keep Estalia safe. They keep an eye on people like this." He gestured to the tunnels. The children. "How do you –"

"I saw every death," she said forcibly. "Mr Montgomery *was* the Guard. He was from their elite. He dressed finer than anyone I've seen, he moved like a soldier and spoke like a noble. Only the Guard have the resources to create a man like that. Only the highest, most powerful people, who want to keep it to themselves."

"Create –?" Tyler tried to question, but Deni was revisiting an important memory.

"He was there to make sure no one left alive. He even killed the guards that came with him." Deni closed her eyes. "My master's friend confirmed it. Hodwick. His research was closed down, too, because of how far Balfair went. I met him secretly. He gave me that *stupid* box, I could've got away –" She paused again, taking a breath. "Doesn't matter. Chetan betrayed me too."

"Hodwick's the man that gave you the note?" Tyler clarified. "And Qait Seyron's name?"

Deni didn't answer. She'd reached the end of her account and gone back to hiding in her own thoughts. Tyler bit his lip. "Is there some other way to deal with these slavers?" When she didn't answer that, either, he moved on. "Why are these slavers the ones after you?"

"Balfair died. They're the ones that gave me to him."

"But you said the Guard killed everyone. How'd they know?"

"Someone must've reported me missing. Blamed me for what happened at the estate."

"Shouldn't the Guard be after you too, then?"

"They're not normal." She shook her head. "Balfair and Sincade, they always told me what would happen. If I left the estate, the tattooed man would come after me. I thought it might be just to scare me. But... they can find things normal people can't. They have my scent, or something. The Guard don't need to come after me now – they can leave it to them."

Tyler didn't want to question it when she'd already trusted him with so much, but he was sure a suspected murderer would never be left to the slavers alone. His instincts said this was more complicated than she knew, or was willing to accept. If people had been murdered on her estate, including the guards, and the main people after her now were those brutal mercenaries, it couldn't be the Guard that were hunting her. And this Hodwick, responsible for the note, had given care of the task over to Qait Seyron, a Border Guard, for a reason.

"I met the guy you were supposed to take those coordinates to. He can help."

"He's a Guard," Deni scoffed.

"It was Hodwick's idea, wasn't it? He must be different. Why not give him a chance?"

"Hodwick is as big a fool as Balfair was," Deni said. "He wasn't interested in helping me, only himself. That guard would betray me the same as everyone else."

"Trust me, we're better off going to someone like him than this lot," he said, indicating the halls again. Her face was blank. She'd said what she needed to. Tyler sighed. "I suppose it doesn't matter, anyway. We can't even get out of here."

"We can. But we're getting my note back first."

It was his turn to go quiet. Her eyes were bright again, lighting up at the challenge with the passion he'd seen when she first addressed Chetan. The same boldness she'd turned on him when she drew that knife. Behind her meekness, there was something burning, and that note was giving it fuel. She wasn't going to leave without it, even if she had no idea how to use it now.

He nodded, slowly. That was their path, then, for now. With all she'd been through, right up to her most recent betrayal, he would help her see it through. And find out if there was anything in this crazy idea about the clouds. But in the meantime all that meant was waiting with her to see what trials the Kennel had in store for them.

12

Deni watched Tyler resting his eyes across the room. She had no desire to rest herself. He was strangely trusting, with no idea what was coming, not even believing that she had a way out. It had been good to talk to him, to someone that she felt had actually listened, just for listening's sake. All the talking had woken her up as clear as if she'd slept a full night. So many words. With him paying attention, wanting to share her problems. Like there was something he could do about them. He was naive, though; he didn't get how dangerous the Guard were. Whoever Hodwick's man was, he might be interested in finishing what Balfair started, but not in helping her.

She considered leaving Tyler there. The last echoes of sound in the Kennel halls had died down. Their barricades were strong from the outside, but on the inside they were soft. And complacent. The first time they'd escorted her in, and out, she had kept careful note of the route and knew exactly where to hide to avoid being seen. If the guards were even still awake. She could move quicker and quieter without Tyler.

He would be trapped here without her, though. They might make him pay.

As Deni turned the idea over in her head, she heard a yawn from another room. Someone else stirring. Was it later than she'd realised? Coming on to morning? She picked at the lock quickly but quietly. It was a marvel that the idiots had left her with her knife, and her pin, not daring to search her. How could she have ever believed Chetan could help? He was a fake king in a pathetic kingdom.

She pulled the door open carefully and peeked into the tunnel as Tyler mumbled unconsciously. Deni looked down at him. He was so peaceful. And handsome, in his way. That was why she'd said so much, she told herself. Tricked by the way he looked, and how kind his voice sounded, just like the women in the stories, the ones who lost their senses at the sight of a man.

What nonsense. She'd seen countless handsome men outside

the estate and they didn't possess some kind of magic. He *had* got her talking somehow, though. Why hadn't she just kept quiet?

Deni hesitated. Of course she couldn't leave him here. That was as bad as killing him herself, and of all the people she'd hurt, he was the least deserving. She cleared her throat and whispered, "Tyler..."

Quiet as it was, her voice stirred him. He sat up and rubbed his eyes with his fists. "Sorry. How long was I down for?"

He held a hand up to her, expecting her to help him to his feet, and Deni stared at it, startled by the gesture. She took a step back, rather than touch him, and he hummed before pushing himself up. He straightened himself out and gave her a small smile.

"You can slip out," Deni said. "On your own. I can show you."

Tyler shook his head. "I'm coming with you."

She gave him one more look. She didn't know how to argue.

It was not far back to Chetan's chamber. Roller had taken them to the room slowly, giving Deni enough time to memorise the turns. Tyler said nothing as she walked, trusting her judgement, not even commenting on the fact that she'd sprung them from the locked room. He was looking around uncertainly, though, not sure where they were.

At the final corner, before the chamber's back entrance, Deni paused and Tyler almost bumped into her. He was still tired, his senses numbed. She shouldn't have let him sleep.

Deni leant around the corner. The stool by the small door was unoccupied, as she'd suspected. The last embers of a torch kept the entrance vaguely lit, but these children weren't disciplined enough to stand guard all night. Hazel and the other one had probably only stayed up before because they were expecting her return.

Deni crept ahead, her practised steps barely making a sound. She shot Tyler a disapproving look when his boots squeaked behind her. He cringed to say sorry. She put a hand on Chetan's door and turned the handle as slowly as she could. It creaked, but not loudly enough to carry. Holding her breath, she drew her knife and pushed the door in.

There was no one inside. Chetan couldn't have been far away, but he didn't sleep directly in his hoard. Deni moved in and scanned the trove of stolen goods. She put the knife away as Tyler brought in the torch from the hallway.

"Over here," Tyler whispered, pointing to the desk. To start, he took the leather bag and swung it over a shoulder, giving Deni pause. From the way he briefly lingered on it, she could see it was his, and important to him. He hadn't said anything about it before. It was pure chance he was getting it back. As the thoughts grasped her, he slipped past and nodded to the papers. They started to sift through them together, a pile of maps and pages of scrawled writing. Deni paused as Tyler's hand brushed hers. He didn't seem to notice. He asked, as quietly as he could, "Do you read well?"

Deni shook her head, but he wasn't looking at her to see it.

"Can't say I'm surprised," Chetan's voice said from behind. They both spun to face him, scattering the last of the papers in their hands. The Kennel leader stood in the doorway they'd entered through, clothed as they'd left him, his hand on his sheathed sword. He was alone, and there was no other light coming from the tunnel, but he looked at ease, smiling his gap-toothed grin. "Guess it figures, you won't be tamed. At least we got that answer quickly, eh?"

He paced into the chamber, the heels of his boots clinking against the stone. Deni positioned herself behind Tyler, as he spread an arm sideways to protect her. Just enough of a shield for her to move her hand towards her knife unseen.

"You know she came halfway across Estalia?" Chetan addressed Tyler. "If you believe her. Came all that way with a slave bangle. That shows some skill – even if she's a lying barrel of scum. Real shame. We take care of each other down here – you would've done well to join us."

"Yeah?" Tyler said. "I didn't see trophies in anyone else's rooms."

Chetan paused. His overlarge left eye locked on Tyler as he drew his sword, quickly. He had the tip out towards them before either could move. He said, "I offer a bigger prize. Security."

"All we want is the note," Tyler said.

"You want it –" Chetan patted his chest "– you'll have to take it the old-fashioned way. Let's make it worthwhile. I'll play fair, give you a sword."

He nodded to a rusty cutlass on the floor, part of the collection, and then he shifted a foot back, holding up his rapier, free hand rising like a scorpion's tail. However untidy and unexercised he looked, Chetan had a trained pose, and his twitching eyes invited a fight.

"I don't want to fight you," Tyler said. Deni edged out from behind him, knife drawn but hidden from Chetan.

"Yes," Chetan smiled, padding to one side, back. "The girl's game, aren't you?"

"Please," Tyler said. "No one needs to get hurt."

"Too late for that."

"Ready," Deni whispered into Tyler's ear.

Without further warning, Chetan skipped forward and sliced, the blade nicking Tyler's arm before the younger man could react. Tyler swung the torch with an arc of flame that made Chetan jump back. Tyler's shirt sleeve showed a thin line of blood.

"Was that unfair? Should I count to three?" Chetan circled his sword-tip before them. "One..." He hopped to another foot, turning side on. "Two..."

"You're mad," Tyler told him.

"Three!"

Chetan stabbed the sword forward and Tyler ducked to the side, barely dodging the blow before thrusting the torch at him. Chetan sliced the torch in two, its flame scattering. Deni shot out from behind Tyler as Chetan spun to strike again. She lunged at the Kennel leader's leg but he parried out of the way, the knife grazing his velvet trouser leg. Chetan spun and brought the sword back around. Tyler pulled Deni down, towards the floor.

As the fallen torch's light dimmed to a vague afterglow, Chetan steadied himself, slowing in surprise at Deni's attack. He prowled towards them, sniggering but holding back from speaking. Flicking the sword flamboyantly, he pounced again. Tyler rolled aside, the blade sparking on the stone where he'd been.

Deni's hands searched the floor and found a chest. She felt metal, grabbed at it and came away with a chain, tangled in other items, clanging noisily as she stood. Chetan spun towards her as she flung the handful of metal at him. He batted it off with his sword and used his free hand to hit her hard in the chest. Deni flew into the wall and down onto a pile of hard objects. Chetan growled, losing some of his cool as he lunged at her. A shape rose behind him and he crashed forward. Deni rolled out of the way and a hand pulled her clear. Tyler pushed her aside as he clambered over to Chetan, patting him for the paper. Chetan groaned, stunned by whatever Tyler had hit him with.

Deni watched, picturing her last moments in the estate. The same movement, probing the tattered suit of Montgomery, the man who'd tried to kill her. The letter she'd taken from him when he'd fallen. The blood across his face. That dead look in his eye, the killer's stare.

Tyler snapped her back into the present, hissing, "I've got it! Come on!"

Deni stumbled, nodding unseen, and they ran out into the dark. She reached for the walls of the tunnel while Tyler kept an arm around her waist, finding his way with the other. They tripped along, away from the chamber, no light ahead.

"Get them!" Chetan yelled, recovering. "Traitors in the Kennel!"

They froze as the shout bounced off the walls and panicked cries came back. A moment later, as they continued through the dark, a bell rang. Then another, and another, their clangs shaking the rocks that surrounded them.

In the rising din, Chetan shouted behind them, his rage building. Light gleamed across the walls ahead: someone carrying a torch around a far corner. Tyler and Deni shared a look. It was either towards the light or back towards Chetan. They chose the torch, and started running.

A few paces down the tunnel, the walls and the ground shook violently, almost tripping them. An enormous crash sounded above.

Dust rained around them as they paused to look at the ceiling. Chetan's approach behind them had stopped, the leader going quiet. The light in the tunnel ahead stopped moving.

With the next crash, the chaos of movement erupted again, footsteps and shouts from all angles, the bells ringing harder, more panicked. Chetan's voice rose above the rest. "We're under attack!"

A dull boom vibrated through the tunnels, and the ceiling cracked. Tyler gasped, "It's gonna come down – we have to get out –"

"Is it them?" Deni said. "They wouldn't –"

The crashes continued above, in a sudden cannon-like barrage.

"Guards!" Chetan screamed, sprinting out from the shadows of their tunnel. The torch-bearer ahead emerged at the same time, light pouring over them all. Chetan pointed his sword at the pair. "You brought the Guard to us!"

Deni shook her head.

The biggest crash yet made them all stumble. Deni banged into the wall as Tyler caught her. He pulled her up and turned towards the torch-bearer. This younger member of the Kennel was staring at them fearfully, ready to run.

"Don't you dare!" Chetan shouted, seeing it. "Stop these animals – they're stealing –"

The boy didn't listen, turning to flee. Tyler and Deni chased after him. The bells grew louder, more frantic, as another crash came above.

"What the fuck is this?" Chetan uttered, slowing down. Tyler scanned back to him as they pushed on, making Deni follow his gaze. The Kennel leader was turning on the spot, caught in a panic. He screeched, "What have you done!"

13

Deni broke into a run.

"Where are we going?" Tyler cried after her, but she didn't answer, bounding down the cave, pushing past the terrified boy with the light. The tunnel descended into a cavern, alive with panicked children. They were screaming, shoving and running in and out of dozens of exits. Towards the middle, Hazel held a blade high above his head as he shouted unheeded orders: "Get to the east escape tunnels! The east escape tunnels! Not that way!" Spotting Tyler, he roared, "Necker!"

Tyler sidestepped an attack as Hazel blundered towards him. They both banged into fleeing children, stumbling, and Deni shoved Hazel from the side. He tripped and fell flat on his face. His blade slid to a handful of children who stopped briefly to look at it, but after a glance at the fallen boy they lost courage and ran.

Tyler did all he could to avoid tripping over the young ones as Deni raced on. Somewhere, down one of the tunnels, a child's endless scream reached a piercing pitch.

"We have to help them!" Tyler yelled, but Deni did not listen, pushing her way towards an exit. A bang sounded closer than before, inside the tunnels. Adult voices followed with calm but aggressive shouts. Deni spun back to Tyler, clearly fearing what the presence of the Guard might mean to him. Could they reason with them? Could they explain that they weren't even supposed to be here? He said nothing but Deni must have read it in his eyes. She shook her head.

Hazel pushed himself up onto his knees. His blade lay a few feet away. Deni ran to it, and made a final lunge before he did. She pulled back and raised the weapon. With the point in his face, Deni said, "How do we get out?"

"There's a hundred exits," Hazel snarled. "But the neckers are getting *in*. They know 'em."

"Can't know all of them," Deni said.

Hazel's eyes flitted towards one of the passages. He said, "East. Like I said."

"Show us." Deni pulled him up.

More adult voices came, closer now, joined by the sound of heavy marching feet. Hazel listened, then ran for the passage, calling to the children, "This way, come on! If you want to live!"

Deni and Tyler followed, along with a handful of the children who had fallen into line. Echoing Hazel's shout, Tyler pushed at some of the children they passed. "Come with us! This way!"

As they made it into the tunnel, Tyler gave a backwards look to the approaching men. A line of Road Guards entered the cavern, shoulder to shoulder, blocking an exit as children bundled over one another to escape. Concealed head-to-toe in slate grey armour, the guards held tall metal shields in one hand and crude batons in the other. Any child close to them was slammed to the floor by a swift baton strike. The line shuffled mercilessly forwards. Faltering, Tyler ran back a few steps to help a fallen child up, pulling the young girl with him as Deni stared, aghast. He caught up again, shouting, "How can they do this? They're kids!"

"Keep moving or it'll happen to you too!" Deni hissed. They pressed on through the cave, Hazel moving faster as he grew more desperate to get out. They crossed another cavern where the guards were already grappling with children and slamming them into the rocks, binding their hands and feet once they'd fallen. As Hazel's entourage raced through the madness, a few were picked off at the fringes. Tyler ducked to avoid being struck by a swinging baton.

Hurrying to the side, he shouted at the scrambling children, "Keep moving! Follow us!"

They bundled into another corridor and kept running, in and out of pools of light, until Hazel charged into a stairwell. Everyone bounded up it, and Tyler tried to close his ears to the screams and crashes they left behind. He could feel his cheeks wet with tears as he faltered up the steps behind Deni and two smaller children. Seeing him fall behind, Deni held out a hand. He took it and tried to move faster. A few more twists of the stairwell, and the stairs opened up to a small square room, walls wooden, not metal, with cracks of light at the edges. Hazel stopped at a door, turning back to the handful of people who had made it up there with them.

"Give me that." He opened his hand to Deni. "There's gonna be trouble out there. You want a chance to get away, you need me."

Deni looked to Tyler and he quickly nodded. She gave Hazel the blade and the boy put a shoulder to the door, telling everyone, "Stay low, move fast. From here it's a hundred, two hundred metres to the city-line, max. Just follow me."

He slammed through the door, breaking it open and letting the morning light pour in. Squinting against it, Hazel ran into the open, blade raised. The children followed close behind, with Deni and Tyler behind them. After only a few paces they froze at the sound of a man shouting, "Sword!", followed by a gunshot.

The children screamed as Hazel flew back through the air and hit the side of the wooden hut. In a split-second glance, Tyler saw him flop lifeless to the floor, and made the decision to run. He grabbed Deni's hand again and pulled her to the side, shouting as he burst through the petrified kids, "Everyone scatter!"

"Runaway!" an adult voice shouted.

They were in a small clearing, slum houses on all sides, with three Road Guards at the edge, one reloading a rifle. The other two dove for the children as the crowd spread out at Tyler's shout. They couldn't cover all the exits. Tyler dragged Deni past a snatching hand, and they raced between huts into the slum. Without looking back, blocking out the sound of the crying children, Tyler ran as fast as his legs would go, feeling Deni stumble in his grip but refusing to let her stop. She shouted from sheer emotion. The sounds of the guards fell behind.

Tyler turned a corner, into another street of scrap huts, and realised he had no idea where they were. The sounds of assaults were rising from every direction. He let go of Deni and climbed up a box, onto a roof, and, crouching down, stared with horror at what was happening.

Armoured guards in red, grey and black flitted between the buildings, bullying people out of their homes. A steam-driven tank on tracks crashed through weak shacks. The throb of propellers sounded above, a twin-prop gyrocopter circling with two men hanging from either side, searching through scoped rifles. They shouted through a metal horn, and swathes of guards rallied in response to their directions. Guards with pistols and rifles fired indiscriminately, so regularly that the smoke made the slum appear to be on fire.

Tyler forgot himself and stood taller, to get a better view. A street away, a teenager sprinted for cover. A guard sprang out from behind a building and slammed an armoured forearm into the boy's throat. Tyler flinched as two more guards rushed in to start kicking the young man.

"Tyler!" Deni said. "Come on!"

"How can they..." Tyler replied distantly. He turned on the spot and saw the city limits, as Hazel had promised. The first warehouses of Bawkley stood a hundred metres from their position. He called to Deni, "That way!" As he did, a man nearby shouted, "There! On the rooftop!"

At the sound of a gunshot, Tyler half-jumped and half-fell off the shack, landing heavily on the ground. Deni helped him to his feet, pushing him in the direction he'd pointed. For once, Tyler was happy to be at ground level as they fled.

The pair continued to the edge of the slum, ran over a rickety bridge and up the nearest flight of steps, moving too fast for the guards to catch up. They rounded a corner and looked back. The guards chasing them stumbled at the bridge, unsure if it would take their weight. They looked out towards Bawkley and scoffed at one another: it wasn't worth it. They turned back to the slum.

Up the flight of stairs, Deni and Tyler took in the carnage from a higher vantage point. The same scenes were repeated a dozen times over. Droves of guards moved violently through the Low Slums like a plague of beetles. Their machinery was deafeningly loud and destructive. Nearby, a wheeled tractor with a mounted harpoon knocked the front off a home as it struggled to fit between buildings. The driver paused, lifting a pair of goggles, and shouted to his comrades, "Can prop it back up, right?"

His fellow guards laughed.

"You're gonna help them do it," another voice shouted, quietening the group. A Road Guard with yellow officer's stripes painted across his arm marched to the tractor. "We're here to help, not to destroy homes."

Tyler watched with surprise, hoping this man would do more, but the exchange was cut short as another shack erupted in a plume of smoke and the guards around it ran back, cheering. They must have dropped some kind of bomb into one of the Kennel entrances. One of the men was shouting, "It's him! Right here!"

A man stumbled out through the smoke as the guards flocked towards him.

"It's Chetan," Deni said.

They watched in silence as the jeering guards gathered around Chetan. He staggered from one side to another, bloodstained, his thin rapier in one hand, the other raised defensively. He shouted something, muffled by the blood in his mouth and the guards' raucous goading. They swung weapons at him whenever he came close to the edge of their circle.

"We need to do something," Tyler said.

Deni said nothing. They were lucky they could even hear the rabble at this distance. There was nothing to be done but watch. A bulky Border Guard shoved his way through the crowd, roaring. Chetan swayed, sword raised to receive him. The Border Guard removed his helmet, revealing a face so scarred that his beard appeared to be made up of dozens of erratic lines. He boomed, loud enough to carry over the slums, "Give up and I guarantee your safety."

The activity further afield seemed to be slowing down, quietening, as word spread of what was happening. Chetan was already wounded, darkened by soot and blood. His big eye probed the group that surrounded him; his ready posture showed he had no intention of surrendering.

"Guarantee it for all the innocents you've slaughtered!" Chetan shouted with a spray of bloody saliva. He eyed the crowd, seemingly satisfied by his audience. He looked up, in Tyler and Deni's direction, and his bloody mouth stretched to a smile. Part of the crowd started to follow his gaze towards the pair, but he snapped their attention back to him with a brief shout: "You can't kill the Kennel, neckers!"

Chetan leapt towards the Border Guard. The guard stepped back as the rapier sliced through his ear, but he barely winced, drawing a wide blade. The guard swung back at Chetan, and the crowd cheered as the two men locked in a duel. Chetan was quick, deftly avoiding the attacks, and he controlled his sword expertly, despite his bulk, just like the Chetan from the stories. He ducked and weaved, slicing back with nicks that chipped at the guard's armour. Even in his wounded state, depleted of energy, he looked like he was winning: the guard back-stepped to keep his defences up, quick enough to block but too slow to return blows. Another slice came close to taking off the guard's head, flicking hair from the tip of the dodging man's chin, and Tyler stifled an instinctive cheer of his own.

At the periphery of the crowd, another guard pushed Chetan from behind. As he rolled to regain his footing, he was shoved from the other direction, the circle closing on him. Suddenly, no amount of dexterity could defend him against the jostling from the crowd. He spun dizzily back into the centre of the ring. He was stopped suddenly by the bearded Border Guard's blade. Tyler caught a cry in his throat, clamping a hand over his mouth. Chetan slumped against his killer, and the crowd went mad with celebration.

"No," Tyler uttered. He looked to Deni for support, to share his horror, but she wasn't watching; her focus was on something further away. He followed her gaze. There was someone directing other guards. A man not dressed in armour, but wearing a long, lightly coloured coat, blond hair hanging loose over one side of his head. Deni said, "We need to keep moving."

Tyler looked back over to Chetan, the animalistic guards closing in on his body. Deni turned and stiffly walked away, jolting Tyler from the scene. He hurried past her and said, "Did you see – they killed –"

"We need to go," she told him, voice and eyes so firm that he froze. He scanned past her, to check the direction she was heading in.

"No, not that way – follow me."

He guided her across a bridge and up more stairs. Back to one of the walkways that he knew led to Bawkley proper. As he hurried forward, distractedly picking out the route, he muttered without sense, "Killed him... and those children..." Two tiers up, they passed more guards coming through the city at ground level, on their way to join the attack. Tyler led Deni higher, cursing as they went. "What is this shit... how could they..."

He climbed to a higher level and pulled Deni up after him, checking the nearby walkways. Tyler slowed down as they continued over a flat factory rooftop. Then stopped. Deni bumped into him, giving him an odd look. The sounds of guards' shouts, weapons and vehicle engines sifted back to them. People had started emerging on the walkways below, asking what was going on.

"You didn't see – Chetan –" he started.

"Not now," she replied urgently. "Keep moving."

"Is this because of us?" Tyler asked. His hands were opening and closing like he couldn't figure out what to do with them.

She said nothing. Smoke rose over the Low Slums.

"Deni?" Tyler moved closer to her, raising a trembling, pointing finger back to the chaos. "They didn't just happen to find the Kennel the same time that we were down there, did they?"

Deni looked into his eyes. Of course, at the point when Deni escaped into the Kennel, the slavers couldn't follow, and this was the result. Whoever was behind this was willing to go to unfathomable lengths to end it. Tyler grabbed her shoulders and demanded, "Why was your master's work so important?" She didn't respond, and he shook her, voice rising. "What's so important about this rocket – why are people dying – you have to tell me!"

Deni gave a light hiss and broke free from him, moving a few paces away. She still didn't answer him, but didn't retaliate either. She was looking back towards the slums. Had to be acknowledging the scale and danger of this thing she'd brought upon the world.

"I already told you," she said, finally, and he frowned at the back of her head. Something that could change the sky? Something that people at the highest levels of the Guard wanted hidden? Tyler checked himself. He shook his head as the reality struck him. If it really was that big, then it would stretch further than this. "Ruke. We have to get back to my uncle!"

Deni spun to stop him, shocked. "No, they'll be waiting!"

"They saw us go in there!" Tyler shouted. "Everyone's here now!" He skipped clear of her, so she couldn't stop him, then ran.

14

Deni slowed down as she recognised the buildings of Tyler's neighbourhood. She wanted to call out to him to stop, to be careful, but he was too far ahead and there were too many people on the walkways above and below. She couldn't be seen now, not here. And Tyler only got faster as he got closer. When the familiar shacks of his street came into view, a few tiers down from their walkway, Deni stopped. She scanned the surroundings, but there was no sign of the slavers, only a woman scrubbing hard at a piece of wet material. If the tattooed man was there, he would've come out by now, wouldn't he?

Deni continued warily, following Tyler onto his tier's walkway, darting her eyes around to make sure it was safe. Tyler found his caution at last, as he stood before his home, turning on the spot, checking for danger. Deni wanted to draw him back, to tell him not to go in, just leave with her. Every second they spent in this place was making danger more likely. She was silent, though.

"Unc?" Tyler called out. It was strangely quiet. The sounds of the city, above and below, seemed distant, muted. "Ruke, we've gotta go!"

"We shouldn't be here," Deni finally managed, moving behind him.

Tyler gave her a warning look, his hand on the door. As she watched him, she saw the tension quivering in his eyes, and she knew, somehow, that he was right to be afraid. The slavers should have been here, still waiting. Why weren't they here?

"We should go," Deni heard herself say. It only made Tyler's eyes narrow. He pushed into the shack and froze in the doorway.

"Unc?" he said, quieter. Weaker. "Ruke?" Tyler went inside.

Deni stood rooted to the spot. There was no greeting from the old man. He'd been okay when she left him. Talking, moving. Maybe he'd passed out.

"No," Tyler said inside. "No no no. No."

His voice shook. Deni stepped into the doorway and looked

inside. The old man was inert in the middle of the floor, bruised and bloody. There was a dark bloodstain on the ripped shirt over his heart, a pained and angry look fixed on his face. He'd been stabbed, once, cleanly. It must've been a quick death, but he looked anything but peaceful.

Tyler knelt at his side, touching the old man, whimpering in confusion and fear. "It can't be, it can't be... no."

"Tyler," Deni gulped, barely able to speak.

He spun back to her, eyes quivering, lips curled in anger. "You said he was okay!"

"He was!" Deni said quickly. "I spoke to him – he was –"

"Look what they've done!" Tyler shouted. He was back on his feet, pointing down. "Look what *you've* done!" Deni cringed, not able to look at him or the body. Tyler's free hand was clenched. She waited for him to hit her. "He never hurt anyone! He was the best –" Tyler turned back to Ruke. "He was the best man I knew. Why – why would anyone –" His anger turned to sobs. He ran the sleeve of his forearm over his nose. He looked back to Deni, pleading. "*Why*? Why him?"

Deni didn't say it. She had been right, hadn't she? About everything.

"Why would anyone do that!" Tyler yelled, making her jump back. "Why hurt those kids! For some damned rocket?"

"To keep their secret," Deni said, quiet but quick.

As she trailed off, Tyler stared at her as though seeing her for the first time. As though looking at something he couldn't quite understand or believe. He shook his head, telling her how foolish she was. This was about more than her safety, and the tattooed man. It had been a childish dream to think that she could gamble with this information to kill the slavers. Whoever was continuing what Montgomery had started in Balfair's estate was taking no chances. The rocket, or whatever was on it, really did have the ability to change the sky, and whoever controlled that ability could control everything, couldn't they? They could make people believe they were gods. That was why Montgomery had come to the estate – him alone, representing whatever group were behind this. *No one* outside their circle could find out. Everyone that got in their way was a target; from an old man to innocent children.

She'd seen him in the slums. It couldn't have been

Montgomery, but someone of his sort. There would be no one who could save her, not from people who could command that kind of power. The more she tried, the worse it was going to get. All that was left was to keep moving. She said again, weakly, "We should go."

Tyler looked down at Ruke's body. Fists clenching tightly, he said, "You go. I'll wait here. For when they come back."

He would really do it. Simply face it head on.

"No," Deni said, and her hand was on his wrist, his flesh in hers as she tugged him away from his uncle. He gave her a startled look as he stumbled after her, out of the door. Then he went rigid and yanked his arm free.

"That's my uncle! They killed him! I'm not *going*!"

"Then what are you gonna do?" Deni replied. "Let them get you too?"

"I'll kill them – like you wanted!" His shout made her flinch and check the surrounding houses, expecting the slavers to emerge. "I'll stay here and kill them!"

"What about…" Deni thought quickly; what could she use to persuade him? "We can go to the guard? The one on the note – you said he'll help us."

Tyler's face was incredulous. "The Guard tore up the Kennel – you said –"

"*You* said he might be different."

Tyler paused. He stared back into the dark shack. He couldn't make this decision himself.

"Look at me!" Deni hissed. "I can't do this alone! There's *nothing* you can do here. Please, Tyler – please. Come with me – we'll go to this man, we'll figure it out, but please – don't stay here – don't let them get you too."

Her own eyes were filling with tears, and he must have seen her desperation, because his furious expression relaxed – slightly. He said, "You'd really go to this guard?"

She nodded quickly. He turned his back on her, though, fully facing the shack. Deni moved closer and tried to soften her voice. "If there's people capable of doing all this – there's got to be others, too, hasn't there – people who can help?"

Tyler didn't move. His breathing grew deeper as he stared in at his uncle, and his arms trembled. Taking in what remained of his home. What remained of his family. Through gritted teeth, without looking at her, he said, "At least help me cover him. I can't leave him like this."

The city seemed empty in the early hours, as though the madness in the Low Slums was of another time and place. Few people were awake or moving, closer to the centre. They would sleep until the world demanded them; they didn't know the people who protected them were absent, carrying out ungodly work against children. They didn't know a harmless old man had been murdered.

Tyler tried not to blink, staring at the dirty walls that flanked him. When he blinked, he saw Ruke, dead. Or Chetan, dying. Or the children, being struck down. A dozen or more images he didn't want to see. He kept his eyes wide, trying to find something else in the world to distract him. The cracked sign of a watchmaker's shop, an overflowing bin. Anything that wasn't violence. A day ago he'd known nothing about what was really going on; he trusted the Guard, and all he wanted was to return a lost note to a stranger. Now, the world seemed like a different place.

He tried to think ahead, instead of back. Qait had to help them. He wasn't like the others, he wasn't out there hurting kids. He'd given up on the Guard somehow, hadn't he? Maybe he knew what they were really like, maybe he was ready to resist them. Even if he was reluctant and washed up and wanted to drown himself in booze, the tracker could be persuaded. Tyler ran dialogues through his mind. This girl had seen things he couldn't imagine. Her enemies were powerful, and didn't baulk at hurting innocents. His uncle had been *murdered*. She was in a position to make this mean something; to get what she knew into the right hands so they could make those monsters pay.

It was earlier in the day than Tyler's last visit to the Raskel Den, and with the massive activity elsewhere in the city, the bar was practically empty. The barflies there were all but comatose from too much drinking, and a barman was taking the opportunity to clean the floor around them. Tyler feared the tracker would be in the same state. Qait was washed up, doing no one any good, but Tyler would hold the man's head in a bucket of cold water to sober him if he had to. Deni had accepted this wasn't just about her; Qait had to accept it too.

For all those children, for Ruke, for Deni and for whoever else had suffered because of this secret she was carrying.

Tyler continued up to the third floor, the grimy atmosphere only strengthening his resolve. Qait *had* to help; the city was at risk, maybe the whole of Estalia. The young man tensed as he got closer, all the more determined, ready for a fight, verbal or physical. This guard had a duty. He was going to fulfil it.

The tracker was waiting, and his ready posture gave the young man pause. He was standing to attention, tall and proud now that he wasn't slumped over a drink. Tyler opened his mouth in surprise, and suddenly all his words of justice and anger and suspicion were silenced. Qait took his rifle from against the bar and said, "You've got the girl?"

"They killed my uncle," Tyler said without thinking. His voice shook as he repeated it, and with the tracker standing over him he suddenly felt impossibly young. "They killed him." Qait's face dropped slightly, a crack in his calm facade as Tyler pointed a shaky finger to his own chest. "Knife."

"You saw them?"

Tyler shook his head, unable to say more.

"You were in the Kennel?"

Tyler nodded.

"And the girl?"

The younger man twisted, indicating outside with a turn of his head. Qait nodded understanding. Tyler quivered as he said, "What happened this morning..."

Qait put a hand on Tyler's shoulder. "Let's talk somewhere more private."

Before they could go, Tyler surged forwards and wrapped his arms around Qait, embracing him in a tight hug. He let tears flow, not caring that the tracker was stiff with confusion. Qait patted his arm, the bare minimum of reassurance. When he spoke his voice was kind, though.

"We'll take care of this. Don't worry."

Part 2

1

The morning chill made Deni shiver as she waited under an eave for Tyler to return with the guard. She was back there again – on the streets, hoping for someone to come and save her. Just like before. She could still smell the piss that burnt her nostrils when she'd been hunting for Hodwick. She pictured it. Ran it back through her head, rehearsing it for the others – it was important. They'd want to know.

Hodwick had found Deni sitting at the side of the road, where she had slept for the past two nights. Huddled in her robes, she had retreated as far as possible into the corner of a doorway to shelter from the cold. He made a quiet noise in his throat to stir her, the same nervous sort of sound she so often made herself. She jumped, reaching for her knife, and he jumped too, holding up his hands. His nervousness calmed her. He was small, mostly concealed by a cloak, hood pulled over a round head with wire-rimmed glasses. He spoke in a hurried whisper: "You've been looking for me. Please come, we don't have much time."

"Hodwick?" Deni questioned, unbelieving. He nodded frantically, scanning around as though afraid he was being watched.

"Please, hurry," he said and scuttled away. He moved like a frightened rodent, heading straight for the darkness of an alleyway between the buildings. He paused and looked back, glasses glinting in the light of a hanging gas lamp. Then he ducked into the shadow and was gone.

Deni hesitated a second more, then raced after him with a hand on her knife. She slowed at the alley entrance. His feet scampered away in the darkness. Bracing herself, Deni ran after him. They crossed half a dozen streets, at a rapid pace, with the small man pausing fearfully at every opening and pool of light. Deni was quiet behind him, not asking where they were going or what he was so afraid of, simply preparing for trouble.

They reached the great river that divided the city, and he guided her across a flimsy walkway. Braving the thin, shaking planks that spanned the water below, and seeing how anxiously he moved across it, she doubted any kind of trap would be worth this much effort. They continued through the cleaner, wider streets of a different neighbourhood on the other side. He ducked in and out of shadows, telling her to keep down and watch her feet. She knew how to do that well enough, moving without a sound. They reached a road flanked by tall houses. Real houses, not like in the rest of the city; these ones had brick walls framed by timber. He took her to a door loosely chained shut and squeezed through the gap. She paused in the doorway. At the end of the road, she noticed for the first time that a great dark shape was eclipsing the night sky, closer than she'd ever seen it before.

The Towers.

Deni followed the man inside and into a hole in the ground. They were silent all the way as he led her along a long tunnel, up many flights of stairs and across a corridor lined with pipes, into a wide room. There, they finally stopped. He closed the door behind them and dragged a desk in front of it. Deni's hand went to her knife again, in the fear that a trap had been sprung after all. But he ignored her, rushing across the room to a table set with wooden boxes lined with brass piping and instrument panels. She recognised their style. Scientific contraptions like the ones Balfair had always been tinkering with.

Hodwick threw off his cloak, revealing an even smaller figure than Deni had anticipated, round all over and dressed in a tatty old suit. He jumped onto a stool in front of one of the machines, a particularly large one with a lever at one side and a series of white cylinders sticking out of the top, each lined with black markings. Numbers or letters.

"You knew Balfair," the man said.

"He was my master," Deni replied.

"You were there when they came for him?"

Deni nodded, but he wasn't facing her. He turned to set his eyes on her. When she stared back, he made a pensive face and turned away again.

"If you can tell me exactly when it happened, I can locate it."

"Locate what?" Deni asked.

"The *rocket*," Hodwick tutted. "This machine does the hard work. It's attached to a series of modules that have been recording activity in the skies for three decades. Obviously it wasn't *supposed* to go up, so no one was watching for it. But it was recorded, somewhere."

"You know about it?" Deni asked. Hodwick gave her another quick look, then nodded with a stuttering little chuckle.

"Know about it, of course. And about the accident, so they called it. I wasn't sure it was true, but when I heard about you – that there was a girl asking my name – well – it sounded familiar. Balfair wrote about you, you know?" Deni hurriedly pulled the letter from a pocket and held it up for him. The letter her master had sent, hoping to enlist this man's help. He smiled as he took it from her and turned it over in his hands. Then he placed it aside, telling her, "Better no one sees you with that. It's no use now." He patted a pile of papers covered with symbols. "These, though. I had an idea that one of these readings had to be it. I fed them half a dozen false readings to keep hold of this collection. Maybe a few high-flying rebel vessels slipped through our radar, but it has to be worth it. So when was it?"

"I don't understand," Deni told him, frowning at all the papers.

Hodwick flashed her another look that told her he had neither the time nor inclination to explain. He just wanted an answer. It was a look she remembered from her master, though at least Hodwick's seemed fearful rather than forceful. He urged, "Please, just think to the rocket. When did Balfair set it off?"

She said, "During the last moon, at least."

"Be exact."

Deni went quiet, resisting the command.

"Are you thinking?" Hodwick said. "There's not much time; I need to get you out of here. If they realise you're here –"

"Who are they?"

"The same people that came for Balfair!" Hodwick exclaimed. "Now, think!"

Deni folded her arms.

Hodwick sighed deeply and slumped, looking over his glasses at her. He said, more kindly, "You're in a unique position, child. Perhaps you don't even realise it. What Balfair was trying to prove is forbidden research. I believe the evidence that rocket contains is historical. Something that shows something unnatural in those clouds. Do you understand?"

Deni nodded.

"I can't be seen to move from the Towers. I'm barely permitted to leave these halls, you see? They monitor us closely. But if you can help me locate the right coordinates, there's a man I know who can find it." Hodwick started writing. "This is his name, and where you'll find him."

"Why?" Deni interrupted him.

Hodwick froze with his mouth loosely open, unable to comprehend the question. He shook his head and said, "The Guard have all of us focusing on the fight with these rebels. The best of us know that we could be doing something more than killing each other. Get me the readings from that rocket and I may be able to do that something. Tell this man that I sent you – that this can *change the sky* – and he'll do the rest."

Deni frowned. He never thought to question that she was there to help. To complete the work that Balfair had started. He hadn't even considered, for a moment, what she wanted. It didn't matter, though. The rocket's location was exactly what she needed to trade with Chetan. She said, "You want to know what day it flew?"

He nodded quickly, enthusiastically, as a happy smile crossed his face. "They think it exploded, in the sky or on impact – I tried to convince them of that. But I knew Balfair wouldn't have designed it that way. You see – with you here – this is a gift – a miracle."

She thought, then, over everything she had been through since leaving the estate.

A night sleeping in the steam-waggon. The next trying to negotiate a room outside Hadersherry, where the men mistook her timidity for weakness. Not after she'd faced Montgomery, no. She was not afraid of them. A third day when she'd managed to trade the waggon and another day to find a slow land vehicle as an alternative form of travel to the more popular public barge. Two days... three days in that moving cabin, sleeping on hay and eating scraps she had to pay absurd amounts for. On the third day another passenger tried to steal what little money she had, before they arrived at the city.

Another three nights in the Metropolis, trying to understand the city, trying to avoid trouble, and finding that the people she found the courage to talk to had no interest in talking back. Then the appearance of the children, inviting her to meet Chetan. The Kennel. The den leader's insistence that she find proof of what she'd told him. Then the days she'd spent hovering around Central Metropolis, searching for Dr Hodwick.

And now here.

"Sixteen days. It's been sixteen days since the rocket went up."

"Perfect!" Hodwick let out a little laugh, rifling through the papers. It took him a minute to find the right one, and he checked up and down, over a few different numbers. He murmured with satisfaction and quickly scribbled down what he had learnt. He laughed, muttering to himself in satisfaction. He spun back to her and held the paper out. Without the slightest suspicion of her motivations, he said, "You'll do the whole empire a service. I'll await your return fondly."

Deni said nothing, reaching to take it, but Hodwick whipped it back, his brow creasing. The same nonsense as her master, the frustrating workings of the engineer who had his own agenda. He twisted away from her and searched through his messy desk, then turned back with a box, into which he placed the paper. He did something to it with rapid movements of his fingers and held it out to her, saying, "This will keep it safe. Don't worry, Qait will know how to open it."

Deni took the box in two hands, staring with alarm. Was he mad? In what world was a box a discreet way to carry a piece of paper across the city? She started to speak, but he tutted her quiet, saying, "Trust me – this is information worth protecting!"

She said nothing more, taking the thing off him. He was no better than Balfair. Another fool in his own world, caring more about his work than her safety. Or common sense. No matter, she'd open the box when she left.

"You're a saviour," Hodwick told her earnestly. "The world owes you a great debt."

Deni nodded silently. She already knew how the world was going to pay her.

2

As Qait Seyron held up the paper she'd given him, Deni reflected on Hodwick's words. She'd told the tracker what the doctor had told her, that simple phrase, *this can change the sky*. Between the violence in the Kennel and Ruke's death, she'd realised the secret of the sky was exactly as dangerous as she'd feared. It wasn't just a fantasy, it *could* change everything, and they were willing to kill for it, again and again. Qait was looking at it with such sincerity that her fear of the tattooed man now seemed utterly childish – she was stuck in the middle of something much bigger than that.

"No one knew you had this?" Qait asked.

Deni shook her head. "Only Hodwick. But they came after me, almost as soon as I crossed back over the river."

"They might've been watching him."

"Who?" Tyler demanded, standing near the door. He was keeping his distance, rather than huddle inside with them, but the conversation was drawing him back in. The tracker's home was high up, the top two tiers of a watch-post that looked out over a spectacular view of Central Metropolis. A brisk breeze came through the doorway, fluttering the edges of maps and notes strewn around the small room, held down by greasy machine parts. The treated canvas walls flapped, too, and must have offered no resistance to the sounds from the nearby horns of Speakers Square. Tyler must have been cold standing on the periphery, but though he had his arms folded tight, his face was fixed with angry determination.

"It's someone high up in the Guard," Qait said. "High enough to order a raid on the Kennel. Vorst must've passed it back to them when you escaped down those tunnels."

Vorst. That was the name of the slaver. The tattooed man. The monster of Deni's imagination who had seemed so unreal for so long. He had a name and the tracker knew it. Deni said, "The tattooed man wasn't there – at the Kennel. And... he'd left Tyler's house."

"Beyond their scope," Qait said. "When it was just you, his

involvement was all that was needed. At the point when their secret gets into the hands of someone with as much clout as Chetan, though..." He trailed off, letting them finish the thought for themselves.

"Chetan didn't believe us," Tyler said. He was frustrated at the injustice. Deni had seen it in the way he watched the den leader's fight, and she heard it again now. Despite the man's betrayal, Tyler hated to see him hurt. He said, "He was toying with us. He didn't want a fight with the slavers, and he definitely wouldn't have gone up against the Guard."

"They didn't know that, though," Qait said. "The same way you didn't."

"Maybe it was a coincidence?" Deni said hopefully, regretting it even as she heard the words come out. As if there was any chance it could be simple, that she could get away easily.

Qait was shaking his head. "I don't believe in that kind of coincidence. An order to raid the Kennel a day after a boy comes to me, specifically, worried about a runaway. Carrying coordinates which came from Hodwick, of all people. Understand this: we've known about the Kennel since its inception. It benefited the Guard, a myth that helped the Mine Guard and the Road Guard operate more freely. They'd need a very good reason to destroy it."

"He was just trying to survive," Tyler stated firmly. "All of them were."

Qait didn't comment. Something about him reminded Deni of Sincade; uncomfortable in his tallness, with sadness behind his striking eyes. He looked across to a map, considering the coordinates they'd given him. Then back to Deni. "Balfair never said anything about what he thought his research might lead to?"

"He said it would analyse the sky and record everything," Deni said.

"And you say it broke through the clouds?"

"I saw the sky. You might not believe me but –"

"I believe you. Many in the city wouldn't, but I've seen it myself, a couple of times. You just have to travel a long way. In the mountains north of Yerth, or beyond the Aftan Ice Tracts. Where civilisation stops." The tracker paused. "Where the clouds thin, it's cold and inhospitable. But where they're thick, over most of Estalia, they become impassable. You can go into them, some way, but not above them. Balfair must've built something extraordinary to punch through it."

"He found a liquid in the swamp," Deni explained. "That's what started it all. A fuel."

"Something that could make it move more powerfully than what we know." Qait nodded in understanding. "It's the first I've heard of anyone succeeding in that."

"How's that a bad thing?" Tyler said. "Why kill my uncle over it?"

"I'd have to know what they're hiding to know that. But there's been paranoia in the Guard since some of our best scientists went mad trying to unravel questions like this. One of them, Rosenbault, turned to creating weapons to try and fix the world."

"The rogue scientist," Deni uttered. That was the spark that started all the inspections on the estate, the hints of stories of bad science that Deni had wanted to use to her advantage. The tracker nodded, almost impressed. Perhaps he wasn't like Sincade. Her fellow slave had never given her a positive look.

"You know those rumours," Qait said. "Since Rosenbault, showing an interest in parting the sky has become the first sign of deviant thoughts. Rosenbault drew some terrible conclusions. Most of it has..." the tracker stalled, seemingly over some regrettable memory, "proved incorrect. But one thing he and his contemporaries had in common was an understanding that the darkening days, and our constant cloud cover, hold some clues as to the destruction of the Gracian Kingdom, centuries ago. And they hold clues as to what comes next. Whoever is behind this, they must know some of those answers already, and think them too dangerous to share."

"Dangerous to who?" Tyler demanded. "Everyone, or just them?"

"We'd have to find the rocket to know," Qait said. His voice suggested he intended to find out. It was clear from the flapping charts and maps that lay around his home that he was, above all, interested in knowledge, and this was a question he wanted answered.

Tyler was becoming increasingly engaged, too, eager for justice. Deni saw that for both of them, this was something that demanded completion. She was not alone in that, at least, even if completion for her meant the onward march towards her freedom. With their help, she could at least understand who, or what, she needed freedom from. The force behind the tattooed man. A force which might have included the man they were with. Deni asked, "Did you ever work with Callison Montgomery?"

The tracker barely hesitated. "I've done the same work, in the past. You've no call to believe me, but I assure you that's behind me."

Deni caught Tyler shifting in her periphery, tensing, but she didn't look away from Qait. What option did they have without this man, anyway? She had to show confidence, for both their sakes. The last thing she needed was Tyler trying to pick a fight on his own. She said, "Truthfully, you're not with the Guard any more?"

"Truthfully."

A loud, tinny trumpet rose from somewhere below, then echoed through numerous nearby horns. It drew their attention to the rising clamour outside. Something was happening, and the central, noisy location of Qait's home made sense, then. He'd never miss an announcement from here. As the other two looked towards the noise, Deni said, "Will you help us find what's there?"

"If you're prepared for the consequences," Qait answered. He navigated the small space to lean over his desk, running a finger over a map. "If Hodwick's numbers are correct, the rocket, or what's left of it, should be easy enough to find. The problem is that the city is locking down. Too many people on the waterways coming in, too many skirmishes in the surrounding towns. If we go out there, it won't be easy to get back in. I want you to consider an alternative to taking this information back to Hodwick. By the fact that they caught up to you, and responded with such force, you have to assume he's already been compromised."

"Compromised?" Tyler exclaimed. "He's the one who knows what to do with this information!"

Qait stopped again, giving him a thoughtful look. He gestured to the door as the sounds of the crowd below escalated. Tyler gave Deni an uncertain look as the tracker passed her. They joined Qait on the small platform outside his home, looking across to Speakers Square, just visible through gaps in the flanking buildings.

The massive courtyard was surrounded by walls lined by arches, designed to amplify whatever was being said. Pipes ran over the walls and across blocks of buildings as far as Qait's tower, emerging in wide brass horns. The square was filling with people. Guards mingled at the edges of the crowd. Word of the events of the early morning must have spread, and people were coming to hear the news. Qait said, "The displays of Guard strength have been getting stronger these past few weeks. They'll announce the Kennel raid as a triumph over the rebels."

A Border Guard procession marched in columns through the crowd, a tall man striding between them. His head seemed small between curved metal shoulder-pads. A red cape hung down his back and his breastplate was decorated with a shining metal emblem, the symbol of the Guard.

"Is that the Supreme Commander?" Tyler asked, unable to hide his awe.

The commander walked onto the stage, clearly visible between gaps in the walls from Qait's vantage point. When the man spoke, his voice boomed through the horns in the surrounding streets, reaching them clearly moments later. Deni flinched at the sound, but marvelled at how it spread through the pipes. "My friends, my allies! You have heard – our united forces have purged this city, once and for all, of the plague of the Kennel!" The Supreme Commander raised his hands triumphantly, and a roar of celebration thundered through the crowd.

As he continued, Qait whispered an explanation to Deni. "These horns are one of the Guard's greatest weapons. Spread a message through them and Estalia *will* hear it."

"The coward Chetan was the first entry point for rebels in our city," the commander went on. "He lies dead, and the traitors' gateway is closed! Hundreds of children are being returned to safety –"

The cheers became too loud for him to speak over. Thousands of people, convinced the Guard had done something good.

"We're on the brink of war," Qait said. "People are scared and angry. The Guard can justify what happened this morning. And what happened to your uncle, the same way. Tell them someone's their enemy, they believe it." Tyler's face reddened and his mouth moved to complain, but he couldn't argue. They'd all seen the rising disquiet in the streets. Qait continued, "However worried you've been about Vorst or Montgomery, you need only look down there to know there's bigger problems at hand. The people who came after you are the same ones that can control a crowd like this. Hodwick is trapped behind their walls. Before we do anything, you have to understand that if we go after that rocket, then coming back here – returning to him – may not be a possibility."

Deni turned to Tyler. This was the city she had come to for sanctuary, the people she thought might be able to help her. If not here, then where? Tyler met her eyes with none of her doubt, though. This was *his* city. He answered Qait firmly: "This is where it matters most. If Hodwick's the man we need, we're not gonna do any good to anyone by running away. Whatever it takes – we put this information to use."

Qait regarded him plainly, betraying no thoughts on the matter one way or another. Finally, he inclined his head slightly, a nod of concession, and said, "That starts with finding the rocket, anyway, doesn't it?"

The top level of the tower, Qait's second room, was dominated by an object at its centre, covered by a sheet. Qait threw back the cover with a flourish, revealing a mechanical contraption as incredible as any Deni had seen Balfair create. A metal chair rested on a tripod of wheels, in front of an engine the size of a cabinet, lined with pipes and gears connected by chains. A long arm extended to a point from the back, finishing with a cross of metal.

"What is that?" Tyler gasped.

"My profession," Qait said, pulling back a rug on the floor. Underneath was a handle, which Qait kicked. A plank slid out from the floor, over the edge of the tower. He grabbed another handle, at the front of his machine, and lifted it with a heave onto the plank. Tyler helped, seeing the strain in Qait's face, and the pair made it precariously out over the teetering platform, a hundred feet up.

"This will carry us over the city," Qait said, thumping the machine. "Anyone after us will flock to it, they'll know it's me. The further out we go, the longer it'll take for them to catch up to us, but they *will* know where we are. Once this thing fires up, we won't be safe. You can back out of this. I can drop you somewhere. A friendly village."

Tyler answered, without hesitation, "No chance. We're gonna stop these people."

Qait responded with little emotion. "You're a brave kid."

"Brave nothing," Tyler said. "This is big. We can change the sky. We can change the world. It's more than just doing the right thing, it's the *only* thing." He turned to Deni. "Isn't it?"

Deni took in the young man's returning enthusiasm. He was already overcoming the tragedy he'd seen, driven by his need to make it right. She nodded wordlessly. Wherever they were going, and whether or not they could come back, she was pleased he'd be there.

3

There was barely room for all three of them on the gyrocopter. Tyler held on tight as the engine rattled behind him. Deni was squeezed in in front of him, her eyes fearful and her shoulder pressed into Qait's back as the pilot hunched over the controls. He flew without commentary. The propeller turned so fast that its individual strokes blended into one throb, and the thick smoke spluttering from its various holes was pulled away from them. Tyler held a hand over his face to protect him from the wind, jealous of Qait's scarf and goggles. Deni, at least, was shielded by his back.

Tyler was used to climbing, but this flight gave him a new perspective. The city spread below them like a map, though the structures were so sporadically stacked that it was impossible to make out any ground-level thoroughfares. Propped together and concealing the life underneath, the city was a mess of towering scrap joined by countless bridges. The urban landscape stretched endlessly, dipping into dull fog before meeting the horizon. The only hint of a break was the barren plain of Height Park, the vast factories lining the river, and the Drain itself, which widened to the east. Even that was full of dark, hulking vessels.

"More floating castles!" Tyler yelled, straining to be heard above the engine. It was no use. Deni followed his gaze without hearing and Qait ignored him, concentrating on flying. The mightiest machines of the Border Guard's navy were resting just outside the Metropolis.

The gyrocopter moved fast, angling downward as it did. People gawked at the flying machine from walkways and streets. Tyler waved, with what little movement he could manage, and he searched the faces for anyone he knew. He half-expected to see Ruke smiling up at him, but he caught himself in the thought and his elation at the journey faded. They passed the edge of Bawkley, over the clouds of smoke rising from the Low Slums. Guards and machines were still moving among it all, the fighting not yet finished.

Beyond the slums, the vast opening of the Mines became visible, all buildings, and land, disappearing into a huge hole in the earth. As they skirted it, not coming quite close enough to see down, the sheer scale of the operation became apparent – a gap in the landscape as big as entire neighbourhoods of the Metropolis. A hole filled with children like the ones in the Kennel. Ones who'd never escaped. Tyler had always known it as a necessary part of their society – and as such he'd never visited it, or so much as given it a second thought. Seeing how large the Mines were now, he wondered if that had been wilful ignorance. How could he possibly have thought the Mine Guard were doing good work?

He looked sternly forward. Had to keep looking forward now. There was no turning back.

Wanderers rather generously called it countryside, these stretches of land interrupted by clusters of rickety huts. Countless communities outside the Metropolis congregated around pits filled by rainwater, or small streams running into the Drain. Their collectives weren't much different to the slums, in the size and quality of their buildings. Just more spread out. There was little movement, and little colour. It looked flat from high up, but Deni knew the terrain was really rocky and irregular, like a never-ending wart. The trees that survived were mostly without leaves. The world was empty and, more than anything, dead.

Deni struggled to get comfortable in the gyrocopter, pressed into place between the bony form of the pilot and Tyler's weight on one of her legs. He was craning out over the side, apparently too fascinated by the sights to fear falling.

That was how she had wanted to feel, when she first ventured out into the world. She had hoped it would fill her with joy, the creatures and societies she'd encounter. All she'd found was ruins, though. It only got more harrowing the more of it you saw.

"Look! Look!" Tyler pointed. Deni shifted to see. A large shape moved across a plain on four legs, bigger and quicker than a person. A tail flapped majestically at its rear as it disappeared behind a wiry hedgerow.

Deni twisted to try and get another look. She said, "Was that a horse?"

"Something like that," Qait replied.

He had barely said a word since they'd left. Tyler neither, too busy taking in the views. It suited Deni fine, as she'd realised that even if she had wanted to talk she was never going to raise her voice above the sound of the engine.

With the panic of the morning's events having subsided and the flight from the city complete, her doubts had crept back in. She watched both men warily, with no idea where this new venture would take them. Neither of them seemed dangerous, at least, but was that a good thing? What were they going to do about Vorst? Let alone the greater force behind him? Qait had basically confirmed her own suspicions that Hodwick's path might not present a solution.

Vorst – she repeated the word in her head. For over a decade she had pictured a nameless monster lurking outside her life. Waiting to destroy everything. She wasn't sure if it made it easier or more difficult to endure, knowing he was a person with a name. Knowing he might answer to someone else, more dangerous than him. He still threatened any life she might create for herself. She still needed to be rid of him, even if there were others that needed to go, too.

Qait called out a warning and they started to descend, the sensation lifting Deni's gut. They hovered over what looked like a road, a wide, gravelly path running up the side of a hill, then set down. A copse of trees sat nearby. Tyler jumped off and pressed both hands into a patch of dry grass. He looked up at Deni, detached from their troubles in his curiosity. "Feel this, you have to feel this!"

Qait moved without saying anything, tending to his machine. Deni stretched her way out of the seat. Tyler held out a hand to help her up, but she stood without him. She ran a tatty boot over the grass and said, "It's rough. Not like home."

She cringed at the word. Home.

"It's grass!" Tyler said. "I ain't never seen so much."

Deni watched him sceptically. He stopped and offered her a faint smile. His face was impossibly disarming, teeth glinting as white as his eyes. She felt at the same time desperately sorry for what she had done to him and strangely happy that she had done it. Forced him to join her here. She turned to Qait, who was folding up the gyrocopter and wheeling it into the cover of the trees. In the other direction, the country ducked into wide, empty fields. Somewhere far away a plume of smoke rose from a settlement. Even this far out, people survived.

Deni searched for some irregularity in the fields, and finally said, "Where is it?"

Qait padded back from the trees, shouldering his rifle and a couple of leather bags. He said, "We're close, but we've got a walk ahead."

"What?" Tyler said. "There's nothing out here."

"There's no guarantee we'll be the first ones there," the tracker replied. "We couldn't risk landing too near. So get moving."

Qait started to march away. Deni watched him uncomfortably. She wished it was over already. That she was on the other side of this, that the full force of the Guard was with her not against her. People were supposed to be good. Civilisation was supposed to help. She was supposed to be free.

But here she was. She scanned the countryside again, worried that they might run into people, rather than elated at the possibility. Her eyes ran back to Tyler, though. He gave her an encouraging pump of his eyebrows, and he straightened his own satchel on his shoulder. She frowned. There were shadows at the corners of his eyes, a downward turn to his smile, but the smile was there all the same, the lightness in his expression overcoming whatever darkness he must have felt. He'd seen his uncle dead that morning, and he must have blamed her for it, but he was pushing any hint of it from his face.

Tyler walked past, towards Qait, and said to her, "I've got a good feeling, now. Don't you?" She didn't answer him, watching as he trotted up to the tracker and called out, "Do you want me to carry something? I've got space in my bag."

4

The trio walked through a canyon of craggy rock, its walls jutting over them. Qait led the way in near silence, occasionally checking a compass and consulting Hodwick's coordinates. He used a nub of a pencil to make notes as they went. Tyler bounced along behind him, asking questions that went unanswered: was it all like this, outside the Metropolis? What did people do out here? Deni fell far behind to avoid being drawn into it. Finding little conversation from Qait, Tyler eventually twisted back to her. He skipped a few paces towards her and said, quietly enough for the pretence that it was just between them, "You're safe, you know. You can talk to me."

Deni gave him what she hoped was a disapproving look. She wasn't afraid of him. He wouldn't accuse Qait of being quiet because he was scared, would he? Why should he think that about her?

"Look, about earlier..." he said.

"I'm sorry," Deni told him. She didn't want to drag him back to the darkness, not when he'd somehow managed to lift his spirits after what he'd been through. "I never... I didn't mean for any of this to happen. I spent all my life doing what Balfair told me and I just wanted to make things better. But it's got worse and worse."

Tyler slowed to a stop, reading her face. She fixed her eyes on the root of a plant growing between the rocks, relying on an old trick to avoid seeing his judgement. Tyler hummed thoughtfully. The tracker had stopped up ahead, waiting by the edge of the rocks.

"You didn't know," Tyler said. "And I believe you. About Ruke. You would've told me if you knew he was in trouble."

Deni tilted her head. That was true, at least. She'd thought the old man was safe.

"Don't blame yourself." Tyler leant closer. "You never met him, but if you had you'd know he'd have said the same thing. You know what he said? Sadness never made no one happy."

Deni murmured, "That's a strange thing to say."

"Is it? I like it. At least I think it was one of his – he borrowed a lot of what my dad used to say, too. Like *always do the right thing*. That was an important one. We all live by that one – we have to. There was a soap seller, on Grest Street, who used to shout it too, like you were making a mistake if you didn't buy his soap. Maybe my dad stole it from him, who knows! But it works."

Deni studied his face again. He didn't speak like anyone else she'd known. He wasn't hard like Balfair and Sincade, or fierce like Vorst and Montgomery, but he wasn't weak either. The opposite of all of them: he was caring, and that somehow gave him a different strength. Enough strength to stay positive even in the face of his uncle dying. Outwardly at least. She said, "I'm sorry you got involved, anyway."

"Rats to that," he replied. "Ruke would've said the same there, and all. He said I shouldn't be chasing you, but if he'd known about this –" Tyler gestured towards Qait "– he'd have been on board. It's the *right* thing. We're gonna help you. We're gonna help everyone, if it's as you say."

Deni grimaced. The more people they tried to help, the more people were going to get hurt. She tried to look away, but Tyler moved around her, making sure his cheerful face was well in her vision, holding her eyes. She frowned. How could he be so cheerful? He was odd – unnatural. Didn't he understand how much trouble was coming? He raised his eyebrows, comically, flashing his teeth in another grin. What a fool. Unable to help herself, Deni's lips turned with a smile.

"There it is!" Tyler let out an exaggerated breath of relief. "Know how much I've wanted to see that smile?"

"Why?" Deni fixed her face again.

"Because people should be happy."

Deni took a breath. Qait was drinking from a canister of water, not looking their way, studying the horizon. He was a professional, on his mission to recover their information, and whatever emotional baggage they brought didn't matter to him. She liked him for that; it made things simpler. With Tyler trying to understand her, paying attention to her, she felt confused. Not sure if she liked it, even if she was becoming fairly sure she quite liked and trusted him. It only made life harder.

"No," Deni thought out loud. "Not everyone gets to be happy."

"That's a hell of a thing to say," Tyler said.

"Sincade wasn't happy. Ever." Deni paused, her voice trembling. "He died that way. With misery on his face. And those children, they're chained up now, if not dead. Where's their happiness? And me... I've only got more people hurt. Where's my happiness? Where's the happiness of those that died without it?"

Tyler watched her carefully, waiting as though sensing she wasn't finished. She met his eyes again, trying to signal how it felt. She'd travelled hundreds of kilometres. She'd seen the city and she'd stood up to the Guard. She'd evaded the tattooed man and she'd survived. Yet the weight of the entire sky's darkness seemed to rest on her. There could only be more running, more violence, more dead faces twisted in misery. Maybe her own. Maybe Tyler's, with that smile wiped clean.

She closed her eyes to push it all away.

Tyler hadn't moved or spoken. Qait was still waiting patiently.

She said, "I want things to be better. But I don't know if there is a better."

Deni opened her eyes again. Tyler was no longer smiling but he wasn't done.

"Tell me one thing," he said, seriously. "When that rocket broke through the clouds, and you saw the sky, how'd it feel?"

She didn't answer straight away, recalling the memory. She let the first word come out, her voice tiny with uncertainty: "Hopeful."

"You see?" Tyler put a hand on her shoulder, making her tense. He didn't seem to notice. "Things are better already. We've got a guard helping us and we've got a plan. We're gonna get to this thing before anyone else and you're gonna see those clouds part again. These people *won't* get away with it. Everything will be all right."

"You heard what he said," Deni said. "We've got nowhere to *go* with this."

"We got exactly the place to go," Tyler's face hardened. He wasn't trying to console her now. "You've already been there. This rocket, it's *meant* for Dr Hodwick – and that's damned sure where we're taking it. It's going to be used for the thing it was built for – we're gonna see what's behind those clouds. You and me, together, we have to do it - we're gonna see that light again."

Deni gave him another weak smile to concede. It was impossible not to. He couldn't know, not really, what any of it meant. But he believed in it all the same. And he'd said they'd be together. Whether it meant taking their findings back to Hodwick, or finding the real means to be free of all this. He'd be there. Her smile widened, just a little, and he winked back at her. That was all he needed; he gestured up the path. "Shall we get on with it?"

He waited for her to start walking, and walked alongside her. As they continued, he asked, "Who was Sincade? Your friend?"

Deni didn't answer.

That wasn't something she wanted to revisit.

They stopped to refill Qait's water bottles at a rock cluster on the bank of a thin river, where no boats were passing. A small boathouse sat abandoned in the shade of the rocks, empty of food or supplies, partially concealed by creeping vines. The air was humid, rain on the way, so they settled inside, where Qait prepared a small fire between rocks and handed out dried meat. They ate in hungry silence as the rain splashed into the stream.

There was something comforting about the sound. Deni was glad to be away from the dense, dirty air of the city, and was glad there was little chance of going back. She could see it in Tyler's face, too; the young man had been taking deep breaths every time he remembered to stop and appreciate it.

When she'd failed to talk about Balfair and Sincade, he'd gone quiet and given her space. She wanted to say more, so he could keep comforting her, but every time she tried to speak, words failed her. As they ate, though, with the loud rain and the crackle of fire between them, it seemed safer to talk. Her voice would be tempered by the other sounds. She ran a hand over the wooden floor.

"It's hard, in the city," she said, quietly.

After another of his smiles, Tyler shrugged it off. "Isn't it tough everywhere?"

"Not tough," Deni said. "*Hard*. There's so much metal. Your walls, floors. Tools. Even the plants, they're hard. Hard dead trees, where there are any. Hard and dry."

"Has to be," Tyler said. "You know, to last."

"Our estate lasted. From before anyone can remember, it was

still standing. With wood and stone. We had storms, floods, and it was a lot of work, but it survived. Do people in the Metropolis not miss it? Touching the world?"

Tyler and Qait exchanged a look. The roofer wasn't sure what to say. What did he know of the world, after all? Metal walls were normal to him. Tyler said, "I like it out here. These hills, trees, rivers. The air's weird. And that smell, the rain, it's... fresh? No, you're right – maybe – it's *softer?*"

"The city grew too quickly for anything else," Qait said. "Even one generation ago, things were different. When the Guard got organised, and exploded open the Mines, that's when people started to learn again. To work together. And people started to spread. No one was thinking about how it looked, or felt, when they built the city. Just how to stop it from all falling down."

"You know about that stuff?" Tyler asked curiously.

"It's my business to know as much as I can about everything," Qait said, as a fact, not a boast. "To track, first you have to understand."

Tyler paused, then asked, "Why were you in that bar? When I first found you?"

Qait raised an eyebrow, not expecting the question, and Deni suddenly wanted to know the answer, too. She had seen the decadence of the Raskel Den, from a distance, and understood the sort of place it was. Such holes were necessary for men of a certain nature; she remembered Frinz, the whoring, drunk tollman from the estate. Qait wasn't like him, though, was he?

"It's difficult," Qait said. "Knowing the truth of the world."

He stared into the fire, eyes glazed by regret. Deni understood his sadness, then; that mood that linked him to Sincade and now, she realised, to her. He knew about Balfair and Hodwick, and other scientists. He knew what their work meant, and what had been done to stop it. He knew about Montgomery's work, and he'd had a part in such activities himself. When Tyler opened his mouth to speak, Deni spoke first. "Did you know the rogue scientist?"

Qait gave her an icy glance, different to any expression she'd seen from him. It was accusing, almost angry. He caught himself before saying anything, but the message had already been conveyed. Her guess had been exactly right – and whatever memory it stirred, he didn't like it. She looked to Tyler warily, and the younger man said, "We're together in this. You can trust us."

The moment of tension in the tracker passed as he looked from Tyler to Deni again. He shook his head and said, "You can't understand."

"Oh, tripe! Of course we can – you think –"

Qait's fiery look returned, his steely eyes fixing on Tyler as he said, "Where you found me – and the way you found me – was the way I needed to be. Leave it at that." He pointedly turned away to prod the fire, with a short, stabbing action.

Tyler twisted to Deni in surprise. He met her eyes, imploring her for a response. She kept quiet.

Deni eyed the tracker for a moment. They needed Qait, and it might be easier to rely on him without knowing his history. Montgomery had been cold and ruthless, Deni had experienced it. Tyler had seen Ruke dead, but not the man who'd done it. Better if he didn't know Qait was capable of such things.

It had been a bad idea to get them talking. Deni bowed her head and pulled her arms in close to her. She tucked her feet under herself and shifted in her robe, as though she might blend into the shadows. Tyler took the hint, though she could feel the disappointment in his gaze. The fire crackled between them.

5

Qait kicked at Tyler and Deni. The tracker had his rifle up, standing as the pair blearily opened their eyes. The urgency in his voice moved them. "There's someone here."

Tyler shot up into a crouch, blocking Deni to defend her, but she scurried across the floor, hand probing for a weapon. Qait crept towards the door, rifle braced in both hands. It was dark, though the dirt and vines covering the windows made it hard to see if it was day or night. A twig snapped outside. Near the door.

"Ready?" Qait whispered.

The moment the door burst in, the tracker fired. The shot shook the hut and smoke filled the small space. Someone yelled, falling away, as another man screamed through the smoke, arm raised above his head with a big blunt object. Qait had no time to reload as the attacker swung at him. Qait rolled aside, and the hammer slammed into the floor. He jammed his rifle up at the man, but the attacker kicked it out of the way with another war cry. Qait dropped back and drew a knife from under his layers. Before he could stab, the man swung the hammer again, barely missing as Qait ducked aside. The man landed on top of the tracker to try and pin him. Qait pushed back, catching the hammer hand, and the two grappled on the floor.

Tyler grabbed a rock from the remains of the fire and threw it. It hit the man on the head and he grunted, dazed but barely interrupted. He was big – ferocious. It got Qait enough room to jam an elbow into the man's neck, though. The attacker fell down and Tyler tried to pull him away. The man swung back over his shoulder, the hammer still in his grip, and caught Tyler in a glancing blow on the shoulder. Qait scrambled up, punching the attacker's face. The man took the blow and returned one of his own, seeming to absorb damage. He roared louder and blindly swung the hammer in anticipation of another attack. Standing over Qait, about to bear down on him again, he didn't see Deni coming.

The jagged wooden plank crashed over the man's neck, with Deni's full weight behind it. It splintered and dug into his skin. He yelled, turning to her as he dropped the hammer. He fell to his knees, clawing at a shard of wood stuck in his neck. Blood oozed around it. His wild eyes locked on Deni, mad and accusing, then they rolled back into his head as he toppled backwards.

The room pulsed with the sound of heavy breathing.

Qait moved first, standing to retrieve his rifle. He chambered another bullet, cocked the gun and left the hut, disappearing into the fog. Deni stood over the man on the floor. Tyler stepped in front of her, putting his hands on her shoulders and blocking her view. "Don't look."

She shook him off, staring at the corpse, taking in its finality. Her defiance forced Tyler to look, too. Standing against her shoulder he tensed at the sight, but did not look away. The body took up most of the floor, open eyes like glass, fur clothing black with blood. Tyler said, "You had to..."

"Doesn't matter," Deni said. Tyler looked at her face, neutral, unfeeling. She'd been through this before. How many times? She snapped him out of it. "There could be more. Get his hammer."

Tyler took the man's weapon. He held it up: a crude device, a scrap of long metal with a leather strap for a grip, the sharp top speared through a stone, cracked around its edges as though constructed with brute force. He looked past it, though, to the body on the floor. He knelt next to the man and raised a hand towards his lifeless eyes. He needed to do something, anything, but with his fingers shaking he couldn't think what. He uttered, for only the dead man to hear, "Sorry."

"You coming?" Deni drew his attention back to her, by the door.

Tyler hesitantly but obediently moved towards her. He reached the door and gave one last look back at their dead attacker. Taking a breath, he strained to let it go, and stepped out into the fog, with Deni close behind him.

It was impossible to see further than a few feet ahead: the world was a cloud of white with occasional hints of life from sprigs of tall grass and the branches of a withered tree. Tyler held the hammer close to him rather than out and ready to strike. He moved slowly, waiting at every step for Deni, and pointed upwards, to the slope of land that ran behind the building. The pair slowly made their way up through the fog, to where it thinned at the top of the incline. Equally tense, they pushed their heads out to see what the morning held.

Above the mist, it seemed brighter than before. The morning light bounced off the fog and cloud alike, the earth ahead stretching out in a grey-green plain, the patches of grass between the rocks twinkling as light caught the dew at their tips. There was no sign of movement, as far as they could see. No people. Just an expanse of wilderness which eventually faded into a white glow, with no discernible edges.

"Qait?" Tyler ventured quietly. When he got no reply he raised his voice. "Qait?"

"Here." The tracker's voice made them start, jumping into each other. He appeared out of the mist at their side, his rifle hanging loose. He said, "Looks like it was just the two of them."

"Who were they?" Tyler asked.

"Bandits. Here by chance. Might be a bigger group nearby."

The tracker passed them, heading down the slope. Tyler gave Deni a questioning look, then hurried after him. "You're sure they were bandits?"

"I'm sure."

The pair followed as Qait returned to the hut. He patted down the dead man and packed away what little of his possessions he'd taken out. When the tracker was finished, Tyler asked, "What if they were sent by Vorst? Or the slavers' bosses?"

"Then they'd have been better prepared," Qait said. He made for the doorway, ready to leave. "You got everything you need, both of you?"

"Hey!" Tyler said. "Can you stop a second? This guy's dead – and what about the other one? Don't you think we oughta talk about this?"

Qait stopped. "There's nothing to say." He looked at Deni, over Tyler's shoulder. "Is there?"

Deni shook her head. The tracker pushed out of the hut and started away, down the edge of the stream. Tyler ran after him but paused, twisting back to Deni. He said, "You're okay with this? Shouldn't we do something? Bury them? Cover them, at least?"

Deni barely hesitated. She shook her head again, and started to follow Qait. Tyler huffed in frustration, desperate to do something, anything. Whoever they were, these people shouldn't just be dead. It couldn't be that simple.

*

Mist hung over the fields like a blanket, floating flat above the ground. It lingered for over an hour of the trio's march, and they had to wade through it slowly to watch where their feet were falling. The fog hid the finer features of the world and foreboding shapes rose on the horizon, which could have been trees, buildings or tricks of the light. They passed a tree, and a basic wooden tower, and finally a vehicle that looked like a waggon made from metal, half sunk into the earth and covered by moss.

"Automobile," Deni commented as they passed the vehicle.

"Huh?" Tyler replied.

She'd taken the word from one of Balfair's books. That was what they called the land vehicles, the ones that ran on liquid fuel, in the time before. Automobiles. Or cars. She said, "Nothing."

"Your master taught you a few things," Qait observed from the front, eyes ahead.

"No," Deni replied. She might have learnt, but no one ever taught her.

"That's specialist knowledge," Qait said. "It's not an Estalian word, it's Gracian."

"I don't know any Gracian," Deni said.

Tyler was watching her from the side. She felt it but didn't want to return his gaze. He wanted to brood over the attack, but she wanted him to work through it. He'd got over the trouble the day before, and he'd get over this, too.

Qait asked, "Did Balfair work on machines like that?"

"He worked on a lot of things."

"It's what Hodwick specialised in," Qait said, and Deni slowed down, ears pricking. "Old machines, theories about the past."

"They worked together," Deni noted.

"Yes. They all did, once," Qait said. "There was a project called ArcTech. They studied things people found, to make sense of the world. Not in the sense of the Fallen Architects – the people who built the Metropolis, and most of what you know, used recovered technology without dwelling on what it *meant*. The ArcTech engineers wanted answers, so they could improve on what went before. My gyrocopter came from them. Many of our finest vehicles have them to thank, one way or another. But the

Border Guard shut them down after the fire in Thesteran. Hodwick disappeared into the Towers, they all faded away."

"But if this rocket has anything of value on it," Tyler concluded, "ArcTech would've put it to use?" Qait didn't answer, ducking slightly as the field rose towards a crest with a cluster of three leafless trees. They didn't need an answer; Tyler gave Deni a look, finally distracted from the morning's events by his apparent confirmation that his plan was validated.

"Keep quiet," Qait warned them. They followed him up, the slope too steep to see what lay on the other side. The tracker moved ahead, gun raised. As they reached the trees, sounds from beyond filtered up.

People talking.

Laughing.

Deni and Tyler moved around the trees. Down a dip lay another wide field of rocks and patchy grass. Towards its centre was the tail end of a massive cylindrical structure, sticking out of the earth at a skewed angle. Around the grounded rocket were half a dozen waggons with canvas tops, and around them stood at least a dozen people, eating, drinking, and tending to their weapons.

6

The crooked cylinder was half the height Deni remembered. The bottom half, upended, with its various mechanical trappings and wide exhaust pipes. The front, the peaked arrow, must have hit the ground first, crumpling into the crater. What remained was dark and dented, with holes where the panelling had split. As she stared she remembered it shaking on the spot, ready to launch. She saw Balfair's face as he shouted at her.

This will tell us why the clouds won't part.

Qait pulled her back, blocking her with his arm as he pressed himself into the tree trunk next to her. "Stay out of sight."

At the next tree, similarly hiding, Tyler whispered, "What do we do?"

"Wait," Qait replied. "Observe."

Perhaps a hundred metres away, the cluster of people below were clearly from the same stock as their morning attackers. The same ragged clothing, rough weaponry and skin darkened by dirt. Possibly the same clan. There were men and women in equal measure, the women as burly and dangerous-looking as the men. At least two children ran playing through the group. A cooking pan steamed over a small fire near the rocket. It was not a raiding party, but a community. The waggons were tied in place, semi-permanent.

"Who are they?" Tyler said.

"Bandits," Qait answered. "Same as before. They're trying to figure out what to do with it."

The question hung between them without needing to be spoken: *what now?*

The tracker took out a scope and studied the camp. He lowered it and kept staring. Finally, he shook his head and gestured back down the hill. He walked ahead. The younger pair exchanged an uncertain look, then hurried after him. Shielded from the camp by the hill, Tyler spoke more loudly. "Can you reason with them? Tell them the Guard need what's on that rocket?"

"You met them this morning," Qait said. "They won't negotiate."

"Where are you going?" Tyler said, jogging up to him. "What are you going to do?"

"Lay low. We settle in somewhere safe, watch them, figure out a way in. Without being seen."

"You said they'd be after us, though – the others – do we have time –"

"There's no other choice," Qait said, so firmly that Tyler stopped.

Deni paused too, and Tyler turned to her. "What we need from that thing, can we even sneak it out of there? How big is it?"

"I don't know," Deni said.

"Could they have taken it already?" Tyler continued rapidly. "Would they think it's valuable?"

"I don't know," Deni repeated, more frustrated.

Tyler went quiet. They both watched the tracker as he moved to the right, angling across the field. Tyler frowned. "Where's he going?"

On the far side of the rocket site, a stream running into the nearby river formed a ditch crested by tall grass. There, the trio lay low, peeking through the grass back to the bandit camp. The sounds of metal pounding on metal had bounced across the field while they skirted the site, as pairs of bandits approached the rocket and tried to chisel pieces off.

"They're not going anywhere," Tyler said. "Not until they've taken the whole thing apart."

"No," Qait agreed.

"So we need to act," Tyler demanded once more. "We've lost half the day figuring out there's no way closer – with them smashing that thing apart all the time. We can't keep waiting!"

"This is how I work," Qait replied calmly. "Rush things and you'll get hurt."

"We've gotta do *something*," Tyler said. "By night there might not be anything left to save."

Punctuating his point, a great creak came from the site with a chorus of triumphant whoops from the bandits. Something thumped on to the ground, a piece of the machine having come loose.

"You said it already," Qait said. "There's no way to get closer.

We need them to move. When they do, they'll either leave behind what we need or take it with them. If they've taken it, we follow them and at the right time we take it back."

"Take it back?" Tyler gaped. "How?"

"As the opportunity presents itself."

"And if they destroy what we came for?"

"Then at least we'll be alive."

"Crap! That's not good enough."

Qait remained calm but his tired eyes showed waning patience. Deni knew the look; he thought he knew best and felt no need to further justify himself. And from the way Tyler averted his eyes, she knew that Qait's seniority would win. Deni cleared her throat, preparing to speak. Neither man looked at her. She cleared her throat again, more loudly, and this time they both turned.

"You could distract them," she told Qait. "Safely. Lead them away."

"There's at least thirteen people," he said. "At best they'd send a few scouts, leave the rest to defend the camp."

"Not if you flew over them," she said. "They'd send everyone after your gyrocopter."

Qait considered it. He shook his head. "Not everyone. Even with one or two standing guard, you two couldn't go in there alone."

"Yes we can," Deni said. "We have to."

"I've already said –"

"Your plan won't work," she continued, before she got a chance to doubt it. "Even if they don't smash up what we need, Vorst will catch up to us. We can't wait."

The tracker continued watching the camp. More hammering rolled back towards them.

"I can get in there," Tyler said. "Alone. I can move real quick."

"So can I," Deni told him.

"You don't need to –"

"I spent most of my life going unnoticed," Deni said. "I can *help*."

"All right," Qait said, reluctantly. "It's possible. If you're sure." They both gave him looks severe enough to pre-empt any further questions. "I can't guarantee I'll get to the gyrocopter and back before nightfall."

"Nightfall's good," Deni said.

"Head for the longer grass, over there. It won't provide much cover if they're looking for you, but lay low and it might just work. If they're distracted."

Qait took out one of his knives and held it up, about to hand it to Tyler but noting the crude hammer the young man was still clutching. Instead, he passed it to Deni. She looked at it carefully. It was about twice the length of the blade she hid on her arm, nicked in places where it had seen use.

"Be careful," Qait told her. "Don't take any unnecessary risks."

Tyler let out a nervous laugh. "Don't worry, Qait. I'll take care of her."

Qait kept his focus on Deni. She stared right back. Not afraid. He understood her, she could see that. Quicker than Tyler, the tracker had an idea of what she was capable of.

"What was it like," Tyler asked, "where you grew up?"

Deni didn't look up from the piece of wood she was digging the knife into. What was it like, she reflected. Busy. No time to stop. The blade twisted in the bark, peeling out a thin spiral. Qait's knife was large, but a toy in comparison to hers. At least it was different. She had carved shapes out of two sticks and was in the process of sharpening this one.

"I never moved too far from where I grew up," Tyler continued into her silence. "Ruke lived a block away from where my parents were. I only lived in the two places all my life. Both Bawkley."

"I only lived in two places, too," Deni muttered back, then went quiet.

Tyler waited a moment and said, "You don't like talking, do you?"

Deni shrugged. *Like* was the wrong word, wasn't it. She liked talking. She had things to say. Tyler was waiting for a response. She said, "No one ever wanted me to."

"Dendra! What about what *you* want?" Tyler laughed, then caught himself. "Sorry, but if you want to talk, just talk, there's nothing to it."

She frowned. To say what? To who? *Why?*

He seemed to understand her concern. "You know what works, if you're worried about what you'll say? Just ask me something, instead."

Deni put the knife down, considering it, then asked, "What happened to your parents?"

"Oh." Tyler paused. "They're dead." Deni's eyes widened, but he waved it off. "No, it's fine. Long time ago. My dad died in a fire. My mum, she was never the same after that. She worked in the factories, panelling by the Drain. Do you know what panelling is?"

"Attaching two bits of metal together. We did that. Made a water tank."

"On your own? Nice! Well, there's people that do it all day. Sitting in lines, running a machine minute after minute, for a few packs of food. Those places are dangerous. The machines shut down, something gets stuck, they have to crawl in to figure it out. Then the machines start up again... people get hurt. You need to focus, working there."

"Your mum..." Deni started.

Tyler didn't waver. "We've all got things to deal with, you know. Life's tough but you get on with it. That's another of Ruke's sayings."

"I'm sorry," Deni replied quietly.

"You don't need to be so sorry all the time. I'll bet you've gone through worse." He didn't ask, though, and she didn't tell. He seemed to have come up with his own ideas already. "Can't imagine what it's like having to go where slavers tell you. Be put in that situation. I was always lucky, I had a trade, I could support myself. And I had a home, with good people around, and the memory of my dad, at least. This," he patted his leather satchel, "this was his. Ruke said he got it as a gift, from a trader who he protected from a swindler. He took care of people, my dad. He knew what it meant to be part of a community." He slowed down, watching Deni, and said, "Sorry you never had that."

"I thought it was normal." Deni thought back to the things Balfair had told her. "I was always told I was lucky. Like most people were suffering worse."

"I don't barely know you," Tyler said, like it'd been weighing on his mind, "but I can see it wasn't right. Maybe there's a lot more that's not right going on, and I don't even know it. I always trusted that the Guard knew best, that things were done, even bad things, sometimes, to make things better overall."

"Better for who?"

Tyler frowned, going quiet.

Deni turned back to the bandit camp. They had stopped attacking the rocket and were drinking, play-fighting and laughing again, around a couple of small fires. As the light behind the clouds dimmed, the firelight cast them in demonic yellows and oranges. The shadows of their grins and grimaces seemed to make up half their faces, larger and sharper shapes than were natural. Deni said, "The Guard didn't know why they were there, in our estate. Only Montgomery did. But they helped him all the same. And now they're working with slavers to hunt me, just the same."

"Qait's helping us –"

"But a hundred others tore the Kennel apart. Probably without knowing why."

Tyler went quiet again and Deni could feel his doubts. The sort of questions she'd faced when she'd seen Frinz's throat cut and Sincade dead on the floor. The Guard were not a force for good, and that made everything complicated.

Beyond the bandit camp, coming from the other direction, a vehicle moved into view. Bigger than the canvas waggons, bumping over the rocks as though they provided no obstacle. Deni sat up straight. Tyler followed her gaze.

"What is that?" he asked.

"It's them. It's Vorst."

7

As the vehicle approached, the chug of its engine filled the countryside like a tribal drum. Large cogs and chains spun amid wheels as tall as a person. Smoke poured from a slightly askew forward chimney and from three pipes that ran towards the back, and pistons rose and fell even as the machine came to rest. The vast engine was connected to a two-stage metal cabin, the front slightly lower, with thin slits for windows, and the back a sealed container bigger than the huts in the slums. The corners of the truck were lined with spikes, and a hatch in the middle of the roof was open, with a man standing out, leaning on the dual handles of a long-barrelled weapon.

It was an apparition that was burnt into Deni's memory as clearly as the face of the tattooed man. She had bounced on its cold floor while it thumped towards Balfair's estate, a slaver leering at her as a Road Guard sat stoically opposite, drowned in the sound of that thundering engine.

Ten seasons, at least, and the truck was still swallowing helpless victims into damnation.

The bandits filtered out between their primitive canvas waggons, old rifles, blades and bludgeoning objects in hand. They approached the vehicle with curiosity, without urgency or hostility. The visage of the terrifying slave truck signalled kindred spirits, it seemed. As the crowd panned out around them, two people jumped down from the truck's cab, one larger, hand resting on an axe hanging from his hip: Vorst. Deni half rose to her feet, fighting the dual instincts of wanting to attack him and flee. Tyler gripped her wrist and pulled her down. "What's wrong with you!"

"They'll get what we're after," Deni hissed back.

"And you want them to get you, too?"

Deni stared ahead. She said, "Look. No one's looking this way."

It was true; as Vorst addressed the head of the bandit community, the others were fixated on the newcomers and their vehicle. The slavers were as stunning a spectacle as Qait was going to be. This was their chance. Without further discussion, Tyler rose in a half-crouch and darted out. Taken by surprise, Deni held back for a second, then raced after him. They ran into the longer grass, as Qait had suggested, patches rising up to their knees, some waist-high. They kept as low as their speed would allow. Seeing the bandits were still turned away, voices rumbling in calm discussion, Deni rose higher to move faster towards the nearest waggon. Tyler joined her at full speed.

They skidded to the side of the waggon, pressing themselves against its wooden frame, exposed at their lower halves, where the base was raised above its wheels. Taking Deni's free hand, Tyler guided her along the edge of the waggon, to position them behind a wheel, and he kept hold of her as he leant around it, towards the rocket. With her heart already pulsing from the run and the danger, Deni found her senses pushed even further as she felt the young man's fingers wrapped around hers. She wanted to pull away, but he was holding tight, protectively.

"Is that it?" he whispered.

Deni shifted past him, free of his hand but pressing into him as she tried to keep close to cover. The wall of the fallen rocket was about ten metres away. It was black from fire, like the kitchen walls after an accident, and it was dented all over, crumpled like paper. The base was submerged in the earth, through rock and soil, with the permanence of a rooted tree. It seemed transformed in every way, but it was, at the same time, that object she had set off in the estate. That mysterious device that had got everyone killed but set her free.

A single object with the power to change.

"There." Tyler pointed with the hammer. Near the centre of the twisted metal, which had been sawed through and pulled apart, was a solid metal box, welded and bolted into place within the now-exposed exterior panels. A set of glass dials, circled in brass, sat at its front, two of them shattered, and a series of cables ran out from the top. One had been severed. The box had been left in place, but the dents around its edges showed that the bandits had already made efforts to penetrate it.

They'd been working on it. A little longer and it would've been lost.

Behind the box, the interior of the rocket was a mess of pipes and poles, an elaborate system that had either guided the missile or supported whatever work went on inside. The parts were broken and intermingled like a tangle of weeds.

Deni moved towards it and again Tyler pulled her back, bringing her even closer to him, his breath on her ear. "Too much open space."

Vorst's low voice rose over the camp. "They find you with it, none of you will be spared."

"Trick talk," a slurring bandit answered. "Fair price is fair trade, don't need words."

"This way," Vorst said. The sounds of dozens of feet moving drew Tyler and Deni's attention. Beyond another of the bandit waggons, the crowd was shifting closer to the slavers' truck. Vorst moved out of view along the side. The others followed, and the truck doors at the back opened. A brief, frightened scream came out. Vorst announced, "I'll give you three."

A murmur of discontent ran through the bandits, their leader replying with a derisive laugh, "For this? Crazed slaver, think we got no smarts?"

"It's fair," another voice said. The woman. "Keep it and you'll all be dead by the morning."

"Bringing threat to us now?"

"Fact, not threat. The Border Guard aren't far behind."

A rush of comments went through the crowd, suggestions and disapproving grunts. Tyler pulled at Deni's hand and hissed, "We gotta do this now."

Without waiting, he ran the short distance to the rocket, through the glow of the central fires. Deni rushed after him, looking aside as the bandits and slavers focused on the truck's contents at its rear. Reaching the box, Tyler grabbed at the knife in Deni's hand but she pulled away with a scowl. After a split second's surprise he whispered, "Cut it free! Quick!"

Deni sliced at the tangle of cables that held the box in place. Qait's knife was weak, catching on the hard material, and she had to saw at it. After a few quick tugs, barely denting the cabling, she growled and put the blade aside to use her own knife, drawn from its tiny sheath on her wrist. Tyler watched with surprise as she whipped it through the cable with no resistance.

The young man turned to check on the bandits as she rapidly cut through the rest.

"Six," one of the bandits was demanding. "At least six. Look at this size. Beauty machine."

"It's garbage," Vorst replied. "And you can keep it. There's only a small thing we need."

"Six is good deal," another bandit agreed with the first.

"Four," the female slaver said impatiently. "Let's do four and damned well get on with this. You see this one – he's special – fetch a high price in the city."

"They're bargaining with people's lives?" Tyler whispered.

Deni cut through the last cable and pulled back. She followed his gaze, to where two of the bandits were visible, slightly apart from the truck and the crowd, a male and a female. The latter scratched her nose with the tip of a machete.

Deni patted Tyler's arm and he turned back to her. "It's free?"

She nodded and he pushed past, wrapping his arms around the box and attempting to lift it. He heaved with his whole back and the box scraped against the metal with the slightest shift. Another heave and it barely moved.

"Get on that side," Deni instructed, pushing him back and placing her hands on the box. He did as he was told and she nodded. They lifted together. She was his equal in strength, it seemed, as they lifted with equal strain. They stumbled to the side and almost dropped the box, but steadied themselves. They shared a worried look, then hurried back to the nearest waggon.

"Only one thing," the first bandit, with the slur, was saying. Footsteps started towards them. "Still loosening it."

"Quick!" Tyler said.

The pair made no attempt to crouch or hide, now, just sidestepped as quickly as they could with the bulky metal box between them, jumping over rocks and weeds as they rushed into the open, away from the camp, towards the stream. Their only hope was that the closing darkness would hide them as the perimeter waggons obscured them.

Tyler's foot hit a brittle patch of weeds that cracked under his weight and they both froze. The sound cut through the dusk, back to the camp. It was met, a moment later, by a baby's shrill cry. The bandits and slavers stopped talking as the scream rose from the nearest waggon. A few on the periphery of the group, out to the side of the waggon, looked past it to the field beyond.

Tyler hissed, "Run!"

Abandoning all subtlety, they raced over the rocks. A stampede of people followed, bursting from between the waggons, bandits shouting to one another.

"Shoot them dead!" the lead bandit roared, but Vorst quickly followed. "No! Alive!"

A rifle cracked, making Tyler flinch and lose his grip. Deni jumped back, letting go as she took the full weight of the box. It slammed into the ground, one corner digging in.

"Stop!"

They froze, holding each other's gaze as the mob of enemies surged towards them. Tyler mouthed an apology. Deni's hand went back to the knife on her wrist. The two nearest bandits leapt towards them with clubs raised. Behind them, others were moving to the sides with rifles levelled. In the middle, Vorst watched calmly, with the similarly armoured woman at his side, their weapons lowered.

The first bandit reached them and went to grab Tyler, club up high. As he touched the young man, Deni sprang forward, driving her blade into his side, under the arm. The club fell from his hand as he twisted and shrieked. Someone far off fired a shot. The misplaced bullet hit the bandit in the back and flung him between the pair. Deni dropped to the ground with Tyler as a series of shots followed. The second bandit closed on them, his club smashing into the ground beside Tyler as the young man rolled out of the way. As the bandit raised his club for another attack, the throbbing of a rapidly approaching engine made him pause. He twisted, looking to the sky. The shouting and movement stopped as the shadow of the gyrocopter buzzed over the camp.

With the crowd watching the sky, one of the waggons exploded.

8

The bang rang through the field as dazed bandits and slavers stirred from the ground. Behind it, the sound of the flying machine's engine beat back in. The blast had knocked people down, and a few closer to the waggons had their hands clamped over their ears, groaning, unable to hear their own voices.

Deni rubbed dirt off her face as she rested on her elbow. She blinked to clear her eyes of smoke. All that remained of the nearest waggon was the shattered corner of its wooden base, a smouldering wheel and a wall of smoke.

To its side, Vorst was one of the first to get back up, shaking off debris. He threw his axe from one hand to the other as he watched the gyrocopter circling. He instructed, loud and calm: "He's coming back. Shoot him down."

The sense that came back to the bandits brought only panic, though. Realising the waggon was gone, a woman screamed and sprinted towards the wreckage. Another bandit tried to hold her back, but she pushed him down and wailed even more loudly. A man ran through the scattered bodies, pulling comrades to their feet, shouting, "It's the Guard! They're coming! Go! Go!"

"It's one man!" Vorst shouted back, but as he did, his female companion gripped his arm and snarled something at him. They turned from the bandits to Deni and Tyler. Deni jumped up moving towards Tyler. The young man was staring into the sky in disbelief.

"Hurry!" she said, dragging him to his feet, and they started an uneven run across the field.

Tyler pulled back, though, shouting, "The box!"

He tugged free of Deni and ran the other way, back to the contraption they'd dropped. Deni froze, seeing Vorst and his companion slowly approaching. Behind them, the bandits were scrambling into the waggons, cranking up engines, shouting incoherently. Two men dragged the screaming woman away.

Another explosion interrupted them, landing beyond the camp, clear of all the panic, erupting in a cloud of black smoke and dirt.

The closest bandits fell down and the shouting and running and screaming started again. Vorst and his companion had paused, looking sideways to the gyrocopter as Qait steered smoothly past, towards the far corner of the field, over Deni and Tyler's heads.

"Come on!" Tyler yelled.

Deni joined him at the box, hauling it up, and between them they continued their difficult run. Across the dark field, the shape of the gyrocopter slowed, then descended. As Deni and Tyler ran with all their energy, the vehicle struck the ground, bounced, then came to a standstill.

"Move!" Vorst shouted. Without looking back, Deni heard them break into a run. She and Tyler had twenty metres to cover, the weight of the box slowing them down, and the slavers were closing on them. A few more steps and they'd be within reach. Deni pushed herself with cringing terror, feeling in the air that Vorst was bearing down on them.

A rifle shot cut off the chase, the rush of a bullet passing narrowly overhead. Deni and Tyler ducked as one, straining to keep their grip on the box, then pushed on. Qait leant out of the gyrocopter, chambering another bullet. As he raised the rifle again, Tyler and Deni dropped the box heavily into the narrow floorspace of the vehicle and climbed on after it. The shaking jostled the tracker, and Qait's second shot was skewed. He cursed, letting go of the rifle to grab the controls.

Deni rolled over him, clutching the central struts of the engine and twisting back towards the approaching slavers. They were stalled but not injured. Vorst was up, and close. He sprang towards them with a roar, covering the final distance as the gyrocopter veered clumsily off the ground. One of Vorst's thick hands caught hold of the rim of the vehicle as it cleared his head-height, the whole thing shifting as Tyler kicked his fingers free. Qait grunted as he leaned heavily on the controls and took them higher, straightening up.

Vorst rolled across the ground beneath them. He started shouting again. His companion was calmer, slowly aiming a pistol up. Deni shouted, "Gun!" just before the weapon fired. The shout gave Qait just enough warning to steer, but not enough to get them clear. The shot twanged into the base of the gyrocopter, making the engine splutter. It whirred more quietly for a moment, then returned to its steady throb as they went higher, up towards the clouds and clear of the camp. The way Qait's shoulders tightened revealed that he knew damage had been done.

Below them, a tremendous flash was met a moment later by a series of bangs. The gun on top of the truck had started firing. Its shots sparked out in bright, ferocious lines, arcing up over the rocket and slowly moving towards them, but the aim was slow and the barrage was unable to follow them as Qait pushed the gyrocopter faster, out of its range.

Tyler uncomfortably climbed over him, struggling not to get in his way, and steadied himself on the central mast, standing over Deni, feet barely on the gyrocopter's edge. She followed his gaze back down to the ruin of the bandit camp, as the truck stopped firing. Smoke rose from the sites of Qait's bombs as the remaining waggons started rolling away, one or two straggling bandits sprinting to join them. Vorst and his companion stood staring after the gyrocopter. Another man had climbed out of the slave truck to watch them, too.

"We did it," Tyler told the others, triumphantly. "We got it!"

Qait did not reply and Deni knew why.

The gyrocopter rose and fell with minute stumbles. Something smelt wrong, burnt and noxious. Tyler laughed again, like he couldn't believe everything was all right. Deni noted his arm looped through one of the vehicle's supports, a hand rubbing his leather satchel, as though for reassurance. Seeing it, Deni understood his laugh. Tyler hid his fear behind happiness. She shifted her hand, the slight distance required in their tightly packed space, and placed it over his, stilling his nervous caress of the bag. He looked at her with a great smile. She nodded back.

Tyler and Deni stood some distance from the gyrocopter as Qait leant over it, tinkering with its various elements. The landing had been difficult, making the pair rub their aching limbs as they stared down at the metal box by their feet.

"Ruke would know how to get into it," Tyler said. "Opened your safety box in a second."

"It's not a safety box," Deni said. "It's sealed the way a vehicle's sealed. Not supposed to be opened, not without the right tools."

"Do you have any, Qait?" Tyler called over. "A torch? A saw?"

Qait kicked something across the ground towards them. It was a small device with a wooden handle clipped to a bulbous canister, shiny like an insect's back. Tyler rotated it uncertainly in his hand. There was a valve where the canister attached to a metal nub, and in front of that a pair of thin pipes which joined the handle as a trigger. Tyler undid the valve and the thing hissed, making him jump. He clicked the trigger. The gas lit up in a sharp lance of heat. Impressed, Tyler crouched by the machine.

"Better step back," he warned Deni. She didn't move.

Tyler ran his free hand over the box, as though there was a way he could tell the best place to start. He took the torch to a corner of the box and very slowly moved closer. As the heat hit the casing, it lit up red, then white, then the wall of the box started to liquefy, bubbling in. Tyler pulled back and turned the valve off. He waited a second, staring at the hole he'd created as the metal started cooling, the colour slowly returning.

"Why'd you stop?" Deni asked.

"What if I damage it?" he said. "You said, in the Towers, there were machines with papers and numbers and writing. What if that's what's in there? We could burn it. Ruin everything."

"How else will we get into it?"

Tyler didn't have an answer.

"Anything?" Qait asked, striding over, rubbing his oily hands on a rag.

"I don't want to damage it," Tyler said.

"Well, we can't carry it," the tracker said.

"We got it this far."

"The gyro did," Qait said. "Not any more."

"You can't repair it?" Deni asked. She had seen Balfair work on a dozen vehicles; he said anything that had once worked could work again. With the right attitude and the right tools. There was a lot she had loathed about him, but she had never seen him proven wrong when it came to machines.

"Not quick enough," the tracker said.

And time. That was the other thing. Sometimes it took a lot of time.

"They're a long way off," Tyler said. "We're not still in danger, are we?"

"Of course we are," Deni told him. "The Guard could be close, too."

"The Guard *aren't* –" Tyler started, but Qait cut in.

"We can't take the chance of staying with it. I brought us down for a reason."

The younger pair looked around them. A small copse of trees stood to their left, hiding them from another anonymous field. To the right, a short walk down a slope, was a wall of reeds. Beyond it was darkness, and as they looked that way they could hear why. The water of a river ran gently by, its surface sucking away the little light of night.

"You plan to build a raft?" Tyler said, gesturing to the trees.

Qait replied, "We can walk. With luck, we'll find a boat."

"Do you know where we are, at least?" Deni asked. "Where this will take us?"

The tracker hesitated. For the first time he seemed to have doubts. He did not admit it, though, telling her, "Towards the city or away from it. But not with that weight between us."

9

"What is it?" Tyler asked, looking at both Qait and Deni for answers. Deni shrugged. Qait didn't move. It appeared to be intact, at least, having survived what must have been a terrific flight, and the tracker had been careful to keep it that way, expertly applying only as much heat as was necessary to carve a lid from the box. Exposed inside were dozens of cables, small brass pipes and glass cylinders containing various liquids and granulated substances.

One component stood out from the mess of the rest. A small roll of paper was held in place by thin metal arms, with a needle against it. Reams of it had unravelled into a space below, crumpled with lines etched over them.

Qait took the paper out, carefully smoothing it and frowning. The etching had long, wavering lines that had somehow been printed against a pattern of dots, without any letters or numbers. Utterly meaningless. He gave Tyler and Deni a cursory look before tightly reeling it back in.

"That's it?" Deni whispered. "What can we do with that?"

"Exactly what I said," Qait replied, unfazed. "Keep it safe, and keep ourselves safe."

"It must've recorded something from the ground up to the sky," Tyler said. "Up above the clouds, even." Qait looked up and around them. Night had fully fallen and it was hard to see far beyond the patch they had landed in. He was trying to read the terrain and observe the world, even when there was nothing to see, to help form a plan. Tyler could see he was looking for some alternative to what they all knew must be true. "This is worthless if we don't get it back to Hodwick. Not just worthless, wasted. We're in the same boat I was in with the numbers when I found Deni's paper. You have to see now – we need Hodwick, the same way we needed you."

Qait said, "No. Our priority stays the same. Protect ourselves first, figure this out second."

"The longer we try to protect ourselves the harder it'll be to figure this out," Tyler said. "Eventually it'll be too late." The tracker didn't say anything. They had narrowly escaped death. More than once. But there had to be a reason for that. Tyler pushed, "They killed Ruke for this. Not for Deni, or anything else. Because they're scared of *this*. This isn't just information – it's a means to change things. To challenge the people who destroyed the Kennel – to *change the sky*. You get that, don't you?"

Tyler had picked up pace in his speech and was breathing more quickly, eyes wide as he stared at Qait, but the tracker looked barely moved. He said, "There's another option. We take this to people who have the means to fight. Let them worry about Hodwick, and the trouble it'll bring."

"You're talking about the rebels? You honestly believe *they* can be trusted with this? If they even exist!" Tyler said. The tracker had that sad look in his eyes that said he didn't have much belief in anything. Tyler turned to Deni: "I know the city. I can get back in, by myself, safer than anyone else –"

"No," Deni said. "Not without me."

There was determination in her eyes, her mind fixing on something as she glared at Qait in a way that showed she had doubts, too. Qait shifted his bag on his shoulder, seemingly deciding as he watched them. He said, "I have no love for the rebels, but this can open a dialogue –"

"This isn't *about* dialogues or rebels," Deni snapped. Her eyes burnt even stronger; she didn't have to go on, that look saying it all. Tyler smiled; his instincts had to be right about her. She was ready to face this thing head on, and she understood it the same as him. She said, plainly, "The rebels haven't shaken the Guard leadership in all this time. *This* can hurt them. This can *end* them. But only if we put it to use – not if we hide it."

Qait stared silently for a moment. He was bigger than them, and a fighter, but nothing in his calm suggested he wanted a fight. He sighed. "To the city it is, then. We'll walk though the night, as far as you're both able. Make camp, rest, continue. Agreed?"

Tyler and Deni nodded.

"Good," Qait said. He held the roll of paper out to Deni. He'd tightened it down to only a few inches thick, small enough to fit in a pocket. "You take this. They'll go for us first; you've got the best chance to get away."

*

The terrain at the edge of the river was difficult, utterly uneven and overgrown, but Deni was used to it. She had walked part of the way between Balfair's estate and the city, after all. She stayed out of sight, sticking to the roughest tracks. It was late, though, and as the adrenaline of the slaver's attack faded, she found her energy depleted underneath. Her eyelids felt heavy, she needed to rest, but Tyler and Qait pressed energetically on.

She stifled a yawn.

Tyler must be tired too, she decided, even as he skipped light-footed ahead. He hadn't said much more, but she could see what was going on in his head. They carried an unspoken secret. The bombs Qait had dropped had killed people. Infants. As well as making sense of Ruke's death and protecting her, Tyler had the weight of the bandit deaths to cope with too, now. The same way she'd struggled for days after the attack on the Balfair estate. Unnecessary deaths in the course of their survival.

Perhaps the tracker knew. If he was of Montgomery's stock, perhaps he didn't care. None of them would talk about it. They just had to think through it privately. Marching back to the Metropolis, to certain trouble, would help them atone. Atone. Find the truth, help the world. At least, take the most likely action to weaken the Guard. So they would stop hunting her. It still wasn't about helping the world, was it? Why help a world that had never helped her?

She knew why, though, watching Tyler bounce ahead. If it wasn't about breaking free or helping Estalia or resolving Balfair's legacy, it was suddenly about him. He'd fought for her. Against the slavers, and the bandits, and the Kennel. He'd suffered, and he was still going, still trying to help. Without the slightest hesitation. She had to fight for him, too. So they would both be free.

He was the only person she'd ever met that didn't deserve to suffer.

Not like all the others. Bitter people, wrong people. Which of them hadn't deserved their lot? But not Tyler. It was in his smile. And his eyes. Something she hadn't seen in anyone else. Something she longed to nurture and keep seeing, to keep close.

Was this love?

The thought confused her. It wasn't the love of the story books, where people aspired to spend all their time in someone else's arms. Where you thought about someone's scent and touch and wanted to ride horses with them. It was more like love for life. For everything. Just looking at him ahead, she knew there was still good in the world, and she wanted to be a part of that.

As Deni's energy waned, her focus shifted. Half-formed thoughts flitted across her mind.

He couldn't do the things she'd done, could he?

Would Qait?

She saw the tattooed man's face and heard his shout as he crossed the field behind her. She jumped. Turned on the spot. There was nothing there. She took a breath and continued, more slowly. The men hadn't noticed, walking ahead.

Why hadn't Qait shot Vorst? He had the chance, and the slaver was so big, how could he miss? Had he meant to miss? Maybe they were working together. He was a Guard. Or maybe he was scared? Afraid to kill? The bombs could have been accidental; he might have been aiming to distract them.

She had learnt one thing for sure. No one could be trusted. Life was a history of betrayal. How would he betray her? Deliver them to the Guard, now they had the rocket's information? Cut their throats as they slept?

What could she do?

She slowed down, squinting towards the horizon. A dark shape stood in the field. Maybe the size of a man. Maybe two. Three. Watching her. Were they really there? Montgomery, he still wanted her dead, didn't he? Was Qait working with him?

"Here," Qait said, stopping. Deni tried to shake the thoughts from her head, speeding up to join him. Nonsense ideas. Paranoia. Not enough sleep.

Qait was standing by a divot in the earth alongside the river, shielded from the world by an arch of tall weeds. The sunken gap was barely two metres wide, flattened by something that had rested here long ago. The tracker pointed with his rifle. "You two rest. I'll keep watch."

"We should keep going," Deni said, trying to pick out the shapes she'd seen watching them. There was no sign of them now.

"I'm okay," Tyler agreed, but in opening his mouth he invited a yawn.

"You need your rest. Both of you. Don't worry. We're safe here."

"What about you?" Tyler asked, Deni in turn watching the tracker.

"This is my work," Qait said, simply. He slung his bag into the space, then took a pouch from his belt and handed it to Tyler. "Eat. Drink. Sleep. I'll return when it's time to go."

Tyler slumped, and suddenly looked ten times more tired as he gave in to it. He placed the pouch on the ground and crawled into the grass space. Qait nodded to Deni and she followed more cautiously, kneeling and feeling ahead with her hands. The earth was hard, rocky under the surface, but it was flat enough, and hidden. She gently reclined alongside Tyler. He yawned more openly, stretching his arms and sliding to the floor.

"Thanks, Qait," Tyler said.

Deni nodded in agreement, but when she looked up the tracker had already gone.

"Here." Tyler turned to her. He placed his leather satchel on the ground behind her and patted it, as though fluffing up a cushion. Deni wanted to protest that she needed no more comforts than he did, but he gave her an encouraging smile and she couldn't deny the gesture. She rested her head on the makeshift pillow, stiffly trying to find a comfortable position on her back, keeping what small space she could between herself and Tyler. She breathed in the scent of the bag; old, comforting leather. And Tyler's smell, with it. The man who had owned this bag before must have been a great person, responsible for the great person with her there. She opened her mouth, wanting to say something, anything. Tyler murmured something that could have been a goodnight, followed by a snuffling sound and a deeper breath. He had fallen straight to sleep. Deni closed her mouth again and sighed.

She stared into the darkness above, determined to stay awake, at least for a little while. They couldn't be safe, after all. Maybe Qait would double back, do something terrible. This would be the right time to do it, wouldn't it?

Tyler rolled in his sleep, pressing into her as he did, and his arm flopped over her waist. It lay there, limp, unintentional, not holding. His touch softened her.

She felt safer.

*

Deni woke with a start at the sound of the dry grass crumpling, and she sat bolt upright. Tyler was stretching upwards, sitting next to her. He offered her a brief smile, saying there was nothing to be worried about, and he started searching Qait's pouch for food. She resisted the urge to pull away from him, embarrassed at how little their closeness meant to him. She said nothing as he handed her some dried meat. She chewed slowly.

The morning light had come during their sleep, the river now visible in the hazy grey. It was wider than she had thought, at least ten metres across, and the water was moving faster than it had in the night. Qait crouched at its edge, filling a canteen.

"Sleep well?" Tyler asked. He sprang to his feet. "I feel like a new man!"

Deni nodded. She had not dreamt. Had barely noticed the night passing, and regretted not having more time to appreciate the calm, alone with Tyler.

"I scouted ahead," Qait called back to them from the riverbank. "We're still clear of them. But we'd better keep moving if we want to keep it that way."

"See anything ahead?" Tyler asked.

The tracker approached before answering. He handed his canteen to Deni and she gratefully drank from it. Watching her, Qait said, "There's a mill. They might have a boat."

Deni looked at his steely eyes and felt guilty. Did he know what she'd been thinking? He was a good man, too, as Tyler was. How could she have suspected him, after what he'd already gone through? It was just tiredness, wasn't it?

Even as she thought it, the doubts came back. Tiredness or experience? Hadn't he agreed to their plan a little too easily?

Tyler tapped her on the arm, drawing her attention back to him. He must've noticed her concern. "Our luck's coming in. You'll see, everything's gonna get easier from here."

Deni wished he hadn't said it.

10

Tyler found his voice again for the walk towards the mill. He asked about where Qait had grown up, where he had travelled to and the things he had seen. The tracker answered in monotone, monosyllabic words that offered almost no insight into his past. Tyler tried with Deni, too, and she took Qait's cue with similarly simple answers. Not because she didn't want to share, but because she had nothing she felt was worth sharing. How could the tinkerings of her isolated master interest someone like him?

Aggravated by her own silence, Deni strained to keep the conversation going. She thought of his advice from the day before and asked what Tyler had seen in the city. His enthusiasm for his home carried him on. He described unique foods from one area or another. The grand architecture of Grenevic. The enormous machines around the Hasting shipyards and Kelp Furnishings Factories. Occasional airship sightings. The theatre shows and acrobatics in Height Park. He described visiting public *glus* shacks and listening to music from live bands, and promised Deni he would show her all these things.

She pictured it and smiled. Not just at the thought of the city's wonders she had yet to see, but at having Tyler show them to her. In his enthusiasm, he bounced closer to her and put an arm around her shoulders, squeezing her to him, saying, "You'll love it! All of it!" Deni slowed down, her smile gone and her eyes wide with surprise at the brief contact. It felt important, somehow. Special. Tyler had quickly moved on, though, a few steps ahead in his eagerness. "Just as soon as we've settled the score with this rocket."

Qait made a small noise of disapproval. "This is the start of something, not the end."

Tyler let the tracker have the comment, not arguing, twisting back to Deni. "And hackball. You need to see a game of hackball!"

"What's that?" Deni asked, but Qait waved them silent.

"Here we are."

They came to his side and took in the mill. A few hundred metres ahead, it was a tall wooden building with an arm sticking out over the river, a vast wheel hanging in the water beneath it. The wheel was turning but the site looked abandoned, with no vehicles in the dirt forecourt. Across from the mill, on the edge of the field, stood another, even larger building, with enormous doors taking up most of one wall. One of the doors had fallen off its supports at the top, and lay partly sunken into the ground.

"I don't see a boat," Tyler said.

"Wait here," Qait said. "I'll look."

"There's no one there."

"That we can see."

"Then we go together. You've been up all night, you can't just wade into trouble alone."

Qait must have been tired, as he didn't complain. "As you like. Follow my lead."

He raised his rifle. They fell into step behind him, moving closer to the river, watching their feet for where the ground had fallen away. The closer they got to the mill, the more impressive it seemed, as large as the warehouses of the Metropolis. It was damaged, though. Part of the structure supporting the wheel was missing, picked off by a particularly severe torrent of water or a badly directed boat. Half of the spaces for windows had been boarded up, too.

The wheel rotated with a steady creak. Deni slowed down to look at the ten-metre structure. A system of cogs rose around it, with poles stretching over their heads and into the main building. Something large turned inside, grinding, the whole device slowly moving.

She wanted to tell the others it still working. She understood machines like this, at least in part, and they didn't turn on their own. You disconnected them to stop the parts wearing down. When she didn't say it at once, Qait voiced the conclusion for her: "They can't be far away."

He steadied his gun as they continued through the passage, out to the other side. It opened onto another empty dirt patch and a few smaller buildings. One looked like a small workshop, with wide-open doors and benches inside. Another ran onto the river, low but long and wide.

"Boathouse," Tyler pointed out.

Qait ventured into the open, turning back towards the house as he did. He watched the windows and doors as he backed towards the boathouse. Halfway across, he waved for them to follow. Tyler and Deni rushed across the short distance and got behind him as the tracker watched their surroundings.

They reached the boathouse in silence, coming to a small doorway, and Qait nodded to Tyler to test the handle. The young man did so and found it locked. The tracker kept moving, along the side of the building, and checked around the corner. The wall was flush, no other way in. He came back to the locked door and put down his rifle. He took a palm-sized stone from the floor and raised it to smash the handle.

"That's enough," a rough female voice shouted from somewhere above. They spun towards her, Qait tightening his grip on the rock in lieu of his dormant gun. The woman was in a small window-frame fifteen metres up, barely visible except for a long barrel that poked out towards them. "You wanted to keep walking I would've let ya. Seen your intent now, I can't."

"I'm a guard," Qait shouted back, dropping the rock and spreading his arms.

"And I ain't shot you in spite of it," the woman answered nastily. "It's the kids that got you lucky. He take you from your folks?"

"No ma'am," Tyler called out. "He's a friend. We have problems with the Guard ourselves. Them and some slavers."

Deni looked from Tyler up to the gun. He wasn't committing to it as she would; they had more than a problem with the Guard, and it seemed this woman would understand.

"So?" the woman replied. "Doesn't forgive you being thieves. Step out in the open, let me see you better."

Qait gave the others a warning look. It would make them easy targets, for sure. Tyler tried again, more insistent. "We're not thieves, just had a bad run of luck!"

"What's the difference?" She was losing her patience.

"They killed my family," Deni blurted out. It wasn't loud enough to reach the woman, she imagined, not properly, but loud enough for her to take notice. She tried again, more loudly. "They killed his family, too. The Guard did. Important people in the Guard. But we have a way to stop them. Please."

They were all still. The gun didn't move for a moment.

Finally, the woman shouted, "You all stay there. I'm coming down."

"Where is everyone?" Qait asked as the thickset lady approached. She was dressed in dusty workman's clothes, trousers and a shirt, her curly black hair tied loosely back. Her gun had two long barrels and a circular chamber near the handle, holding additional ammunition. She held it confidently, one hand under the barrel, as she marched towards them.

"Where you coming from?" she demanded, ignoring Qait to address Deni.

Deni hesitated, looking to the men and willing one of them to take over. Tyler opened his mouth to speak, but the lady wasn't interested. "Not you. I'm talking to her."

"Far west," Deni said, "originally. Now –"

"Speak up," the lady ordered. "You got something to say, better make sure I hear it."

Deni cleared her throat. "Originally the west. But I made it to the city. We're headed back there."

"That's a long walk."

"We thought this place was abandoned," Qait explained. "Otherwise –"

"What, you would've come knocking? Didn't hardly check, did ya?"

"We're sorry," Tyler said.

"Yeah yeah, save it." The lady sidestepped around them, keeping her distance. She kicked Qait's rifle out of reach. Still addressing Deni, she said, "They hurt you, miss?"

"They're my friends," Deni said. The word felt weird in her mouth. "The Border Guard –"

"Oh, I know all about the Border Guard!" the lady spluttered, her anger stirring a nervous sort of energy. "They're the ones – to hell with them!"

"What happened here?" Qait said.

"What didn't?" she snapped. "Same that's happening all over, by my estimation. Guards on the run, taking advantage. People following their example, pecking at each other for scraps. Whole lot of good folk dead!" The lady stopped and eyed Qait. She moved slightly further away, saying, "You wear the uniform and want me to believe you got problems with them?"

"I took up this armour when it meant something good. I still believe it does. But I've been separated from the leadership for some time."

The lady eyed him, not convinced. She nodded to the boathouse. "Now you come looking to steal, is that it?"

"Like I said, we thought there was no one here."

She looked from him to Deni again and started shaking her head. "I oughta shoot you down right here is what I oughta do. Thieves and liars, I see that well enough. But damned if I'd stoop as low as the rest of them. You're just kids. Damned kids." Her face toughened again. "Shouldn't be out here at all. You even eaten anything today? Any of you?"

"A little," Tyler answered.

"Yeah, I know what that means. Here's what we'll do. We'll get you fed and we'll get some measure of you. Then see where that takes us, huh?"

"There's people after us," Qait warned. "Our time's short."

"Then you'd better get to doing what I say and quit talking back, hadn't ya?"

"About a moon ago, they came through here. Packs of them. It started with a couple of Border Guard ships, big ones, barely fit in this river. You saw the damage out there? That was them. They took what supplies we had. Food, drink. There must've been fifty men on board, all of them tired and angry. What could we do? My husband, he told them we didn't have enough to go round, and you can guess what happened next. They took what they wanted anyway."

"Any idea who they were?" Qait asked.

The lady gave the tracker a cold look. She'd introduced herself as Wallen and brought them into her dining area where they sat around a plate of dry biscuits. She answered, slowly, "What for? You gonna get them to bring back what they took? Undo what they did?"

Qait responded confidently, "They all answer to someone."

She barked a vindictive laugh. "And here I thought it was a joke when you mentioned leadership. You're a dreamer. There

141

was worse to come, anyway. These bandits, that's what they were, they left us to rot with no food and a few bruises, but they left us all the same. Then came the Road Guard. A group of maybe a dozen. We had nothing to spare, then, so they got mighty mad. Said if we can't have food, we'll have people. There was trouble coming, rebels in the hills, they said, Border Guard needed everyone able to go with them. Help fight it. Like hell, we told them. For what? You see any hills near here?

"There was six of us. We said we needed everyone to keep this mill running, had people counting on us in town. They said town wouldn't be there much longer, at this rate. Wouldn't be a mill either, without their protection. Two of our hands chose to go, got convinced they needed to join this fight. That left Ialn and me, one lad and our daughter. About your age." She nodded to Deni.

"Those bastards, they never came back," Wallen continued. "Ialn, he took the lad and went into town to see what was happening. Trading post of twenty, thirty homes, about a kilometre east of here. That's..." She swallowed her emotion. "That's the last I saw of him. The lad, he made it back, all shaken up, and said everything was gone. Buildings burnt, bodies in the road. No one left, not alive. Ialn wanted to go further, to see if there was anyone they could help, or some way to get a message out. A little way down the road they got ambushed. A couple of guys in furs, don't know if they were from the town and got desperate, or from further away." She tensed her jaw to push the emotion down. "The lad, he ran. Off through the fields. He made it back here and told me what happened. The guys that did it, they followed... we had trouble. A lot of trouble."

"What'd you do?" Tyler asked, horrified.

"Well," Wallen said, "I'm still here, ain't I? No one else."

"Dendra," Qait cursed, drawing a look from Deni. The tracker looked as affected as she'd ever seen him.

"Haven't had a look in from Dendra in seasons," Wallen scoffed. "Just Hrute on the back of Modo. It's anger and suffering that's brought this on us. And you know what? Those men that came back here, dressed in their furs, their faces were familiar. Maybe someone I saw in town. Maybe someone I saw in the Guard's armour one time." She thumbed her nose in disgust. "We've had rumours of rebels, sure. Movements in the woods two or three towns over. Friend of a friend, always, never heard anyone that'd actually seen one. Kandish bandits would stick out like a long-barge, wouldn't they? No foreigner's come through here in a decade. Only the Road Guard taking tribute and the Border Guard shipping up to the north. Haven't even had a sniff of the Water Guard in seasons, they stopped coming by, left us to shore up the river ourselves when the rains came. In the midst of everyone panicking over these invisible rebels, the thugs in the Guard started doing things for themselves."

"It's the war," Qait said. "Come down from the north."

"Whose war?" Wallen snarled. "My home's destroyed. Everyone I ever knew is dead or gone, and I never saw nothing about war. Your people did this, only they make the world think it's someone else's fault – playing a damned sick game of Aftan Whispers."

"They're not all bad," Tyler said, his quiet voice lacking conviction as his eyes rested on the tracker. Qait wasn't defending his colleagues, though. Wallen grunted, seeing no need to argue. The truth of it was out there, weighing on them.

"Better in the south, isn't it?" she said. "You can't fight against it here, but you can join them, there. I've got grain enough to grind for a few days yet, so that's what I'm doing. I'll fill up the barge and trade my way into a new life."

"The city's south of here, isn't it?" Tyler asked. "You can come with us. We'll help you, make sure you're okay."

"Out of your own damned goodness, sure," she replied bitterly. "Without a lick of me knowing who the hell who you are. You're off the mark, though. I ain't going to no Metropolis, not when that's where the Guard are pooling. Anywhere but. I'll go further, maybe Brofton. Maybe somewhere in the country, anywhere as long as it's away from the empire and their shit. From what I hear, that's where it's all going – the cesspool. We can't trust what we hear, though, can we?"

"No," Qait said, gravely. "Nothing's been the same since the Thesteran Fire, and people haven't been told what's really happening. Not even the Guard. The rumours of the rebel attacks are true, but those rebels aren't responsible for all the fighting. There's regular people taking up arms. Some against the Guard, joining the rebels. Others on their own, just trying to take advantage. That's what happened here. In the north, they're calling it the Fall of the Guard."

Qait gave them a moment to process that. He kept his eyes on Wallen but clearly wanted the two younger ones to appreciate it, too. He continued, "I got out. Just before Thesteran. I avoided getting back in. I believed there was no hope. But this girl, she uncovered something. We have information that a man was murdered for. It can bring about change."

"And what," Wallen said, "would that information be?"

Qait gave Deni a look as though suggesting she should be the one to explain it. Deni was quiet, though. It had been easy enough with Tyler, on their own in the dark, and with Qait, on the tail of their frantic escape from the Kennel. Now that there were biscuits and an audience of three, the words were more difficult to find.

"It's to do with the sky," Tyler offered for her. "The clouds. A guy in the Metropolis can use what we've found. When we get back to him, it'll change everything – break the clouds, stop the darkening days, even."

Wallen eyed him, then Deni again. She was drawn to Deni, that much was clear. She took a breath and said, "More of the same, isn't it? Stories about stories and a lot of hot air."

"It's not stories!" Tyler insisted. "Deni has seen through the clouds! Tell her!"

Deni seized up for a moment. She said, meekly, "It's true. I saw the sky."

"We could all see the sky!" Tyler rolled on. "It can bring light to the world – in every way! The Guard, they're keeping people down – trampling them into the ground – and they know – they know that whatever this is, this thing can make the heavens open and something – *something* can be done!"

Wallen eyed him warily. Her hesitation alone said the idea interested her, and it was easy to see why, with Tyler's passion. He wasn't talking madly, he was smiling, genuinely hopeful. Deni watched him, wishing she could join in.

"Bring light?" Wallen commented. "You know how that sounds? When we've had season upon season of withering crops? Bring light. How exactly would that work?"

"There's researchers," Tyler insisted, again surprising Deni with how complete the idea seemed to be in his head. "A big group of them, who've been working on things like this for years – but the Guard have been trying to stop them. They have the understanding, and the means, and this – what we've uncovered – it'll give them the last push they need to act on it."

"If it's something that big," Wallen grumbled. "ain't the city the most dangerous place for enemies of the Guard to be?"

"It's more dangerous here," Deni said quietly. Wallen turned to her, now. Deni picked out a knot in the wooden surface to fix on so she wouldn't have to look at her. She went on, almost in a whisper: "It's more dangerous wherever I go, because they're trying to cover it up. They're following us, and they'll come this way and kill you just for talking to me."

Wallen shifted uncomfortably, her thick hand closing around her cup. She said, "Sounds mighty like the Guard telling me there were rebels in the hills."

Deni shook her head, still not looking at her. "I don't want to take anything from you; I'm only telling you the truth. We can leave without you, or your boat. But if you stay here, you'll die. Come with us and we can do something important, though. More important than anything, maybe."

Wallen kept her eyes on Deni. Tyler and Qait were staring too. Were they surprised? It was all true, wasn't it? The mill owner said, "You *really* seen the sky?"

Deni nodded slowly.

"When? How?"

"There was a rocket that went through the clouds," Deni said. "It brought light. Colours like I'd never seen."

"Warmth?"

Deni nodded.

Wallen bit her lip. "You know what that would mean? Sunlight? Real sunlight? You know half the food in town was generated in those artificial lungs? How much more we could've done with *real* light..." Wallen paused. "You got any proof?"

"There's a lot of people dead," Deni said. "With no other reason than how powerful this thing is. That's the proof."

Wallen nodded, finally conceding. "All right. All right. I already told you I'm set to travel – maybe we do work together on this. That don't mean I'm going to the city – but you want passage with me, you can help me load the boat. We can see where this takes us."

145

11

There was a good-sized barge, big enough for fifty sacks of grain or a few dozen people, with an engine straddling the back third of the vehicle, attached to a paddle-wheel on either side. It moved slow, Wallen had told them, but it was powerful, and once they got it started it wouldn't be stopped unless they decided it. Qait had been impressed enough to ask for a closer look at the engine, and their chat turned to how he might get it to move faster. He knew a few things about engines, after all. The pair's conversation became inaudible as they disappeared inside the boat.

They'd almost been friendly, Tyler had noticed, as he left the boathouse with Deni. That's all people needed. Some connection to interest them both. Then they started treating each other like humans again, not enemies.

Tyler was watching the road while he tried to think of a way to do that for Deni. He kept an eye on the site's entry point rather than look at her. She didn't want attention. He knew it had been tough for her, speaking up in there, and before. Still, she stood close to him, even with the whole mill for space. Not a foot away. Maybe she was warming to him. They'd had a lot of closeness without much choice, in the Kennel and sleeping out here, but this was different. Now it felt like she wanted it.

Just as he didn't want to push her to talk, though, he didn't move any closer himself. Best to give her some space. They had the time, now. Even if the slavers might roll down that road any minute, for the moment they had time. Even if the *Guard* came rolling down that road. That was what they were dealing with, after all. Qait had confirmed it, clear enough. He'd known it since the Kennel, anyway, he just hadn't faced it. The Guard were the enemy. The people he'd believed helped the world run smoothly. It was one of them who had killed Ruke.

"What's Aftan Whispers?" Deni asked, drawing him from his thoughts. He turned to her and couldn't help but smile again. She was pretty, even more so when her face was fixed in concentration, as it was now. Had she been trying to figure out the expression without ever having heard it?

"You never played it as a kid?" he replied. He knew at once he shouldn't have said it. She probably hadn't played anything as a kid. She didn't look hurt or offended, though, just shook her head, an honest *no*. He said, "It's a game. You whisper something in your friend's ear and they whisper it to someone else, and you do it round a whole circle. Except you each change it a little bit. Then the person at the end says it out loud and it's something totally different. It comes from Afta, you know, across the Southern Sea, because it's so big out there, and if you could imagine anyone trying to get a message from one side to another..." He trailed off, seeing that Deni was concentrating harder, a step behind. She didn't need the trivia; she was processing the phrase against what Wallen had said. About how the Guard spread stories about the war to hide the world's troubles.

"It's true, isn't it?" Deni said. "That's the way it is."

"I guess so. I've heard ten different things that could've happened in Thesteran. Must be sixty different descriptions of the Short Queen, and a hundred stories about how Supreme Commander Klant died. People like telling stories, they don't care that the truth gets a little mixed up along the way."

"It matters, though," Deni replied.

"Yeah, it does."

"How many stories have you heard about why the clouds don't part?"

Tyler paused. The question made him look up, considering the blanket of grey above them. It was slightly lighter than usual, almost white with its background glow. He answered, "It's not a question people ask. There aren't any stories. It's like asking why water's wet, isn't it?"

"No. Not really."

Tyler went quiet. It was another stupid thing to say. But it was true. In all his life he couldn't recall a single person suggesting the sky should be any different. It glowed bright, it glowed dark, it changed at night when the moon grew or shrank and it all got worse when the great storms came. But the sky was what it was: clouds that blocked the heavens beyond, sometimes thick and sometimes thin but always there. "People should know about it,"

Tyler said. "They'd want to hear it. Like stories of the storms at sea and the creatures in the Aftan plains. What's beyond the clouds. You could get people dreaming."

Deni said nothing.

"You could write it down or something, find another way to do it. You shouldn't worry, people would want to hear you talk. I like hearing you talk. You've got a nice voice." Her expression was sceptical. Like he was making fun. "I mean it! You're different to the girls in the Metropolis – they're loud, and the ones that don't care what people think, they're the worst. You think a lot, I can see that. Someone that thinks a lot, instead of saying any old thing, it makes it special when you talk."

"No," Deni said. She looked up the road. Glum, not taking his compliments seriously. "It's just making trouble. It's like the Aftan Whispers, like she said. We talk and people don't hear it right. The things we say make bad things happen, even when we don't mean it."

Tyler shifted closer to her then. He took her hand in his and she looked sideways at him, frightened. She didn't pull away. As he took her other hand, she turned to face him fully, eyes on his. He said, "Whatever's happened in your past, that's not now. Don't you believe for one moment you shouldn't share your troubles. Those people that told you not to speak, they were wrong. I can only imagine the things they did to you – they shouldn't have, and you deserve better. You're not a slave, Deni – you can't let them keep controlling you."

She wrenched her hands free from his and pulled back, saying, "You don't know. Not about any of it. It wasn't what anyone said, it was me."

"Like hell it was – you –"

"You don't *know*!" Deni snapped and moved away. He held his empty hands up.

That time, he thought he'd been saying something right.

She skipped across the clearing and rounded the workhouse building. Tyler took a few steps after her but stopped. He was only going to make it worse, wasn't he?

The engine in the boathouse started up behind him.

*

Deni planted herself on the floor, back against the wall of the workhouse, and screwed her eyes shut. Idiot. Idiot.

He was trying to help but he had no idea. Of course she'd said things she shouldn't have. It was her words that got everyone killed. The more she said the more damage she did, and he didn't get that. How could he? Probably spent his whole life talking to people and having people listen to him and never had anything bad to deal with. Never said a wrong word that made a difference to anyone, only said things that made the world better. Even here, even with Wallen, he'd talked about the future like it was a great and positive thing and all she could say was how much suffering was still to come.

There was no doubt in him that they were on a path to something special. She still saw that something special as a chance to cut these people down so she could be free. She was a liar, a cheat. Whatever majesty parting the clouds might bring, that wasn't going to stop whoever was behind the tattooed man, whoever controlled Montgomery. That was what *she* needed.

She rubbed a tear away with her sleeve, the old, dirty material scratching her.

What use was changing the world, if it wouldn't save them?

The sound of the boat engine rose from behind. A throaty mechanical churn. They'd be travelling in that tight space and he'd keep trying to talk to her. They all would. They wanted to know her, to connect with her. None of them could understand, though, could they?

The road turned up a gentle slope, away from the mill, flanked by trees and messy hedges. It went out into the unknown, the open countryside where the only thing she knew she'd find was a town where everyone had been killed. Maybe that's where she belonged. Roaming, alone, through the graveyards of Estalia. Not in the city where there were still things left for her to damage.

As she stared up the road, Qait's voice called out, "Deni! We're gonna load up. Won't be long."

She didn't answer.

She'd done it before, she knew what was out there. More people that wanted to hurt her, or control her. People that she didn't mind hurting. Tyler was too nice. She liked him too much. She buried her face in her hands as the thought struck her.

She *liked* him and that was dangerous. What could she do, other than mess it up?

"Deni!" Qait raised his voice, with a hint of impatience. "Where are you?"

She choked back the emotion, pushing herself up. They didn't need her now; she could leave Balfair's research, they knew what to do with it. This was her chance to get away. To stop getting in the way. They'd said it, hadn't they – no one had ever *really* been after her – only after what was on that rocket.

She took a breath.

"I didn't mean to," came Tyler's voice, the pair of men hurrying through the clearing. "I was trying to cheer her up."

Qait didn't say anything.

Trying to cheer her up. Like she needed someone to help her be happy. Deni hesitated. She could get to the hedgerow in seconds, they'd never see her. They wouldn't know where to look, she could stay low and just keep moving.

Qait came into the open first, striding around the building. He gave her a look, glancing first to her then out to the road ahead. She froze as Tyler joined him, the young man's face a picture of concern.

Neither of them asked why she hadn't answered, or what she was doing there. The tracker knew, though. She could see it in his expression. All he said was, "Come help us move some of these sacks. We're about ready to go."

12

With its engine rumbling and the paddles turning, the barge was even louder than the gyrocopter. They stayed up front, in the raised cabin room where Wallen stood at the wheel, with one of them only occasionally having to dip below to stoke the coal chamber. Deni tucked her feet under herself in the corner, on a side bench, while Tyler kept his distance with Qait, by the far window, watching the world roll by. Both of them had been giving her concerned looks since they had moved what was left of Wallen's stock into the massive cargo hold, but they hadn't said anything. She dreaded when they would. She knew the words would stick in her throat when she had to reply. Without knowing what those words would be, or the questions, she knew they'd be hard to form.

She was trapped, drifting back into the Metropolis. Even as Tyler strained to look ahead, making an effort to hide his glances her way, she knew he was concerned. He'd left his satchel on the bench, near her. She gazed at it, wondering if he regretted leaving it so close to her. Did he realise it wasn't safe here? Did he think she was crazy? The girls in the city probably talked to him all the time without thinking too much. None of them had mad secrets or dark pasts. None of them had got his family murdered.

"How'd you learn all these things?" Tyler asked Qait, searching for some distraction. "Like, where we'd find the rocket? Where the river goes?"

"I've been doing it a long time," Qait said, plainly. A look on his face said he knew Tyler would only ask more questions, so he continued. "Part of tracking is studying the world. So you can work without a map. I study things like the direction moss faces on a tree, or the way the wind moves flags."

"Have you used this river before?"

"I don't need to recognise it to understand it. Most waterways south of Hasseran, west of Feldoh, end up joining the Drain, one way or another."

"Hasseran..." Tyler tested the word. Deni didn't know it either.

Perhaps there were more alternatives to the Metropolis than she knew. Tyler didn't ask about it, though, as she'd have liked. Instead, he said, "And you know we're going in the right direction?"

"Sure," Qait said. "You just follow the flow."

Tyler nodded with the focus that said he was trying hard to learn this information.

Deni twisted to kneel on the bench and look out of the window, to avoid thinking about them. The countryside's edges were softened by mist again, flat fields stretching into a white haze. A dark, living shape moved in the distance, making her flinch, but when she kept looking she saw it was only an animal. Not as big as the one they'd seen from the sky, but unlike anything she knew. Its back was arched, legs thick and short, and it had a long, flat head. It looked furry. It disappeared into the mist.

"You believe in Providence?" Wallen asked, glancing at Deni.

Deni didn't reply, unsure where the question had come from.

Wallen nodded to her robes. "Or is that just some kind of disguise?"

She looked at the clothing, remembering the clever idea she'd had when she'd taken the holy woman's outfit. People would respect her, she'd thought, and leave her alone. But some had asked questions, others wanted blessings, and they all got angry when she kept her mouth shut and avoided them. She'd smeared the robe in mud to hide the signs of Providence, enough to convince people she wasn't a church leader, just a lowly penitent. The worst she got, since then, was people tossing a few chips her way with dutifully mumbled prayers. Deni answered distantly, "It's a disguise."

"Well, it's an ugly one that you've only made uglier. You want a change? We've got spares below. I can help you pick something out. The boys can keep watch up here." Wallen said it pointedly, drawing looks from Qait and Tyler.

Deni nodded quickly. Somehow she felt it'd be easier below, with just Wallen. Less suffocating.

"How long you been with them?" Wallen asked as she dug through a chest of clothes. Deni watched cautiously; there'd been shiny, silky dresses and colourful scarves, already discarded. She dreaded the idea of floral patterns or, worse, short sleeves or skirts that would reveal her thin, pale flesh. Wallen hadn't been impressed by anything so far, which suggested she was looking for something particularly striking. Deni shrivelled at the thought.

"Not long," she answered as the mill owner tossed a brown cloak aside. Deni watched it mournfully. That looked like her sort of thing. A bit big, and formless, precisely the trick.

"Don't like to talk, do ya," Wallen told her without looking up.

Deni said nothing.

"I respect that. Had a nephew like you. Always hiding in his thoughts. His dad tried to beat it out of him when he was young but that only made it worse. Turned out, when we left him to it, this boy was plotting to improve the farm. Found him tinkering in the workshop one evening, adding an extra wheel to one of the trailers. All on his own. It was a little adjustment, but it made it easy to steer the thing. That was just the start of it." Wallen pulled back from the chest, holding up a frilly blouse, white with a hint of red. Deni looked at it fearfully, but Wallen tossed it aside with a look bordering on disgust. She tapped her head and continued, "He didn't know how to say things properly, not really. But he had ideas. Lots of them. I didn't get it at first, felt terrible for my brother with this dumb kid. But I got it in the end."

Wallen sighed and started thumbing through the clothes again. It was an excessive amount of unorganised clothing. A look of sadness crossed Wallen's face as she took another dress out and placed it aside, and Deni realised why it was all here. Wallen hadn't just been taking the stock with her to trade. Wallen finished her thought, voice quieter. "You don't want to talk, don't. The world needs thinkers, too."

Deni watched for a few moments longer. She wanted to talk. She closed her eyes, thinking of what Tyler had said. How to make it easier. She said, "What happened to your nephew?"

Wallen stopped, dwelling on the question as her fists closed around the next item of clothing. "One of the few that made it away. Thankfully. A few seasons ago. He'd done a lot around the farm but he was no use in the field, nor in the mill, so my brother took him off to the Metropolis to find him work with the Tail Mechanics."

"Not the Guard?" Deni asked.

"Hrute no," Wallen scoffed. "You go to work with the Guard, it's because you've got no guts or you've got no choice. Great big security blanket or a great big boot in your throat, that's all they are. No, it was between the Tail Mechanics and the Upenders. You know them?"

Deni shook her head.

"Upenders are salvagers. They customise recovered tech from the Mines, or wherever, and make it useful again. The Tail Mechanics take things like the Upenders have created and make new versions, though. He was doing well with them, last we heard. My brother considered moving some of the family down to join him. Didn't happen soon enough, though, did it?" She grunted in frustration. Wallen held up something long and grubby, the colour of swamp water. She smiled at it. "Here we are. That's more what I had in mind."

She turned to Deni and stretched it out. The clothing combined a square torso and two legs, trousers that went all the way up over the shoulder. It looked hard-wearing but pliable, scuffed and a little torn in places, and had straps fastened with brass buckles. Deni frowned; it was a size smaller than anything she'd worn before.

"It's clean," Wallen told her. "Even if it don't look it. And it's good material. Made locally. Most important, it's normal for people like us. You won't be drawing attention to yourself with this."

Deni gingerly took the outfit off her. She wasn't so sure. Though the material was thick, people would see the shape of her body. And there were no sleeves. Wallen tossed another item over, though, which Deni fumbled to catch. A canvas shirt. "This'll go with it. And there's some fresh socks, underwear. How long since you changed yours?"

Deni didn't want to answer, so she simply shook her head. Did she dare? Don't draw attention to yourself, don't be a distraction, that had been Balfair's principal rule. These clothes weren't feminine, but they wouldn't exactly hide her, either.

"You'll look good," Wallen assured. "Like a real woman."

Deni looked back at her, eyes only widening at the thought. Wallen had a kind face. Big and warm, like the rest of her. However hard she sounded, and acted, there was a contrasting softness there that Deni didn't quite understand. She realised, though, that the mill owner's clothing wasn't too different to what she'd been handed. Bigger, definitely, and the shirt patterned with brown lines, but the same overall outfit. The clothes in her hands, she realised, would make her look like part of the family.

"Do you know where to find your nephew?" Deni ventured.

Wallen's expression shifted, grimly. She turned back to the chest, looking for something else, as she said, without joy, "Sure I do. He'd be over the moon to see me."

"You'd be able to start a new life there," Deni said. She doubted it, but the mill owner needed reassurance. She thought of the words from Sincade's books, the ones that had first filled her with hope, and said, "The city is... full of opportunities."

Wallen gave her a humourless smile. She said, "You know what that expression means? *Over the moon*? You'd think it should mean something impossible. No one's ever seen the moon – what's going over it? How's that thought mean we should be happy?"

Deni didn't respond. There was something else going on, something Wallen wasn't saying.

"Now let's get this off you," Wallen reached over to take Deni's cloak, where the sleeve hung over the knife. Deni pulled back, shaking her head quickly, putting her other hand over her wrist to hide the weapon. Wallen looked at her oddly. "Yeah. I suppose you want to be alone."

She paced past Deni, towards the exit, then paused and looked back, face fixed with concern. "This guard, you really trust him?"

Deni looked up, picturing Qait. "He's helped us so far."

"Think he knows best?" Wallen asked. "Think he knows better than the boy?"

Deni paused. The mill owner was getting at something. They had spoken in private, hadn't they, she and Qait? Had he told her something he hadn't told them? Deni answered carefully: "I think he knows where to take us. I don't know much more than that."

Wallen nodded at this and made a thoughtful noise. "That's what I thought. But what the boy said, tell me – is it just a story you made up to get him on side?"

Deni gave her a confused look.

"The clouds," Wallen said. "They can't really part, can they?"

155

"They can," Deni said. Qait *had* said something, undermining Tyler. Wanting to defend him, Deni pressed on. "My master was obsessed with the idea. And he made things happen – he made machines that would make your nephew's work look like toys. He broke through the clouds – and we found the rocket he left behind. This thing is real, and it's important to the Guard. It can take power away from them."

Wallen gave Deni a lingering look, mulling it over. "How sure of that are you?"

Deni held her gaze, questioning it seriously, on the spot. In Wallen's face she saw that the mill owner was asking for hope, now. Asking for Deni to tell her that things could genuinely change; that their lives and their world could improve. After all she'd been through, and all she'd lost, worse than Tyler, perhaps even worse than Deni herself, Wallen needed hope. Deni took a breath and asked herself the same question. How sure was she really? Forgetting the damage she'd done, and the possibility of freedom, what if the clouds really did open? Tyler believed it. She knew it was possible. What if they really *could* change everything? There was no choice in it. She said, slowly, "I'm certain. It's not just possible, it has to happen. We have to make it happen."

Wallen's face didn't change. Deni's words hadn't given her the lift Deni thought they might. Hadn't she said it clearly enough? Didn't she have Tyler's passion? Before she could try again, though, Wallen said, "We'll go a little way further, make sure we've put distance between us and these brutes chasing you, then we'll take a breather and have a good chat. Make sure we're all on the same page. I want to be clear that I was happy to move, and move quickly, on the strength of what's chasing you. That doesn't mean I made any decisions in advance, not completely."

Deni frowned; what decisions was she talking about? Going with them to the Metropolis? How did that involve Qait? She kept the questions in, staring.

"You get those clothes on, why don't you? Then get upstairs and enjoy the view."

Wallen plodded away, leaving the unspoken thoughts still there. Had Qait given Wallen some reason to question their journey? Had she been wrong to give up her doubts?

13

"How is she?" Tyler asked as Wallen thudded back up onto the deck. She pushed Qait out of the way to take the wheel.

"How should she be?"

"I upset her," Tyler replied. "I didn't mean to."

"That girl's been through a few things," Wallen huffed. "Which bit was you?"

"The part where she started to get help," Qait answered for him, though Tyler was less sure. The tracker moved to the side window, watching the terrain.

"We safe, guard?" Wallen asked roughly.

"I don't know. The closer we get, the more trouble we're likely to see."

The floorboards squeaked and Tyler spun to find Deni re-emerging. She'd made it up to the cabin without making a noise on the stairs, moving like a ghost. That was only part of the surprise. The dark, buttoned dungarees and brighter shirt held her slim figure well. They made her look cleaner and lighter, her face clearer without the shadow of the cloak. They showed off the curve of her hips. She gave Tyler a quick, nervous look, just to see his reaction, and he smiled. He gave her an enthusiastic thumbs-up, but she'd already turned away. She climbed onto a bench and looked out the window.

"See, I told you it'd look good," Wallen said.

Tyler watched Deni as she ignored him. He'd had this from girls before. When they didn't like it that he did stuff with his friends instead of them, or when he disagreed with something they said. All he'd done was try to encourage Deni, though. Taking a breath, he determined to resolve it. He approached her and asked, "Can I join you?"

Deni said nothing, watching the river go by. Tyler pulled himself up next to her and gave her a quick look, then followed her gaze down to the water. To give them some privacy, he whispered, "You look really good."

She didn't answer. Her brow was creased with the same

concern he'd seen from her before, concentrating hard on a problem. Was he the problem now?

"I'm gonna stop talking in a sec," Tyler told her. "I don't want to make things worse."

Deni's eyes shot to him, worried.

"But I just wanna say, first, that I meant it. I figure maybe you thought I was making fun, or just wasn't serious or something, but I meant it. You're right that I don't know you, or what's happened with you. I'd like to. But I still think you're good, and worth knowing, and speaking to, whatever you say. So. That's all."

Tyler nodded, satisfied, and pushed away from the window. Deni's hand touched his before he could leave. She looked into his eyes and said, "It's something else."

"What?" Tyler frowned. "I don't –"

Deni nodded towards Wallen, eyes serious.

Tyler followed the gesture. He whispered, "Did she do something...?"

"No," Deni said. "But something's not right. Look."

Deni tapped the window, and Tyler looked down at the water. It was dark and choppy, breaking with splashes as the barge lurched through it. He didn't understand. "What?"

"Qait said the rivers here flow to the Drain. *Look.*"

Away from the boat and its wake, Tyler saw the ripples she was talking about. The water was flowing in the other direction. They were moving against it.

"Holy –" he exclaimed. Deni caught his wrist in her hand.

She said, "Qait knows."

Tyler glared at her. It wasn't possible. He shook his head. "You're wrong –"

"He's a guard. The same as Montgomery. We can't –"

"No," Tyler said, more firmly. He only just managed to keep his voice quiet enough to stay between them. "He risked his life to come out here with us."

"He *knows* where we're going," Deni told him coldly. "How could he *not*?"

Tyler glanced back across the cabin. Wallen had her back to them, her gun propped against the side of the wheel. Qait was standing on the opposite side of her, his rifle close by, too. Tyler felt the soft touch of Deni's finger on his forearm and turned to her. She nodded to her other arm, where he knew she kept that vicious knife. He shook his head. What was she thinking?

There was no time to discuss it. Deni sprang off the bench and moved without sound across the cabin. Qait half-twisted to her, seeing her too late; she kicked his rifle to the rear wall. Wallen spun instinctively towards her own gun, but before she'd turned Deni had the knife out and up. The mill owner froze. She said, "What in Hrute's hell? Didn't I say we'd have a talk when the time's right?"

Wordlessly, knife raised in front of her face, Deni sidestepped around Wallen and took the gun with her free hand. She backed off, away from all of them, until her legs hit the side bench. The contact made her flinch, betraying her nerves.

"Why?" she finally said, to Qait, voice barely audible.

"By the heavens," Wallen muttered. She raised her voice, talking sideways to Qait as she steadied a hand on the wheel. "Didn't I say to tell them? This is too –"

"Why?" Deni raised her voice.

"Is it a better route?" Tyler ventured, watching Qait hopefully.

The tracker had barely moved, and still wasn't talking as he looked into Deni's fierce eyes. Tyler waited for one or the other of them to back down, to relieve the pressure; it was a misunderstanding, that was all. Qait knew what they had to do, how important it was.

"Truthfully..." Qait said. His voice was calm, rational. "I didn't think you'd get it. Not in the time we had."

"Qait?" Tyler's voice rose in disbelief. Deni's knuckles tightened around her knife. Her eyes looked dangerously focused, threatening, even with the full width of the boat between her and the tracker.

"Put the knife away, Deni," Qait said. "Then I'll explain."

"You lied," Deni told him quietly. "Just like the rest."

"For your own good," he said. "There's nothing simple about this."

As Wallen directed the boat, she looked expectantly at the tracker, and Tyler put the pieces together. In the brief time she and Qait had had alone, the tracker had made a case against their plan. And she'd gone along with it because he was the adult, and Deni and himself were two youths who didn't know what they were doing. Tyler tightened all over. His voice cracked. "We discussed it – it's what we *need* to do – why didn't you ask us –"

"You're the same as him," Deni cut in, her voice unstable.

"Who?" Qait said.

"It *was* him, wasn't it?" Deni went on. "I didn't believe it – in the field – I *saw* him – I should've trusted myself. They're here. Waiting for us. You're leading us to them. I can *only* trust myself –"

"Who are you talking about?" Qait asked more firmly.

Deni bared her teeth as she spat the word. "*Montgomery*."

Her quietness, and stillness, was frighteningly wrought. She was ready to snap. Maybe into tears, maybe something worse. Tyler wanted to touch her, but seeing her shoulders shaking he wasn't sure she'd let him. He said, "Deni – let's hear –"

"Turn the boat around," Deni said. She stepped back, up onto the bench, looming over them all. Tyler looked over his shoulder at her, fearing she might jump across the room with her knife struck forward. "You're taking us to *someone* – someone as bad – somewhere bad. No. *No!*"

"Tell them, damn you," Wallen cut in loudly. "Go ahead and tell them – the same that you told me, before you drive her nuts!"

"Yeah, tell us! We're not children, dammit!" Tyler demanded, moving closer to Deni, trying to keep a barrier between her and the tracker. He looked up at her, trying to meet her eyes and calm her, but she was rattled, glaring at the tracker.

"There's no Montgomery," Qait said. "I assure you – that's not it."

"Then what!" Deni demanded shrilly.

Qait took a moment. "You've got the hope of youth." Tyler started to complain, but the tracker continued: "Nothing I could say would quiet that. We can't go back to the Towers, not now – and the chances of making a difference there are so slim –"

"Qait?" Tyler cut in, unbelieving, eyes wide. Qait stared back at him, coldly, unapologetically. It was true. The tracker had no intention of going back. He had never wanted to follow through what they had started. He had only ever said what they needed to hear. "*Why?*"

"He told me," Wallen said, voice bold, impatient, "there's people in the rebels as learned as them in the city. Who can use this thing you've got just as well –"

"Rot!" Tyler snapped. "He tried that line with us, too. Hodwick is the one who knows about opening the sky! ArcTech have the resources –"

"Opening the sky," Qait echoed, like it was exactly the childish idea he'd expected to hear. "They say prayers to Dendra can do the same. Converting to the Fire. I've even heard it said the Short Queen communes with the sun."

"This is *real*," Tyler snarled.

"I'll tell you what's real," Qait said. "As long as there's war, the research is dead. The rebels want change, but they're bringing a world of destruction with them. The Guard offered protection and stability, but now they've faced problems they're panicked and dangerous. Neither side will sit down and talk. This research – this idea about changing the world – it's worlds away from being *real*. But with the Guard desperate to suppress it, it's a bargaining tool. We can get them to talk, Tyler, don't you see –"

"That's gutter sewage!" Tyler said. "It wouldn't be a bargaining tool if there wasn't something behind it. They wouldn't have killed my uncle!"

"It's a bargaining tool because it can make them look bad. That's all."

Tyler paused. Deni moved behind him, to the side. Her breathing had deepened. Whatever ideas Qait was giving her, they weren't helping.

"You're just scared," Tyler said. "You just want to get away from the fighting."

Wallen alternated her gaze between Qait and the river. The tracker returned her look without feeling. He had no desire to argue, no passion either way. "He's offering you safety, kid," Wallen said, though she sounded uncertain. "Even if you don't like it – isn't that better than going up against the Guard? The chance to get away."

"No!" Tyler said. "We're *not* running! We're going to act – we're going to help –"

"It will help," Qait said. "Highness Elzia can get the Guard's attention and *talk* to –"

"The assassins," Deni said. "The worst of their kind. That's who you'd invite to trade the code. Montgomery, after you – straight to her hide-out – it'd get you *in* there – get him *in* there –"

"You don't know what you're talking about," Qait replied curtly, finally losing his cool. "This is not –"

"You're a *snake*."

"Hang on!" Wallen called out, silencing them all. The boat slowed, and they all braced themselves to keep their balance as it reached a bank. It listed, coming to a stop, and Wallen spun back from the wheel. She said, "Right. My turn. We all know any guard is as good as another, which is no good at all – but this man has a point, don't he? Isn't there a way to work this without going to the city? Someone else who –"

"We don't need someone else!" Tyler said. "There's no time for someone else! We have to do this – because they don't want us to!" He shook as he continued, "And they killed my *uncle* for it!"

"What can you do?" Qait fired back. "Even if you opened up a valve in Speakers Square, and amplified your voice for everyone to hear, what would *those* people do? All that matters to anyone right now is surviving. You'd need the support, and protection, of the Guard to continue the research. You'd need their support to get that research to the people. You'd need *peace* before any of that. Going to the rebels, that's a step towards peace."

Deni jumped down from the bench to move around Tyler. Her knife was still up, shaking in her hand, as she took a step towards Qait, locking on him. She said, "That's not enough. That doesn't stop them."

"Trust me, Deni, it can," Qait told her gently. "I'm not your enemy."

"Not my friend," Deni said. "You don't care – you're only thinking about the war – like *them* – thinking about how it benefits *you*! Sacrificing to survive!"

"Hence," Qait said, "I thought you of all people would understand."

Deni's eyes were alight with fire, glaring at him. She had frozen. Tyler watched her for the slightest movement. Qait's words meant something to her. However much he wanted to say it, that she shouldn't listen, that it was nonsense, Tyler couldn't. Of course it was true. She wanted to save herself. But she wanted what was best too, didn't she? He waited. They all waited for her to stay something, until it looked like she would say nothing at all. Qait's mouth turned at the corner, satisfied. He started, "You see –"

"No." Deni cut in. She still wasn't moving, but her eyes had taken on a greater intensity. "I don't want to run. I don't want to be free, I want to make them pay – I want to make this matter. I *want* to. I'm not like you. I'm *not* like you!" Her voice took on a higher pitch, a desperate sound. "I'm not like you! I'm not!"

She backed off, as far as the side door, leading onto the boat's surrounding skirting platform. No one else moved. Deni shook her head, voice sounding more vicious by the second, defiant. "We don't need you. We don't need this boat. We'll walk, all the damned way – just Tyler and me. Together. We didn't go through all this to get safe in the countryside. People didn't die for *this*."

Qait stared at her in silence for a moment, Tyler and Wallen watching him, waiting for his response. He finally said, "It might be best that we part ways."

Tyler flashed him an unbelieving look. He would go on without them, after all this? Tyler said, as strongly as he could, "You're not getting what we took from the rocket. That's ours. Just because you're scared – that's not gonna stop us."

The tracker eyed him, for the first time appearing unsettled by their situation. He wasn't going into the wilderness without some leverage. "I'll make a copy."

"No you won't," Deni looked over her shoulder, out to the water as though she was prepared to jump if she had to. "No. You fucking won't." Tyler took a step towards her as she edged out, but she stopped to throw a look back at Qait. "It's ours. It's *mine*. You're not taking it – you can't be trusted – you're the same as *them*."

"That's as may be," Wallen intervened, at last. "But *I'm* not. I've heard enough. If this boat's going anywhere, Deni, it's with you, you hear me?"

Deni watched her, trying to read her. It had disarmed her, defused some of her anger. She opened her mouth to ask something, no doubt to confirm it, then looked to Tyler. He nodded, trying to reassure her. She shook her head, though, and ducked out through the door. Tyler gave the others a quick glance and rushed after her. As he reached the door he heard Deni's feet clattering up the side ladder.

"Give her a break, boy," Wallen called out, making Tyler stop. He turned to find her almost smiling, as though proud that Deni had stood up for herself. "She's not going anywhere." She turned to Qait. "For someone who left the Guard behind, you've done a damned fine job continuing their work."

14

Deni had her back against the top of the cabin as she sat on the roof of the cargo hold. With Wallen having restarted the boat and pulled them away from the bank, the river was becoming narrower, a corridor of reeds guiding them between trees on one side and rocky inclines on the other. The surrounding land had become more interesting as nature took over, but less hospitable. It wasn't as flat here, or light, and it was harder to see far from the boat, with more obstacles in the way. Deni wrapped her arms around herself as they passed a partially crumbled brick building where an unfriendly looking man drooped over a balcony, leering at her. She didn't move, and neither did he.

Let him stare.

"Can I come up?" Tyler's voice called from the side, where the ladder rungs were bolted to the wall. It had been at least half an hour since the clash, since Qait had backed down, and Wallen had taken control of their route. They had turned into a waterway that the mill owner insisted looped back to the main river. Deni had lost her cool, but Tyler had handled things better than she could've hoped. She felt that she really wasn't alone, for once, even as Qait had betrayed her. Tyler had stood up for her, hadn't he?

"You know I didn't want this," Tyler said.

Deni said nothing. There was truth in what Qait had said, though. And hypocrisy in what she'd said. Shouldn't they flee, still? Run to the mythical rebels, find somewhere to hide. Why had it choked her, this need to get back to the city? To complete this task?

"I'm sorry, anyway," Tyler said. "Qait just wanted us to be safe."

"He thought we didn't matter," Deni replied, barely loud enough to be heard.

Tyler's boots clanked against the rungs as he pulled himself up. The top of his head poked over the roof on which she sat. "It wasn't right, what he did, but he wants to protect us. All of us, not just himself. Can I come up?"

Deni looked away. He pulled himself onto the roof but stayed clear, sitting at the edge, giving her space. He said, "It's a setback, that's all."

"It's more than that," Deni muttered.

Tyler nodded, conceding. He went quiet like he wasn't sure what to say, then. After waiting a moment, watching the countryside, he scooted across the roof towards her. He sat back against the cabin wall, too, and didn't speak. The boat rocked gently under them, passing more trees. He checked their surroundings and his lips curled, like he wanted to smile, like he had some comment to make. Probably about how he'd never seen anything like this, how different it was to the city, again. A bird made a noise up ahead, a chattering call that drew Tyler's bright-eyed attention.

It seemed to take all his effort, but he refrained from commenting.

Deni frowned. He raised his eyebrows encouragingly, but then looked away again. She was usually the first to look away. Unsure what he was up to, she kept staring.

"When we get to the Metropolis," she said, "I'll go to Dr Hodwick on my own."

Tyler gave a little nod, but still said nothing, watching the riverbank.

"I mean it," Deni said. "It's better that way."

"Qait still wants to help us," Tyler said. "He thinks there's a way to get things working differently – to get the rebels and the Guard talking. This is different, though, isn't it? It's bigger than that. He knows that, too. Just doesn't want to admit he's scared."

"You don't get it. What people are really like."

"Neither do you," Tyler replied without offence. "If he really wanted to betray us, it would've been easier to take us back to the Metropolis. Deni. I'm not just saying it. That's how he persuaded Wallen it was the right thing to do. He knows people who could hide us. It wasn't a betrayal exactly, just the way he thought was best to make a difference."

"I'm *not* hiding." Deni shot him a fierce look.

Tyler shook his head, smiling again. "Me neither. Deni…" Tyler put a hand on hers. She looked at it, resting there, and felt herself softening despite her efforts to stay hard. His touch was warm, comforting. He told her, careful to sound gentle, "This Montgomery. He wasn't out there – and he's definitely not working with Qait. We're all tired, scared, it's normal to look for the things we fear. Qait is alone, just like us. That's the whole point. He needed something to trade with, to escape."

Deni looked into his eyes. Was that truth any better? She'd seen the burning image of the tattooed man in her mind, in her dreams, for years, but she never saw him lurking in the shadows. Not like she'd seen those apparitions in the field. The familiar shape in the Low Slums. She said nothing, though. Just let him keep his hand there, and looked into his eyes, trying to relax.

Tyler let out a light laugh. "You know how happy I was to hear you say it? No matter what, we're going to go on – and finish this together."

Deni kept staring at his hand, resting on hers. She wished that things were different.

The waterway curved back to the right, a turn bolstered by wooden slats that must have been decades old. The water was still before the barge hit it, not flowing one way or another, a man-made canal returning to the river. While they drifted in relative quiet, Deni heard bits of Wallen's conversation with Qait in the cabin below. Wallen criticised him for not trusting the young ones, though he replied that it was necessary if they wanted to survive. She said, "Since when was surviving enough?"

Something in her tone said she was happy they'd changed direction. Deni suspected their chat, and Tyler's arguing, had given Wallen a better idea of what she'd really wanted when they set out from the mill. She had family alive in the Metropolis, after all. And she knew what a difference the darkening days had made.

Tyler had fallen asleep alongside Deni, sliding slowly towards her, down the wall. He hadn't quite collapsed, and started to snore while still semi-upright. She couldn't do the same. She watched the land change, as they drifted south, and the woods and rocks fell away towards flatter fields. Then the canal curved, again to the right, and she felt sure that they were going the right way, completing a circle. She stood to look ahead, eager to see the river.

They approached a wooden bridge, on stilts high above the

canal, supported by dozens of slanted beams. It was sturdy, with high walls, and bore the emblem of the Road Guard, making it part of a major thoroughfare. Deni looked to its left, seeing the paved track that joined the bridge from the field. Then to its right, towards the north. The road stretched across another open field, and on it was a large shape, trundling away from them.

Her heart tightened.

As the barge got closer to the bridge, and the road, Deni heard the sound of the vehicle's engine over theirs. Smoke rose from its funnels, puffing behind it. Not enough to obscure it from view. It didn't have mirrors; there was no way for the drivers to look back. But someone might be watching from the rear, where the double-doors had barred windows, facing their way.

Deni swallowed fear, standing as they passed under the bridge. She wanted to call down to Wallen or Qait, but didn't want to make a noise, in case it alerted the slavers. Qait had been doubly wrong; it hadn't just been a mistake to hunt for the rebels, Vorst had guessed that was what they would do, too. And at the speed that the truck moved, over a paved road, he would soon have caught up to them.

The boat had looped back behind Vorst, though, just late enough to go unnoticed. They were safe, surely.

She looked ahead. The river was a hundred metres further, at worst, closer by the second. Once they turned they'd start putting twice the distance between themselves and the slavers. She glanced back towards the truck, willing it further away.

It was slowing down. Stopping.

Deni stared, transfixed, as the rear door opened. A stout man dropped out onto the road. He was recognisable, even from this distance, as the one from Bawkley, with his goggles and beard. The one she'd cut on the side. Deni took a step back as the man stared directly at her. Her foot caught Tyler and he stirred on the floor, grumbling. "What are you..."

Deni shook her head quickly as he looked up, and the worry in her expression fully woke him. He jumped up, as the stout man thumped on the side of the truck. The shout was loud enough to reach all the way back to the canal: "Eyes on them! Behind us!"

15

"Don't look like guards," Wallen said as the barge swayed, veering further out across the river to put as much distance between them and the bank as possible.

"They're not," Qait answered simply, at the cabin door, rifle in hand as he traced the truck's approach. It hit the bridge hard, like it might fly off the other side.

Tyler came to the tracker's side, itching to do something. "You got a spare gun?"

"Mine would take your shoulders off," Wallen said. "But look in there." She gestured to a trapdoor, then twisted to Deni, who was watching from the far wall. "You, too. They board us, you'll want more than that fruit-knife to fend them off."

Tyler opened the hatch to reveal a recess in the floor stuffed with weapons. Blades, hammers and long hooks. He sifted through the top ones and took a short sword, one he could actually wield without falling over, though it was chipped and loosely frayed around the handle. He gave Deni an encouraging look and hurried back to Qait.

The truck was all but alongside them, bouncing over the uneven road with all its funnels spewing smoke. The lanky slaver, Grunberg, pushed himself out of the top hole, manning the huge weapon mounted on the roof. Qait moved out of the cabin, putting a foot on the boat's side for support. He crouched, aimed and fired without warning. The slaver flapped his arms above him, dropping back into the truck; the bullet must've come close.

As the tracker chambered another bullet, the truck rolled off the road, hugging the bank of the river, and an armoured window on the driver's side swung open. Vorst was behind the wheel, splitting his attention between the ground ahead and the boat.

"Tracker!" he boomed, his low voice impossibly louder than the engines of the barge and the truck. "Our fight's not with you!"

Qait slid down, partially behind the side of the barge, rifle trained on the truck. Watching him, Vorst varied the truck's speed and weaved, closer to the river, then further away. He looked fearsome as ever, dark marks across his rabid face. He growled something into the truck, and Grunberg's hands probed up out of the roof, searching for the mounted gun. Qait took another shot, which twanged off the edge of the gun with a spark, and the hands dropped back down.

"Try it again," Qait shouted, "and the next one's for the driver."

"What are you waiting for?" Tyler asked, crouching behind the door. He could feel the sword loosening in his grip as his hands got sweaty. "Can't you just shoot him?"

Qait didn't answer. They had the full width of the river between them and the truck, and with the combined sway of the boat and the bouncing of the land vehicle, it'd take a miracle to hit anything with accuracy. That he hit the mounted gun had to be some kind of fluke. It had done enough to inspire caution in the slavers, though.

"Tracker!" Vorst roared. "You don't know what you're into here. That girl is not who she says she is."

"She's under my protection!" Qait shouted back.

Tyler gave Deni a glance. She was crouching, too, a long pole with a hooked top in her hands. Her eyes were wide, fearfully watching Qait rather than the truck, as though waiting for the completion of his betrayal.

"She's a murderer," Vorst shouted. "And a thief."

Qait didn't look back, not interested in Deni's reaction. Wallen looked, though, and Tyler warned her off, trying to use his eyes to tell her not to listen.

"She killed her master!" Vorst shouted. "Her friends, who cared for her all her life! The guards who came to help them! Killed them all!"

Deni was frozen. Wallen gave her another worried look.

"Told you it was the Guard that did it, didn't she? She was always one of my worst acquisitions. Slow down! You don't want a fight – you know it's true!"

Tyler stared at Deni, willing her to deny it. Of course it wasn't true, but these adults had already shown how fickle they were. She needed to say something, anything. She didn't, though. Her grip tightened on the pole and her eyes stayed widely, rigidly open, like she was reliving the memories that the slaver was stirring.

"Think we'd be out here for some runaway?" Vorst shouted.

"It's not about the girl," Qait called back. "You know that."

"There's nothing else!" Vorst shouted. "We wanted the rocket because she was obsessed with it. She wanted to destroy the last traces of Balfair's work. You know that?"

The truck hit something and had to swerve away from the river, giving them a second of relief. Qait twisted to face Deni, finally showing some doubt.

"You kill your master, girl?" Wallen spoke up.

"I..." Deni gaped, mouth open. "I..."

"They'll say anything!" Tyler said, loudly.

The noise of the truck's engine suddenly got louder as it veered once more towards the river. With it came Vorst's renewed shouts. "Burnt down the whole estate! Didn't even leave bodies to find – lucky there was a survivor. Tracker, are you listening to me? There's dozens dead because of her!"

Dozens? Tyler mouthed. Deni met his eyes, then, not with denial but in apology.

"If that's all it is," Qait replied, half-rising from behind the boat wall, "then why'd you murder the boy's uncle?"

There was no answer for a moment, Vorst turning back into the truck. He finally shouted, "Who says we did?"

Qait glanced back at Deni.

"It was my fault," Deni uttered weakly. "But I didn't kill them. I didn't kill anyone."

Tyler took a deep breath and said, "Qait, for the love of Dendra..."

"It doesn't matter," Qait grunted. "They won't let any of us walk away from this."

"Last chance, tracker!" Vorst yelled.

Deni held Tyler's gaze, imploringly, as he stared back. He didn't believe she'd lied, not about any of it. These people had been threatening and dangerous from the start. He reached a hand towards her and began, "We're with you –"

The gun on top of the truck opened up with a thundering roar, and bullets ripped through the cabin around them. Wallen let go of the wheel and threw herself to the floor, the ceiling above her splintering and glass from the windows exploding in. Tyler dived towards Deni, dragging her down, both dropping their weapons as the barrage continued. The wall of the cabin was shredded, fist-sized holes being punched through one after another. The bullets stayed high, though, like they were trying to knock the roof off.

Tyler twisted to Qait on the floor. Only the tracker's feet were visible as he'd fallen to the side. He fired back. One shot, then another. The cannon stopped firing.

The boat turned, the wheel spinning unchecked. Wallen pulled herself across the floor on her elbows to grab her gun. As she rose to a knee, the slaver opened fire again. Holding her weapon against her shoulder, Wallen fired back, joining the sound of Qait's gun. The din was tremendous, smoke and its cordite stench filling the room as it rained wood and glass.

The truck's gun went quiet again. Wallen rushed to the cover of what was left of the cabin wall, spinning the wheel at the back of her gun to reload it. She paused to look out. Then she leapt for the boat wheel. They were turning to the side; the attack had stopped because they were no longer alongside the truck. Tyler rose to a crouch, watching the bank of the river fill the view ahead of them.

Qait rushed through the room, low, going for the opposite door. He leant around it and raised his rifle again. Fired without aiming.

"You need to go," he called back into the cabin.

"*Go?*" Tyler cried. "What are you –"

"Over the side," Qait ordered. "I'll distract them. Move through the field, get behind them."

"You can't –"

The boat banked heavily as Wallen braced the wheel. She turned it with a groan, putting all her weight behind it, but the sway knocked her off balance and it swung back again. She yelled, "Hold on!"

Before impact, Qait bent back and shoved Tyler, hard, in the chest. Tyler fell onto his behind and slid across the floor, towards the other door, where Deni caught him. As she pulled him halfway up, the boat crashed into the river bank. Tyler fell into Deni and together they rolled into the shattered cabin wall. Wood snapped over them and they flipped, hitting the side of the barge. With a creak and the sound of a dozen planks snapping, they jolted still. Tyler looked up in time to see Wallen's body smack the wheel and she fell back, wheezing. Qait had a hold on the doorframe and was already reloading his rifle.

Tyler tried to stand, to get to the tracker, but Deni caught him around the waist and pulled him back. She directed him over the side of the barge, where the wall dipped, but she paused. She reached out quickly, retrieving something from the twisted bench, then she jumped past him into the water, without hesitation. Tyler glanced back towards Qait. Before Tyler could call to him, Wallen knocked him over the edge.

He was only airborne for a second. The water shook him with a freezing rush, overtaking his whole body. He surged back up with a gasp, legs kicking, and dug into the riverbed. It wasn't deep here; he was able to stand, the water up to his waist. He spun, surrounded by grass that rose from the high river bed. Wallen was already wading past him with big strides. Deni was jumping in the water, careful not to let it get above her waist. Tyler took her by the shoulders and helped steady her. "I'm here, I'm here!"

She calmed, slowing her breathing, looking into his eyes.

"This way!" Wallen hissed, pointing ahead. The riverbank was high and uneven, with a ditch running off to its side. Tyler took Deni's hand and splashed through the water after Wallen. As they moved, Qait's rifle went off above. Tyler twisted back to the grounded barge. Its front had crumpled against the bank, risen up so almost half the boat was stretched out of the river. The engine was still on, grinding noisily as its paddle-wheels turned ineffectively, barely touching the water now.

The gun went off again, and another replied from further away. Then another.

The slavers were out, firing rifles, or pistols. Advancing on the boat.

16

Crouching, they were all concealed by the muddy bank that joined the field, but the ditch didn't go far, an inlet of only a few metres. They had a nook to hide in, but no way to get around the slavers. The gunfire had slowed down, but continued, with Qait letting off a shot followed by one or two in return. Deni pulled herself up next to Wallen, raising only her eyes above the grass, ignoring the big lady's hisses to stay down. Deni rested one hand on the river bank, the other on Tyler's retrieved satchel, hanging over her shoulder.

A shape moved twenty metres ahead of them, one of the slavers who'd run out to the side. The bulky one with the goggles. He plodded a short distance to a rock, showing his side to them as he watched the boat. Beyond him, the edges of two others were just visible, one within a copse of trees and the other holding a piece of metal like a shield. From his size, the biggest of the three, that had to be Vorst. A rifle shot from the boat hit the metal, but it didn't move; Vorst took the blast with his weight, snarling loudly. The one in the trees, the woman, leant out and fired her pistol, a hopeless shot at that distance, another thirty metres or so from the boat, but enough to silence Qait's gun as he ducked for cover.

The truck sat far behind the skirmish, the rocks and trees offering sparse cover over the full length of a grassy field. The cannon on top still had a man standing behind it. There was no chance of them getting there without being seen.

The gunfight lulled, and in the brief respite Vorst started shouting again. "Tracker! She's not worth dying for!"

Qait didn't respond. The man closest to them edged around his rocks. He must have made his dash unseen in all the chaos, now coming towards Qait's flank. Deni wanted to attack him. To warn the tracker. It would give their position away, though, and there'd be no escape from the others.

"Do you know where I found her, tracker?" Vorst shouted. "It was more than ten years ago now. She was just a child."

Silence from Qait. He must've been doing something;

reloading shouldn't have taken this long. He couldn't have just been listening, could he? Vorst's distraction was too obvious for that.

"Her village was burnt to the ground," Vorst went on. "Everyone killed except her. We saved her from the fires, but she was rabid. The most vicious child I've ever seen. Among the dead were two bandits. Two *she* had killed. As a child."

"It's not true," Deni whispered, for herself more than the others, her hand tightening on Tyler's bag. She remembered the flames, and being pulled away by the slavers. She remembered the Road Guard in their bulky armour demanding answers. Blood and screams. She hadn't hurt anyone, though. She'd run, hid. She remembered being afraid, beyond anything else.

Deni found Tyler's eyes, and he couldn't hide his own questions. He looked away.

The man in goggles started out across the field. Keeping low, partly concealed by the grass. It left the route to the truck unwatched. Wallen nudged Deni, nodding to the rocks the man had left behind. "Stick behind me, keep the rocks between you and the trees."

"Qait..." Tyler said, his head appearing next to theirs, watching the slaver with fear.

"He's doing it for us," Wallen said, then gently pulled herself up over the edge of the ditch. Tyler pushed Deni up after her, and they crept silently through the grass. The man with goggles was turned away, getting ever closer to the boat. He froze as Qait's voice came from the barge.

"How well did you know Balfair?"

The slavers looked to Vorst for the answer. "Well enough to know he didn't deserve a violent death."

"Well enough to know how the Guard protect research done by men like him?"

"Making what she did all the more tragic."

"You don't know," Qait told him, louder, as Deni's group reached the rocks. Wallen waved at them to keep behind her, low. It was barely enough cover to conceal them, and they trod a careful balance between being exposed to the man with goggles on the right and the woman in the trees on the left. The tracker continued, "You're not out here for her, even if you don't know it."

Vorst gave a discreet hand signal, as he replied, "Enlighten me." The man in the goggles edged closer to the boat. A short dash away; once he got past the taller grass at the riverbank, he'd get a view through the tatters of the cabin wall.

"Doesn't matter," Qait said. "You'll keep coming anyway."

"I'm a reasonable man, tracker," Vorst said. "Not what you think."

Qait didn't answer. Vorst checked the lady in the trees. Ready to move. Tyler shifted alongside Deni, looking back to the boat, around her elbow, and she put a hand in front of him, shook her head. This was their only chance.

"I've heard of you, you know," Vorst shouted. "Is it true that you travelled to the Deadland?"

No answer again. His patience exhausted, Vorst waved a hand above his head, and the slavers made their move. He and the woman in the trees started shooting, and the cannon on top of the truck opened up again. At the same time, the man in goggles vaulted the last few feet of the riverbank, up to the side of the barge, gun raised. Their bullets tore into the wood for only a second before the boat exploded.

Deni flinched as the shockwave swept over the field. She knocked into Tyler, twisting away from the flower of black smoke and shattered debris that spread from where the cabin had been. The man in the goggles was punched back through the air, pirouetting over the edge of the field and down into the ditch behind them.

The blast rang in Deni's ears, and she couldn't make out what Wallen was saying. The mill owner pulled her along, though. They were all up, suddenly, and running across the field. Deni tried to take in the scene, her legs carrying her at full speed. The female slaver had broken free from the trees and was racing towards the ruin of the barge, pistol raised, as the remnants of the boat creaked and snapped in the middle, toppling back into the river. Vorst had thrown down his shield to pace heavily after her. The man in the truck leant around the mounted gun, trying to see through the smoke. As her ears cleared, Deni heard him shouting, "…can't see him!"

"There, dammit!" Vorst roared. Grunberg twisted in their direction.

With only a short distance to clear, the trio sprinted to the truck as he turned the gun their way. It moved too slowly to target them, and didn't pivot low enough; they reached the vehicle, and ran out of sight, before he could fire. A pistol fired to their right, though, from across the field, and Deni twisted to see Vorst marching towards them. Wallen pulled her out of the way as another shot rushed past. They skirted the truck, towards the back, and Wallen tore open the rear doors as the lanky man swung down from the ceiling hatch. He launched out, his whole body knocking Wallen back. As they rolled, she thumped his ribs and pushed free of him. Tyler and Deni ran to pull her up, taking an arm each.

"Get the truck going!" Tyler shouted, shoving her and turning back to face Grunberg. Wallen wasn't about to leave, so Deni shoved her too. "Hurry!"

Wallen ran around the far side of the truck. Deni peeked back around the corner. Vorst had broken into a jog, coming towards them, and the woman had turned back from the boat, further away. Ducking into cover, Deni found the lanky slaver squaring off against Tyler, grinning a crooked-toothed smile as he drew a long, curved blade from a sheath at his belt. Tyler stood his ground, unarmed, arms spread, ready to do whatever he could. Tyler waved a hand at Deni without looking. "Get in!"

Deni dumbly rushed past him, up the steps into the back of the truck, Tyler's bag slapping against her as Grunberg lunged forwards. Through the grill separating the front cabin, she saw Wallen climbing into the driver's seat. Deni flashed a look back as Tyler ducked an attack. The man's blade twanged off the truck. Grunberg took another swing, shouting wildly as he did, and again Tyler dodged. They moved out of range of anything Deni could do to help, Tyler dodging across the grass as the man took one swing after another. A slight limp was holding the slaver back, the leg injury she'd given him staggering his strikes. It wasn't enough to give Tyler room to retaliate. Wallen let out a shout of success as the truck engine choked into life, the vehicle shuddering around Deni. Tyler slipped and the blade caught him, ripping his sleeve. He dropped to a knee as the slaver arced his blade above his head, about to deliver a finishing blow.

The side of Grunberg's head erupted in a mess of brain and bone at the sound of a gunshot. He stayed upright for a second, blade held stiffly up, then he toppled rigidly to the side. Tyler pushed himself up and dived towards the truck. Deni caught his hands and pulled him in as she looked out to the field. Qait was behind the rocks they'd used for cover, down on a knee, cocking his rifle for another shot. Stepping over Tyler as he rolled across the truck floor, Deni leant out of the truck to check for the others. The woman was back in the trees, taking cover, but Vorst was missing. Had he ducked into the longer grass?

The truck rolled forward, then veered to the left, turning in a wide circle. Deni stumbled as the rear doors slammed shut. She caught hold of the ladder in the middle of the cabin and pulled herself up, struggling against the force of the vehicle's increasing speed. She climbed through the hatch in the ceiling and grabbed the handles of the gun as they kept turning. Wallen was steering them around the field, back towards the rocks where Qait was hiding.

Another gunshot, and something rushed past Deni's head, making her duck down. She ventured another look and saw Vorst, in a crouch, tracing their movements with a pistol. Before he could fire again, Qait fired and made him duck. Then the woman fired from the trees, aiming at Qait. The salvo made Deni slip down into the safety of the truck. She twisted on the ladder to watch through the front as Wallen drove them speedily towards Qait's rocks. Even with the erratic bounce of their ride, and the limited visibility of the narrow window slot, Deni saw in snatched, bouncing images that something was wrong ahead. A dark shape on the ground.

Deni's eyes widened as they approached the rocks.

Feeling that Wallen wasn't slowing down, Deni sprang the short distance to the truck cab. She was blocked by the metal grid separating the back from the front. She shook it violently, shouting, "No! Stop!"

The truck was already turning away from the rocks as Wallen silently concentrated.

Tyler appeared at Deni's side, a hand pressed into his bleeding shoulder as he craned to see out, too. He bumped into Deni as they banked, turning too fast, and they both turned to look for another angle. There were no windows in the rear of the truck, only the barred gaps in the doors. Deni turned back to the view of the field ahead, as Wallen guided them towards the stone road. The slavers, left behind, let out a last few shots that pinged into the side of the truck but didn't go through.

"We need to go back," Tyler said, quietly. As the truck steadied and they moved in a straighter line, he ran to the rear doors, looking through the bars. Clinging onto them, he shouted, "We need to go back for him!"

Deni loosed her grip on the metal grid, just slightly, trembling as she looked past Tyler to the field behind them. He was shaking as he repeated it, more desperately: "We need to go back!"

Wallen said nothing, eyes ahead. It was all she could do, Deni knew it. To stop would kill them. They had to keep moving and make it mean something.

Tyler knew it too, of course; he just hadn't admitted it yet. He kept staring out the back of the truck as they got further away. Deni kept her distance. She didn't want to see.

17

It was a while before Tyler realised they weren't alone in the back of the truck. He didn't care; he couldn't care. They weren't in danger, so what did it matter. Qait was gone. Left lying in a random field, at the hands of these monsters. Cut down as he'd been doing all he could to save them. In the few days he'd known him, Tyler had understood, without doubt, that he'd been a good man, and he spoke the words that said it all. "It's not fair."

Wallen had offered no words of comfort. She kept on driving, and merely called back to them, "We're moving till it's safe."

What use was stopping now, anyway? They weren't bringing Qait back.

Deni didn't reach out to him, stiffened by her own shock. She must have known it was wrong too, whatever disagreements they'd had. She sat close on the truck bench, pressing into Tyler with her shoulder and leg, probably the nearest she could get to affection or comfort. She was staring into the shadows of the truck, and looked like she hadn't blinked since it had happened, nor would again. She had Tyler's leather satchel on her lap, hands probing its material, just for something to do.

Tyler's mind raced, not just over how unfair it was, or how wrong it was, but over how confusing it was, too. The slavers had attacked them, and done everything they could to kill them. They were bad people. But if they were so bad, why did they say that about Ruke? Why lie about killing him?

The truck jolted over an obstacle that made Tyler brace his arm against the wall, and the pain brought him back to the moment. He was bleeding, though the cut seemed minor. It just hurt when the vehicle moved suddenly. He put his hand to it again, applying pressure, and blood seeped warmly between his fingers. It was an almost welcome contrast to the cold damp that chilled the rest of his body, his clothes heavy with water. Should probably take them off.

Looking down, to where some of the water was pooling around their feet, he saw Deni's legs were sodden, too. Her new trousers and leather shoes were soaked through. He looked up at her, remembering. "The rocket?"

Deni met his gaze, her brow furrowing as she interpreted what he'd said. She put a hand into the pocket of the dungarees, at her stomach. Tyler watched her fearfully. Her clothes weren't wet all the way through, though. Her shirt was dry. She hadn't fallen in the water like he had. She pulled out the roll of paper and held it up. Untouched.

"Thank Dendra…" Tyler let out a breath of relief.

Deni turned it over in her hand, as though seeing it for the first time. Taking stock, she noticed, too, the bag she was holding. She hurriedly took it off and held it out to Tyler, eyes imploring but saying nothing. He slowly took it from her as she explained in a whisper, "I took it. For you."

Tyler looked dumbly at his father's bag. She'd managed to pluck it from all the confusion. He frowned, but before he could question the gesture, she asked, "What now?"

Tyler didn't say anything for a moment. He wanted to reassure her and say everything would be all right. Of course they'd find a way, and of course she wasn't alone. But it was difficult. Difficult to find hope. He needed to trust her and what they were doing. He couldn't let doubts start to creep in; that's what the slavers had wanted. She'd rescued his bag, for Dendra's sake. He cleared his throat to say something, anything, and a voice from near the front of the truck cut him off.

"Who are you people?"

Tyler and Deni looked up with unified alarm. The man was huddled in the far corner, a thin shape shackled around the hands and feet with chains that ran under the bench. His clothes were little better than rags, his skin blackened with dirt, and he looked like he hadn't eaten in days, bones jutting through his flesh. Tyler shot to his feet and stood in front of Deni, blocking her from him, but the man gave him a sardonic smile, holding up his chained hands. "You're in no position to be afraid, now. I'm but a humble actor – Helious by name. Tim Helious. And I can see you are ferocious fighters. Please, I would beg of you, can you help me?"

Concealed in the shadow of the trees at the side of the road, the group gathered outside the truck. The road had worsened since it diverged from the river's edge, getting narrower and more uneven as they rolled up between hills of rock. The sides of the truck caught on thick bushes and trees that threatened to branch across the path and block it off forever. Without the expansive emptiness around the river and the fallow fields, this road was succumbing to nature; a sign that the Guard had retreated from the area. The truck was powerful enough to muscle through, though, making the overgrowth a blessing as it hid them.

It had been an hour, perhaps more, since they'd abandoned the boat, and Wallen had finally agreed it was safe to stop. Over the better roads, they'd moved more quickly than any boat was likely to, so the chances of the slavers catching up seemed unlikely. Tyler had stayed quiet, for once, even with their guest in the truck trying to engage in conversation. Deni was thankful for it. Helious made light references to his work, boasting of the theatre that travelled across Estalia and the messages his company could spread in their honour when he got back to the Metropolis. She could think of nothing worse.

"First up, I'm sorry," Wallen told the younger pair as they joined her outside the truck. She paused, staring at Tyler. "You okay?"

Deni had found a scrap of cloth in the truck's supply chest, along with some rubbing alcohol, and had messily bandaged his wound. It had looked all right, but the darkness of the truck had been more forgiving than the limited light of day outside. The blood had soaked through. Combined with the mud that had washed over his wet clothes, he looked like he'd been dragged from a grave. His chilly silence made it worse. Deni had no idea what he was thinking, but was sure it wasn't good.

He nodded, though. Likely he wouldn't complain even at the point of dying.

"You'll freeze," Wallen warned. "Ride up front with me, the engine's warm, it'll dry you off. Probably better if you take all that off, though."

Tyler shrugged, not bothered. Riding in the front sounded good to Deni. The back was too grim a reminder, to say nothing of their strange passenger.

"Okay." Wallen ran a hand through her matted hair, regrouping. "Where'd I start? I'm sorry. He was a good man, of sorts, and I wish to the gods we didn't have to leave him like that. But you saw it as well as me." She spoke specifically to Deni. "There was nothing we could do, was there?"

Deni let her silence stand as agreement.

"Next up, I know you're shaken, but trust that we're okay for now. This baby moves." Wallen thumped the wall of the truck. "There's plenty of fuel in the chamber. Can't promise I could fix it if something goes wrong, but it's simple enough to operate, we used to have a tractor with a similar engine. I can take us someplace far away. And there's some supplies out back?"

"Food for a few days," Tyler nodded. "And chips to trade with."

He didn't mention the weapons. There were two rifles racked near the rear door, and blades under one of the benches, as well as chains running the length of the truck, enough to hold ten people in place.

"What about our passenger?" Wallen asked.

"Says he's called Tim Helious. They picked him up a few days ago; he's been wandering since bandits raided his acting group. The slavers traded off their other prisoners, to move quicker, but they thought he'd get a better price in the city. He speaks kind of funny."

"Actors do," Wallen said. "We can cut him loose in the next town."

"There's no keys," Tyler said. "We looked. They must've had them on them."

"We'll figure it out. Now..." She turned gravely to Deni. "Before we go another step. Was there a word of truth in anything that man was saying about you?"

Tyler immediately moved in front of Deni. "Don't."

His voice was quiet, and, from the way he'd been refusing to look at her, Deni knew he wanted to ask the same thing. It was his fear of the answer, not his loyalty to her, that was holding him back.

Deni brushed him aside with the back of her hand. She was ready for the question. She'd run through Vorst's claims in her head a thousand times since the shooting had started. She said, "Some of it. Some of it was true."

Tyler and Wallen shared the same concerned look as they waited for more.

"There's a lot of people dead because of me," Deni admitted. Her throat felt small, and she picked up speed, in case it closed altogether. "But only a couple I killed myself. My master wasn't one of them. I wished him dead but I didn't do it. It was a man called Montgomery. With the Guard."

"Sent to silence him," Wallen confirmed.

Deni nodded, and quickly turned to Tyler. "I swear to Dendra and all the gods, I had nothing to do with what happened to your uncle. They hurt him but he was fine when I left –"

"You knew they'd hurt him?" Tyler gaped.

Deni froze. What had she said?

"You didn't tell me that!" Tyler pulled away. "When I went with you into the Kennel – you said he was okay."

"He was," Deni trembled. He stared back, faltering.

"I could've gone back, could've helped him..."

Deni said nothing. It was true. She'd got Ruke killed, the same as all the others. Tyler's shoulder tensed as though he was going to hit something, but he didn't. He walked a few steps away, then spun to her. Deni met his upset gaze. The least she could do, now, was own her shame. He bit down his frustration, and said, "What *exactly* did you see? Who killed my uncle?"

"I don't know," Deni said. It sounded too quiet, not convincing. She couldn't allow it, not this time, not with Tyler. She spoke more firmly: "Vorst hit him, but he didn't stay. I asked your uncle where you were and he was okay, I swear – I didn't think anyone was going to hurt him. Vorst left him, though. Left him alone."

Tyler didn't lash out. He didn't hit her or accuse her. He just said, "You swear, Deni? That's all you saw? You didn't..."

Deni watched him. He was conflicted. Reconsidering standing beside her, at last. She said, as clearly as she could, "I would've told you if he was in danger, I *swear*. But that part, what Vorst said, it could be true. It wasn't necessarily them that killed him."

Tyler was glowering, furious. He swore under his breath, "The damned Guard..."

"The Guard," Wallen intervened warily. "Here's this idea again. Like Qait with his nonsense talk of leadership. *Who* in the Guard? They work in small groups; a community's Road Guard unit, a boatload at sea under one commander, a team of bridge builders. Where's the unit responsible for hunting children with stolen scientific information? Knowing it's the Guard doesn't tell us a damned thing."

"That's not true," Deni said. "There are hundreds of people working together in the Towers. Planning the world."

"You're sure of that?" Wallen said. "Because I saw a crew of slavers out there, not an army of guards."

"I'm sure of it." Deni gave her a firm look. "I lived in a swamp, and guards from the city came to monitor my master's work. No one out here seems to realise how organised they are." Deni paused, though, thinking of Qait and his fears about going back into the city. She drew the dreaded conclusion. "We *have* to return to use this information. Whatever Qait thought the rebels might do with the rocket, it wouldn't have put the research to use. The Towers are the only place it can go."

"Making it a monumentally obvious place for them to catch you," Wallen snorted.

"Don't come," Deni said. "Just get me close. I can go unseen."

"Get *us* close," Tyler corrected, his hand finding hers. His smile hadn't returned, but his eyes were determined. Whether he still trusted her or not, he would do the right thing, as his uncle and his dad had taught him. He wanted to make Qait's death mean something. And Ruke's. She felt it too, something that was now unavoidable. As she'd said on the boat, but now had to believe. Her lonely life couldn't be all that they had died for. They and the others, they couldn't have died for Deni to be Deni.

Wallen looked at them both carefully, the same sort of calculating look they'd received from Qait. All those times when he must have been thinking there'd be no persuading them, and that it was better he make his plans in secret. When Wallen spoke, though, there was warmth in her voice that he'd lacked. She told them, "To hell with it. You think I'm going to let some kids stick it to the Guard while I go out to pasture? When you've got a way to *open the sky*? Just tell me how we're going to get these murderous sons of bitches."

Part 3

1

Though the Metropolis was fed by countless waterways, there were few good roads that led into the city. Deni had seen that on her first journey there; the ground routes converged, bit by bit, until they all ran into the wider paved pathway of the West Entrance. Wide enough for five carriages abreast, it ran into the city like a welcoming carpet, lined on both sides by tall fire-sticks, increasing in number the closer you came to the gates. The entrance itself was a gap in an enormous fortified wall, a remnant of past wars which was now overrun by traders and craftsmen selling wares. The gates, vast iron doors three storeys high, were always open, and what had once been a moat, a dry ditch either side of the road, was filled with trading stocks; crates of goods, barrels of drink, old machinery parts.

The West Entrance was guarded by Road Guards on foot and a few watching from the towers to either side of the gates, many of them carrying rifles, but there was little sense of security. There were no raiding parties large, or stupid, enough to come this close to the city, with numerous outposts more likely to spot them further afield. And besides, ground traffic was minimal, with only the closest farmers likely to visit the Metropolis by waggon or carriage. Long-distance travellers stuck to the water routes, the nearest of which was visible on the approach to the gate.

The River Lither joined the city there, twenty metres wide. Narrowboats, barges and bigger vessels were crowded in the water on their way to the city. Their passengers lingered around the sides and roofs of their vessels, trading and chatting as they went. In contrast to the relaxed, market-style atmosphere of the West Entrance, the river's path through the walls was lined with a mix of Road and Border Guard at various heights, watching like crows. They slowed traffic, checking the cargo passing through. As Wallen drew the truck to a halt, a pair of Road Guards were carrying a crate away from a canal pilot who was waving his arms in frustration.

"Vultures," Wallen sneered as she watched. "An institution of shit."

Deni looked at Tyler, expecting him to say something, but his face was grim. He had no words left to defend the Guard.

"Cargo?" a man demanded from nearby.

Wallen put on a warm smile as she faced the Road Guard below. He had a full face helmet on, a grey panel hiding his expression. She leant out and replied, "One man, actor from the wetlands. You got a need for someone who talks too much? Yours for sixty chips."

"Sixty?" the Road Guard replied, unclear whether he thought it high or low.

"Fair disclosure, he needs a wash."

The guard shook his head, unimpressed and disapproving. "That's all you've got?"

"It's slow out there," Wallen told him. "Everyone's coming to town, aren't they?"

"Yeah." The guard looked to the river. "Know where you're going? Know the rules?"

"Absolutely," Wallen said. "Beeline for the Mines, if we don't snag a buyer before."

The Road Guard nodded, not interested, and stepped aside, waving them on. As Wallen pulled them forward, Tyler let out a breath. Wallen smiled. "First bit of luck for the day. One thing you can guarantee is that no slaver's an easy target, and it's only easy targets they're interested in."

In the back of the truck, Tyler and Deni watched Helious as they waited for Wallen's return. It was even darker now that they'd reached the city, where the buildings blocked what little light came through the clouds. Helious was smiling, as he had done awkwardly whenever they looked his way. He held up his hands and rattled the chain to show his eagerness to finally be loose.

Over the course of the journey, he'd spoken only about himself, never seeming to listen when they replied. He told them of different places he'd been, and plays he'd put on. Mostly stories about heroes of the empire. Deni had once found it fascinating, the idea that there was such entertainment to be seen, but hearing him talk, knowing what she knew about the Guard, she resented the idea of people promoting such tales. It was probably all lies, used to persuade all corners of Estalia that the Guard were protecting them. Continuing a tradition of justice. When Helious spoke about their latest play, The Flight from Thesteran, Deni shared a look with Tyler that told her he was thinking the same thing. There was nothing noble about the way the Guard had fled the north.

Deni suspected she would feel just as relieved as Helious would once he was finally set free.

"Where will you go?" Tyler asked.

"Oh, Sebank Street," the actor replied without hesitation. "Perhaps you know it? The finest of places, the very finest. Honest as the day, this hasn't been pleasant, but it's turned out very well, very well indeed."

"What's on Sebank Street?" Deni said.

"Dreams, my dear, the very finest dreams!" His voice was too loud in their metal confines.

"It's where the best theatres are," Tyler explained. "Only for rich people."

"For your help, they'll sing your names on the stages," Helious insisted. "Louder than anywhere in the city, bar Speakers Square. Unless you want to hijack their horns – I'd proudly shout it in the square, too! It'd do well to have theatre on *that* stage!" He laughed at his own joke. Deni caught the thoughtful look on Tyler's face. Was he trying to figure the actor out? They didn't dwell on it, as Helious bowled on. "You mark my words, watch the theatres – the heroes of the western waterways, your names will be lauded!"

"No thanks." Deni shook her head. The more he talked of his work, the less she wanted to be associated with it. She said, "It was chance we found you, anyway."

"You say chance," Helious said. "I say *Providence*. I know that's not your walk, I heard you speak the names of the Old Gods, and they have a fine place in my heart too, but there's little as majestic as the workings of Providence, as we see here, with me on the road to Sebank, when only two days hence I shared piss pots with a crowd destined for the worst of lives. They will *sing* this adventure."

The truck door creaked open, just enough to let Wallen back in. She kept her voice low, shifting between them with a mottled pair of bolt cutters. "It's not pretty out there. They're talking about closing the gates, searching outsiders. Apparently a floating castle was sabotaged near Brofton, making its way back here."

"Sabotaged?" Tyler said.

"An explosion blew a hole in it. They're blaming a group of fishermen. Sympathetic to the Kandish rebels." Wallen opened the cutters over the shackles as Helious held up his hands. He flinched as she clamped the handles shut, the metal snapping between their jaws.

"Oh seven blessings," Helious gasped. Deni watched him rubbing his wrists with relief, remembering the feeling. He had endured only a few days of it and he looked like his whole life had been changed. Suffering that indignity had been her life. He said, "This story will spread, my friends. The Flight of Helious. That the world may be a better place, hearing of misfortunes turned fortunate."

Deni didn't want to speak, in case she said something insulting. She looked at Tyler. The young man was staring at Helious thoughtfully. Did he buy this fawning praise?

"Will you not take up my offer and continue to Sebank?" Helious asked, stretching as he stood. "I have friends, yet, and you will be most welcome."

"Not tonight," Wallen said. "It's getting dark and we need more of a plan than that."

"This vehicle, you know –" Helious reached up to pat the ceiling "– would be a fine travelling waggon. The theatre is always in need…"

"It's yours if you want it. We go any further in it, we'll be found out. They'll be looking for it, though, once word gets back that we escaped."

Helious' smile didn't fade but there was worry in his eyes. Remembering that exposure could be dangerous. He nodded. "Rightly so. It's very well. Nevertheless, do come calling. You'll always be welcome where you find me."

He moved to exit the truck but Tyler stood and said, "Wait."

Helious turned a faint smile to him.

"You think we've got a story worth telling?"

"Established hence," Helious answered oddly.

"You want to tell people stories that matter," Tyler went on haltingly. Preparing to suggest something that might be a very bad idea. "Tell them about the sky. They were hunting us because of the sky."

Helious frowned, not following.

"There's... something the Guard are doing. They hired those slavers. Deni here..." he moved closer to her, raising a hand to indicate her, and she cringed. "She saw the clouds part. The Guard don't want the clouds to part." It was coming out strangely, it sounded like he was building up to it, developing the idea even as he said it. The confusion was clear in Helious' face. Tyler continued, "They don't want people to know. Beware of that. You start telling people, it could get you in danger. But this is important. A really important story. This girl, she's seen the sky, and she can help pull the clouds back, so everyone else can see it too."

"So the world can be warm again," Wallen offered, as though it was an image she'd been considering herself. "And we can see the light."

"But the Guards don't want anyone to know about it," Tyler said. "They'd rather kill us than let things change. Because change..." He looked at Deni, reading the words in her uncertain face. "Because if we change the world, they might not be on top any more."

It was unclear whether Helious believed him. Face blank, he replied, "You'd make enemies of the Guard."

"No." Tyler shook his head quickly. "They made enemies of us."

The actor's face lit up at this, his eyes almost sparkling. He clicked his fingers and said, "Oh yes. Yes, that's wonderful! The poetry of rebellion. That is passion. You *must* come to Sebank."

"We've got other places to be," Tyler told him. "But if you want to tell a story, that's the one. She saw what was behind the clouds and it... it was beautiful."

Without elaboration, Helious nodded enthusiastically. The ideas were clearly forming behind his eyes; ways that he could describe such beauty himself. He didn't need their words for it. He thanked them again, chuckling at the idea, then finally ducked out of the truck. They waited, listening, as he greeted a stranger and skipped away. Happy to be alive. Deni said, "You shouldn't have told him that."

"Why?" Tyler said. "He got me thinking. Qait got me thinking – *you* got me thinking. The Guard's power's in the storytelling, isn't it? People believe what they hear about the Guard, and what they hear is what the Guard tell them. If we want this to go somewhere, people need to start listening to something else. They've done everything to keep it quiet, we oughta start doing everything we can to make a noise. We need to be careful, for sure, but we need to do it, all the same."

Wallen nodded slowly, but Deni was less sure, tightening her arms around herself. Involve more people, that's what he was saying. She should've seen it coming. He still trusted in the goodness of others. Even with all they'd been through. He'd keep trusting people, and it would get them noticed and it would get them killed, one way or another.

Tyler was waiting for her response. He put a hand on her shoulder and said, voice softer, "If we don't do it, if something goes wrong, and we disappear, then this whole thing disappears with us."

Deni didn't answer him. It wasn't a good idea. It was the first step towards disaster. She had to get ahead of him, before it got out of hand.

"Deni?" Tyler said, more concerned. "Trust me."

"Okay," she said. She had an idea of her own. It had only been a nub, before, a distant possibility, but he'd confirmed it was necessary. He smiled, and she forced a faint smile back. To stop him moving quickly forward, she turned to Wallen, hoping to change the subject. "Do you know where your nephew is?"

"I've an idea," Wallen said. "But what I *do* know is that I need to get you two someplace safe, and it don't feel safe here. Damned if we'll do it by night, though. We'll lock this tin can up and get some rest, hike out in the morning."

Deni nodded. That was all the chance she needed to get away.

2

Tyler stirred with an ache in his side, the hard surface of the truck bench having dug into his hip. The cut on his arm had scabbed over and barely stung now, except when touched directly, and his other aches were easing up. The morning light came through the front window in a dull grey-blue. He cleared his eyes to pick out Deni. They were almost there. Together, they were going to solve this, he was sure of it. They'd find justice for whoever had killed Ruke, and the others. More than that, she'd get her life back. She'd suffered for too long, and he'd realised, as his mind had settled overnight, that whatever mistakes she might have made, she couldn't be blamed. She'd endured terrible circumstances, and it was all to her credit that she'd survived this long. Damaged and confused, worse off than most. He'd keep her safe, yet. Open the skies, as she'd promised.

It was time to get to it, rested, ready for action.

Tyler swivelled on the bench and scanned past the bulk of Wallen in the middle of the floor, snoring loudly, to the shadows of the far bench. He squinted, in his semi-conscious state, slow to register what he was seeing.

Deni was gone.

Watching the morning glow spread up from the horizon, Deni clung tightly to the railing of an exposed stairwell. She wasn't sure what the thin cylindrical structure was for, encircled by a fragile, rising walkway and swaying in the slight breeze, but it served the purpose she needed, unguarded and tall. Halfway up, she got a good view of the city ahead. Peaks of shadow in the haze hinted at how far the Metropolis stretched, but she could see far enough to pick out the rivers. Near the West Entrance, the buildings were different to the stacked homes in Bawkley; broader and squarer, built of sturdier material framed by thick iron girders. It was no less crowded here, but there was something more orderly about the thoroughfares, with a wide road at ground level running towards the city centre, and the broad Lither carving a similar gap a few blocks over.

The path to the Drain was clear, and from there Deni knew she could get to the Towers. If she stuck to the north side of the river, she'd see the Towers looming to the south eventually. They'd be east of here, for sure, following the flow of the river towards the sea. That was still how it worked, wasn't it? Once the waterways of Estalia reached the Drain, they pushed east towards the sea...

She took in the rest of the city, what was visible of it, hoping some other clue would confirm exactly where she needed to go. As she turned on the spot, the walkway creaked and she clung more tightly to the railing. The platform tilted out, the bolt holding it to the tower loosening. With her breath quickening, Deni froze, not daring to move. It was twenty metres down, at least, the people small below.

Holding her breath, she gave the city another glance. To her left, far beyond the homes, was a huge, empty expanse, where the buildings fell away. It interrupted the wall to stretch far beyond the city limits. The massive hole in the world she now recognised as the vast Mines. The Mines covered a huge swathe of land to the northwest of the city. The road they'd taken came in south of it, it must've done. So she was right: she could follow this road and get exactly where she needed to go.

Deni wished she could ask Tyler. It would be easy for him. She couldn't, though. Difficult as it was to be alone, the decision had been easy. Qait had known Tyler wouldn't let go, and she knew it too. She understood why the tracker had done what he did; the latest betrayal in a life of them, this one had a good reason. And now it was her turn to do the same.

There were dozens dead because of her. Vorst had told the truth.

She wasn't going to add Tyler to that list.

Tyler pushed his way through people starting their days, knocking a woman and scattering a basketful of clothes from her hands. He ran on without apologising, searching faces, jumping to get a view over shoulders. He sprinted for a set of stairs and went up onto the roof of a building, then along its edge, scanning the street below. There were too many people. First thing in the morning, they were already up, trading, busy in open-fronted workshops, some just *moving*. In the way. The road was too wide, there were too many places to look.

A walkway rose off the end of the building and bridged the gap to another. Tyler ran for it, whipping from side to side as he tried to spot her.

He didn't know how long ago she'd gone. Didn't know what direction she would've gone in. She must have aimed for the Drain, but that didn't mean she went the right way. A tier higher, Tyler found the view no more helpful; she could have been right before his eyes but with all the people crowding into one another he wouldn't see her.

When did the city get this busy?

Tyler pulled himself up by the railing and kept searching with his eyes. The new shirt Wallen had bought him was already darkening as his cut reopened. He looked from it back to the crowds, willing the gods to help him. She couldn't be out there alone. He needed to help her. Needed to make them pay for Ruke. For Qait. For all they'd been through.

She had no right to keep that from him.

He closed his eyes, catching himself in the thought. She had no right. She'd had no right to keep Ruke's injuries from him and she had no right to drag him into this whole mess to begin with – and she definitely had no right to exclude him now. Yet he couldn't hate her for it. She needed help, that was all. She'd never had help before, and he knew, somehow, that doing that for her would make everything okay.

He opened his eyes and let out a breath he hadn't realised he was holding.

A movement caught his eye. Someone purposefully racing in his direction, searching, the same as he was. He straightened up hopefully. Not Deni, though. Wallen, pushing through the crowd less subtly. She shouted his name, then Deni's. Tyler watched as she grabbed a slighter man by the lapels and demanded to know if he'd seen two children. She had the same desperation Tyler felt, and he knew then she had no intention of letting this go, either. But as that thought encouraged him, Tyler noticed more movement, further back. Less urgent, but equally harsh, another large figure pushing their way through.

"Wallen!" Tyler waved, keeping his voice to a hiss. The big lady slowed down.

Seeing him on the walkway, he saw the concern in her face wasn't for finding Deni, not right now. She pointed to the side, towards the alleys, saying nothing. Tyler gave another look to the crowd. Squinting, he made out flashes of fur. The bald head thundering through the people. It had to be Vorst. How had he got back so quickly?

Tyler waved to Wallen again, directing her to the side, where they could meet in the shadows, and he raced down a stair to meet her coming up. They squeezed into a gap between two buildings, a storey up, in a recess from the main street where they wouldn't be seen. Wallen said, "No sign of her?"

Tyler shook his head.

"Me neither. But damned good thing we were out looking for her. They got to the truck just after we left."

"How?" Tyler mouthed.

Wallen didn't have an answer, but leant around the corner to watch the crowd. Tyler joined her, making out the big slaver and his female companion, almost upon them, walking straight ahead. Vorst was muscling his way forward with angry impatience.

"Bloody roof-rat, isn't he?" the woman was snarling, loudly enough to be heard over the hubbub. As she said it, Vorst looked up, reminded to check the walkways, and Tyler pulled Wallen out of view.

"I'm done trawling through this shit," Vorst grunted.

Tyler leant back out, just slightly. The pair had paused in the road, looking at each other in silent conference. The woman didn't say anything, but they seemed to agree to keep moving. Vorst took his frustration out on the nearest passer-by, with a shove that knocked the man to his knees. They weren't looking up, not any more, not scanning the crowds at all.

"They're going," Tyler told Wallen, in a hushed tone. "Not looking for us."

"Not looking for us? They found the truck," Wallen said. "Are you gonna tell me how a bunch of slavers stranded in the wastes got back here as quick as us?"

The same thing he wanted to know. He said, "The ones after Deni, they had the resources to attack the Kennel, they must've had the means to keep in touch with the slavers. And bring them back here. But if they're not hanging around..."

Wallen followed his gaze, out over the crowd. The slavers were barging their way towards the Drain. She said, "They're going back to whoever's hired them."

Tyler nodded. "Deni said she had a secret way into those Towers. I have no idea where that is, I don't know how we can follow her. They might, though. It's our best shot."

The expression on Wallen's face said she wasn't happy, but Tyler knew that seeing the slavers was a blessing. This was a chance to spin things around. He said it out loud: "We follow these bastards, maybe we can see where all this is going."

3

At the river's edge, Deni saw a city different to the one they'd left only days before. The Drain was even more crowded with warships, bunched together with planks going from one to another, and the people flooding over them had created a carnival atmosphere. Tradesmen had flocked to this hub to peddle food, tools, clothes and animals, while guards milled aimlessly in the throng, drinking, shouting and singing. They weren't working, and maybe didn't understand why they were there; they were merely enjoying being together. It would have been a tremendous river-wide party, if not for the looming monstrosity that Deni understood to be a Border Guard floating castle. She had seen it from a distance before, but it was now firmly rooted in the centre of the menagerie, five storeys high with its impenetrable walls, fortified towers and guns jutting from every possible gap in the defences.

Deni crept to the corner of the vast bridge known as the Grenevic Passage, which was teeming with loud people and lined with makeshift buildings. She couldn't find the gangway Hodwick had led her over, only smaller bridges that were carefully guarded, so this crossing seemed like the safest option, packed as it was. But at its entrance, Deni found it as closely watched as the other footbridges, with a Guard watch-tower raised over the milling people and the floating castle only a short distance down the river. There were at least a dozen guns pointed her way.

Would anyone know who she was? Surely not.

She wasn't sure herself, now, if the Guard were actually looking for her, or if it was all the work of a few madmen. She'd passed a group in the street who hadn't so much as looked at her. The bridge was a focal point, though. It was a border, from the ordinary world of the north Metropolis to the affluent neighbourhoods of the south. She understood that from her journey with Hodwick, and now it seemed even truer than before.

Ten metres away, two armoured guards were checking the bags of a traveller, as they'd been doing on the boats at the West

Entrance. Deni backed off. Further on, beyond the massive boats, was a footbridge that rose twenty metres over the river. It didn't go all the way across, though; they'd removed the centre to allow boats to pass.

What were they all doing here?

"I saw him, you know," a male voice said near her ear. She turned to find a pear-shaped man staring at the floating castle. He had a round head and a swollen, red nose, thumbs tucked into the waistband of his trousers, chest puffed up proudly. Everyone else was moving busily, not paying attention; there was no doubt he was talking to her.

She said nothing in response, hoping he'd simply go away.

"Dniren," he clarified. "He came down here, two days ago. Looking for clothing. Strong presence. Very strong. We should be glad to have him here. You know the things they've done on Command Post 3? Protecting the empire for more seasons than you and I have together, I'll wager."

Deni followed his gaze. Command Post 3 didn't look that old, and although it was clearly a structure of war, it looked untouched by battle. The black paint made it hard to see for sure.

"It's safer on the other side," the man said, turning to Deni. She didn't meet his eyes. Why was he talking to her? Was he going to try something? "But it's not for everyone. You might get as far as the south bank but they're checking anyone that goes down the Parade."

"What Parade?" Deni asked quietly.

"Ah ha," the man said, nodding as though she'd confirmed his suspicions. "Not from these parts. Look. Everyone that's come south wants to keep going south." He pointed across the bridge. She noticed what she hadn't seen before. The shifting throng of people reached a halt about halfway across, blocked from going further.

Had it been this bad before? Hodwick had smuggled her across and back with ease, but he used alternative routes. Coming back, no one had been looking anyway; no one cared if you went north. Maybe it had got worse. Maybe she'd found Hodwick's bridge and didn't even know it, with all the people and guards surrounding it.

Deni bit her lip. Even if they weren't looking for her, they might not let her pass. She let it out without thinking: "But I need to get to the Towers."

"What business have you got there?" The man spoke with curiosity, rather than accusation or hostility. Deni resisted the urge to ask what business it was of his. She thought of Tyler, though. Despite everything, he still believed in people, he'd still talked to the stranger Helious as though he was a friend – he still clung on to the hope that some people were simply willing to help others. What she'd dreamt of when she first left Balfair's estate. She took a breath.

"I have something to deliver," Deni said. "But the Guard don't necessarily know about it. Or might not believe me."

The stranger said, "They don't always, do they? Forgive me, but you're not a courier?"

Deni met his gaze, finally, and ventured, "Can I ask... why it interests you?"

The man smiled warmly, nodding to the Drain again. He inhaled the river air and said, "I'm not wanting to impose, and don't think myself nosey by nature, but when I saw you I thought you didn't quite fit in. We've had a thousand people sweep through here since the troubles in the north began. Before we even had talk of fighting and fires, just when it was the darkness that had people scared. I know the look of someone that's not just going with the flow, though. The way I see you looking at those boats, calculating how it is you're going to get something done. Standing here without a possession on you."

Deni hesitated. She felt uncomfortable, knowing that someone had noticed her. And noticed her so well. She said, "What do you do?"

"A cooper, by trade," he said. "You know coopering?" He pointed to a waggon across the busy street, piled high with large wooden barrels. "As it happens, I've got a delivery for Grenevic. I wouldn't say no to a second set of hands."

Deni eyed the waggon sceptically. It was all too familiar, like the cartloads of goods she'd had to shift into the estate. The aches she'd felt in her back, the resentment at having to do it all alone. That was what this was? Another man after her labour?

"I give fair trade for fair work," the man continued. "Help out and I can give you the passage you need. They won't ask questions of me. And I won't ask questions of you. Think you've got the muscle for something like that?"

"I can move barrels," Deni said, defiantly. He was a foot taller than her and probably twice her weight, but she was fairly sure she could shift his cargo as adeptly as he, and he had no right to think otherwise.

He held out a chubby hand. "Do we have a compact?"

She paused, considering how else he might try to trap or betray her. She held up her hand to shake his, though, mindful of the knife on her wrist. Let him try it.

4

The Golden Barrel, a celebrated haunt for merchants, sat in perhaps the only passably clean area of the Metropolis north of the river. Part brick and part wood, the structure looked older and sturdier than the predominantly metal buildings elsewhere. Warmly lit by lanterns, its wide-open hall was lined with massive timber tables, and the occupants were dressed in finery: gilded coats and brass-buttoned suits. Near the entrance, a man with a monocle was studying a gem, a large pile of chips out on the table next to him. Between the traders were occasional guards and mercenaries, as big and fierce-looking as Vorst but with an air of civilisation, concealed in cloaks and more presentable armour than the slavers'.

Tyler watched Vorst making his way through the crowd. The slaver looked out of place with his darkly inked, dirty skin, and Tyler caught glimpses of disgust on his face. Tyler moved to the side, ducking low to hide between the bigger people milling about. The drinkers chatted loudly, and somewhere a tier above, up a wide set of stairs, someone played a string instrument.

Vorst approached the bar, which ran the full length of the hall and was staffed by a dozen fast-moving people in shirts. He pushed to the front and gave his order, interrupting whoever was ahead of him. Tyler hovered at the far end of the bar as Vorst's companion turned to survey the room. She looked as irritated as he did.

"What's your poison?" a chirpy voice said from near Tyler's shoulder. He found a bar girl staring at him expectantly. She didn't look much older than him, pretty but tired. When he smiled at her, she smiled back.

"Oh, I'm just looking," Tyler told her.

"Oh? Some free advice." The girl was still smiling. "If you're not drinking and you're not meeting someone, you're not welcome."

Tyler fumbled in his pocket for chips. "Okay. Something small then, please. It's still early." He passed the chips across. The girl took them and turned away, picking up a small glass and going to one of the many stacked barrels. Tyler turned back to Vorst. The two slavers had large tankards in their hands and were moving away, towards the stairs.

"Modo forbid anyone should come to a bar to *drink*," said a burly man on Tyler's right. Sitting on a stool, he was dressed in trader's leathers, with a knife sheath hanging conspicuously from his belt. As the girl returned with Tyler's drink, the man finished his thought. "Fucking tourist."

Tyler flashed him an uncertain smile. He said nothing, aiming to stay discreet, and twisted away from the bar to check the room. Deni would've stood out here, even more than him. There were plenty of female traders and fighters, but they were big and tough, at least tall or wide, or scarred in some way. Deni's figure was too light and gentle. His probably was too. He came from a lean family, their strength didn't show.

Up the stairs, where the balcony was darkest behind a decorative drape, Vorst and the woman found a table. They didn't look like they were saying much, and they were facing the wide stairs. There was no way he'd get up there without being seen. Tyler turned back to the bar, hoping to ask the girl if there was another way up, but she was gone. The grumpy loner hadn't looked up from his drink, even if he'd found time to miserably engage. He looked like a resident here, as Qait had been in the Raskel Den. Tyler couldn't head into the open, to find someone else to talk to, so this guy would have to do. He said, "There's two people up on the balcony. Closest to the steps. Do you know who they are?"

The man gave him an irritated glance, but rather than outright dismiss him he looked up. He grunted and turned back to his drink. "Slavers. Shouldn't be here any more than you. Shouldn't even be in the city."

"That's what I thought..."

"They've got permission, though."

"From who?"

"You're getting on my nerves," the man said. Tyler had the feeling this was going nowhere good. He turned away, about to leave, when the man rumbled on. "This is a place of business. Used to be, anyway. Now it's everyone scratching around for scraps. Bloody wasters rolling down from the north, cut-throats offering dirty work done. Kids, bloody kids, thinking they can come in from, what, Kelp?"

"Bawkley," Tyler corrected.

"Bloody Bawkley. You're what's wrong with this world, you know? Countryside's falling apart and everyone's running here for cover – what do the rats do? Try and take advantage, forget their place."

Tyler scowled at him. There were a dozen things he wanted to say, but any moment those slavers might spot him. He backed off, keeping quiet, scanning the bar.

"Rats like you making the sky darker, you know that!" The man raised his voice. He must've been drunk, looking for a fight. Tyler hurried away as faces turned to him with interest. He bent low again, slipping through the crowd, keeping an eye on the balcony. Vorst had reclined, looking up to the ceiling.

Tyler crept through the room, holding his drink carefully, smiling and apologising as he went. He reached the stairs and ducked to the side, under the balcony. There was a low rumble above, probably Vorst's voice. Tyler wasn't going to be able to keep an eye on them here. He searched the wall ahead. A man burst noisily through a small door. Tyler rushed to it and found a stairwell, up to the next floor.

In the doorway directly above, he peered from behind the slavers. Perfect. The woman had her back to him, now, and Vorst wasn't looking his way. He found a space on a bench, between a man in street-armour, twisted sideways in conversation, and a couple of old, quiet men with a spread of empty mugs in front of them. Tyler settled into position, one hand on his drink and the other shifting his leather bag onto his lap, as Vorst spoke, two tables over.

"Head straight for Nexter. Get as far from this as possible."

"What's for us in Nexter?" the woman replied.

"A simpler life," Vorst grumbled.

They both went quiet, focusing on their drinks. Tyler wished he had Deni's knife. He could slip up behind them, unnoticed. Do for her what no one else had been able to. Do it for *him*. And Ruke, and Qait. These monsters were right there, and they hadn't seen him. This might be the only chance he'd get to take them unawares, no matter the consequences.

Tyler's eyes ran to the man next to him, who had his leg armour on but chest plate lying aside, on a separate stool. By the chest plate was a short sword in its sheath. Tyler could take it. Run it through the woman from behind, swing it into Vorst's face.

"There's a ship due for Afta, out of the Extraner," the woman said. Vorst made an uninterested noise. "Two, three hundred people on board. They hit trouble, you've got dozens of stranded, desperate people."

Vorst's silence suggested they'd discussed this before and he wasn't going to address it again. He looked away from her, to the room below. She stared at the side of his head, not happy.

"We need to do *something*," she hissed, finally.

"How about when he gets up here I crush his skull with my bare hands?" Vorst replied levelly. Tyler tensed. Did they know he'd followed them? He ducked, pretending to drink, looking at them from over his cup. They were both staring down the stairs, though, attentive.

"It was a monumental fuck up, wasn't it?" a man's voice said, climbing towards them. He spoke well, the sort of clear accent Tyler would expect from someone out of Grenevic. As he stepped into view, Tyler's eyes widened, as he realised in an instant who the man was.

His face was framed by a jagged scar, discoloured as though only recently healed. His shoulder-length sandy hair was swept to one side. As he moved, offering the slavers a crooked smile, his hair shifted, revealing another scar. Just visible past the tables, his light grey suit had been adjusted around one leg to accommodate a metal brace that supported his knee, and the hand on his hip pulled back his jacket to reveal a pistol holstered at his chest.

Deni's descriptions had been simple but unmistakable. Something about those scars told Tyler he was exactly who she'd feared he was, who she was afraid she'd seen in the slums – not someone similar. He should have listened to her, not assumed it was in her imagination. As Vorst greeted the man, confirming it, Tyler's heart stopped in his chest. "The monumental fuck up started with you, Montgomery."

The man stood over their table, looking from one slaver to the other with a lizard's smile. Vorst had barely moved, slumped in his chair, not deigning to sit up straight, let alone rise and greet the man.

"Tell me you have a line on them, at least," Montgomery said.

"What we've got," Vorst answered, "is two dead men and a beat-up damned truck. They're back on your turf, now, your problem."

"You're going to make me spell it out to you again?"

Vorst gave Montgomery the same silent treatment he'd offered the woman. He opened and closed his fingers over the tankard. Whatever had gone unspoken between the slavers in the street was stirring in the silence again here.

They didn't like working with Montgomery. Maybe they were being forced into it, even; maybe Qait had been right, that they didn't even realise what they were involved in.

"The truck arrived last night." The woman took over, her tone businesslike. "They've had the morning to get across the Drain. If there's any chance of the girl getting back to the Towers, she's all but there by now. What do you expect us to do?"

The suited man's thin smile didn't leave him but his eyes looked venomous, like he'd cherish hurting these two. He spoke through clenched teeth. "I expect you to find them."

"In Grenevic? *Us*?"

"Do your damned job," Montgomery snarled suddenly, all pretence of friendliness disappearing. "Think for your-fucking-selves – rather than sitting here drinking like a pair of idle dock-workers. Go out and *end this*. I want to hear you've done something – not that you're stranded, not that you want to talk, not that you've left any loose ends untied."

"Tell us about the rocket," Vorst said.

Montgomery locked on him furiously, daring him to say more. He did.

"She had a friend of yours with her," Vorst continued. "Border Guard. Why would a man like Qait Seyron help a murderer and a thief, exactly?"

"Seyron?" Montgomery replied carefully, revealing a crack in his control. He hadn't known about Qait. "The man who helped deliver bombs to the rebels?"

"The rebels," Vorst echoed. "Which rebels would they be? The ones that didn't blow up Thesteran, or the ones that didn't sabotage that ship off Brofton?"

"You're getting cute, Vorst. Do you have any idea –"

"Starting to get some, yeah," Vorst said. "Whatever it was we didn't recover out there, it was more important than the girl herself, wasn't it?"

"The sort of important that might be worth that much more in danger money, don't you think?" the woman added.

Montgomery said nothing, eyes unblinking, calculating.

"It's simple," Vorst said. "We don't give a shit that you want information hidden, we give a shit that it makes the job harder. Don't tell us it's a kid you're after when we're looking at maverick Border Guards or, what, potential rebels?"

"Show us that much respect," the woman agreed.

Montgomery took a long, nasty breath. He looked at the woman. "You really think they could've made it to Grenevic? These children?"

"She got the drop on you, didn't she?" the woman replied.

Montgomery stared at her hatefully. He said, "I don't want you across the river, no. If she's got that far, I'll find her myself. But you *will* keep looking, in case they haven't made it to the Drain. You'll keep looking until I tell you otherwise, is that understood?"

Neither slaver spoke, but he took that as agreement. Taking another breath, he turned to leave, without a farewell. As he moved down the stairs, Tyler half rose, bumping the man next to him and receiving an annoyed grunt. Montgomery's head disappeared from view.

He could follow him. Unravel whatever trap the man might be laying for Deni. But Montgomery would be going over the river, probably into the Towers – he wouldn't be able to keep up, certainly not unnoticed. Instead he looked to the slavers. Vorst was gulping down the remains of his drink.

There was another option. These two had to have some idea of what Montgomery's plan was, and might draw him out again. More importantly, they didn't like him, or what they were doing. And from the way that brief meeting had gone, Montgomery looked ready to do away with them.

Keeping his eyes on them, Tyler lowered himself back onto his seat. He whispered an apology to the man next to him and took another sip of his drink.

The question was, what could he say to convince these savages?

5

The cooper introduced himself to Deni as Fulora and explained his work, helping to fill and deliver barrels across the Metropolis. Most of his recent deliveries had been made to the Guard in Grenevic. In the daylight, Deni got a better look at the buildings than she'd had before, with their carefully carved stone pillars, large glass windows and arched doorways. They rivalled Balfair's estate for size, but were in far better repair.

Expansive and impressive as they were, it wasn't as calm as it should have been. Groups of guards, in all shades of armour, rolled dice over crates in the cobbled roads. One of the mansions was barricaded, with sandbags in front of the doors and dozens of guards nearby. Many appeared idle, as they had been around the Drain, but others were improving the fortifications, shifting guns into place and installing sharp-edged metal fencing.

"Why are they here?" Deni asked.

"You've come from out of town, you tell me," Fulora said, keeping his eyes on the road. The waggon was a crude machine, using a combination crank and coal engine. The chamber at the front, which he'd stoked before they set out, turned the wheels slightly faster than walking pace, while he used his feet to pedal, creating additional drive from the rear wheels. He continued, "This is the last line of defence, isn't it? Should the forces out there get as far as the Drain. Hrute forbid."

"The rebel forces," Deni said.

"Rebels, traitors, the lot. They'll tear this whole place down, give them a chance. Except we won't give them a chance, will we?"

Deni didn't answer.

"You oughta be thankful," Fulora said. "It's why you're here, after all."

Deni tensed. There was a greater purpose, wasn't there? A trap? Her hand shifted slowly towards her knife.

"With the trouble, I mean," he went on. "I'd have hired this work out, before the Guard came back. Now there's too many people in the city, they're going through all the *glus* quick enough to recycle their barrels. Otherwise I'd be making the barrels full-time and hiring out the delivery, instead of bartering with strays for extra help. Once the *glus* plant gets its act together, there'll be plenty more business, but right now here I am."

"Supporting the Guard," Deni said, bitterly. She regretted it at once.

Fulora went quiet. He turned the waggon slowly around a corner, and only when they'd straightened out did he reply, "I don't follow."

"Nothing," Deni said.

"You got some problem with the Guard, is that it?"

"No."

Fulora stopped pedalling, opened a release valve and pulled a brake lever, bringing the waggon to a trundling stop. Deni's eyes darted ahead to a group of Road Guard at the gates to one of the mansions. The road continued past other large houses into the middle distance, all walled off with little cover. The Towers rose above to the left. Still a way off.

"What say you tell me what's going on, then?"

Deni looked away, saying nothing.

"You're not making things better," Fulora said. "We've got wolves at our door, missy, and I know you've got something to hide – but I thought we were talking loved ones already moved over – or looking for safer shelter."

"I've got nothing to hide," Deni said quietly.

"Except why you're here? If it's something more – the Guard –"

"All I meant is they're taking over the city," Deni told him, and stopped in surprise at the boldness of her voice. She'd interrupted him, made him go quiet. She quickly carried on. "It's crowded, isn't it? And difficult."

Fulora kept staring, judging her. He nodded up the road, to the gathering of guardsmen. "And if I took you to them? Asked you to explain your business here?"

"I'm looking for loved ones," Deni said, with little conviction. "And shelter. I exchanged honest labour for safe passage." The cooper shook his head, not buying it. She didn't expect him to. As he prepared to say it wasn't enough, she followed through. "Or I could tell them the truth. I'm here because I know something the

Border Guard are killing people for. And I could tell them that you know it too." She nodded to the Road Guard. "They'd let the people after me know about it. Then *those* people would kill all those guards, and you too, just because I talked to you."

The cooper looked horrified, a mix of shock at the threat and alarm that this innocent girl could be so malevolent. It didn't matter which side he fell on, really, as long as he was intimidated. Deni held his gaze without faltering. This was what it felt like, she realised, as he held his tongue. She was in control.

"I don't want to get you killed," Deni told him, impressing herself, now. "But I can guarantee if you say a word about me to anyone, they'll come for you. Sure as they came for my master, sure as they came for the kids in the Kennel. It's what they do."

"The kids in the Kennel," Fulora echoed.

"I was there." Deni nodded darkly. She could see it in his face: he believed her. "But if you take me to the edge of the Towers, that'll be that."

"The edge of the Towers..."

"On the south side. Please."

The cooper kept staring at her, stunned, as he reactivated the engine.

The street Deni alighted in was mercifully quiet. As it had been when Hodwick brought her here. He'd chosen this entrance deliberately, after all, in one of the rare abandoned spots of Grenevic. The nearness of the imposing Towers made these buildings undesirable. The houses were still more impressive than the shacks of Bawkley, but they were mostly wooden, close to collapse with holes in their walls and empty windows. She recognised the second building from the end, with its door loosely chained shut. Hodwick's secret entrance. Though she took care not to show it, it was a huge relief. They'd snaked through half a dozen roads to get here and she'd feared they'd never find it. But here it was.

Deni waited in the road for Fulora to leave. He watched her as he turned his waggon around the corner and headed back the way he'd come. They hadn't exchanged another word beyond her brief directions, when she started to recognise the area. He had looked like he wanted to say something, and was on the verge of getting it out, but he never quite did. Deni enjoyed the silence.

Only when she got off did he comment, "What on earth are you going to do here?"

She didn't answer.

When the sound of his engine had faded, Deni squeezed through the doorway. She crept through the dilapidated building to the tunnel. The hatch was still open, as she'd left it. No one else had come this way. It was still safe. Qait might be right, they might've been looking for her in the city, and known she'd come back, but it seemed they didn't know about this place. Hodwick had kept it from them. There was still hope.

Deni climbed down, into darkness, and felt her way along. She didn't need to see. It was a narrow passageway with only a few turns. Long but simple. Her hands finally met the metal rungs of a ladder and she pulled herself up. This trapdoor was shut. She put an ear to it, listening for sounds from above. When none came, she gently forced it up with her shoulder. The door creaked, jolting up, and she caught it with her free hand as she pushed into the room. A semblance of light crept under the door.

Deni closed the trapdoor and slid a tatty rug over it, checking around her. It was the same room she remembered; a collection of dusty chairs and shelves, untouched. The door opened onto one of the building's maze-like corridors. She slipped out into the hallway, a blank tunnel that stretched in both directions with a dozen doorways into rooms and other hallways. Large pipes ran along the ceiling, occasionally rumbling to life as something passed through them. Small gas lamps lit the corridor at irregular intervals. There was no one as far as she could see, and no sound of anyone coming.

Six doors down, on the left, she went through another corridor and found the tight stairwell. It was like in Balfair's estate, the narrow passages and trick entrances. You just needed to know where to go.

Deni climbed seven floors up and entered another hallway. Hearing people approach, she ducked into the stairwell and waited. When they were gone, she carried on; two corridors across and she found the door to Hodwick's workshop. There was no sound inside. He might not be in. But that was better than finding him with company.

Bracing herself, checking up and down the hallway once more, Deni entered. The room was as she remembered it. Dozens of tools lay idle on the worktops; machine parts, clamps for holding them, handheld devices for manipulating them. A large chalkboard ran along one wall, covered in words and diagrams. Far across the room, the opposite wall was dark glass, looking out to Grenevic.

Deni ventured slowly into the room, scanning some of the projects Hodwick had been tinkering with. She touched the measuring device that had given them the coordinates. Had it been used again, somehow, to direct the slavers after them? The only person outside their group to have seen those coordinates was Chetan. And he hadn't believed in them enough to make notes. Vorst and his team had caught up to them so quickly, though.

It had seemed natural that the demonic man should be able to pursue her like a hound. She'd always expected that. But he hadn't come to her. He'd gone to the rocket. It dawned on her then.

They knew exactly where it was.

The door squeaked on its hinges and she froze.

"Deni," a familiar voice said. She turned slowly to face him, her heart stopping in fear that it might be someone else. The man's small frame and inoffensive eyes softened her slightly, though, and she couldn't help but smile at Hodwick. She'd made it, and she'd kept Tyler safe. They were going to change the sky, as the doctor promised. Hodwick ambled into the room, carefully pulling the door to behind him. He spoke quietly: "You shouldn't have come back."

6

Terrified of being spotted at every step, and continually ready to take flight, Tyler strained to keep his breath steady and his movements calm as he followed the slavers through the side streets of Central Metropolis. He kept his distance, without hiding, simply trying to look like he belonged, turning his attention to a store window when he feared they might look his way.

They were walking down increasingly quiet roads, in a part of the merchant district reserved for trading offices. Few guards loitered here, and it was becoming difficult to take cover. The slavers finally turned into a small courtyard overlooked by a terrace of houses, all seemingly empty with no lights in the windows. They went to a central building and paused, Vorst with his hand on the door. He turned back and Tyler jumped into a doorway.

There was no movement for a moment. Then a lock clanged and the door opened. Tyler leant back around to see the pair of slavers going inside. He couldn't follow them now; they'd see him coming down this empty road, and even if they didn't, the building was old, the only entrance noisy.

Looking it up and down, Tyler knew this was it. This must have been their city hide-out. They weren't going to lead him anywhere else, not any time soon. He had to approach them. To put himself on the line. It would've been better to do it in the inn, where there had been people who might have helped him if things had gone wrong. But he had waited too long – been too unsure of what he might say, or why.

On the long walk through town, he still hadn't found any inspiration.

Could they really help? Would they fight off Montgomery, for their own sakes? Distract him, maybe? They were violent mercenaries, he knew that well enough; might they just turn him in to partly complete their job?

No. They were still *people*. They had wants, and presumably some kind of morality. They'd tried to persuade Qait, after all, by insisting they were doing something right. It might've been a lie, or they might have simply not known the truth, but they showed an understanding of right and wrong. They had to be willing to listen, to get some idea of who Deni really was, and what she and Tyler were really doing.

How could they refuse to help, then, knowing what he'd been through? They certainly weren't working with Montgomery out of shared beliefs.

Tyler stepped into the road. He'd know if this was a good idea or not soon enough. He'd walk right up to that door, knock on it loud and clear, and tell these slavers exactly where they stood. He'd put it in the hands of the gods, or Providence, or whatever force was watching over him.

Bracing himself, Tyler started towards the building but stopped at the sound of boots marching behind him. He spun to find eight guards heading his way, two abreast, batons and blades already out. Tyler recognised the man leading them, the only one without a helmet, marked by yellow stripes on his arm and carrying a rifle. It was the big bearded brute that had killed Chetan. They were moving with a fixed sense of purpose, right towards him.

"They resist, they die," the leader instructed. "And they *will* resist."

As the guards approached him, the leader grunted wordlessly for Tyler to get out of the way. They weren't aiming for him, but for the house. Tyler darted to the side, narrowly avoiding being knocked down. The patrol marched straight to Vorst's building. There was a flash of movement in one of the windows.

Tyler's instinct had been right; there was no love lost between Montgomery and these mercenaries, and he'd had the same idea as the young man. That the slavers might be turned against him. They were coming to kill them, the same way they'd murdered Chetan. Ruke. How many others? Tyler searched the surroundings for a solution. Other than locked doors and boarded windows, the street was empty. There was just a single gas lamp opposite the building. Scanning the road again, he spotted a hand-sized bit of rubble.

"Slavers!" the officer shouted. "By the Border Guard's command, come with us!"

"We're done talking for the day," Vorst's voice shouted from the building. He hadn't realised it was a threat, assuming Montgomery was merely summoning them again.

"You have five seconds before we come in," the guard replied, even more loudly.

A curtain shifted in a window: the female slaver looking out.

"Five," the guard started counting. The woman ducked back in, about to say something, but she was too late. The door burst open and Vorst lumbered out. The guards collectively backed off, raising their weapons; all except the leader.

"I fucking said –" Vorst started.

The leader stepped in without warning, his rifle smacking Vorst in the gut. The slaver dropped, reaching a hand up defensively, as the guard aimed the gun at him.

Tyler ran, sweeping up the bit of rubble and throwing it, barely aiming. He was close enough for the lantern to be an easy target; the glass smashed and the gas fire burst out in a brief but wide flash. The guard's gun went off, but his aim was thrown by the distraction. Tyler yelled a useless warning: "They've come to kill you!"

Half the guards turned towards Tyler, and their leader gave the briefest look up – all the mistake he needed to make. Another gunshot came from inside the house, the doorway lighting up as the bullet burst through the opposite side of the guard's neck. He collapsed, gagging and clutching a hand to his throat, rifle dropping in front of Vorst. Vorst grabbed it and rose as the other guards faced him.

The two guards quickest to come to their senses launched at Vorst as he slammed his shoulder into one of them. At the same time, he got a hand onto the second guard's knee and wrenched it aside, bringing him down. The others remained frozen in uncertainty, their batons seeming pathetic in front of this beast, yet one found the courage to shout a war cry and advance. Vorst's fist cracked his jaw, through his helmet, and in the same movement he arced the rifle towards the next guard, the butt catching the man in the unprotected neck. The guard fell choking as the woman ran out, pistol raised. The remaining guards backed off, one throwing his hands up and dropping a blade. The leader was on his knees, choking on his own blood with wide, terrified eyes.

Only one guard was still moving, away from the slavers, lurching towards Tyler.

"Stop!" the woman shouted, and he half-twisted back.

Tyler back-stepped, as Vorst flanked the group, rifle up, and the woman kicked the leader onto his back. The slavers moved past the routed guards, towards Tyler. He stared, unsure if he should run, if he could find the sense to move.

Vorst bore down on him, as large as ever now he was up close, tattooed skin flecked with blood and eyes burning with murderous fury. Tyler flinched, thinking he might knock him down, but the slaver stopped in front of him. He said, "You're the boy."

Tyler squeezed his eyes closed, took a deep breath and thought of Deni. He opened his eyes again and stood up straight, raising his chest. If he was going to face these monsters he wasn't going to show fear. Looking Vorst in the eye as the woman came up alongside him, Tyler said, "I want you to help me."

Vorst and the lady exchanged a look. The woman frowned, looking back to the group of guards watching them. A grim smile crossed Vorst's face as he turned back to Tyler, his gold teeth glinting.

"You're a fucking idiot," Vorst said. His thick hand grabbed Tyler's arm, and, as the younger man cried in protest, the slaver pulled him away.

7

"Deni," Hodwick said. "These are most unfortunate circumstances."

They were alone. She'd made it back unseen and she had what he needed, but nothing about his tight, anxious posture or the words he was saying gave her any confidence. As he came further into the room, she backed off, towards the window.

Hodwick gave her a nervous smile. "I am sorry for what you've been through. You must have questions, and..." He let out a little laugh, at some private joke, and pushed his glasses further up his nose. "You have the readings?"

Deni ran a hand over her wrist, feeling for the knife. The doctor watched her.

"There's no need for violence," he said, but gave the smallest look back over his shoulder. To the door. They *weren't* alone. And he knew she had the knife. He'd spoken to someone who *knew*. Deni backed up further, bumping into a desk. Hodwick let out another chuckle. "Now – now, dear – of course you've had a tough time, you must have, but you're safe – it's only, rather complicated –"

Hodwick took a step closer and she darted to the side, knocking a stool over. The knife was out, then, suddenly in her hand, waving towards him, and the doctor let out a yelp as he put both hands up. There was a good ten metres of space between them, but he didn't dare move. He let out a few more uncertain noises, looking over his shoulder again.

"Deni – I want to help you –"

"Who's out there?" Deni hissed.

"A colleague, that's all," Hodwick said. "No one to fear. Please. Let's talk."

There was no sign of movement beyond the door. Hodwick offered his pathetic smile again. It felt dishonest. He hadn't wanted to talk on her last visit; he'd been in a rush, hoping to get her in and out unnoticed. Now he wanted to take things slow, to trap her. She should have known. She was stupid for not guessing that he, like everyone else, would turn on her. Had he reported her as soon as she left the Towers? That's how Vorst had caught up to her so quickly afterwards. But why? Why bring her here and set her loose, why not bring the Guard to her the moment he found her?

"Okay," Hodwick said hesitantly. "Okay – yes – you're right to be worried. Obviously this got out of hand. You've been hunted – hounded. I know what happened – what happened in the Kennel was because of you. Yes?"

"I didn't want it," Deni replied.

"No – of course not," the doctor laughed again. Seeing her fierce expression, he turned more serious. He indicated his hands, still held up, asking if he might put them down. She didn't move, and he slowly lowered them. When he spoke again, his voice was quiet and grave. "You did something fantastic, didn't you? I doubted it had survived, I doubted *you* would survive, but you did it. Can I see it? Please."

"You've betrayed me," Deni told him, flatly.

Hodwick didn't deny it. He waited a moment, no doubt considering in his genius scientist brain that there was no sense in trying to trick her. She was stuck in this room with him, after all. He said, "I can interpret what you've found. Whatever else comes from this, dear, I can tell you what it means." He held a hand towards her, inviting cooperation. As she kept staring, he added, "Don't you want to know?"

Deni lowered her knife. She did. And if she was trapped – so be it. She should at least know why. She dug the rolled-up paper from her pocket and held it up. As Hodwick's smile threatened to return, she said, "Come take it."

The doctor's face went blank again. He tried to laugh it off and failed. She kept the paper up, between them, waiting. He said, "You can't be... you really..."

She held the knife higher. "Come."

Hodwick hummed awkwardly, but edged forwards. He held a hand well out in front of himself, reaching for the paper. She made him move all the way, not going any closer, and he gingerly touched it. He plucked it away from her and immediately scuttled a few steps back. Exhaling with relief, he unravelled part of it and scanned the numbers.

"Why did people have to die?" Deni asked.

Hodwick paused. One hand started to play with his glasses, adjusting them uselessly as he mumbled, "Of course. That is, I suppose, a place to begin. With my apologies. My sincerest apologies. I heard about Qait. That was incredibly unfortunate."

"*Why?*" Deni said.

"There was..." Hodwick continued to fiddle as he searched for the words. He tilted his head to one side, thinking of something then deciding not to say it. She thought he might go quiet. Why bother explaining to her, after all. He nodded, though. "You already have some idea, don't you? I mean, there's only one good reason."

Deni frowned. She had her idea, all right, but it didn't make enough sense. Controlling the sky was a form of power: keeping the world the same guaranteed the Guard stayed where they were. But if the clouds could open, couldn't that bring a different kind of power? Wouldn't they want that? Unless... Hodwick nodded to the paper and offered his smile again, suggesting whatever she had in mind was right. She said, "It's the Guard's fault. The way the sky is. They don't just want it kept the same – they *made it* that way. That's why they don't want it studied."

Hodwick rocked a little on the spot, head bobbing somewhere between a negative and a positive. "Mm, yes and no. It's a little simpler than that, what this shows. These numbers – the things Balfair was measuring in the sky – what they demonstrate is that there's something *unnatural* in it." Deni waited as he thought this over again. He said, "Let me start somewhere earlier. Will you let me do that?"

Deni glared, unmoving.

"I want you to understand I had no malice, in my part of this. I was being closely watched when I received Balfair's final letter. Asking for my assistance. The letter was read by others and they tried to force me to tell them who sent it, but I – well – I played the fool. There was no way I could get word back to him, though I wanted to help, truly I did. I devised a way to extricate myself from this place. The tunnels we used. The one you used to return to us, yes?" He chuckled again. "Very good. They still don't know about it. It was a complication when you went to the Kennel, but it at least deflected suspicion from me, to let them believe you were working with those children.

"Anyway. By the time I had found a way to get free from the

Towers unseen, the Guard had started asking more about Balfair. His theories about the sky were already well known, of course. Everyone had theories, about the world before. He might've stayed, might've proved it some other way – if things hadn't changed..."

Hodwick veered off into the memory. He sighed.

"ArcTech was still running when Balfair left. Myself, I was researching the origins of the Mines. They tell us awful things about the world's history. I thought – we *all* thought – that if we got to understand how Estalia came to be, then we could see a way to recovery. There were more animals before, fantastic machines. Civilisations the world over. Do you know how small this part of the world is? And yet so many fossils and fuels are concentrated right here, on our doorstep, under the ground."

He eyed her, smiling, hoping for a response. She didn't give him one.

"Well." The doctor shuffled, slightly affronted. "While I was looking down, Balfair was looking up, and the findings of this rocket, they tell us another story." He held up the paper again. "Do you know how clouds work?"

He waited once more, and again she gave him no answer. Who would ever have told her such a thing? He read it in her eyes, and continued almost sympathetically. "From your actions after you left here, and what I have since learnt about you, I believe you weren't close to Balfair. He didn't share his work with you?"

"No."

"Mm. Then it's time someone did. Even the lower ranks of former ArcTech researchers could tell you these readings demonstrate an unnatural chemical composition in the higher strata of the clouds. If I – if we can..." He looked over his shoulder again, checking for whoever was in the hallway. "Perhaps if they understand your ignorance – they can see your resourcefulness – maybe I can convince them you might work with me –"

"Work?" Deni snapped, unable to hold it in. She had scrubbed floors for a decade to serve projects that had been hidden away – how dare he suggest it now? "I know of your *work*."

Hodwick put up his hands quickly, making hushing noises. He lowered his voice to say, "It won't be like that again. There are ways – things we can say – if we are careful. Very careful. But that starts with building trust. Let me finish. Let me explain. I never wished to betray you, but you see –" His nervous laugh again, again adjusting the glasses. "I thought I was the only one who knew. It was said that no one survived the disaster in Balfair's estate. But the day after you left, Mr Montgomery came looking for you."

Deni jerked upright, fingers tightening around the knife.

Hodwick didn't notice, continuing, "I was so surprised – there was no way I could hide it. They told me things about you that – well, of course I didn't believe them. But what choice did I have? I told them what we had exchanged, between us – and they made efforts to recover the information you took. It was difficult – near impossible – but they have found the rocket, now. They have. I'm so glad you got there first – I might never have seen this otherwise. They wouldn't have told me."

"Is Montgomery out there?" Deni demanded, nodding to the door.

Hodwick slowly shook his head. "Not yet."

Deni moved quickly, pushing past the doctor as he flinched aside. She flung the door open and burst out into the corridor. The way was blocked. Two guards stood either side of the exit, in slate grey Road armour. She spun, knife raised, as they watched her.

"Get out of my way!" she said, loudly, but they didn't move, and she got no closer. They were unafraid, batons ready. They didn't know her knife could cut through their armour, but to surprise one of them wouldn't be enough. Deni spun back to Hodwick's lab, looking through the doorway to the wide window. This high up, the fall would kill her.

Hodwick told her, weakly, "There's nowhere to go, Deni. But we can at least talk."

"Talk about what!" Deni surged back into the room, knife up again. One of the guards followed her as Hodwick backed off. Deni turned the knife towards the guard and got a reaction this time, a flinch. He raised his baton, ready to strike her, but the doctor intervened. "No! Please, we're not done here!"

The guard's eyes, visible through the slit in his helmet, glanced from Deni to Hodwick, all three of them still.

"I've been watched," Hodwick hurried to explain. "This laboratory has been monitored since they learnt you were in the city – after our talk. But you have to understand why. Before you panic, Deni – let me explain –"

"You're a snake and a coward," Deni hissed. "That's the explanation."

"This is over," the guard said. "She's dangerous –"

"Please wait outside!" Hodwick replied in a shrill voice, losing his cool. "You're making a difficult situation worse. I must talk to her!"

The guard grunted in irritation. He didn't respect the doctor, and seemed to have authority, but he did as he was told. His boots clicked against the floor as he walked back out. Hodwick waited until the door was closed and the man was out of earshot. He moved quickly, closer to Deni, but he didn't react to her wavering knife this time, whispering on. "Listen. Balfair's theory – it says something about the world. It's more than a – what would we say – more than a question of changing the landscape. Fixing the sky. It's a message. There aren't many clouds outside Estalia, did you know that?"

Deni did. Exactly the detail that had concerned Qait.

"But they hang over our empire like a blanket. This thing – this idea – that there's something in the clouds – it suggests the Estalians did it. Not the Guard, no – to be more precise, the Gracians. The people before. They *created* this world. And it is the same darkness we find hints of in the secrets of the Mines. You understand?"

Deni tried to. It wasn't science, it was history. Not a matter of the dangers of technology or what might happen to them if the clouds were explained or fixed; it was about the danger of knowing who they were. Where they'd come from. She said, "We created the clouds to save ourselves... only ourselves."

Hodwick responded with rising enthusiasm. "Worse than that, though, isn't it?"

Deni met his eyes. She concluded his thoughts. "If the Gracians were able to save themselves, they were prepared... for what destroyed everything else."

"This is why the Guard shut down ArcTech." Hodwick shifted a little closer, speaking even more quietly. "The more we learn about what created this world, the more we understand that it was not done *to* us, but *by* us. And it reflects upon them, the ones in control, those who inherited this legacy. They know this already, you see?"

"How?" Deni demanded, accusingly. "You're the ones researching it, how could they know!"

Hodwick quickly shook his head. "Look around you! How much have you really seen – of the way the Guard really operates? This Tower itself stretches into the clouds – but I've never been higher than this floor. What goes on up there? Who else is working with them? ArcTech – it wasn't something new – not to them. They have been running this empire for longer than any of us realised there *was* an empire."

"What are you going to do about it?" Deni said.

Hodwick paused. "We need to be very careful –"

"Now?" Her voice rose slightly. "Why not before? I could've run. Could've been free. I thought you'd do something! Make a difference, you said – change things!"

"I want to! And we can – but there's a war, and the Guard need focus. They won't compromise, they'll hurt anyone that gets in the way."

"Fuck the war! This could end it!"

"It can't!" Hodwick said. Footsteps were coming down the hall. His eyes widened imploringly, voice quietening again. "It's not enough to make a difference – it's just an idea. We'd need resources we don't have – to even begin to unravel this. What we need, before anything else, is *time*. We need to survive."

"She's in there?" Montgomery's voice announced his arrival.

Deni skirted to the side, clamping both hands onto her knife. He had survived. He was back and he was there. She could cut him down before she succumbed, at least. Make *some* difference. She had to do that much.

"A minute, for goodness' sake!" Hodwick called back, flustered. He turned his pleading eyes to Deni. "Work with me. Tell them who you've spoken to and what you've said, cooperate. If they think it's over, there may still be hope. We need *time*."

Deni eyed him furiously. Hope for him, he meant. He'd slipped up, helping her in the first place, and rather than embracing it he'd gone the opposite way to her. He was ready to throw it all away to re-establish his oppressors' trust.

"I promise, it's the best solution," Hodwick said.

All she'd wanted was to get rid of the tattooed man. How had she let Tyler persuade her the world deserved her involvement, when this man, the only one who could supposedly help, was no more concerned for others than she'd been?

"That's enough."

The door opened and there he was. Leaning against the doorframe, pistol in his hand. With his leg brace and scarred face, he had none of the charm he'd shown when he first arrived at the estate. For a moment, back then, Deni had dreamt he was a saviour. Now she knew he was more monster than anyone.

"Just tell them – whatever they want to know," Hodwick whispered. He looked more afraid of Montgomery than she was, and it only strengthened her resolve. She was better than this man, this mouse of a man. "They have machines, Deni. Terrible devices to make you talk. There's no need –"

"Enjoyed your chat?" Montgomery asked. His voice was rougher than Deni remembered, but the self-satisfied tone was still there. Deni edged away from Hodwick. There was still the window; might it be better to smash through? Give herself up to the gods.

"She's innocent," Hodwick insisted. "She had no hand in Balfair's work –"

"Innocent," Montgomery sneered. "Look at my face. Does this look like innocence?"

Deni adjusted her grip on the knife, breathing heavier, preparing for his attack.

"Please." Montgomery aimed the pistol at her head. "Don't make this too easy."

There was too large a distance between them, and the four guards still waiting in the hall. Her knife barely extended a few inches from her hand, and his pistol would knock her down before she got anywhere near.

"Put down the knife."

8

Wallen was drinking with a group of filthy men, laughing as Tyler entered the tavern. He managed to force a smile as he approached, but she didn't return it, humour fading as she clocked the slavers behind him. The friends she'd made tensed. She snarled at Vorst, "You step away from him."

The area around the bar went quiet. Some patrons looked pointedly into their drinks, while one or two braver hands slipped towards sheathed weapons.

"It's okay," Tyler said shakily. "We're going to talk, that's all." He turned to Vorst. "Isn't that right?"

"Stop fooling around and get behind me, boy," Wallen said.

"Stand where you like," Vorst said, shoving Tyler. The young man stumbled across the floor, bumping into a drinker who shied away when he saw the slaver. Vorst's face was black on both sides now, smears of dried blood matching his claw-like tattoos. His eyes glistened all the more clearly, white in the black. His chest-armour hung slightly askew. At his side, the woman looked equally dishevelled, her hair tangled over half her face and blood staining her bare right arm. The barkeep lowered a hand towards some concealed weapon.

"This isn't your problem," Vorst said to him.

"You're in my bar."

"The lady doesn't want any trouble," the woman said.

Tyler looked to Wallen with all the reassurance he could muster, then over to the barkeep, whose hand was still dipped out of view. The man looked tough, but he was old. And the other patrons looked no more able; a lot of dirty faces, ragged clothes and tired weapons on drinkers who might not baulk from a fight but certainly wouldn't win. Tyler said, "We're not going to have any trouble. Just gonna talk."

As Wallen and the slavers exchanged vicious looks, Tyler moved to one of the tavern's free tables, a large circular one. He pulled out the nearest chair. The slavers walked through the inn unimpeded as dozens of eyes followed them.

"I'm warning you," the barkeep said, but the slaver lady shot back, "Do your job and get us a round of *glus*."

A murmur of disagreement ran though the room, and the barkeep made a disapproving noise, but he turned to pull their drinks from a towering metal tap. As Wallen joined the slavers and Tyler, she said, "There's no love for the Guard in here. Nor their lackeys."

"I'm no one's fucking lackey," Vorst said. "And I don't threaten easily."

Tyler could see the anger in Wallen's eyes, and knew she'd do whatever she could to take this man down. He also knew she wouldn't stand any better a chance than the others in there. He put a hand to her arm and said, "We need this."

His touch and his smile eased her, slightly. The slaver woman moved away from them, saying, "I'll get those drinks."

Vorst pulled out a chair and sat as she walked to the bar. Wallen gave Tyler one more cautious glance before sitting too, as far as possible from the slaver. Vorst stared unblinkingly at Tyler, and the young man stared back. Whatever kind of monster this man was, Tyler wasn't going to show he was scared.

"Things have taken a turn, you know," Wallen said. She gestured to the bar. "People are talking. We were only a mite ahead of the rebels when we got here. They're marching on the Metropolis. There was a battle outside a market town, two days' hike from here. The Guard lost."

"Good for them," Vorst replied. "The real fight will start when they get here."

The woman returned with a tray of metal tankards, each foaming with ale. She placed one in front of each of them, drawing another nasty glare from Wallen. As she sat, the tattooed lady said, "My treat."

"Let's start properly," Tyler said, trying to sound friendly. "My name's Tyler, this is Wallen. How about you?"

The female slaver's eyes sparkled with humour as the other Vorst receded into quiet hostility. She said, "You're special, aren't you?"

"Tyler," Wallen said, voice thick with restraint. "What're you doing?"

"The Guard are after them, too," Tyler said. "We're in the same situation, now. Please. Give this a chance." He looked at the slavers again, imploring an answer. They both stared with calculating glares. The lady finally caved.

"This is Vorst, one of the most famous Finders in Estalia."

"Finders," Wallen snorted. "Call yourselves what you are, filthy slave traders."

"Hey," Tyler cut in. "Enough. Give this a *chance*. You are?"

As the lady paused, Tyler took her in properly, up close, for the first time. Her elegance was a strange contrast to Vorst's appearance, face slim but soft in features, skin clear where it wasn't marred by blood and dirt, eyes shimmering with intelligence. Her hair was partially braided, swept to one side and shaved high around the ears. She had a V emblem etched on her bloody forearm and an ornate, armoured bird wrapped around the left side of her neck. Vorst introduced her: "This is Cetherine. She'd be as famous as me if she let people talk about her."

She offered Tyler a smile, showing off a few metal teeth of her own, as he said, "Nice to meet you."

Vorst took a swig from his drink and wiped the foam off his mouth with his forearm. It smeared black and red across his cheeks. "Where's the girl?"

"Gone," Tyler replied.

"She left you to dry." Vorst turned a knowing glance to Cetherine. She rolled her eyes and gave him a chip from her pocket, some bet settled.

"She's smart," Cetherine said. "You kept going even after she'd ditched you?"

Her gaze was harder to hold than Vorst's. He was a brute force that could be met with simple resistance. With her, it felt like the more time she had to look at Tyler, the more power it would give her. He didn't look away, though. "Deni was telling the truth," he said. "About everything. You wanted us to doubt it, but I saw how that man talked to you, in that tavern, and I saw them coming for you. He thinks you can't be trusted, the same way they thought we couldn't be. You can't ignore it."

"And what? You think that makes us friends? That we can save the world?"

Tyler's mouth fell open. What if he did? Didn't they? Words escaped him for long enough that Vorst cut in.

"What I told the tracker was true. Her whole estate burnt down. Everyone was killed, bar one man. She'd gutshot him and cracked his skull with a rock. He saw her setting the fires, saw her shooting off rifles. She cut a man's throat. You want to tell me she's honest?"

"The man who survived," Tyler said. "Was he the same one who just sent people to kill you?"

Tyler's eye was drawn away from Vorst by the smile on Cetherine's face. She said, "I like this kid. Okay. Montgomery can't be trusted either. So what?"

"Don't you want to do something about it?"

"You know how we operate?" Vorst said. "How we're *allowed* to operate? The price of running our business is dealing with prick guards threatening to remove our trading status every now and again. We wade through their bullshit, we move on. Sometimes their bullshit gets out of control and we leave it to dissipate. That's all we need to do."

"But you saw the rocket," Tyler said. "You know what happened in the Kennel. You must see how serious this is." Getting no response, he picked up speed, frustrated. "They lied to you! They've been killing ordinary people over this! My uncle – he didn't do anything wrong, didn't even know anything. How can you not care?"

"Caring gets good people killed," Vorst answered coldly.

"They sent you to hunt for Deni, they'll send even worse people to hunt for you."

Vorst smiled, showing his gold teeth. He shook his head without needing to say what Tyler knew he was thinking. *There's no one worse.*

The young man took an exasperated breath. "Who *is* this Montgomery?"

Vorst took another swig, finishing the tankard. He looked around the room briefly, as though deciding whether or not to bother. "He's an asshole. When he came talking about this lunatic girl, with his face mashed up like that, we got the idea it was personal. He's got important friends, though. It makes *personal* dangerous, coming from someone like him."

"It's not that simple," Tyler said. "Deni met with one of their scientists. He said this thing was real – it's not just Montgomery looking to hurt her –"

"Mr Callison Montgomery," Cetherine interrupted. "Once cut a man's ears off because he thought he was *prettier* than him. A man who owned a tailor's on Farrough Street, supplied some of the wealthiest people in the city. He was paraded as a traitor, dragged through the streets and pelted with stones. His shop was burnt down. All because Montgomery got jealous of him. What do you think he'd do on account of someone that smashed his face in?"

Tyler gave Wallen a glance, imploring her to try. Her face was knotted with concern as she took it all in. She asked, "How's a man like that got any power at all?"

"He was a tracker, like your man in the flying machine. Doesn't advertise he's part of the Guard, so he can get to places the Guard aren't welcome. He's done important things for very important people."

"He's an assassin," Vorst corrected.

"Like Qait," Cetherine shrugged.

Tyler frowned, but they continued too quickly for him to ask.

"The point is," Vorst said, "however big an asshole he is, and however innocent you think your girl is, this man ruins lives for a living, with the support of the Guard. And this whole damned city belongs to them. Making whatever Deni was fighting for amount to a fart in the wind, as far as we're concerned. I appreciate the chat, kid. Whatever you think of us, we do prefer to know where we stand. You've cleared it up, at least, and there's no part of my mind that says we need anything more to do with you. But wherever else you thought this was going, it's not."

Tyler hesitated, mind racing in search of some way to convince them. He thought back over what they'd said, where they'd come from, and he blurted out, "You knew Balfair, didn't you? You knew the sort of work he was doing?"

"And?"

"That rocket was designed to change the sky. The days are getting darker and Balfair had an idea why. The Guard know why. Maybe how to stop it. Montgomery might be running this, but there's more to it than him trying to stop Deni. They wouldn't have killed my uncle if that's all this was – they wouldn't have –"

"They might have," Cetherine said. "Listen, kid, with the fighting that's coming, no one's going to care a damn about these fantasies."

"That's not true," Wallen said, before Tyler could explode in frustration. "I've been talking to people in here half the day. There's a rumour come from over the river. A wanderer who claims to have met someone who'd seen the clouds part. At least a theatre full of people have had their ear chewed about this tale. The girl who saw the sky. People were impressed enough to share it, for it to reach us here."

The table went quiet for a moment. Tyler couldn't keep the smile from his face. Helious had told their story, after all. There was some hope in his idea. He looked at Vorst eagerly, imploring. "The Guard spread more stories than anyone, about the good they do, and soon those stories are gonna spread about you. *Vorst, the most famous Finder in Estalia. A traitor!* But we've got a different story. One that says there's hope, if we do something about the people in charge."

Vorst shifted in his seat. "So spread your stories. We're not gonna stop you."

"We need you to fight!" Tyler slapped a hand on the table, surprising the slaver. He took a moment, and a few breaths, staring hard into Vorst's eyes. "I'm not a fighter – but I know what's right. I'll damn well *do* what's right. The people coming for us, they're dangerous – we *need* to be able to fight them. You don't look like someone who'd back down from that. Or run away."

"You're not talking about fighting," Cetherine sighed. "You're talking about telling stories until they come to cut your throat."

"No. I'm talking about standing up for Deni," Tyler said. "She has the proof. And she's my friend. You can save her from them."

Vorst let out a bass chuckle. "Out of the goodness of our hearts, right?"

"I don't believe you wanted to kill us," Tyler said, more quietly. "Not on the boat, not before, not now. I don't believe the world is bad, or that all people want only to help themselves. I can't believe that. And I don't believe anyone who could see the right thing to do would walk away from it. No matter who they were."

The slavers kept staring at him, Vorst giving nothing away and Cetherine appearing more amused than ever, one side of her mouth turned up in a smile. Vorst nodded, finally, making his decision, and shoved his chair back. He said, "We've got a truck to fix, since you handled it so carefully."

Tyler shot up from his seat, mouth open, wanting to say more, but he couldn't. They were proving him wrong that very moment, as they stood. Cetherine swallowed her drink. She said, "Thanks for the pep talk, anyway."

They nodded to Wallen by way of farewell, and turned away.

"Wait!" Tyler panicked. "What if I paid you? I've got some money – or – I can get some. I can pay it off – whatever your price."

The slavers gave him a pitying look. Cetherine no longer looked amused. They didn't even bother to answer, and his voice fell weakly as he pleaded, "You could take me. Sell me, whatever it is you do – I don't care – isn't that worth something? I'm a good worker. Skilled. Just... get Deni back. Do something about this. I know you can."

Vorst took a step towards him, and Tyler held his breath. The slaver's eyes ran over him, assessing him – considering the possibility of taking him as payment? Or something else? Vorst's eyes narrowed, a shadow of something passing over them – a thought he didn't voice. He shook his head. though. He turned away again, and Tyler shot forward. "You have to –"

Wallen held him back. "Easy, Tyler. Give it up, bless you. You're the proof that not all the world's rotten. It's just that most of it is."

The slavers didn't respond to her comment, making their way out. Tyler watched their muscle-lined backs as they thumped across the room. Vorst's shoulders were lower, his steps slower, as though in thought, but he was walking away all the same. As the pair reached the door, Cetherine glanced back one last time. Her eyes rested on Tyler too, similarly assessing him, seemingly serious now. Her mouth bunched to one side, as though she couldn't quite figure him out. She shook her head, too, and said something inaudible to Vorst as the pair left.

9

In a tight chamber, barely big enough for the platform that ran along its back wall, Deni stared hard at the bulkhead door, imagining what she would see when it opened again. She had got there in a daze, barely able to focus after Montgomery had jammed a fist into her gut. There had been no question of running, nor fighting, in the end. It was a strange miracle that he hadn't killed her already.

Then, it was a hellish curse that he was alive.

The one monster she was certain she had overcome, through her own volition. He was alive and she was at his mercy. But he hadn't killed her. He had merely ripped her knife away, shoved her into this room and locked her there. Keeping her alive to exact a worse kind of revenge.

When the door creaked open, she jumped back, hitting the wall. Montgomery shifted into the light, the brace around his leg clicking as he entered. He wasn't alone; a woman in a long white overcoat entered alongside him. Her face was devoid of any emotion, her shoulder-length hair cut at straight angles around her face.

"We need to hear your story," Montgomery said. "Everything."

Deni said nothing. She had no story to tell them. They had known she was coming back, which meant they had heard from the tattooed man. Hodwick had talked to them, too, at some point. All she could hope for was that Tyler had run. Escaped all this.

"Make this easy," Montgomery said. "Tell me everyone you've spoken to."

Deni's eyes bored into his. The scar she'd left him with made his leer a grimace. There was a flicker of aggravation, his eyes moving slightly to the side, as he appeared to sense she was judging it.

"Do you know what a flaying gauntlet is?" he asked abruptly. He paused for effect. Of course she didn't, she knew nothing of his world. "It attaches over your forearm. The screws wind into your flesh, bracing it there. A rotary device hangs over your arm with a set of tiny blades. It falls very slowly. Very slowly. Tiny blades... peeling away your skin."

Deni wanted to make him stop, unable to avoid picturing it. She had seen the weapons of war Balfair made: the fastest and most efficient ways for the Guard to kill people. She could imagine that they had people working on the exact opposite. Still, she was quiet. He wanted her to suffer, wanted her to plead. She wouldn't give him that pleasure.

He didn't have his pistol out. There was barely room for her to move, but she could jump him. Squeeze his neck. It'd be like wringing clothes dry. If she moved quickly enough, she might get a grip before he could beat her back. Would she be able to hold on? What weapons did this woman have under her coat?

"She does talk, doesn't she?" the woman asked dryly.

"Yes," Montgomery replied. "Perhaps we should stick to single-word answers. How many people have you spoken to?"

No. Deni knew she wouldn't be able to hurt him, but she could at least get under his skin. Make him angry by not giving him what he wanted. Let them torture her. She wouldn't let them get to Tyler or Wallen. She'd do nothing that could hurt her friends.

"Deni," the lady said. "My name is Inquisitor Napier. It is my job to make people talk. I want to be clear that you will answer to us, one way or another. We have to know who you spoke to."

"They're dead." The words came easily, although she'd never meant to say them. In the surprised silence that followed, Deni realised what she was saying. Something that might help. She rushed it out: "They all died. In the boat. The slavers tore it apart. It exploded. Tyler was... he tried to help the lady out."

"No one got off the boat?" Napier confirmed. Deni paused.

They must have known she'd escaped in the truck with Wallen and Tyler; the slavers would have told Montgomery that. She'd said one thing and already messed up. Unless she went all the way with it. She could be convincing, couldn't she? Taking a breath, she said, "I stole the truck to get away. Alone. The same as when I left the estate."

"Nonsense," Montgomery sneered.

"Qait escaped the boat. He shot one of the slavers," Deni said. "But I left him behind. It was just me."

"Why would the slavers lie?" Napier responded, her voice as flatly emotionless as her face.

"Because it's embarrassing," Deni addressed this point to Montgomery. He narrowed his eyes. She said, "There might not be much left, but if you search the remains of that boat you'll find them. And I told no one else. You killed Chetan; now you've killed Tyler and Qait and the lady, too."

Napier turned to Montgomery. He shook his head, but said nothing.

"The slavers," Deni added quietly, trying to cement it. "I told them, too. The tattooed man and the woman with him. I thought I could persuade them." She took a chance. "They said they didn't know. That you said I was just a murderer."

"They spoke about me?" Montgomery raised an eyebrow.

"Yes."

"And you told them about the rocket."

"What I knew," Deni nodded. "They said..." She pictured Vorst, scheming behind his glittering metal teeth. "It was worth double."

Montgomery shifted, unable to hide his discomfort. It wouldn't matter how much he believed; if he at least doubted Vorst, she might get something back from this. They had killed others for knowing less. The slavers had seen the rocket, after all.

Napier said, "If you're lying, you'll suffer more, you understand?"

Deni said, "I wouldn't have come alone if I wasn't alone."

This seemed to satisfy the woman. Without another word, Napier left, but Montgomery stayed behind. As he stared at Deni, his smirk returned. "You're a fool, and you're done, you know that, don't you? You think you're clever. That maybe you inherited something from that moron Balfair? It doesn't matter. Whatever lies you have left to tell. Tricks to play. There's no escape."

"I've told the truth," Deni whispered, as if it would help.

"By now the slavers are already dead," he confided. "Your tricks won't make the slightest difference. Your friends, too. For real, this time. You're alone, Deni. And all you've got left is to wait to die."

Deni determined to give him no more of her fear. She had defied him once and she had to do it again. She had to, because she could see in his face the need for her to suffer. He hated her because she'd bested him. She said, "I was alone before. When I made you a cripple."

Montgomery surged forwards. Deni jumped up onto the bench, but there was nowhere to go; her back hit the wall as his hand clamped over her throat and squeezed. Deni gagged, clawing at his wrist, but the initial impact drove most of the strength out of her. He drove her into the wall and didn't let go. She squeaked as the air was pushed out of her, fingers barely able to grasp him, and he drew his face up next to hers. His eyes were mad, like an animal's, though he'd somehow found his smile again, enjoying his own rage.

"I know you…" His spit flecked into her face. "I told them of the work you did for Balfair. Persuaded them how much *use* –" he shook her as she gasped for air, another jolt into the wall knocking the last of the fight out of her "– how much use you could be!"

Deni's vision went dark, her attacker blurring as her last gasps left her.

His grip relaxed and she fell to the floor with a huge intake of breath. Dropping onto her knees, eyes flooding with tears, she had no chance to recover. His hand closed over her hair. He yanked her up, forcing her neck back as far as it would go, and he drew her knife from his pocket. He traced the tip down her cheek and stopped it against her neck.

"You remember, don't you?" he said. She fixed her terrified eyes on him, unable to make a sound, much less move. She saw past his face, though, and past the knife. There was blood on the shoulder of his suit. "I had a better measure of you in minutes than your master ever did. You're poison in human form." He twisted his words cruelly into her ear. "You're going to suffer for me."

She blubbed, recovering just enough air to utter, "Please."

"I knew you'd come back," Montgomery continued. "None of these fools listened. I knew you would lie through your teeth, but still they didn't listen. But now it's my turn. I know how to make you suffer. And you will. You'll wish you'd died in that swamp. You'll wish it was those road animals who caught up to you, instead of me."

Deni tried to shake her head, to somehow resist him, but he shook her again and pressed his face even closer. He said, "You see me? What you made of me? Do you know how it feels to have everyone stare? You will. Imagine it. I promise it to you. Everyone will stare."

Montgomery shoved her away and she got a hand up just in time to keep herself from striking the bench. He paced around her, straightening his jacket and recovering his calm. She felt his boot on her side and was tipped over by a short kick, unable to defend herself. As she rolled onto her back and weakly protested, he pulled a roll of paper from his pocket and unravelled it. *The* roll of paper – from the rocket.

"No." Deni raised a hand towards him. He wasn't looking at her. He held the paper up like a string and took something from his pocket. He flicked it open and clicked the top. It sparked.

A flint.

That paper – the rocket's findings – the answers to the sky – it was everything there in his hand – at a flame's tip –

The spark caught the paper's edge and it flashed up.

"No!"

Montgomery waved his hand as the fire spread, then let go. Deni's eyes flared open as she watched Balfair's research erupt in a rain of embers. She screamed, "No!"

The opening of the clouds – the light she'd seen – the hope of change – it drifted to the floor. A pile of ash. His boot came down on it, close to Deni's face, and she gagged as he ground what was left into the tiles.

Everything they had fought for.

Gone.

Deni couldn't breathe, staring at the ashes. She couldn't blink, even as her vision blurred from tears; she couldn't move as her hands dug rigidly into the floor. It was the gateway to the sky. It was their way out, their only weapon. It was the light in the dark – the thing she and Tyler were going to see *together*. She tried to make a sound but couldn't.

Montgomery removed his boot. He was soaking up her distress. He said, "A piece of you is dying. The first bit. There's plenty more to go."

Deni wrenched her gaze from the ashes, up to him. This man. This one, vile man who was prepared to ruin everyone's chances of change. She locked her hate on him. She imagined his bloody face, the deathly body she'd left behind at Balfair's estate, the memory that had haunted her as clearly as the threat of the tattooed man. She never should have stopped. She should have kept hitting him until there was nothing left.

She needed a second chance.

She needed him to die. Painfully. Brutally. Infinitely slowly.

"There it is," he said, her expression apparently pleasing him. "Save that rage, you little witch. You'll need it when the world comes out to see you die."

With that, he strode out of the room. Deni slumped forwards, a hand sliding through the ashy remains and scattering them with one last dance before her. She breathed quickly and deeply, trying to regain control of her body. How could he – the animal – they *wanted* the world to suffer. He'd damned them all – the bastard – *how could he*.

She collapsed forward, bringing her arms up over her head, trying to hide from it all. She groaned loud and low. No. *No.*

Outside the cell, she caught the sound of quiet talking. Napier had been waiting, maybe another guard with her. They didn't care about what he'd done. Montgomery was unhinged, and his vendetta was personal, and he'd damned them all and they didn't *care*. They were letting him do it. They wanted the world to suffer.

They all needed to die. *They* needed to suffer.

Deni sat back on her haunches and took a deep breath, gritting her teeth, ready to let it all out. She stared at the door, furious, willing them to see her, to hear her, to know her. She took another deep breath. Another.

Their footsteps retreated down the hall.

She swallowed it. Tasted it. Listened to the shaking sound of her own breath.

They were doomed. All of them, doomed.

10

There was no hope of getting over the river. Every person and carriage that ventured onto the bridge was subjected to a gauntlet of two or three inspections as guards loitered behind barriers, rifling through bags and angrily turning people back the way they'd come. In the space of only a few days, the city had become increasingly locked down, and the populace seemed happy about it. Catching the look on Tyler's face as he stared at a guard emptying an elderly lady's basket, a passer-by had commented, "Better this than the alternative."

Tyler didn't need to ask what the supposed alternative was. Street-criers were making it known from every corner, delivering messages ten times madder and more violent than the ones he'd heard in Bawkley.

"Outpost 12 have secured victory in the Mystle Ruins – another Kandish force has been put down, and those that lost their homes to the rebels are being cared for!"

"The Bandit of Kelp has been captured – trial set for tomorrow! The food stalls of Blanker Square are safe again!"

"Rallying cry for all men of age – Hunterwell Road Guard open for recruits!"

The subtle rumours about the girl who'd seen the sky barely resurfaced. People in taverns talked about the cloud-parter as though it were an old fairy tale, as a joke and a distraction, but that was as far as it seemed to go. No one was sure exactly what it referred to: had this girl herself parted the clouds? Was there a machine capable of doing it? Was it a metaphor? Tyler and Wallen tried to drop it into conversations, with little luck.

"I heard a crazy story about a girl who saw the clouds part," Tyler would begin, smiling over a drink, like it was nothing. "Apparently they're talking about it in Sebank."

"You think that's a good one," came a typical reply. "I heard about a reptile in the sewers – apparently these chemicals they dug out from the Mines made the thing huge."

It became a competition, to see who could produce the most

outlandish tale, and the cloud-parter barely factored in their imaginations.

In between trying to spread rumours, Tyler stalked the bank of the Drain, concealed in a fisherman's cloak, asking if anyone had seen someone of Deni's description. The streets and waterways were so crowded, people said they'd seen too many people to know one way or another. It was hard to offer a distinct description of her, anyway. If only she'd had some identifying mark on her. Except then the Guard might find her more easily, too. It wasn't until he asked a trapper that he got a different response: "What's the price on her?"

The man had taken him for a tracker, or a finder, assuming Deni to be a wanted woman. There was a chance, wasn't there, that if she hadn't resurfaced, the Guard might have spread a wider net for her. Tyler thought, then, to check the Hunt Bulletins.

He found the nearest Guard Station to the Drain and started searching the many thick flaps of paper that covered its external wall. The Hunt Bulletins could be found throughout the city; dozens of crudely reproduced faces, each as ugly and unclear as the next, printed on coarse papers pinned one over another. The messages on them were clear, even if Tyler didn't understand the writing: the criminals were labelled with one or two words summarising the evils they'd done, and a big number showing how many chips their capture was worth. There were men and women, thick and thin, bearded, bald, ugly, normal-looking. None of the faces looked real, the simple line-work depicting the basic identifiable details of these monsters. A nose-ring, a glass eye, a cheek scar.

Tyler's eyes fell on one that startled him still. A half-painted face and teeth on show in a snarl, to draw attention to their texture: a sheen like metal.

It had to be Vorst. Was the slaver still around, or was this old news?

He searched the nearby pictures but didn't see another. There was no sign of Cetherine, and nothing similar to Deni.

Tyler took the picture and crept warily into the Guard Station. They had no call to recognise him, did they? No one knew who he was, and if there weren't pictures up for Deni then there surely wouldn't be guards out looking for him. Not ordinary guards, at least.

He approached a low desk, where a lightly armoured Road Guard was writing a message with an ink pen. Tyler cleared his throat, and when the man didn't look up he placed the poster down in front of him. The guard paused, scanning the image, and shook his head.

"Bullshit. If you'd got him we'd have heard it."

"I want to help bring him in," Tyler lied. "What can you tell me?"

The guard looked up at him. He was only a little older than Tyler, and his face was patched with thin adolescent hair. He replied, "Don't go there. The whole Guard's out for his blood. You'd only get in the way."

"What'd he do?"

"Seriously?" The guard regarded Tyler oddly. "You didn't hear about the fires in Grenevic? Two guards dead trying to stop him. More, over here. This guy's a monster."

Tyler paused. Maybe it was the Guard's propaganda at work again, damning Vorst the same way they'd spread stories about the rebels and traitors and all that was happening outside the city. Exactly as he'd expected to happen. Or maybe the slaver was actually up to something. Had their conversation somehow got through to him?

"Something else?" the guard prompted, drawing Tyler back into the room.

"Yeah," Tyler said. "There was someone I saw a few days back, thought there might be some word about her. A girl, a little older than me. Dark hair. I'm not sure how else to describe her, but..." Tyler stopped. The guard was already looking at him with an impatient expression. "What?"

"You're subtle, I'll give you marks for that, but that doesn't make you any better than the half-dozen other leeches I've had in here this morning."

Tyler frowned. "I don't follow?"

"Right." The guard pushed back in his seat, exhaling. "You tell me you saw her doing something suspicious, you tell me you signalled some guard about it and saw them go after her, but you left them to it. Then you heard who she might be, and realised you might've been the one that helped get her caught. Thinking, oh, maybe there's a reward for that?"

Tyler shook his head.

"All you chancers swinging in trying to get a piece of the action. Happens every time word gets out that someone high-profile's got a trial coming."

Tyler burst into the tavern bedroom to find Wallen hunched over one of the narrow beds, busy organising a small pile of belongings. Before he could bring her his news, she said, "Pack up, it's time to go."

"What?" Tyler stalled, noting her battered attaché case. In the few days since they'd returned to the city, she had collected enough clothing to fill it.

"I've found my nephew," she said. "He's got a room for us. Near the Mines. And not a moment too soon; we need to get away from here, I can feel the vultures circling."

"But..." Tyler could see in her resigned slump that she wasn't just saying it was time to move. She was saying it was time to give up. He shook his head. "Wait. Listen. I've just been to a local Guard Station. Do you know what they're saying?"

"Sure," Wallen said. "They're rounding up enemies of the Empire. Everyone's a suspect, everyone's a potential informer. Huey, down the hall, they took him last night. Apparently he'd been promoting traitorous messages."

"Huey..." Tyler recalled. One of the men she'd been drinking with. A harmless drunk. "Why would they..."

"Because they *can*," Wallen snapped. "The closer the fighting gets, the more they're taking advantage. We've done what we can, Tyler, and it hasn't worked – Qait was right. No one cares about the sky, or what the Guard might be hiding, or that an innocent girl might be missing. These rebels and these traitors they keep talking about have everyone thinking only about how to protect themselves. It's time to get out from under this – we've got no money left, and we're only making it more likely for someone to find us, hanging around talking to people. It's safe at my nephew's. From there we can see about getting you home."

"No!" Tyler said forcefully. "What use is *home*? What am I gonna do, return to roofing, with what I've seen – what I know? *Listen* – they're saying they've caught someone. A girl they're blaming all these fires around the Towers on. A terrorist – in league with the rebels. The Guard are going to address everyone – tomorrow – and lay out what's going on. You know, *explain* to the city where they stand – where we all stand. They're gonna make an example of her."

"They're spreading more lies," Wallen replied warily.

"Wallen," Tyler spoke desperately. "Do you hear what I'm saying? They've got Deni. And they'll make her answer for all the crimes in this city – for the rebellion itself, if they can get away with it. People have already started talking about her, thinking she's some villain. We have to do something. We have to be there to answer back."

"Answer back?" Wallen said. "How do you expect to do that?"

Tyler paused, breathing deeply to recover from his outburst. He'd pictured the crowds gathering to hear from the Guard and knew he had to stop them. To speak up and be heard. He pictured the stage, and the speakers, and imagined the volume of it all. Helious's words came back to him. Not just anyone was allowed an audience in Speakers Square. The Guard made sure of it. But Qait had made an offhand comment about it, too; those pipes could be manipulated. Tyler gave Wallen a look as the idea formed more clearly in his mind. He told her, "There's a way. But it's dangerous. You should go to your nephew. Be safe. Leave it to me."

"Oh hell!" Wallen thumped the bag on the bed. "Not on your life."

11

Deni held her knees tight to her chin, staring into the darkness. The warnings of Balfair and Sincade circled around her head, telling her that she had been lucky. Isolated in the estate, doing good work, comfortable. Lucky that she wasn't free, fending for herself.

They had been right. Qait had been right, too. She had let Tyler get to her, with his ideas about goodness and helping. His kindness was useless. If it worked for him, he wouldn't have been caught up in this mess and he wouldn't have lost what was left of his family. He wouldn't have been living in that shack scraping around for a living to begin with. Did anyone ever get anywhere worthwhile by *doing the right thing*?

She should've stayed ruthless, all along. Right back to when she'd left Montgomery bloody on the ground, instead of finishing him off. She was fool to believe anything could survive in this world without being utterly ruthless.

The cell door creaked open and Montgomery entered, alone. She shot away from him, but he did not come closer, pulling the door carefully to. He was wearing his cruel smile again, about to share something terrible. He held a vial of liquid up in one hand, but didn't explain it, waiting for her to recognise the sounds of celebration just audible through the crack in the doorway. There were vaguely distant drumbeats.

"Do you hear it?" he asked sinisterly. "The city is gathering for you."

Deni glared at him. Why would anyone care about her? Why would *he* want them to see her, after he'd gone to such pains to silence her?

Reading the questions in her eyes, he said, "It's over. The rocket is gone, along with all traces of it. We even found the bandits that were near it." He smiled at her confusion. "They're gone too, before you try and tell me you spoke with them. We all know your propensity for lies. It's a good thing, really, for you – they're convinced that torture would be pointless. The best we can do – all we need to do – is put you on show to draw out whatever sympathisers you have left." He crept slightly closer, lowering his voice. "That seemed to me the finest, and only, torture that would matter to you anyway. The people are waiting, ready to believe what we tell them. They will hate you, and in death you will bring ever more suffering, as you burn for whatever sins you might have accused the Guard of."

Deni said nothing. The thousands they could turn against her were the same ones she had once dreamt might help her. Sincade had *always* been right, and the goodness she had imagined in society was a lie, her own creation. They were all rotten. It was a rotten city and being surrounded by more people had only ever put her more in danger.

Still.

At least she'd removed any doubt.

"I know you won't *want* to say anything," Montgomery continued. "All you ever really wanted was quietness, wasn't it? But they have insisted on this measure nevertheless. You've surprised people before, after all." He took the lid off the vial of liquid and a pungent aroma wafted out. "You've no idea how happy I am that we can prove it to you, fully and completely, that you *never* had any hope. Every choice you ever made was bound, inevitably, to bring you a miserable life and a miserable death."

What she took from his message wasn't hopelessness or fear, though. If death was guaranteed, and a horde of people somewhere out there were calling for it, then she had nothing left to worry about. She would not suffer in the way he thought she would. These people did not matter. When the braying masses took her life, she'd know that her failings were meaningless. Tyler had convinced her to try and save the world, instead of just herself, but this world didn't deserve saving. It didn't matter if they hated her. They didn't matter.

The one thing she could do, at least, was to share some misery with this vile man who wanted to control her death. She told him, voice as clear as she could make it, "You can kill me, but I'll always be the maid that ruined your face."

Montgomery's smile faltered, but he wasn't swayed. He said, "Is that all?"

Deni took a breath. No. She had more. She had hurt him more

than she knew, judging by the venom that he showed her. She answered carefully, chest swelling with defiance. "It's all I need. There will always be something wrong with you. Your flesh will always be marked and your leg will always click. And you will always think of me. Every time a child gets scared of your face, sensing from your appearance what's true in your heart. There will *always* be something wrong with you, and people will *always* know it, no matter what you do to me."

Montgomery's face twisted with the first hint of irritation. Her words did mean something to him. She was right. He told her, almost angrily, "You chose a bad time to find a voice. This could have saved you from the pain." He tilted the vial, and the first drops seeped out onto the floor. "It'd be an awful shame if there wasn't quite enough. Don't worry, it'll still keep you quiet. But you'll feel everything. Consider it my final gift."

With that, he launched at her, a hand gripping her neck as she tried to buck away. The other hand thrust the vial towards her. She gagged and cried out, her calm defiance forgotten as he forced the inadequate portion of poison into her mouth.

The approach to Speakers Square was blocked by a sea of people, five streets deep, passable only through slow jostling. Wallen wasn't happy with the plan, but Tyler was proud to see she'd stuck with him, even as they waded into trouble. She felt the same way about Deni and the rocket's secret as he did, even if she'd offered so many words of caution along the way. She'd seen what the Guard did to her family, after all, just as they had to his. They needed exposing, and change had to come – whatever it cost them.

More nimble than her, used to slipping through crowds and eager to get to his destination, Tyler found himself moving away as Wallen struggled to keep up. The din approaching Speakers Square was immense, far busier and more raucous than Tyler had ever seen it before. The festival atmosphere that had been spread over the city reached a pinnacle here, with the music of makeshift instruments colliding from all directions, and people's voices rising ever louder to compete with them.

The Guard were out in large numbers, various colours of armour visible in clusters throughout the crowd. They were joining in the merriment with more drinks and games, or hemmed in by the busyness of it all. With the resentful looks Wallen was giving them, Tyler worried some would take notice. They didn't appear to be looking out for anyone in particular, though. There were people under those suits of armour, after all, and whatever they stood for, this was a day of celebration that they must have simply wanted to be involved in.

He only hoped that would be enough to give him the opportunity he needed.

Half the city were gathered there, and the means to talk to them was available, if he could say enough before the Guard stopped him. It was a big risk, a dream, that the pipes of the square's horns could be manipulated. But it had to work. The Guard couldn't silence everyone, not if they all found out the truth at once.

"Hold up, Tyler!" Wallen called. He twisted back; she was a short way behind, separated from him by dozens of bodies, distracted by something to the side. Tyler slowed down, trying to follow her gaze, but with so many people he couldn't see what she'd picked out.

"What is it?" he called back. She moved towards him, sideways, as she kept her eyes on whatever she'd seen, bumping into people.

"Thought it might be them," she said.

Tyler looked again, still unable to follow. "Who?"

"Never mind," Wallen muttered. "Could've been anyone."

Tyler continued with concern that there was already a threat in their midst. There weren't many people in the city Wallen was likely to recognise, so he allowed himself the brief fantasy that it might have been the slavers, somehow returned. Was what the guard had said about Vorst true – had he really started fighting against them within the city? Perhaps they weren't entirely alone.

The square came into view ahead, its towering walls lined with arches clear between the gaps in the buildings. Tyler ducked and dived across a group of people, picking up speed as he got closer. He kept low, slipping between legs, offering rushed apologies, and heard Wallen's complaints behind him, the larger lady finding it difficult to make her way through as the throng of bodies only got denser.

The sounds of revelry quietened as people shouted at them, "No cutting!"

"We waited hours for this space!"

As Tyler rounded another group of people, a man snarled at Wallen to stop, blocking her path. "Go back, you got no right."

"Let me pass, you gutter-swiller," Wallen snapped. "Before I flatten you."

They were nearing their destination but it was getting harder to move and the people were understandably irate. Getting into the square must've required a lot of time and effort for those who'd already made it; they had no patience for people who were stealing their spaces. As Wallen argued with the man, Tyler searched the nearby walls for the pipes.

Qait had said that once the valves were opened, you could speak into them. These pipes stretched for miles around the nearby buildings, but he was confident he'd have to use one of the ones in the square, before they split off in different directions, if he wanted to be heard. He had to keep going; this wasn't close enough to the centre. The crowd was too thick, though, and it would only be moments before another angry bystander blocked the way.

A whistle sounded from the edge of the crowd. Guards started coming towards them, taking an interest in the commotion. Wallen glanced to Tyler. As she stared past him, to the increasingly thick crowd, he read her eyes. She couldn't go further, not without trouble. He couldn't either, not without a distraction. She was going to do something stupid. He held her gaze for a second, partly willing her not to, partly apologetic because he knew she had to.

Tyler ducked past more people, head low, as Wallen started shouting behind him, met by shouts from the guards: "I'm warning you – step aside or I'll break your face!"

"Try it, you oaf!"

"What's going on here? Stop in the name of Estalia!"

The first wall of the square was just a short distance away, the brass pipes almost within reach. There was a sudden press of movement as someone lurched into action, knocking the crowd into a wave. Tyler jumped up through the last lines of people, putting his hands on the nearest shoulders and finding a foothold on a barrel being used as a table. Amid protests, he scrambled over heads, moving quickly and knocking people off balance. As a clutch of angry voices cursed him, he flew the final few feet and caught hold of the brass pipe, ignoring the pain that lanced through the cut on his shoulder. He found footing on the pipe's brackets and pulled himself up. Gripping one section of pipe after another, he clambered out of reach of the furious people trying to drag him back down. They bellowed in annoyance and disbelief. "Get him down from there!"

Wallen's yell rose above the others. "Move, I got every right to be in the square!"

Driven to get clear of the danger, Tyler kept climbing, up past a window in the building that flanked the square, where a group of spectators flinched back inside. At the next window up, someone leant out to catch him. Tyler dodged to the side as he continued past the man. A flapping hand fell short and the man shouted, "The broom, get the broom!"

Tyler sped on before the man could return. A few metres further up, he could see a connection in the pipe near the relative safety of a lip of concrete that jutted from the wall: the top of one of the acoustic arches. He reached it and pressed his behind into it for support, seizing the palm-sized nut that held the pipe closed.

The pipe vibrated under him with a tremendous rattle and he slipped, clutching the nut and the wall to stop from falling. A sound followed a moment later, rising into the arches; a rumbling announcement horn.

The pipe rattled again as the horn sounded two more times.

The vast throng of people in the square below went still, a thousand parties pausing in anticipation. Tyler froze too, taking stock. He was twenty metres up, and could see right across Speakers Square to the main stage, where twenty clean-armoured guards stood in wait, an announcer blasting his trumpet into the pipe opening at the stage's centre.

The ground was hidden under the shoulder-to-shoulder press of people. The crowd below put their frustration with him aside to search for the source of the announcement. A short distance into the crowd, Wallen had stopped, one hand raised ready to strike someone, the other pushing people back. A handful of guards had surrounded her, closing in, but they had paused too.

A rush of quietness swept over the square.

"Ladies and gentlemen," the announcer on the stage bellowed into the pipes. His voice repeated itself a hundred times over from various spots around the square. "Prepare for the Coming of the Guard."

Deni's senses were slowly returning as the carriage reached the square. It had been a sedative, not a poison; Montgomery didn't mean to kill her yet. As if she needed further restraints, with her muscles already withering from so little food or water since her capture.

The streets were alive with celebration, and it was hard to tell what was real and what she was imagining in her confused state. A series of road vehicles moved around her, faster, as though her carriage was moving slowly to give everyone a good look. She wasn't the only one. At least two or three other cages were rolling nearby, with equally bedraggled-looking people inside them. In the closest one was a skeletal man with a thick, matted beard. He gave her occasional glances, eyes filled with sadness.

A machine trundled past on inconceivably high wheels, metal circles surrounded by hard rubber. Its walls and roof were armoured, with spikes along the edges, surmounted by a circular tower with guards hanging out of the window-slits, waving at the crowd. Behind it came a group of bikes, like the couriers used but bigger. Noisier.

Trumpets blared. People cheered. Something throbbed above.

Deni leant to the side, trying to look up. Beneath the clouds was the belly of a flying machine, a carriage of metal with a canvas balloon above, enormous propellers sticking out on arms at the sides.

The mass of machines, with their coughing engines, spewed a cloud of smoke that masked the crowd. Faces appeared and disappeared, running close to the vehicles to get a clearer look, then fleeing to avoid getting crushed.

Horns sounded ahead, another trumpet blast announcing their arrival. Deni watched lines of people parting for her. Their faces were demonic, spitting in her direction, shouting vulgar things she could barely make out.

Why did they hate her?

Who did they think she was?

She retreated towards a corner of the cage, but they were jeering from all directions. Hurled projectiles twanged against the bars. With nowhere to hide, the safest spot was in the middle of the mobile room. She curled up, hands over her head, trying to block out the noise. Wishing herself away.

There were hundreds of people watching. Shouting at her, wishing her harm. All the people in the Metropolis, crying for her blood. She shuddered, tears forming in her eyes. Uncontrollable, weak tears.

They gave her no time to cry. The waggon creaked to a halt and the doors opened. Rough hands clamped onto her shoulders and, as she tried to kick and break free, something – some*one* – struck her hard across the face. Knocked into a fresh daze, she went limp as they pulled her between the gnashing faces of the crowd, banging against people, and steps, her feet dragging.

A distant, tinny voice reached her above the clamour. "...present to you Enemies of the Empire. In their vanquishing, we open the gates for a prosperous, *safe* future."

Deni was thrown down again, her knees smashing into the floor. A hand gripped her shoulder fiercely, holding her up and still. A wave of roaring voices hit her, the occasional vicious faces now replaced by a field of them. Ten thousand angry eyes wildly staring at her, the black circles of countless open mouths screaming in her direction.

Deni couldn't move, staring back at them. Everyone was watching her. Hating her. She couldn't flee, couldn't so much as draw her eyes away from the horrific scene. Everyone was here for her now. And they wanted her death.

12

Tyler raced to unscrew the pipe nut as the crowd focused on the Guard's parade. Occasional announcements came through the pipes, delivered with the audacious showmanship of the circus ringmaster. Great machines moved down the wide street flanking the square, visible through the square's entrances; the steam-engines, armoured bugs and cannons on wheels were a noisy collection of riveted panels, smoking pipes and exposed mechanics. Some of them came to a halt around the square, towering over the crowd like watchful guard dogs. A gasp of awe swept through the square as an airship floated overhead.

The nut came loose with a thump of air. Tyler pulled himself closer.

"...for the planned fortification of the Mines!" The announcer's words blasted out of the hole, into Tyler's face, almost making him fall. The change in volume from the nearby horns was clear, though, with the announcement travelling nowhere near as far. The faces below started turning his way with concern.

"You're ruining it!" someone yelled. Tyler took a moment to scan the crowd again. In the distraction of the parade, Wallen had moved, and the guards approaching her were packed in tight. Tyler couldn't see where she had gone. It didn't matter, as long as she was safe.

"But before we celebrate the successes to come," the announcer continued, "let us celebrate what we have achieved. It is my greatest pleasure, and greatest honour, to introduce the Supreme Commander – and the enemies of the Empire that he has personally vanquished!"

As the crowd cheered, Tyler looked back to the stage. Eight people in ragged clothing were kneeling there, four on each side of the podium. Each of them had a guard in black armour standing behind them. The announcer moved to the side, and Supreme Commander Felez took his place to speak into the pipe at the centre, armour shining with its ceremonial grandeur.

"You've been waiting a long time, so I'll get straight to it. The people gathered before you have been captured through the tireless diligence of your loyal guardsmen. First, the Bombers of Brofton. These two rebels temporarily disabled Outpost 7, but could not evade capture. They confessed their plans to destroy the Southern Sea forts on behalf of the murderess Elzia. They are all that remains of a team of four. Their so-called Scourge of the South Sea is over."

One of the indicated men started shouting, but whatever he said was drowned out by the violent retorts of the crowd, as righteous anger spread through the square. Without warning, the guard at the man's side drew a pistol and fired.

There was barely a second of surprised silence before the cheers started again. The man collapsed, blood pooling around his head. The people at the front, sprayed by blood, were jumping and cheering more enthusiastically than anyone.

"Their terror is at an end!" Felez joined in the cheers, his amplified voice barely louder than the din. A second shot followed, and the next man in line crumpled. Tyler let out a sound of protest, desperate to do something.

"Now – your fears over the Fewhaven uprising have been heard! Meet the factory worker who poisoned a hundred good men, persuading them to take up arms for *his own greed*. This wretched traitor plotted to supplant the Mayor of Fewhaven, and conspired with rebels to arm his renegades. So that *he could take charge*. The armoured fist of the Guard has ensured that the threat is over, my friends! Fear. No. More."

Another gunshot answered the ferocious demands of the crowd. Another prisoner fell. The next in line started wailing, a howl just loud enough to be heard above the shouts. Another shot cut him off.

They were halfway down the line. Four people dead, people who might have been anyone. Tyler was so transfixed in disgust that he hadn't noticed who was next. On the other side of the speaker was a slighter figure, female, in dirty worker's clothes. Her head was tilted down, her short dark hair covering her face like a hood.

The crowd heaved with enthusiasm, some of the shouts reaching Tyler.

"Crush the rebels!"

"Keep them from our doors!"

The Supreme Commander held up his hands, waiting for the yells to die down. The crowd kept shouting, but their volume decreased enough for Felez to talk over them.

"Uncertainty and rumour are the lifeblood of the traitors and rebels. We have hunted out the truth for you. Our next prisoner is very special. You may have been led to believe the Fire of Thesteran was caused by an act of rebellion. You may have been told of a scientist who escaped from our research facilities and set off a great weapon."

Felez waited through roars of agreement and demands for answers.

Tyler stared with horror. How could they connect this to Deni.

"We lost many great people in that disaster, including the heroic Border Guard commander, Retical, and his team on the trail of this diabolical scheme. But we have continued their hunt, and I can finally confirm what really happened in the north." Felez turned towards the back of the stage. Twenty or more guards were lined up behind him, and in their mix were a handful of differently dressed individuals. The man in the suit was there. Montgomery. Was Felez looking to him for some kind of go-ahead? The commander continued, "The person you have before you is a liar and murderess equal in crime to the fiend Elzia, though you may never have heard of her. You may, though, have heard rumours of a girl who claims to have seen the sky."

A wave of commotion ran through the square. Without waiting for the commander's explanation, people were making feverish calls to kill her on the spot.

"Mad! She's mad!"

"Destroy her!"

"Cut off her head!"

Felez was patient. He was making this show count. By addressing them directly, he was ensuring they had no doubt about the dictated truth. He said, "It was not our own scientists who turned against us, it was the people they trusted to help them. This girl worked for the great Balfair, one of our most celebrated minds. She killed him and stole his secrets, to sell to the rebels. Hers is a wicked mind, devoid of morals. The fires in the Towers a week ago were her doing – and her undoing. In her latest attempts to steal Guard research, she was finally apprehended. The monster responsible for Thesteran. A menace that took the work of great men – work that would benefit us all – and tried to use it for her own gain – to make the traitors stronger."

"No," Tyler said, breaking from his shocked trance. "No, you can't believe it..."

"Our research into the clouds – the one futile thing she had left to sell – proved useless as a weapon." Felez's voice grew louder as he reached the peak of his point. "So she spread insane stories about the sky! I am here to tell you: *no more*. No more of her lies – no more of the corruption of using our own research against us. Like the rebels in the plains, she has no place in our society. She would see our whole world burn. Like the Short Queen Elzia, she has incited violence to bring us to our knees. But like Elzia and her rebels..." He was shouting, the crowd joining in rabidly. "We have resisted her, and we will continue to resist all like her! Like Elzia, and all traitors that come to our walls, she is not strong enough –" he swept a hand over the crowd, gesturing towards the surrounding war machines "– to fight the Estalian Empire!"

The din shook the walls as Felez waved at the man in the suit. Montgomery limped forward, drawing a pistol. The bastard meant to kill her himself.

"It's lies!" Tyler screamed into the pipe. "Don't believe him!"

The crowd was still shouting, the message barely penetrating their noise, but his voice had travelled through the pipes and gave the men on the stage pause. Tyler shouted again, face fully against the pipe, using all the air in his lungs, "The Border Guard are lying to you! She's innocent – they killed Balfair themselves! It was *that man* who did it!"

Tyler's voice echoed through the pipes with enough volume to quieten the rabble. Felez turned on the stage, searching for the source of the disturbance.

"She's a good person!" Tyler hurried on, as Felez barked orders at his men. "She didn't want to hurt anyone – she wanted to help!" The people below started shouting. Guards moved nearby. "He's lying – her master never built the Thesteran bomb – a man named Rosenbault did – and the rumours about the sky are *true*! Her name is Deni – she's a good person – she's my friend –"

Tyler flinched at the crack of a gunshot beneath him. The brick above his shoulder erupted with dust scattering into his eye. Blinking to clear his vision, he leant towards the pipe again, and another shot came even closer, this one sparking on the pipe and making him jump backwards in shock. He lost his grip, and as he grabbed at the wall his fingers closed on empty air. He'd fallen clear of anything to hold on to.

Looking up at the sky, and the impassable cloud, Tyler fell.

13

"Cut off his head!"

"String him up!"

The cries for justice made Deni look up, tracing the movements of the pack of guards as they dragged Tyler towards the stage. He was moaning loudly, the sound of a wounded animal. The sort that drew predators. Her lip trembled as she watched them haul him up the steps, through the shoving, slavering mass of citizens. Their whole beings were focused on his destruction.

Tyler was bloody all over, his clothes ripped. She had barely seen the fall, he had disappeared into the crowd so quickly. One of his arms was twisted the wrong way. His face was a mess of dark colours, bloodied and bruised, bits of his skin scraped off. He was alive, though. His other three limbs were intact, and his legs were vaguely twitching.

The guards tossed him down a few feet away. For a moment, his eyes rolled from side to side, and back into his head, as though he'd lost control of them. Then they focused on her. As he saw her, his moans died. His breathing slowed.

The worst thing had happened. The very thing she wanted to avoid.

He was damned, the same as her. Because of her.

"This is all they have," Felez announced loudly, his voice echoing off the walls, even louder than before, drawing the rabid crowd to order. The guards on the stage panned out around Tyler, moving out of Felez's way so the whole gathered city could watch. "You have before you our show of strength – and *theirs*."

"Don't die," Deni mouthed to Tyler. The slightest hint of a smile came to his crooked mouth. His lips parted to reveal teeth lined with blood. One was missing.

"For decades, the Guard has avoided involvement in the everyday life of the Estalian Empire. We have created a safe civilisation, without impeding your freedom. Without leaders. Without rules. But we are too many, now, and our enemies – they *do* have leaders. Enough to inspire this mania, taking advantage of our freedom. We. Need. Order."

The crowd started cheering again. Some were clapping.

Rules. Order. The words of the slave master Deni had left behind.

"We must give no more power to the savages!" Felez shouted. "We did not resist the Aftan Horde to open our doors to all. We did not purge the Norgang raiders without direction. We in the Guard have practised for these decades what the whole empire must do now. You, the Estalian people, you must do the same! Help us repel the Kandish invaders! Join with us to stamp out the plague *within our own city*!"

Roars of agreement and celebration spread through the square again. The stamping of so many feet felt like an earthquake.

Tyler was gasping on the floor, barely able to move. The shock focused Deni, the blurry, distant feeling giving way as her senses returned more fully. Her eyes were dry. In moments, they would both be killed. She looked up at the commander. He had swollen with the fervour of his own grand rhetoric. He was more than a man, an icon before these people, a growing force.

The crowd was turning more savage by the moment, like they'd been poisoned by some unnatural chemical. She swept her gaze over the animals and caught sight of an especially big man pushing through to the front. Not jumping up and down or cheering. Of course, he completed the nightmare. The angry, horrible scowl of the tattooed face, partly hidden under a hood, watching her like death, here to take her to the other side. He met her eyes and she didn't look away.

"No *more*!" Felez continued shouting. "There will be no more hiding in our city! Look at these people! They are the ones that start fires! They are the ones that take advantage of your freedom! It stops today! We will have order! We will be safe!"

According to you. Deni glowered at him. *Trust in the results*, Balfair had always said. She wasn't to question him, only to accept that he knew better. Did all these people believe the same of Felez?

"We bring you the message of the future. It is lying here before you. The traitors are weak – together, we are strong!"

The nearby guards joined in the cheers with an orderly stamp of their feet. Hidden behind their helmets, they were without expression: drones feeding this terrible machine. Deni picked out

Vorst again. When she caught his eyes, they flitted to the side. Indicating Montgomery behind her. Deni twisted, as slowly as she could.

"For the good of Estalia, we will establish *order* under one united Guard!"

Deni found Montgomery's face as he spotted Vorst. His pistol was in his hand. There was something wrong. He was more focused on the tattooed man than he was on her. Underestimating her again.

"The gates to this city mark the first line of defence against the savagery without. Here – now – we root out the savagery *within*!"

The crowd roared as he pointed at Tyler. A nearby guard raised a rifle, taking the commander's cue.

Deni shot up, driving her shoulder into Montgomery's crotch. As the people screamed for blood, she clawed a hand through his trouser pocket, ripping the material as she pulled her knife free. As she'd hoped – he'd kept it there to goad her. She sliced across his wrist and surged forward, too fast for anyone to stop her.

The shouts and screams ebbed with surprise, then stopped entirely. The sudden flurry of movement was over; the two dozen nearby guards who'd drawn their weapons were still. Some had rifles pointed at her, others had their guns only halfway up. Montgomery, to her side, clutched his bleeding hand, pistol on the floor.

Felez stood a foot taller than Deni. Her chin pressed into his breastplate as he pushed his head back to look down at her. The fat of his neck folded over the top of the knife, holding it there. There was no way for him to move without the knife cutting him. With his extravagant armour and arms spread to the side, and hers tucked in close, he appeared twice her size. Deni was a tiny target at his centre.

The commander said nothing, dark irises shimmering with anger, teeth bared.

I had a master, before, Deni told herself. No different to this man.

"You're dead," Montgomery growled a shaky promise.

Nothing new.

The quiet of the square was immense. Tension and fear had spread all the way to the back. Even the ones who couldn't see what was happening were holding their breath.

"I'm not a rebel," Deni whispered, finally, barely audible even to herself. She looked sideways to the crowd. Thousands of faces, watching her. Waiting for her to act. The world of people she had wanted to join, every last one of them hanging on her actions.

Felez tried to take control. "For Hrute's sake, someone –"

Deni pushed on the knife, drawing blood and a wheeze of fear from Felez. He rose up on his toes. In her periphery, she saw one a guard making a move, about to speak, but he was cut off.

"Give her space," a female voice snapped from behind Deni. She didn't turn as she sensed someone closing on her, crossing the stage. Deni prepared to dig the knife in harder, about to return some kind of threat, but the voice continued: "A single one of you moves, your hero's stuck and his captain loses his head."

Deni gave a quick glance back.

The tattooed lady had two pistols out. One was aimed her way, the other off towards the back of the stage, targeting the finely robed announcer. The man was quaking, hands up in the air. Cetherine came closer, guns up. The only person in the thousand-strong crowd with the nerve to break the stillness. What was she doing? As she passed Montgomery, she kicked his pistol across the floor, past Deni.

"Big fucking hole you've dug," she told Deni, stopping close to her.

"Is it true?" a gravelly voice asked, beyond Felez. "What the boy says you saw?"

Keeping herself pressed close to the commander, Deni slid her head to the side. Vorst had climbed onto the stage, too. The guards around him were frozen still, none daring to move lest it trigger some terrible conclusion. Vorst picked up Montgomery's gun. Deni could see from his movements, and the grim looks he was giving the guards, that he knew something. The way he looked at Tyler, she could see they'd spoken, somehow. Tyler, the brave, stupid fool. He couldn't have persuaded them to help, could he?

"It's true," Deni said. Again her voice was too quiet. She cleared her throat and spoke up. She had to answer the tattooed man properly. "It's all true."

"So tell them," Vorst said. He was oddly calm. He turned to take in the scene himself. They were three people, now, threatening the leaders of the Guard, holding everyone else still.

Her single action had turned the whole population to stone, and the company of these two frightful mercenaries had cemented it.

"I'll take care of this one," Vorst continued, moving closer to Felez. He put the pistol against the commander's head. Armour shifted audibly as the surrounding guards' muscles tightened, but still no one was willing to take the deadly initiative and act. Vorst raised his free hand to Deni's knife. She stared at his big, rough fingers. The middle nail was cracked and black.

There was no getting out of this, not with ten guns pointed her way. The best she could do would be to stab one of the many monsters on the stage there, with her. The monster that had haunted her dreams for so many years. Or the worse, bigger monsters. The one who had haunted her dreams more recently, or the one who had haunted this whole city, with the population's say so. She had to choose just one. She wouldn't survive any more.

"Tell them," another voice croaked, and Deni's eyes fearfully turned to Tyler. Laid on his back, he was unable to move. When he managed to speak, his face creased in pain. "Whatever else happens... tell them everything..."

Deni shook her head. How could she? How could she talk with the tattooed man right next to her, his animal eyes burning into her? With Montgomery at her back and his equally lethal gaze? Countless others who simply wanted her dead. *Why* should she, now? The damage was done. They believed in Felez. They hated her.

She should say nothing. Simply choose from the three terrible men who deserved to die. Give her life to remove one of theirs.

"This asshole tried to kill me," Vorst said, his voice measured and calm but loud enough for the crowd to hear. Deni followed his gaze to Montgomery. "And he's had me beholden for too long. I trust myself, Deni, no one else. And if I'd known what you knew when all this started, I'd have taken him down a long time ago."

Deni stared, barely understanding.

"You don't know –" Felez started, but his head tilted stiffly as Vorst pushed the pistol harder against his temple.

"The Guard have been manipulating us," Vorst shouted, with such volume that it carried through the square without need for the pipe. "They hired me to hunt this girl, then they tried to kill me when they caught her. She's innocent, like the boy said. He's even

259

more innocent than her. He's a god-damned roofer from Bawkley, it's nothing to do with him. He's one of *you*."

Murmurs of concern started to go through the crowd, as though they'd been given permission to breathe again. One or two comments sifted up to Deni. "Who is she?"

"I would've walked away myself," Vorst boomed on. "But the boy raised questions. And it turns out there's things they don't want anyone to know. There's whole operations in the Guard they don't want you to know about – whole floors of the Towers packed with them."

"A dozen guns on you," Montgomery said. "Where do you think this gets you?"

"It gets her an audience," Vorst answered readily.

"No one's listening," Montgomery sneered.

Another shout changed the tone, though. A frightened young voice, crying, "Tyler? By the gods, is that Tyler?"

Rushes of curiosity spread around the sound. Someone was moving, pushing to get closer. A young man about Tyler's age, a little taller and thinner, and alongside him a long-haired girl that Deni recognised. The girl Tyler had been with before.

"Why's he up there?" Sila cried. "What's going on?"

"He's the best person I know!" her friend shouted. "It's true, he's just a roofer! What have you done to him!"

The confusion started to spread. People weren't screaming for blood, now; there was enough uncertainty for them to want answers. They *might* listen. They were looking imploringly to Deni, though. No one else.

"We're not walking away from this, Deni," the tattooed woman said. "Even with a knife at his throat, none of us gets out of this city alive. Not unless you convince these people you're not the one that deserves to die."

Deni looked at her with alarm.

Convince them. Talk to them.

Change something. Change everything.

Her hand started to shake. Felez's eyes narrowed as he sensed her uncertainty. He said, just for her, "She's right. You're done."

Deni pulled back and released the knife. A gasp of surprise ran through the nearby onlookers, and the tension in the watching guards redoubled, but Felez hadn't moved. The knife hadn't moved. Vorst had taken hold of it as Deni stepped back; it remained pressed against the commander's neck. The slaver drew the pistol back to target Montgomery.

Deni hurried a few short steps to the lectern and the pipe, feeling the guards' rifles follow her as she went. Facing the packed square, she had the city rapt. To her side, on the stage floor, Tyler lay crumpled, looking painfully up at her. She met his eyes.

"Tell them," he wheezed.

The tattooed lady was right. It was the only way, now. There were no numbers from the rocket and there was no Hodwick. No rebel force coming from the wilderness to save them. Only her and her words. Her and her weak voice.

Tyler took a sharp breath. He might die, without help.

They'd all die, without help.

She leant towards the pipe and cleared her throat. Digging deep, summoning all the volume her body was capable of, she addressed the crowd.

14

"I was a slave, and I got my master killed, that's true," Deni said, and the murmurs started up again. Tyler's friends snapped at the people around them for quiet. She closed her eyes and raised her voice, determined to drown out the negatives. "I didn't mean to. It was only because I sought the Guard's help."

Her voice bounced out of the pipes at various heights around the square. It spun through the archways and sprang back to her, as if a hundred bigger, louder, braver Denis were talking for her. Hearing it, she felt better. More able to talk.

"I brought that man into our home." Deni pointed at Montgomery. "My master died because of me. But *he* was the one who pulled the trigger. He killed everyone."

The comments died down. Deni searched the faces. Many still looked angry, even in their confusion, like they wanted to hurt something. Anything. They were the ones who mattered most. She focused on one of them, a moustached man with heavy eyebrows and a scruffy shirt, a few rows into the crowd. Looking directly at him, she continued, "They trick you into being angry at other people when you should be angry at them. I was forced to work for my master, who was forced to work for them. *Everyone's* forced to work for them."

"Forced?" Felez erupted. "We provide safety – we provide security!"

"You provide fear!" Deni replied, her voice rising louder. "You're everything that's wrong – your *safety* killed my master, you want to kill *me* – and Tyler – my *friend* – he never did anything wrong! He believed in the Guard! *I* believed in the Guard – but *he* –" Deni eyed Montgomery. He'd toyed with her and wanted her to suffer, and it had given her the chance to speak. His malevolent look told her he knew it.

Deni turned back to the crowd. They were hanging on her words.

"He wants to tell you –" Deni leant closer to the pipe, pointing back at Felez "– that you have enemies. Me. Or him." She pointed at Tyler. Then Vorst. "Or him. Or the wild rebels no one's ever seen. The worst things I know of were done by them, though. My master killed, by them. My friend's uncle, killed by them. A family murdered in the countryside, because of them. And I've seen maybe one beautiful thing in my life, which the Guard don't want you to know."

Deni stopped to take a breath and in her moment's silence she felt the crowd waiting. There were no murmurs, now, no comments. She spoke more quietly.

"I don't know how to..." She hesitated. "I don't know how to make you believe me, like him. That's what he does. I can only tell you what I know. Balfair *did* make weapons. But only small ones, for the Guard. Nothing that could hurt a whole city. He made one thing that was bigger, to research the clouds. I *saw* the clouds part – they opened onto colours we've never known. Light that changed the way I saw the same building I had seen for ten years."

She took another breath and looked at Tyler. In his broken heap, he was smiling, faintly, impossibly, to encourage her.

"I didn't know what it meant. I *did* want to sell the idea, because I knew it was important to them. I hoped to buy myself protection. So I could be free. I understood, though... this was too important to run from." Deni paused. When she found the angry moustached man again, she said hopefully, "The Guard's engineers have discovered things about the world. Dangerous things. I understand only a part of it – but I understand that part well, now."

"By the gods, someone –" Felez started again, making one more attempt to quieten her before it was too late. Vorst growled into his ear like an animal. Deni quickly continued.

"A long time ago, it was something unnatural in the sky that kept us safe. The Guard know about it – they know more than the scientists, even. It's not keeping us safe any more. The world's getting darker – maybe because of whatever is up there, keeping the clouds there. Whatever it is can be better understood – changed – maybe made better. I don't have all the answers, but I *do* know they don't *want* us to have them."

The crowd were whispering, in such numbers that the hushed discussion built to a great static noise. The whispers turned to talking. Deni strained to focus, turning back to Felez. She said, "Tell them it's not true."

"Of course it's not true," Felez replied. Vorst eased the knife slightly away from his neck. "We're the empire's protectors, what reason could we have to hide anything that could help?"

"Yeah," Deni nodded. She turned back to the pipe. "He spoke to you before with the same language my master used to control me. He made me believe in his rules, like your commander wants you to. To invite change was to invite destruction. That's why they don't want you to know." Deni's hands gripped the lectern. She felt energy building inside her. "As long as things get worse, then we *need* them, and we cannot question them. They don't care about making things better, only about making themselves stronger. That's *why* they would hide something that can help. Look at them, swarming over this city, over this countryside – *taking* from all of you. And giving what? Messages of fear, and hate!"

Deni stopped, almost out of breath, staring once more into the eyes of the moustached man. Believe it, she implored him. *Know* it's true. His mouth had turned, the grimace replaced by the first hint of doubt. That was it. She said, "You all know the same as me, now. The thing they wanted to kill me for. That's *all* it is. But it's everything."

The guards on stage were looking at one another, with the same doubt as everyone else. One lowered his guns, then another. One man took off his helmet, revealing a young face and ginger hair. He was staring at Felez questioningly. Of course – they weren't all in on it. The commander stared right back.

"Silence this murderess," Felez rumbled.

"I've seen *him* kill people," Vorst said loudly. "But has a single person here seen her do wrong?" He scanned the surrounding guards. "Any of you?"

Deni watched Montgomery. The one man who could testify to her past. He kept quiet, fearing the change in the crowd. To draw attention back to himself now would make him the biggest target. When Felez locked angry eyes on him, Montgomery was motionless. He was as cowardly as he was treacherous.

"It's the tallest tale I've ever heard," Felez said. "There's not a lick of proof –"

"Because you destroyed it!" Deni shouted. "What happened to ArcTech? Where's Dr Hodwick now? Balfair? Why does no one know about it? How can you say *I* had anything to do with Thesteran, when I spent my whole life hidden as a slave?"

"The traitors and rebels feed you fantasies!" Felez roared, matching Vorst for the volume of his voice. In his response he all but pulled away from Vorst. "They spread lies in taverns and from street-preaching boxes, hoping you'll believe whatever you're told! The Guard keep you safe from these lies – we –"

"The Guard *create* lies!" Deni shouted, cutting him off. She closed the distance between them. However tall he stood, and however broad his armour, she felt bigger now. "Prove that Balfair created a weapon! Prove that this –" she pointed down at Tyler "– this good man, who only tried to help people – prove he did anything to deserve this!"

Felez glared at her, full of hate. His jaw was tight, his fists were clenched. She knew him perfectly, then. An arrogant, selfish manipulator. The same as the man who had murdered everyone she knew.

"You set the fires," Felez replied, not done. He raised his voice for the crowd. "She burnt the research, two nights ago, when she fled the Towers. She set fires three days ago. Fires a week ago, destroying everything she could – she should be shot, right here – she should –"

"We were in central Estalia, two days ago," Vorst said. "Following her. On your orders."

There was a moment's stillness.

"I vouch for it!" a lady shouted from the crowd. "I own a mill south of Hasseran, I saw her there, before I made my journey here!"

Deni twisted to find the face. She couldn't see her, but it had to be Wallen. Incredibly, another voice joined her. "I saw them come in the West Gate – I remember their slave truck – bold as brass!"

"Tyler was with *me*," one of Tyler's friends shouted. "A week ago – he couldn't have been helping set *fires*!"

Then a man, way off. "Wasn't she on the waterway, near Fewhaven, not a day ago? I was there, on my way south!"

More voices stirred up agreement, inventing facts to side with Deni. Solidifying their uncertainty with created memories. Then the demands started again. The crowd had turned. "He's lying to us!"

"Where's this research?"

"Where's your proof!"

Felez tensed, a small, nervous movement that conceded guilt.

"They're the ones that should hang! The lot of them!"

It was working. There *was* good out there, there was no escaping judgement for the Guard now. It was a chance to make –

Montgomery moved, and as Deni turned a gun went off. Deni dropped back and her shoulder rammed into the lectern. The collision spun her and her face hit the floor. Another gunshot followed, and another. Dazed, with a burning hot sensation in her side, she tried to push herself up, making it just high enough to see Tyler. He reached out his good hand.

She reached back, fingers grasping to touch his. As they failed to connect, booted feet jumped over them and more gunshots went off. Blood sprayed across their faces, and the thousands of gathered people cascaded into panic. Deni twisted back as two walls of guards collided; Montgomery disappeared between the shapes, but Felez was down. His large hand clutched his neck as blood oozed between his fingers, wide eyes staring in horrified disbelief. Other commanders were rallying the Guard.

"Stop them – destroy the rebels!"

Deni jammed a shoulder into the floor and pushed forward with her knees. She caught hold of Tyler's hand. He pulled her closer, the action making him cry out in pain. She slid into him as someone jumped over them.

The world rumbled with gunfire and screams. Everyone had erupted into the moment with no clear idea of who they were fighting. A great weapon sounded from the edge of the square, shaking everything with a tremendous report – and the shouts and screams escalated.

Tyler said, "Hold on to me. Hold on."

Deni wrapped her arms around him and pressed her face into his chest. Warmth expanded between them. Soaking through her clothes. Her warmth, flowing out of her.

Her blood.

"Hold on," he whispered into her ear, as though that was all that mattered now, as the world crumbled around them. Thousands of voices were shouting. Thousands of boots beat against the floor.

Death screams and cannon blasts roared over them.

It wasn't the whole crowd that had turned against the Guard. Just enough to cause an unstoppable, devastating collision.

She'd done this. She'd murdered them all.

"Thank you..." Tyler said, his voice quieter, seeming to fade. "...you..."

Deni looked at him with alarm, her eyes widening as his closed. *Thank you?*

A force pulled her back and she spun, thrown into the nightmare of movement around them. The tattooed man's face blocked it all, fiery and raging, gold teeth glittering between dark smears of blood. The way she remembered him, imagined him, feared him. She screamed as she tried to break free, barely hearing his voice. "You're not done!"

She squirmed, desperation overriding her wound, wanting nothing but to get back to Tyler. She bucked and lashed out, but the monster's grip was too tight. She inhaled, to recover her lost breath, and gagged on the smell of gunpowder. Spluttering, she caught glimpses of activity around them. A guard punching a man's face, pinned against the lectern. The tattooed woman, crouched low, firing as she ducked a blow. Felez, motionless now, face in a puddle of blood. The skeletal, bearded man, pounding a guard's head against the floor. A man in black armour firing a rifle into the square as a line of people clawed to get up. A buzzing machine, flying low past the walls, pouring smoke. Flames, licking up the side of a wall.

Tyler, lying motionless on the floor, eyes closed.

There one moment, hidden behind someone the next.

"Tyler!" Deni cried, above the riotous sounds. She was still moving, pulled away through the madness. They were receding, away from it all, sinking into the impossible depths of a dream. As she struggled and screamed, her energy faded, Vorst's arm braced around her waist. She yelled, "Go back! Leave me – get Tyler!"

They dropped off the stage, and the madness disappeared from view. Her last glimpse of the scene was a mess of angry violence, Tyler nowhere to be seen. They were moving between two buildings, bodies thumping into walls left and right as Vorst smashed his way through the crowd. Deni twisted in his grip, trying to break free, desperate to go back, shouting, but with each movement her vision seemed to blur more. Her energy was seeping out through her open wound, and each sound she made seemed quieter, less effective. As the world went dark, the sounds of violence subsided, and the last thing she heard was Vorst's voice, huffing as he fought onward.

"Hold on. You're not done. You're not done."

15

The chaotic din had faded but not gone. It was far away, sporadic and muffled like a half-forgotten memory. It lived on, though, in the darkness. A shout, followed by silence, followed by a longer shout. Another gunshot, a firecracker on the other side of the world. A siren, whining with a circular sound.

"I know people in all quarters." A low voice came between the noises, nearby. "It's a question of getting out there."

"We're still here because *out there* helps no one," a woman's voice replied.

Deni strained to open her eyes. There wasn't much light to open them to, with the charred surface of a ceiling above. A wisp of fair hair hung from a wooden beam. How did that get there?

"Everything's gonna be locked down," a different female voice said. Firm. Bold. Wallen? "The whole damned city's a fort and however many rebels there are in the world they're not getting in here, not now. So what are *we* going to do?"

"What *we*?"

There was that smell again. Not gunfire though – charcoal. A fire. And a subtle aroma behind it. Meaty. A broth.

"You saved them for a reason," Wallen said. "Not the kindness of your hearts."

Quiet for a moment. Someone moved.

Deni blinked to clear her eyes. She rolled her head to one side. Three big, dark shapes, shadows in front of a tall, broken window. There was barely any light outside, and the fire in the iron stove only highlighted the edges of things with its slight yellow glow.

They looked like demons. Wicked black spirits that glowed along the lines of their muscles and grim expressions. Half of the light that hit Vorst and Cetherine's flesh was sucked back into the abyss of their tattoos.

"I'm no one's lackey," Vorst said. "Two of our people died because of them – because of *this*. Their lies. But it doesn't have to concern *you*, now."

Deni tried to move, to push herself up, and felt a flare of pain in her left side that spread like an explosion over her body. She eased down onto her back, wincing.

"Deni?" Wallen said.

She didn't dare move again, breathing into the agony, trying to understand it. She'd been shot. Montgomery had sparked off the whole riot to kill her. To provide a distraction for his own escape.

The trio moved over to her, Vorst asking roughly, "How is she?"

When she opened her eyes again, three large faces were looking down at her. The tattooed man in the middle. His eyes looked strangely gentle. Concerned. Deni stared back at him, wondering if she had died. The fears of her life would be meaningless when she died, after all. It didn't have to make sense in death, that the monster could care.

"You're okay, Deni," Wallen assured her, with an encouraging smile. Her expression was comforting, something you could embrace and hold on to. She tapped Deni's shoulder. "Try not to move. Not just yet. We'll get some soup down you."

"Tyler..." Deni rasped.

"He's here," Wallen nodded. She glanced to the side and Deni tried to follow her look. There was nothing there but shadows. "Don't worry."

"Where..." Deni said. "Tyler..."

"You dumb kids," Vorst said, not unkindly. "Should've left all this alone."

Deni looked into his eyes. He was still staring at her. Not angry. Not violent. Curious. Like she was a puzzle he didn't understand. As her fears faded, she felt something similar about him.

"Why..." Deni breathed slowly, the pain lancing again. "Why are you here?"

"Where else would we be?" Vorst turned away and crossed the room.

Deni didn't know what to say.

"From the Drain, as far as Bawkley," Vorst announced, drawing Deni's attention to the window where he'd stopped. "Across the Speakers Square and as far as Height Park, the city's on fire. You lit it. The Short Queen would be proud."

"The Guard commander..."

"Felez is dead, honey," Wallen said. "But their command's not. Half a dozen psychopaths were waiting to take his place. That snake Montgomery got away, for one."

"Some of the guards fought with us," the tattooed lady commented. "But their war machines are still blocking the streets. They've got a fleet in the Drain and a fortress in Grenevic. Guns on every gate, eyes on every wall. You started something that's not going to end easily."

Deni blinked again, holding back the pain. She scanned the room again, hoping to find some hint of Tyler in the shadows. He was the survivor that mattered. Had they really saved him?

"How did we get here?" she asked.

"Lot of people died," Vorst said. Maybe an explanation, maybe just a statement.

"Because of me..." Deni said. Wallen's hand found hers and patted it, but she pulled away. Deni pushed herself up onto her elbows, wincing but pushing Wallen's hand clear. She swung her legs off the bed to face Vorst.

Deni stood, fighting against the pain, and Cetherine pulled Wallen clear of her, warning, "Let her be."

She hobbled across the room, every step agony. There was a doorway, rotten and hanging loose at the edges of the frame. She passed through it as the two women followed. "Tyler?"

There was a body on the floor in the next room. Motionless, under a thick, heavy blanket. A leather bag next to him. No other furniture, just a broken window and a cold draught. Deni stumbled the last few steps towards him and dropped down at his side, putting her hands on his arm. He was warm. Immobile, eyes closed, but warm.

She looked up tearfully to Wallen as the big lady stood in the doorway. Her sadness told Deni all she needed to know. They were alive and they had escaped, but that didn't make it all right.

"It was a good thing you did," Wallen said. "Both of you. It's going to change everything. You might not see that now, but it will. Estalia's gonna thank you, one day."

"One day," Deni repeated quietly, eyes locked on Tyler's motionless face. "What use is one day? Everything I touch dies..."

"That so?" Vorst said without sympathy, approaching. He caught her by the shoulder and wrenched her up off the floor.

271

Wallen surged after him as Deni yelped, but he had already stopped. Deni was standing, free of his grip, next to the window. He said, "Take a long look. This has been going on as long as there's been the Guard. You've opened their eyes."

Deni looked. Their hide-out was ten or more storeys above the city, looking down on a vista of multi-tiered towers. Lining the walkways and overcrowded streets were emotionless suits of black and grey armour, watching people, shoving them, brandishing weapons. Armoured vehicles sat dormant with the ready vibrations of spiders about to pounce. Civilians had their heads low, avoiding eye contact, trying not to be seen or heard.

On one walkway, a group of five men charged at a guard, using tools for weapons. A rifle went off and one of the men fell back, dead. More guards swarmed down on them from an adjoining path, the groups clashing in a messy sprawl.

"When that boy came to us, and we started asking the same questions you did," Vorst said, "you opened *our* eyes. This isn't the way it needs to be. People will get hurt, but what you've done was necessary."

A siren whined again. Over the horizon of buildings, a pillar of smoke rolled up into the sky. Deni followed it, to where the black of man-made catastrophe met the grey of the all-compassing clouds. Maybe they were man-made too.

She looked at Vorst, heeding his words, and realised she had no idea who this man was. He wasn't the fearsome construction Balfair and Sincade had made of him; not the unholy monster she'd believed would drag her into some kind of hell. He had his own reasons for being there, and for his risking his life in the square. The words came out of her in a whisper: "Who are you?"

"No one special." He watched the men grappling with the guards below. Two of them had a guard up against the rails. They were winning this scuffle. "But you. You're someone this city needs."

"The research is gone," Deni uttered. "I've got nothing left..."

Vorst glared at her, forcefully, as though her doubts were meaningless. He said, "You've got as much as anyone."

Still, she twisted away from him, back to Tyler. "I couldn't even keep him safe."

They all went quiet as she stared. Tyler's chest was rising, breaths coming in deeper. She moved to stand over him, looking down at his face. He looked so peaceful, so innocent in sleep, like he was dreaming of good things. Better things than the world held.

She knelt down and her eyes fell on the bag. Gently, she puffed the satchel up and lifted Tyler's head, pushing the bag under him for support. Then she took his hand in both of hers, rubbing his skin. She felt the other three moving behind her, gathering in silent comfort.

"You're going to be okay," Deni told Tyler. "I promise. You're going to wake up and we're going to be okay. Because you were right, Tyler. There's goodness left in this world. We'll find it, together."

Tears ran down her face as she watched his eyes. His lips. Searching for the slightest movement. For the slightest sign that it was true. As she held him tighter, his eyelid twitched.

Acknowledgements

Massive thanks are due to my fantastic editors, Jodi Henley and Carrie O'Grady, as well as my team of beta readers, and my fans who've been asking for more since *Wixon's Day* – especially Kat and Lou Fish. I'm also in debt to Jessica Bell for the superb cover art throughout this series, and to Marta, my wife, for her ongoing faith and support.

About the Author

Phil Williams is the author of the Estalia, Ordshaw and Faergrowe series. Living in Sussex, UK with his wife, he also writes screenplays and spends a great deal of time walking his impossibly fluffy dog, Herbert. You can find him online at:

www.phil-williams.co.uk

Join his mailing list for news and free content.

You can also connect with Phil through:
Facebook: **www.facebook.com/philwilliamsauthor**
Twitter: **www.twitter.com/fantasticphil**
Email: **phil@phil-williams.co.uk**

Enjoyed reading?

I am an independent author who relies on fans like you. Reader Reviews and word of mouth do more to draw attention to my books than any advertising can. Only through an enthusiastic and loyal readership, writing honest reviews and encouraging their friends, can my books reach a wider audience.

If you enjoyed *Aftan Whispers*, I would be incredibly grateful if you could take a few minutes to leave a review online (even if it's short – to be concise is a virtue, after all).

Also by Phil Williams

Balfair's Confinement (Estalia Series)

The novella that started Deni's journey.

Isolated in the derelict estate of the engineer Balfair, with only a miserable fellow slave for company, Deni dreams of changing her arduous life. When her master drags something new from the swamp and excludes her from his secretive project, she finally sees her chance. Deni will do whatever it takes to break free - even if it means bringing the full weight of the war-mongering Guard down on Balfair.

The results may be devastating, but they will notice her at last - and she will be free.

Wixon's Day (Estalia Series)

The novel that started the Estalia series.

He just wanted to see what was left of the world. He never meant to join the war to save it.

Marquos drifts through the cloud-concealed Empire of Estalia, searching for hope of a better future as he scavenges to survive. In the Deadland of the North, they say the sky is clear, and the stars shine. Marquos believes there is beauty there.

With rebels plaguing the canals, and the authoritarian Guards pursuing Marquos for his attempts to liberate a child, the route north is wrought with peril. The militant rulers and the ragged resistance fighters vie for the boatman's support, drawing Marquos into a war many don't realise exists, and revealing secrets about the world that threaten to wipe out what little is left.

A Most Apocalyptic Christmas (Faergrowe Series)

On the night before Christmas, mercenary Scullion's ride home is ambushed halfway between the last surviving cities in America. Concerned only with getting drunk for the holiday, his reckless journey leads him on a collision course with a barbaric community who have utterly distorted the seasonal spirit.

This is one madcap night he cannot survive alone, challenging his perceptions of the meaning of Christmas.

Printed in Great
Britain
by Amazon